Ghosted

Also by Jenn Ashworth

A Kind of Intimacy

Cold Light

The Friday Gospels

Fell

Notes Made While Falling

Jenn Ashworth

Ghosted

A Love Story

SCEPTRE

First published in Great Britain in 2021 by Sceptre
An Imprint of Hodder & Stoughton
An Hachette UK company

1

A CIP catalogue record for this title is available from the British Library

Hardback ISBN 9781529336764
eBook ISBN 9781529336795

Typeset in Sabon MT by Hewer Text UK Ltd, Edinburgh
Printed and bound in Great Britain by Clays Ltd, Elcograf S.p.A.

Hodder & Stoughton policy is to use papers that are natural, renewable
and recyclable products and made from wood grown in sustainable
forests. The logging and manufacturing processes are expected to
conform to the environmental regulations of the country of origin.

Hodder & Stoughton Ltd
Carmelite House
50 Victoria Embankment
London EC4Y 0DZ

www.sceptrebooks.co.uk

1

That last morning the May sunshine had spilled into the room through a gap at the top of the curtains and woken me before the alarm. One of the curtain hooks had slipped its ring and left the top edge sagging. I had asked him – my husband, that is – more than once to sort it out. I turned over in bed, away from the window and the job still undone, and towards the sleeping shape of him: a mountain under the duvet, radiating heat. I put my hand in his hair. When we were first together I used to tell him he had hair like a bear. I made a fist and held the thick, dark ruff of it in my hand, then let go. I'll admit I was pissed off with him, however unreasonable that was.

'Are you awake?'

We were an odd couple. Me, short and slight – wispy somehow. Pale, like a ghost. Him, like a brick shithouse. I never found his size and solidity alarming. There was pleasure in it, still, even after fifteen years, twelve of them as man and wife. The feel of him. His weight. Ironic, really. I'd always put myself down as the insubstantial one.

I huffed, pulling at the duvet, and he opened his eyes. He lifted his hand from where he had it tucked between his legs, like a little boy, and put it on the back of my neck.

'You didn't fix the curtain,' I said.

'What?' He blinked, baffled.

'You said you'd fix it. I asked you. It's too high for me. You said you'd get one of the kitchen stools and sort it out.'

He has always been slow to come online in the morning. I took advantage of this sometimes and used the moments he remained not quite with-it, wondering who this angry dream-wife was, to say things I wouldn't usually say. I knew he wouldn't remember, you see.

'I don't know what you were doing all day,' I said. 'Lying around surfing the internet while I'm up to my eyeballs. Me at work, you at home, doing God knows what. Nothing. You don't do anything.' I turned away from him. 'You're a lazy get.'

He squeezed my neck. Used his other hand to pull me towards him. It is instinct for him, in the morning, to want sex. We sleep naked. He nudged my thighs apart with his knee, pulled me in tighter and pushed himself, with some difficulty, inside. I was still quite dry.

'Did you sleep all right?' he said, properly awake now.

'No,' I said. 'You were snoring.' That was often the case, but he had slept peacefully that night, as far as I'd been aware.

'Sorry,' he said, automatically. He thrust into me. It was more of a burrowing really – a persistent pressure until he was all the way inside. He held me very tight. We lay perfectly still.

'Nice?'

'Hmm.'

It was better that we did it like that in the morning, his belly against the small of my back. We often had bad breath when we woke up.

'What time are you in work today? Early?'

I nodded and he bit my neck gently. I made a little high-pitched growl – something like the noise a cat would make if you stood on its tail, but under my breath. Not a purr. The noise – halfway between a quiet yowl and a suppressed groan – had over the years become a kind of private joke between us. Or the remnant of a joke, the way the fossil trace of an ammonite pressed into a rock is not an ammonite, but only a reminder of one. The original joke was something to do with pussy, I think, and the doggy position. We used to be crude in the way we spoke to each other in bed and I suppose the cat noise was a way of reviving the atmosphere of those days. I wriggled my backside against him but his cock had gone soft already. I did what I usually did in those situations and pretended not to notice. We lay still for a few more minutes, not talking, until my alarm went off.

'I'd better get up.'

He withdrew. Little sad mouse sliding out of its hole. He rolled out of bed and turned off the alarm on my mobile. He retrieved my glasses from the top of the headboard, where I always stashed them just before I went to sleep, gently opened them, then passed them to me, ready to wear.

'I'll make your tea,' he said, just as he always did. I was extremely hung-over, just as I always was.

It's hard to know how other couples live their lives, but all of this had become utterly ordinary for us. I told the police as much, later. *I left for work while he was still in the shower. I don't know what he was wearing that day. No, he hadn't seemed unusual in any way that morning.*

The officers – they sent two, a man and a woman who both refused a hot drink and made notes on a tablet instead of in a notebook – seemed frustrated by the fact that no matter how they phrased their questions I had nothing to add – no suspicious or out-of-the-ordinary behaviour on his part – to my account. I didn't tell them I was pissed off with him, but I am telling you now.

But it may not have been the sagging curtain that caused me to be annoyed with him. I had been dreaming – one of my regular dreams about being accused of something very bad. The details were hazy – the dreams were more like emotions than pieces of theatre. There was some kind of courtroom or lecture hall and I was improperly dressed for the occasion. I knew I was supposed to speak and defend myself.

The stakes were always high in this type of dream. Sometimes I had been brought to stand before my accusers from a cell on death row and the courtroom was an American one – grafted into my consciousness from the televised O.J. Simpson trial. At other times there was a religious element, and the people I had to speak to were wearing the black robes of clerics. The implication was that either the stake or eternal damnation were waiting. The nature of the offence was never quite revealed to me and, under scrutiny, the inner certainty of my innocence gave way entirely and the inevitable guilt and terror flooded me with a kind of frozen clamminess. *Yes*, I thought, as I opened my eyes, *I have done something terrible, and I must have forgotten what it was.* I woke up and was teleported home to the marital bed in order to regard the cobwebs and warm morning light around the curtain rail, carrying the emotions of the dream world into this one.

I didn't tell the police about my dream. They deal only in facts and a dream is not a fact. I didn't tell them I was in a bad mood. A feeling is not a fact. Instead, the woman tapped the details I reported to them into her tablet while the man searched the flat. Unscrewed the bath panel and looked inside the suitcases that we stored under the bed, would you believe? Sinister, though I didn't put it together until after they'd left. They were looking for his body in case I was reporting him missing to cover up the fact I'd actually murdered him.

Is there anywhere you can suggest that he might have gone? A friend? A family member?

I promised them I didn't know anything that would help them. I emphasised again: his mood was unremarkable. Our interaction was commonplace: one morning in an entire series of them. I told them, truthfully, that his mother lived in Portugal and his passport was still in the kitchen drawer.

The police didn't ask about the history of our relationship: it wasn't like it is in the crime dramas, where the accused gets a good opportunity either in a police interview room, or in the dock, to explain. And it wasn't as if I tried to tell them. It's only now I am able to understand some of the strangeness that had been hidden inside our lives for a long time before he vanished. It had been there for months, through all our daily wakenings and couplings and comings apart. If I am trying to find a beginning, I need to go back further. Not to the day he vanished, but the day he arrived.

I met Mark at a wedding. I was only invited to the night do, being a colleague of the bride and not a member of the family or in her intimate circle of friends. Not that I minded. It was a relief, really, not to have to sit through a ceremony and a seated formal meal making polite conversation with people who I didn't know, or to have to worry too much about an outfit. I borrowed a dress from my mother that I hoped would pass as vintage and turned up a little late, when the dancing was in full swing. I remember the cake: it was made of four square layers stacked between glass cubes filled with coloured water. This was fifteen years ago; things like that were fashionable then.

I avoided the dancing and made my way to the bar. The disadvantage of being a solitary evening guest is, I discovered, that the other guests have had time to strike up conversations and form themselves into groups and your task is to somehow break into those. Vodka would steady my nerves and prepare me for the task at hand. It was a cash bar, and while I was groping about in my borrowed clutch bag for the twenty-pound note I had tucked in there and giving my order to the barman – the DJ was playing 'Brown Eyed Girl' at an astonishing volume – I became aware of two people talking animatedly at the bar next to me.

'She's crying out for justice. She's telling me everything. I don't get a choice in when or where. It just comes to me.'

I took them for a couple at first. He was wearing a shabby suit and his tie was crooked. He was sweating heavily and kept pulling a serviette out of his pocket and dabbing at his forehead. She

5

was a little older and was wearing a black sleeveless dress with a silver thread running through it. Her hair had obviously started the day in a chignon of some kind but had unravelled slightly. I accepted my drink from the barman and stayed at the bar, listening.

'The murderer has some of her things. Her shoes. Her school bag. They weren't found with the body. The police are going to find them hidden in his workplace, not at his home.'

I gathered they were talking about the case – it had been in all the local and national newspapers for weeks – of a little girl from our city who had disappeared from her own front garden two months earlier. The police had just found her body buried in a ditch beside a field near the Caton wind farm and were transferring their efforts from locating the girl to finding her killer.

'You can't know those things for sure,' Mark – he'd introduced himself to me later, in the taxi back to his flat – was saying.

'But I do,' she insisted. 'I've written to the detective inspector in charge of the case. I'm not just some nutter,' she laughed, and another lock of her hair fell from the chignon. 'I've done work like this before.'

'With the police?'

'Don't sound so surprised. Lots of police forces use mediums to help them when their investigations on the material plane come to a dead end,' she said patiently. I edged closer, unashamedly eavesdropping.

'Name me one case you've worked on,' Mark said, a little belligerently. 'Name me one case where your evidence has been presented in court.'

'Blake Barrett,' she said, without hesitation. 'York. The police force paid for my train ticket. I sat in their incident room holding his lanyard from work – his mother had brought it in for me because it helps me make a connection if I have something material from the deceased – and it came to me – where he was, what he'd been doing. They'd been looking for him along the route he was supposed to take – down the riverbanks and under bridges, places like that. They had a map on the wall with his normal way home marked out on it in a yellow highlighter. He wasn't a well man. *Still water*, that's what he told me. Still water, over his head and all around him. I told them to change tack. To check the canal. *It's out of his way*, they said. *Check it anyway*, I said. *A diving team costs a fortune*, they said. *Check it anyway*, I said. And that's where they found him.'

Mark had been looking at her sceptically all this time, but smiling too – as if this was a debate he took pleasure in having with her. Not a couple after all, I thought. A husband or boyfriend wouldn't be so scathing about his partner's profession in a public place, not when drink had been taken. He'd know better. This was different. It was almost like flirting.

'He wanted to be found. To be put to rest. Everything that had been troubling his mind, his worries, his illness, the wounds from his childhood, it all lifts off when you pass the veil. They tell me – my spirits – that's what death is like. All the earthly and material things that get in the way of bliss just lift away and dissolve. He was happy. But there was this one last thing in the way of his rest. He wanted his mother to know where he was.'

Mark shook his head, then looked directly at me. I looked away – feeling that I'd been caught out doing something wrong.

'Have you heard of this guy? Blake Barrett?'

'No,' I said truthfully. There was a third stool near to them and he patted it. I sat down.

'Joyce here is just telling me about her job. She sees things. Dead things. She talks to dead people.' He glanced at my glass, waved a hand at the barman and ordered another round – vodka for me, a pint for himself, and a large glass of white wine for Joyce. I liked it that he bought her a drink, even if he thought she was a lunatic and was talking rubbish. I liked that about him.

'Joyce,' he said, once the drinks had been supplied, 'are you telling me that if I went and looked up the court records or the police archives or whatever it is – public documents, they will be – that show how the investigation was conducted, are you telling me I'd find your name in there? Find out that the evidence you provided was central to solving the case?'

Joyce laughed. She wasn't a bit rattled or embarrassed. In her shoes, I'd have been writhing.

'Of course you won't,' she said, as if it was Mark who was missing the point. 'Police forces only call me in when they're struggling. It's almost an admission of failure. They're hardly going to advertise that, are they?'

'And that's what the Lancashire Constabulary have done? Found Connie Fallon's remains then phoned you up to ask for the address of her murderer?'

That was her name. The little girl who had gone missing and been found dead. There were photographs of her everywhere, and of her front garden, her pink bike lying abandoned on the patio where she had been playing with it.

'The police haven't commissioned me this time,' Joyce said gently. 'She found me herself. They do that sometimes. She doesn't understand what's happened to her. She wants her mum to come and get her.'

Mark shook his head and looked at me – a 'can you believe this' expression on his face.

'I'm going to get in touch with her mother. Offer my services directly. I can't ignore Connie's voice.'

'Jesus Christ.'

I don't know why I did this – it wasn't like me at all – but I put my hand on his arm. I wanted to both comfort and restrain him, I think.

'Mrs Fallon might find it a consolation,' I said, in as concilia-tory a manner as I could manage (for I too was more on Mark's side of things in this argument). 'It might help her with her griev-ing. People go and light candles in a church, don't they, and there's no science to that.'

Joyce smiled. 'Maybe. Maybe it will work like that. But my work is with Connie. She's the one asking for my help.'

'How much will you charge her mother?' Mark asked.

He was drunk and bolshy and this gave me a misleading impression of him, because Mark is not usually a brisk or argumentative man, even when he's had a few. Even so, that night I admired his stridency and his outspokenness in defence of Connie's mother. He was obviously imagining her as a woman made credulous and imbecilic by grief, about to open her heart and wallet to a charlatan. His protectiveness was attractive. I found Joyce's calmness and unshakable faith in the reality of what she was saying appealing too. I had never been sure of anything at all, and I caught myself wanting her to put her hands on my head and tell me what was in there and what was going to happen to me next while Mark stood guard over both of us. I would have paid her for that, if I'd had any money.

'I never charge for this sort of work,' Joyce said. 'None of us do. Not the proper ones.'

Mark shook his head again and I could see he had given up. I still had my hand on his arm and he placed his palm on top of mine, just briefly. He wasn't brushing me away; he was acknowledging me.

Joyce clocked it – a little movement that Mark seemed unaware of himself – and smiled.

'You two,' she said, 'you have a real connection. I don't see it very often. Where did you meet?'

She had mistaken us for a couple. Mark leaned back and put his arm around me. My dress – which in comparison to Joyce's was certainly not passing muster as vintage and could well be described as dowdy – rustled a little around my shoulders. It was that type of material – stiff and shiny, smelling like loft spaces and charity shop back rooms do. I became self-conscious about it.

'Us two? We've been knocking about together for donkey's years,' he said. He leaned over and kissed my cheek gently. He smelled of beer and aftershave. I fluttered a bit. It had been a good while since I had been kissed and these things do have their normal physiological effects.

'You look good together,' Joyce said. 'You've got complementary energies. Earth meets water. Soil and rain.'

Mark pulled me in tighter. I knew what he was doing but because I liked the feel of his arm around me I let him do it anyway, tucking myself in under his shoulder. Later, I'd see that the makeup I'd put on my face had applied itself to the lapel of his suit: a little pale impression of my cheek and nose impressed on the material, like the Turin Shroud.

'I'm lucky to have her,' he said. It was only pretend, but even pretend compliments are something.

'There's a special link between you two. No, there is. Soil and rain. It makes the flowers grow.' Joyce lifted her glass and slid off her stool. 'Now I have to go and congratulate Sharon. But I think there's another happy couple in the room tonight. I've not seen anything as strong as this,' she waved her hand at us hazily, as if to indicate an aura of some kind that only she could see, 'in a very long time.' She paused, put her head on one side and beamed at us. 'You two really do love each other, don't you?'

I ducked my head against his shoulder again. I was blushing – blushing incandescently – and although Mark was laughing at me, I could see that he was feeling a little coy too.

Now I wonder who the victor was in that little skirmish. Maybe Joyce knew what she was doing all along, and just wanted to knock Mark off his perch of certainty and discomfit him a little. She drifted away to the dance floor, holding her glass up high as she weaved her way through the crowd and vanished from our sight, leaving Mark and me at the bar to get to know each other. He took me back to his flat that night and from then on, up until he disappeared, we were very rarely apart.

* * *

In the aftermath of that first visit from the police, I thought about the early days of my and Mark's relationship often. I kept trying to work out when the pretence started and ended and which one of us ended up being the butt of the joke. Was it auspicious that we met at a wedding? I wondered about contacting Sharon, the colleague who was getting married that day. People make contact with old friends all the time. We could reminisce a little about Dorry and his strange habits. I could even find a way to ask about her friend, the medium who claimed to have good results working occasionally with the police.

'Joyce?' she'd have said, brutally, frankly, directly. She was that type. 'What do you want Joyce for? Are you planning a séance?'

I talked myself out of calling Sharon in the end. We lost touch a long time ago. I no longer worked at the garden centre and I suspected she might be living an entirely different kind of life to the one she was living when we conducted our superficial acquaintance in the staffroom of Dorry's Home and Garden Supplies. Her marriage would have lasted. She, no doubt, had several children and a house with a garden and a drive on which to park a respectable-looking car. I do not recognise that wedding guest in the borrowed dress, game enough to involve herself in a conversation that had nothing to do with her and to go home with a stranger. Today I live only in the present because the consequences of things going wrong are easier to see and more frightening to imagine than they were back then.

The police also wanted to know why I was back from work later than usual that afternoon. I thought it might have looked suspicious to them. *I went to see my father. He's unwell.* I was afraid I was going to get into trouble. So I veered between clipped, short answers – name, rank and serial number only – or I babbled, uselessly.

I still had a key to my father's house, which is on a hill to the south of the city. I passed it every day as I went to and from the university where I worked, and that day, because it had been a while, or because I was still feeling the remnants of my bad mood and wanted Mark to worry about me being later than usual, I stopped off to see him on my way back home. *It would have been mid-afternoon. Around 4 p.m.* That's what I told the police.

Olena and my father were in the living room, the telly on too loud. I called through to them as I took off my coat and hung it on the overloaded hooks in the hallway. In better times my father had been a keen gardener, and his fleece and heavy jacket were still hanging on the hooks, slightly mud streaked and smelling of damp. Olena had taken the house in hand since she'd been coming more regularly, but there was still more to do, and I had to edge in between crates of the second-hand books that my father liked to collect and a stack of old coffee tins, the labels removed.

'You're here!' he cried, looking away from the television. It was a documentary. Something to do with wind farms, if I remember correctly.

'How are you, Dad?' I asked, and held my breath.

I had a great number of fathers: an embarrassment of them, you could say. There was Angry Father, Disgusting Father, Happy Father, Shoplifting Father, Mournful Father, Unfounded Accusations Father, and – my favourite father of all – Doting Father. Since he'd become unwell I had been making the effort to see him more often, but I never knew which one of his incarnations would be sitting on the brown settee waiting for me when I arrived.

'Never mind how I am, love. How are you? Are you healthy? Are you happy?'

Doting Father! I was relieved, sat up close beside him and held his hand. Olena kept him nice. He smelled like Nivea cream and Daz washing powder.

'I am happy, Dad,' I said. He squeezed my hand.

'I can tell you are. You've got a look about you. You're not pregnant, are you? Has that man of yours put you in the family way? You're not going to make me a granddad, are you?'

We'd been through this before. I smiled and stroked his arm and put my head on his shoulder – he liked to be petted when he was in this kind of mood, and I liked doing it.

'I'm too young to have a baby,' I said, in my little voice. 'I'm still your baby.'

Olena, who had been ironing in front of the television, laughed. 'Your father has been asking after you all morning, Laurie. It's so good you could come.'

Was there a veiled criticism there? Probably.

'Where's your mother, petal? I've been waiting for her. She neglects me, you know.'

Mournful Father made his appearance. Sometimes he thought Olena was my mother, who has been dead for six years, and sometimes she played along.

'I'm here, Dad.' I said. 'Tell me about your programme. What are you watching?'

He squinted at me suspiciously. I wonder if we all have lots of versions of ourselves tucked up inside our heads – a whole choir of possible understudies in there, some more trustworthy than others, but all waiting impatiently for their turn onstage. I feel them inside me sometimes, flickering in a great silver shoal, arguing between themselves, never quiet, never unanimous.

'I'm trying to watch the television but your mother keeps disturbing me. I don't know how to cope with her. Did I tell you what she's been up to?'

Olena and I looked at each other. She didn't quite roll her eyes.

'Amazing, isn't it, how big those turbines are? Did you hear what the woman said, Dad? About all the geese getting caught in the blades? It's a shame, isn't it?'

'She's not herself, you know. She's been acting up again.'

'We could get Olena to take us on a drive sometime, if you like. There's loads of them on the way to Heysham. We could take a look.'

'The man from the Prudential was round yesterday. He brought the paperwork to go over our policy. Your mother was sitting in that chair – right there,' he pointed at the armchair under the window. Olena became engrossed with her ironing, smiling under her breath.

'We could go right into the village. Get an ice cream from the café,' I said desperately.

'She had her going-out skirt on. Her knees aren't what they were but all the same. No tights. She looked the poor man in the eye and uncrossed her legs. You could see everything.' He clutched at my arm for emphasis and raised his eyebrows. '*Everything.*'

'Dad, you know that's not right. Stop it.'

'Tell your mother. She was the one . . .' he lost his thread. His eyes flicked towards the television, then back towards me. 'You could see *it*. You know what I'm talking about, don't you?'

'You're being disgusting, Dad.'

He took this personally. 'I won't have you speak to me like that,' he said, his bottom lip trembling. He kept hold of my arm and shook it, as if he was trying to convince me of something.

'Your mother . . . she . . . where is she?'

'You're getting yourself worked up. Mum didn't do any of those things. That's *Basic Instinct*. It was on telly the other week. Did Olena let you watch it?'

'I don't know why you're doing this to me!' he said, his eyes full of tears. The broken veins in his cheeks reddened and darkened and I worried about a blood vessel in his head or neck exploding and damaging him permanently, or even worse. That was how he got Olena to let him have his own way all the time, I suppose.

'Mr Spencer! Gerald. Gerald!' Olena loomed over him. She's fat and has an enormous floss of curly bleached-blonde hair and tits that are, even in the blue and white tunic she wears for work, frankly obscene, and I think her physical appearance – so much more present and vivid than mine – was one of the things that helped her take charge of him when she needed to. She takes up space. I mean that as a good thing.

'Gerald. You're missing your documentary. You've been asking for it all afternoon and now you're spoiling it for yourself.'

'Have I?'

He looked doubtful. And ready to trust. She nodded decisively.

'You have been bothering me to death about it.'

He let me hold his hand again and I patted and squeezed it, but he waved me away.

'Give me half a minute, Laurie,' he said, 'I've had an awful day at work. I'm bloody done in. All I need is five minutes. Go on and pester your mother, will you?' he gestured towards Olena, who was back behind her ironing board.

'Everything's fine, Gerald,' she said lightly. She never called him 'Mr Spencer' when he had her mixed up with my mother because it upset him. 'You have a rest now. You deserve it.'

He settled himself back against the settee cushions and, mollified, turned back to the television screen.

'I don't want you to let him talk about my mother like that,' I said quietly.

'He doesn't know he's making it all up. It's not like he's deliberately lying to you,' she said. My father, engrossed by the television, showed no signs of hearing. Still, I lowered my voice because it felt strange to talk about him when he was sitting right there.

'My mother wasn't like that.'

She shrugged. 'And I don't suppose your Prudential man comes to visit any more, either. It is what it is.' She had a little plastic spray bottle of water: the kind used for dampening the leaves of houseplants. She used it to moisten the cuffs of my father's shirt then took the iron to them.

'It doesn't do him any good to go along with it.'

'What's the harm? Would you rather he knew how much he'd forgotten?'

'My mother wouldn't want him remembering her in that way,' I said. His stories, unchallenged, were contaminating the past.

'Your mother is dead. She isn't wanting anything.' She used the pointed nose of the iron to get between the buttons. She was good like that. Every day a clean, ironed shirt for my father, and a tie too, if he felt like wearing one. It made extra work for her but she seemed to like doing it. And I did pay her by the hour from his savings account or the cash he kept lying around the house for emergencies.

'He's obsessed with sex,' I said.

'Your father is very innocent. His past is all gone,' she made a 'pouf' gesture with her hand. A magic trick. Disappearing rabbits. 'It doesn't matter what he fills the gap with, does it?'

Olena isn't a nurse – she's just a cleaner, like me, who started with mopping and hoovering but took a liking to my dad and began doing his meals when she noticed he was getting a bit too unpredictable to handle the cooker. It grew from there. We'd got to the point where she fancied herself the lynchpin of his care and read articles about vascular dementia, which is what he had, in her spare time. I worried constantly that she was buttering him up so he'd leave her the house and assumed that the mad old bastard had made a new will out to her benefit.

'I better get going.'

'Why don't you stay, Laurie?' I have always liked the way she says my name. Something exotic about the vowels. 'I'm going to make chops.'

'I've got to get back and see to Mark,' I said, though in truth I was still interested in being noticeably late in order to get him wondering: the little revenge I'd concocted over the business with the curtain. I loitered for quite a while in the kitchen, checking my father's stocks of tea and coffee, going through the unopened mail and inspecting the seedlings he had planted the week before and left to germinate in trays on the kitchen table.

It was past five o'clock when I finally left Olena to finish her ironing. My father, in his Pervert Aspect, was beginning another story – the one he liked to tell about the time he lost my mother on holiday in Spain, and found her on a pleasure boat, fucking a local.

'Did she really?' Olena was saying, as I closed the door. 'And you hit him? That sounds brave.'

Mark wasn't at home when I got back from visiting my father. The bed was unmade. The mug I'd drunk from that morning still on my bedside table. I called out for him, even though the flat is so small there was nowhere for him to hide. I assumed he had gone to the garage on the main road for more tobacco or milk and I considered walking around the block a few times, just so he could have the experience of returning, as I had, to an unexpectedly and unpleasantly empty flat. I didn't worry. And when night came and I caved in, tried to call him and heard his mobile phone ringing in his jacket pocket, which was still on the dirty-clothes chair in the bedroom, I only thought he was out drinking and teaching me a lesson over the business with the curtain. In the morning when I woke I cried a little in my loneliness, then got pissed off at him for causing it and vowed to carry on as usual, by way of revenge. I deleted my call from his phone, so when he got home he wouldn't know I had worried about him.

The morning after that, even though I'd never known him to be the type of man to go out on a spree or a bender, I called the hospital – in case, like Blake Barrett, he had fallen in the canal on the way home from the pub. The woman on the switchboard asked me what he'd been wearing.

'I don't know,' I said. I opened the wardrobe door and looked, mystified, at its ordinary contents. Many of the hangers were empty, our clothes draped over the backs of chairs or heaped on the bedroom floor.

'Jeans, probably?'

'Right,' she said. I heard the sound of typing. 'And you're really sure you have no idea what else he was wearing?'

I felt stupid and neglectful when I couldn't answer. *He was in the shower*, I wanted to say.

'No,' I said. 'Just ordinary clothes.'

'I see,' she coughed lightly. 'Well, there's no unidentified man been admitted in the last week, I'm afraid. But I only do accident and emergency and referrals. If you want the mortuary, I'm going to have to transfer you.'

'No. No, it's all right,' I said hastily. I was embarrassed more than distressed. If Mark and I were having a skirmish, then he was winning.

'You can phone back in a few hours,' she told me, 'we update the systems at the end of every shift.' I thanked her, but I didn't call again.

I didn't call the police for another five weeks, and when they arrived at the flat they were very interested in this time lapse. At the time I found it almost impossible to satisfy them with my account for the delay, or for the fact that I'd gone to work as usual in the meantime and spoken to nobody about Mark's disappearance. I appreciate this was unusual behaviour: I will try to illuminate it now.

It is true that during that period nobody would have been able to tell what was happening – or not happening – in my personal life. Apart from my private crying jags on the balcony at home, I lived as if Mark was somehow always watching me. I don't mean this in a spiritual way, as if he was a ghost or a guardian angel checking up on me and even standing by to comfort me or protect me from harm. That's not the feeling I had at the time. And it was more of a feeling than a fully worked-through belief, but if I could try to put it into words now, I would say that during those early weeks I had the general impression that Mark was very close by and observing how I reacted to his nasty little vanishing trick. That, because of the business of the curtain, he was determined to punish me and see me upset, so he would be hovering behind a hedge as I waited for the bus for work, looking for a sign that I was in turmoil.

Each morning I stood in the bus shelter exactly as I usually did, impassively staring at the street before me, sometimes listening to true crime podcasts on my phone, because that was what I always did in the morning. I took care to dress as normal, and some mornings – when the impression he was watching me was particularly strong and I was almost convinced he was about to leap out from behind a parked car or artfully placed wheelie bin – I decided to hum a little, or whistle. 'Oh What a Beautiful Morning!' or 'What a Wonderful World' were my particular favourites, and sometimes I would dissolve into laughter while murmuring the words to these songs in the shelter, the warm spring rain streaking down the window and dripping off the roof.

While it would have been difficult for Mark to follow me all the way to work and discover where on the large concrete campus I had been assigned to perform my duties then to navigate the twists and turns of the labyrinthine passages between the lecture theatres, seminar blocks, offices and halls of residence, the impression he was nearby remained with me. On the assumption that pretending to be happier than I really was hurt nobody and might just show him what I was made of if he had happened to work out my rota, I carried on with my plan. While I cleaned and vacuumed and emptied bins and cleared away screwed-up pieces of paper and dried-out whiteboard pens and empty water bottles from seminar rooms in the morning dusk or late-night dark, I still acted as if he could see me, smiling as I worked and generally looking cheerful and unperturbed by his disappearance.

But the truth was, no matter how she looked to the outside world, poor daft sap Penelope had a terrible existence waiting for her wandering husband to come home and so did I. I didn't plan to inhabit her indeterminate life – faithful wife to an absent lover – for the rest of my fertile years. I won't go into that first five weeks further except to say I finally told the police because the pain of the not-knowing had become greater than the fear of finding out, and when I did call them, it was with a sense of both fury and humiliation: Mark had won – he had managed to continue his stunt to the point where I had really no choice but to report it to the authorities.

'There was no argument?' the woman officer had asked, for the third or fourth time. 'Not even about him losing his job?' I had told them it was perfectly normal for him to be home in the day when I was at work because he'd been made redundant from his job at the power station and they got a bit fixated on that.

'No, nothing like that. He brought me a cup of tea in bed,' I said.

She raised her eyebrows.

'But you thought he'd left you?'

They're trained to be incredulous because most of the people they talk to will be lying to them. I tried not to take it personally. Did you know that over the course of a normal life all of us come across seventeen murderers? That each of us is lied to at least forty times a day – even, or especially, by those we're in a close relationship with? It isn't surprising to me, and probably accounts for most of the discomfort I feel when I am around other people – that sense that I am on thin ice, about to fall through. But how much worse it must be for a police officer. It must drive you a bit mad, being lied to the whole time. I tried to say something to that effect. They wouldn't let me make them a tea or a coffee. Did I mention that already? It was very strange. On the television they always let you make a cup of tea so they can look around your living room and talk about you when you're in the kitchen and I wanted to give them the opportunity to do that.

'It was just an ordinary morning,' I insisted.

'But you thought he'd ended your relationship, which is why you didn't ring us?' she said. 'What made you think that?'

'It seemed more likely, at first. Statistically it was more likely than him just walking off without telling anyone.'

'Or coming to harm,' she added. It was like sitting the French oral exam, the teacher making heavy-handed hints as to what topics she wanted me to cover next. She looked puzzled. As if I should know all this already.

'Yes.' I tried again. 'It seemed statistically more likely that he had ended our relationship, which is not a police matter, than he had decided to walk off somewhere or disappear, or that he had come to harm. Which is why I didn't call you.'

It all felt impossible. To explain about the trick I thought he was playing on me. About why I'd phoned the hospital, then regretted it.

'I think I must have been in a kind of shock,' I said weakly.

She frowned slightly and tapped at her screen to make a note.

'For five weeks.'

'Yes.'

'Any history of mental ill health?'

I shook my head. Did she mean Mark, or me? I didn't ask.

'Family problems? Issues with money? Drugs?'

It was hard to concentrate. We were sitting on the settee, our knees nearly touching, while her companion was crashing around in the hallway, opening doors and checking inside the wardrobe.

'Any children?' she asked, as the other one opened the door of the small room.

'No,' I said. She paused, as if that was something else I should explain. I said nothing.

'Is he a drinker?'

I shook my head.

'And is he under the doctor for anything? Regular medication he needs to be taking?'

'No.'

She swiped at her tablet, revealing the next set of questions she was supposed to ask me, I think.

'You've phoned his friends? His work colleagues?'

'I already told you, he isn't working right now. There wasn't really anyone to—'

She interrupted me, bored. 'So you're worried about him now. You've,' she looked at the screen in front of her again, 'finally decided to call us in. After five weeks.'

Every time she said 'five weeks', it sounded less like a statement of fact and more like an accusation. I clenched my fists on my lap, saw she had noticed it and forced myself to relax my hands. Under her gaze, that didn't look right either.

'Why is that? Why did you call us today?'

'I had a change of heart. A chance to think things through more clearly.'

'I see. And what do you think might have happened to him?'

I shrugged. 'I really couldn't tell you. I wondered if he'd fallen and lost his memory. Or was lying in a coma. People fall, don't they? Into canals?' I was thinking about Blake Barret again, and had the sense not to elaborate. Instead, I told her about calling the hospital. I was trying to redeem myself. If whatever Mark had done, or had been done to him, was my fault – which I was afraid was the conclusion they were coming to – then I'd hardly have called the hospital, would I? This seemed to surprise her.

'So you *did* think he might have hurt himself?' She looked at me sharply. As if I'd tripped myself up, which in a way I had.

'An accident,' I said vaguely.

'You're going to have to slow down and go over this again with us, Mrs Wright.'

I wanted them to look on their computers or do whatever they did with the security cameras in town and find out where he had gone. And I wanted them to bring him home. But I didn't want Mark to know I had made it happen. I didn't want him to know how worried I had been, just in case he was still trying to upset me. It was not possible to explain this to her.

'I thought there might have been an accident. But someone would have called me by now, if that had happened, wouldn't they? So then I thought, probably not.'

'We'll check the hospitals again,' she said. 'And we'll need a list of his bank accounts. Can you do that?'

'Yes,' I said.

I jumped then, because a clatter from the next room startled me. The noise was actually the other officer taking the panel off the side of the bath to look into the dusty cavity underneath, though I didn't know that at the time. I thought instead that a bird had flown into the house through an open window and was fluttering around the kitchen, knocking jars off the spice rack in its fright and panic and haste to be away. That happened now and again, when we left the door to the balcony open late at night.

2

Penelope? Don't you dare be surprised, just because of what I do, that I read. Please note: when I eventually got bored of working at Dorry's and the cleaning job came up at the university, there was another one going at the hospital, which was both nearer to my house and very slightly better paid. I chose the university position because I thought that as a 'valued part of the campus community', I would also be entitled to a library card, although in fact it turned out that I was not.

You'd have thought that the uncomfortable, unsettling and largely disappointing experience of seeking help from the police would have knocked me off balance. I will admit that I expected and hoped for much more in the way of sympathy than I actually got. But afterwards, I did the washing-up and emptied the bin and carried on carrying on as usual at work. What other choice did I have? The end of the exam period was upon us, the graduation ceremonies were looming and, however I felt, there was a lot to do. I told myself I was far too busy to sit around brooding.

In the summer term it worked like this: just as we – by which I mean the domestic facilities and estates teams – needed the campus to be looking its shining and pristine best in time for all the parents and relatives to descend, dressed up as if for a wedding, and wanting to know, for sure, the investments they had made in their child's education had really been worth it, the children themselves, finally released from lectures, seminars and exam preparations, went a bit mad and started having parties and collecting road signs and traffic cones and vomiting and

pissing down the banisters in the communal areas. We were –
students and domestic and estates teams – pulling in two different directions, each party's effort cancelling out the work of the
other, until the only sensible thing would have been for both
parties to just down tools and leave things as they were.

I was sharing this theory with my friend Eddie, as we stood
behind the bin store, smoking.

'You'd think so,' he said, 'but you're not factoring in the natural process of entropy. Even if every single Wanker in the place,'
(we called the students 'Wankers' and the academics 'Staff
Wankers', just to distinguish them from each other, though in
practice, there really wasn't much difference at all) 'ceased their
efforts to make our lives utterly miserable, the universe itself
would carry on fucking us. The dust would still settle. The rain
would still streak the windows. The leaves would still blow in
through the doors and crumble into the carpet on the communal
stairwells.'

He waved his vaper around. I liked it when he talked like this.
It made me laugh. In my heart of hearts I knew that Mark was
not really watching me and as telling the police had won me not
sympathy and condolences, but merely humiliation and suspicion, I decided to tell Eddie too.

'Mark's gone,' I said. Just out of the blue like that.

'Gone where?' he said.

'I don't know. He's just fucked off.'

'Temporary?'

I shrugged. 'It's been over a month.' Precisely, it had been
forty-four days.

'Laurie. You never said.'

I looked at my feet. Eddie paused for a few seconds, playing
with the settings on his vaper. I got the impression he was weighing up what to say next. How could he show an interest without
prodding me so hard my composure would fall apart and he
would have to deal with my tears and hysteria by himself? I

wanted him to prod me. A good cry and the associated coddling that would come with it would do me good.

'Did he say why?'

'He's not said anything.'

'What a cunt.'

'I've had the police out,' I added. Eddie was not reacting as I had hoped he would.

'Shit,' Eddie exhaled vapour into the air between us. It smelled like strawberries.

'There's not a lot they can do,' I said. 'It's not illegal to go missing. Unless they think he's particularly vulnerable, or mixed up in something dodgy . . .'

'They're not going to do anything?'

'Check his bank accounts. He left his phone behind. His wallet. So it looks as if he didn't plan it.'

'And?'

'I'm waiting to hear.'

'You told Shaw?' (Shaw was our supervisor.) 'You'd get compassionate, wouldn't you?'

'I want to be busy,' I said.

'I don't blame you. It didn't do you any good before, did it?' he said. I shook my head.

Eddie was delicately – by his standards – referring to an extended period of sick leave I'd been forced to take at the beginning of the year. Shaw, to give her credit, had been reasonably sympathetic. But Eddie was right. In that case the time off had done me no good at all and I had no intention of repeating those endless days cooped up in the flat, staring at the television and mindlessly drinking. In practical terms, with no wage from Mark coming in, I simply couldn't afford it.

Eddie vaped meditatively. 'I can't get my head around it.'

'Me neither.'

'Are you worried about him?'

'He's either a cunt, like you say, or he's dead in a hedge. I've to be either furious or grief stricken. And until I know which it is, I've got to wait.'

'Can you do both at once? Multitask?' he smirked. I laughed smoke out of my nostrils, in spite of myself. No sympathy would be forthcoming from him, but he was certainly going to do his best to cheer me up.

'Not yet. I've been practising though. Best I can do is to flicker between the two.'

'You oscillate.'

'I do.'

'I've always suspected. You dirty bitch.'

'It's exhausting.'

He laughed. I didn't join in. He put his hand out, tapped my shoulder, then put it back in his pocket.

'And after everything you've been through,' he said, and shook his head. 'I'm going to go for cunt.'

'I hope he is a cunt,' I said, 'and not dead in a hedge.'

'Don't be daft,' he said, 'he's just . . .' Eddie let the sentence trail away and I think his inability to complete it helped him to realise how I was feeling and how it might be to live in the space at the end of that unfinished sentence. Just down the shops? Just in a different city, living with someone else? Just pretending? Just . . . *what*?

The silence grew awkward and I couldn't look at him. I wiped my eyes with the heel of my hand.

'Fucking hell. That's pathetic.'

'Course not. Anyone would be in bits.'

'Don't,' I said. I thought I'd wanted the sighing and patting and condolences, but even the hint of them had released something I did not have the wherewithal to deal with. He stepped towards me and I waved him away. It would have been excruciating to be caught embracing behind a bin store by a couple of Staff Wankers wafting past on their way to the library.

'Don't you cry. Don't you dare,' he said, helplessly.

'I won't. I won't.' I said.

'He'll be fine. I read an article about this. *Ghosting*. That's what they call it. He's ghosted you. Sign of an immature personality. You're well rid.'

'You read an article about it?'

This was a lie so transparent as to be almost laughable. Eddie, although one of the cleverest men I have ever met, is also – due to what I suspect is probably undiagnosed dyslexia – barely able to read. For the first year that we worked together he used to bring me his rotas and payslips and asked me to read him the 'headlines and main points' because he had a headache, or had forgotten his glasses, or was too hung-over to focus on the print. I caught on after a while and though we've never addressed it directly, that little unspoken truth between us stuck us together and we've been friends ever since.

'My sister had an article about it in one of her magazines. She said, "That's you, that is." It's a thing. She gave me the highlights. The Wankers are all doing it to each other left right and centre. They don't bother dumping each other any more.'

He could probably have quoted the article word for word. He has that kind of memory. You can't ever tell Eddie anything without him storing it away and keeping it for later. Sometimes it felt as if all his knowings about me were hoarded as ammunition; at other times, it felt more like being held in mind and cherished.

'You're not a ghoster,' I said.

'I know,' Eddie agreed eagerly. 'I lay it out for them. All of them. No commitments. No staying over. No meeting the parents. Recreation only. I'm a free spirit.'

'You're a shagger, Eddie.'

He nodded and doffed an imaginary hat. 'Nothing wrong with that.'

'He left his stuff, though,' I said.

'Doesn't mean anything. I once left a leather jacket – nearly brand new – on some girl's settee. Walked out and left it. Three hundred pound, it was.'

Eddie was trying to find an explanation that would leave me angry rather than upset.

'I remember that jacket,' I said. 'Why did you leave it?'

Eddie smirked. 'She was asleep on top of it.'

'Jesus, Eddie.'

'It'll be all right,' he said. 'Someone would have phoned you if he'd washed up in a hospital somewhere.'

I threw my fag end onto the floor and tapped it out with the toe of my trainer.

'We should get you out,' Eddie said.

The radio on his hip started to fizz and chatter. Someone – Wankers, probably, as it didn't seem like the type of trick Staff Wankers would pull so late in the academic year – had drawn a giant spurting cock and balls in the main square. We were needed.

'Friday week? You. Me.' He pointed. 'We're going to get out and get some pints in us. We're going to play pool. We may even have a kebab.'

I smiled.

'Right you are,' I said.

By the time I got home that afternoon, I had decided Eddie was right and my husband probably had ghosted me. I took a hold-all from the top of the wardrobe. Mark was not one of those people who had boxes of old school exercise books or concert tickets or anything like that. I'd already been through his chest of drawers, his bookshelf, his phone. There was nothing to find. But now I was not searching, I was clearing out. I opened the top drawer, and loaded socks and underwear into the bag. He took antacids at night, and there were loads of the empty blister packets down his side of the bed and on the floor in front of his drawers. I put those in too. Packets of tissues. Pens and pencils and sudoku books. An Ursula Le Guin paperback. A tin of Tiger Balm. The next drawer down was for his jeans and T-shirts. I worked methodically, emptying the chest from top to bottom.

When the bag was full, I zipped up the holdall and left the flat. Took it down in the lift, then went out through the double doors and looked around. Right in front of the doors? The car park? The communal bike shelter? Sling it into one of the giant Biffa bins we all shared? Leave it, even more contentiously, *next to* the Biffa? Was I leaving his belongings for him to retrieve or throwing them out? I couldn't decide, so I told myself I'd pop the bag into the bike shelter just in case it rained – that way it would be dry until he could come and get it. He couldn't be angry with me: lots of wives would have put everything he owned down the chute, and I hadn't done that. I realise this does not sound very sane. I was not thinking clearly.

When I got back to the flat, my mobile was ringing. I laughed. I'd made a crazy bargain with the universe – half spell, half prayer – while I was creeping around the bike shelter.

I'll leave his stuff out for him, and he can come and get it.

I'd imagined him being attracted back to the block, knowing, somehow, that his socks and jumpers and jeans were out there waiting for him. That he'd need them. And that he'd come back to get them. I'd see him, crossing the car park and edging towards the bike shelter, his hands in his pockets. I'd shout down from the balcony.

What would I shout? Something self-contained, and heartfelt, and witty. I would be invulnerable. He'd look up and I'd say my piece. A short piece, but an effective one. And he'd say something back. I didn't know what my words would be and in my fantasy I could see his lips moving – could even see the expression of sorrow and fear and longing for me on his face – but I could not hear the words he spoke. Even at my most self-serving, I could not imagine a sob story I would be able to accept.

We were on the sixteenth floor. Would there be a Romeo-and-Juliet-type moment? Probably not. Maybe I'd just throw what was left of his stuff down at him. There'd be satisfaction in that: seeing his jumpers rain downwards like the ghosts of men, jumping. I imagined his face. He had been expecting a warm welcome. My arms wide open. Me, tear stained. All is forgiven. The man would be disappointed. Crestfallen is what he'd be, which is not a word I use often.

My mobile continued to ring, and I laughed again because he was telephoning me to beg forgiveness, and I had suddenly become powerful. Disgustingly powerful. I decided (it only took a split second for my mind to go through all this) I probably wasn't going to answer my phone to him. He could wait a while. Leave a message. I lurched towards anger. The cheek of him to assume I'd be available, just because he felt like talking to me. I closed the front door to the flat and grabbed at my phone. A withheld number.

'Hello?'

'Mrs Wright?'

It was the woman police officer – the blonde-haired sceptical one – and when I heard her voice my knees went.

'Yes? It's me. It's me. Have you found him?'

'We don't have him, Mrs Wright,' she said quickly. I paced up and down the hallway. The front door, the kitchen door, the bathroom door, the small room door, the bedroom door. Touched each of them with the finger on my spare hand as I passed. She was saying something about a fight. A fight at work.

'That's not right. He was made redundant,' I said, 'a couple of months ago. Back in April. I told you?'

'You did,' she said, 'and we went to speak to his boss and his old colleagues. It sometimes helps us to get a more rounded view. We were trying to find out if he was especially vulnerable. If there was something in his life – a part of his life that you didn't know about – that he might have been trying to run away from.

If there was someone who, and I'm sorry to say this, Mrs Wright, might have wanted to hurt him.'

'And did you find anything?'

'As I was saying: your husband told you he'd been made redundant, but his employer has confirmed today that he actually resigned after an altercation between him and a colleague.'

I cast my mind back to the month before he had disappeared. The day when he'd come home a little late, and a little drunk, and told me he'd been let go because of a budget overspend that required his team to be consolidated. He told me he liked his position as a security guard at the power plant well enough but losing it was no disaster. The work sounded boring to me but he'd claimed he enjoyed walking the perimeter at night, alone with his thoughts and the faint buzzing that sent the energy to the grid. Still, it wasn't exactly a career. He said it was all right. That it didn't matter. That he'd find something else soon enough. I believed him. It took hardly any effort at all.

'Someone hit him?' I asked. I knew nothing about that. I'd have noticed my husband coming home bloodied or bruised.

'No, he was the instigator – or that's what we're being told. They would have sacked him on the spot for gross misconduct but he walked out, and they decided to take it as his resignation.'

'I see.'

'He didn't tell you about this, Mrs Wright?'

'I think it's pretty clear he didn't, don't you?'

'We need to talk to the man he was fighting with. Find out what caused it. There might have been something on his mind. But I should also say at this juncture that we've had the reports back from the bank and I'm afraid it doesn't look good.'

'He's not using his account?'

'That's right. Could he have cash?'

'I thought he might. Redundancy money perhaps. But now you tell me he wasn't made redundant.'

'Yes. I know it must be difficult. But we are working on this. We'll be in touch. We'll need to come and see you again.'

'Of course.'

'Will you look out a photo of him? As recent as you can.'

'Should I bring it to the station?'

'You can email it to us,' she said.

I didn't want to end the phone call. But there was nothing more to say. I waited for her tone to move from the business-like to the sympathetic and for her to offer me some kindness or reassurance, but it did not.

She could have told me a fact that I had heard on one of my podcasts: that within the year, 99 per cent of missing person cases are resolved, and only 0.04 per cent of them end in the discovery of a body. She could have said that – that the odds were very, very good. I already knew, but it would have reassured me to hear it. She didn't. Perhaps she was bored or resentful. This would be a dull, plodding job. Mark's case would never end up on the news, like Connie Fallon's had. He wasn't a vulnerable child or a pretty teenage girl who would get a slot on *Crimestoppers* and a filmed reconstruction. Our city wouldn't hold a candlelit vigil and nobody would ask me to record a tearful appeal for information that would be broadcast on the evening news.

Did you know – because I didn't, not then – that over 300,000 people go missing every year? Most of them men, as it happens. That's a good-sized town, vanished into thin air. A rapture of husbands, fathers, sons and brothers. Maybe my policewoman's lack of sympathy stemmed from her boredom at the sheer routine nature of the case. But perhaps it was – and this is what I thought at the time – suspicion. She was holding me at arm's length the better to observe me because both of us knew full well that if harm had come to Mark, the prime suspect for the cause of that harm would be me, his wife. It's how it always is in crime dramas.

'He wasn't having an affair,' I said.

33

I looked up at the ceiling. Our neighbours, Tim and Katrina, would be up there having their tea or playing with their baby. Watching the telly or playing a board game or sweeping the floor. I thought about Katrina. Tried to imagine her lying in bed wearing something slutty and silky, the sheets artfully arranged around her, her eyeliner smudged. It was easy to imagine.

'We've found no evidence of that,' she said, carefully.

Was she lying? I didn't know what the rules were in these types of investigations. If they found something out about Mark – that he was, for example, popping upstairs whenever he said he was getting tobacco at the garage, and slipping Katrina one while Tim was at work . . . well – would they tell me? Would they have to tell me? Most of the terrible things human beings can do to each other aren't actually illegal. Even missing people have a right to privacy. Even missing bastards have a right to privacy. That's how my thoughts ran on.

'I'm not asking. I'm telling,' I said, trying not to sound like a madwoman. 'I'm just saying. In case it was in your minds. That he's run off and left me for another woman. Or that he was cheating on me and I found out about it. That didn't happen.'

'Okay,' she said. And, 'I think you should get some rest. Leave this to us for a little while, if you can. We will be in touch.'

I wanted to talk more. I kept thinking of that story – the woman who had killed her husband by braining him with a frozen leg of lamb. I can't remember what it was he was supposed to have done. Perhaps he was boring or annoying or emotionally unavailable. Perhaps he was having sex with her friend, right under her nose, and insisting that he wasn't. Whatever the backstory was, she'd killed him with the lamb then cooked the joint and served it to the police officers who were in her house searching for the murder weapon. I understood her motivation: a strange, self-cancelling urge to parade your darkest acts anonymously, to be there and not there, to linger at the scene of your own crime, pointing out the incriminating evidence while protesting your innocence.

After we hung up I went down in the lift and out to the bike shelter again. I retrieved the holdall and brought it back into the flat. The lift was broken and *of course* Katrina was there, struggling with her pram. I tried to hide the holdall. She must have noticed Mark's absence. I don't think I really suspected that she was hiding him under her bed – Tim would surely have mentioned it – but I turned my head as our paths crossed, and didn't offer to help her lift the pram up the stairs. We used to be friends but it seemed as if she wanted to avoid me too – she bent over the pram and busied herself fussing with her baby as I moved past her.

Once at home, sweating and breathless, I unpacked the clothes and underwear and bric-a-brac onto the bed and refolded all the clothing and placed it back in his drawers, neater than the way I'd found it. I arranged his empty blister packets of antacids in his top drawer. I wiped the dust from his books and stacked them neatly on his bedside table. It didn't take me long. All the while I thought about Mark fighting someone at the power station. Tried to imagine him swinging a punch, his fist flying through the air and connecting, in slow motion, with someone's face.

What's happened to my stuff, Laurie? he'd ask, when he came back and marvelled at the orderliness of it all.

I wanted to make things really nice and tidy, I'd say. *Things looked a bit dusty and in need of a freshen-up.*

I'd tell him it was my way of welcoming him home.

I also anticipated that the police would want to look through his things when they came next to update me on the progress of his case. There'd be no point waylaying their investigation by explaining that I had prematurely, and in high emotion, decided to dispose of all my husband's worldly goods. An unsympathetic eye would see a guilty wife disposing of evidence. I smoothed out the stacks of T-shirts and gently closed the drawer.

The next part is a little difficult and involves me confessing to a minor infraction. After I'd finished replacing Mark's things, I went into the living room and in a box under the coffee table where we keep our magazines and Scrabble set, I retrieved his laptop. The police officer had asked me if he owned one and I – not in the most orderly state of mind – had said that he hadn't. (His phone was a bog-standard Nokia – he had strongly held beliefs and concerns about the way the Deep State would use the location tracking services of the more modern smartphones – and after a cursory glance, they were uninterested in it.) I'd lied to her because, in January, when I had been home sick from work and at a loose end, I'd installed a keylogger programme on his machine.

I had a dim awareness that this act was illegal. When asked directly by the police, and knowing, because of the way the keylogger sent detailed records of all Mark's online activity directly to my email account, that there was nothing there of interest to them, I felt it would have been both foolish and unnecessary to incriminate myself and to distract them from more fruitful lines of inquiry.

My only defence here is that after a long period of marriage the other person feels less like a separate human being and more like an extension of the self. An act against them – and the installation of the keylogger was, by the standards of the world we live in and by the law itself, a very minor detrimental act (I had never used my secret knowledge to steal his money or harass him anonymously, for example) – feels less like aggression and more like self-harm, albeit against a part of the self that was mysterious, disconnected and apt to disappear at any moment, as it turned out.

My mother once told me – perhaps thinking of my father and what he got up to on his mysterious impromptu conferences and business meetings – that a person had no right to subject another to scrutiny of the minutiae of their life. Her knowledge of my father, I gathered, was limited to the broadest of brushstrokes and, other than a few notable exceptions, their marriage was based on a kind of tolerance characterised by distant civility. Which is why, in the end, he was able to surprise her with such horrible consistency. Accountants don't have conferences and meetings that require overnight stays in seaside bed and breakfasts and meals for two in gastropubs in the Trough of Bowland. I could have told her that.

I didn't want to be surprised in that way, but while I might have expected to find evidence of an affair with Katrina or a gambling addiction on Mark's computer, actually he just spent nearly all of his free time posting as NightGuard1980 on a variety of conspiracy theory websites. He avoided the rough and tumble or outright insanity of 4chan and Q-drops, preferring the older, gentler stories about the assassination of JFK and the murder of Marilyn Monroe. He got into arguments sometimes and, in these arguments, conducted entirely by posts stuffed with links to other websites and images that were intended to back up his theories, the joust would be about the truth, about seeing with naked eyes, about not falling for the nonsense that the Powers That Be were feeding the Sheeple.

I don't know why he was so bothered about it. How it all affected him, or what difference it would have made to his life if Marilyn Monroe had accidentally taken an overdose of her sleeping tablets or been murdered by the CIA. It wasn't like he was ever going to know for sure. But sometimes he did win these arguments, with a persistence and enthusiasm that I never saw in our real lives. We never argued like that. He'd give up, or change the target of our disagreement to one that suited him better, or just take himself away for a walk or go and sleep on the settee with his headphones on.

One evening, in the period after I'd gone back to work and before he'd left the power station, I sat in bed drinking wine with my phone in my hand and watched him, through the email reports the keylogger programme sent to me, argue with someone about the 1969 moon landing. He started his shift at 10 p.m. and the evenings were supposed to be our time, but instead he spent them having arguments with these people.

Mark has always believed the moon landing to be a huge international hoax, though a poster called FlatEarthTruther57 mocked him for it – calling it a step too far, even for the milieu they found themselves in. Mark outlined a theory about faked telemetry tapes and related some scientific analysis of photographs and film footage of the landings with persistence, confidence and enthusiasm. He seemed to believe – and had encouraged others to believe – that NASA had sent robots into space because the Van Allen radiation belts would have killed anything living. He argued that – he posted a photograph of Aldrin emerging from the lander marked up with various annotations – ray tracing proved that the lighting in this image wasn't right at all.

It looks like it was made in a studio, he'd written, and alluded to a rumour he admitted he couldn't prove, but found very appealing, that suggested Stanley Kubrick himself had been commissioned to make the footage.

The whole thing was astonishing. He converted not only FlatEarthTruther57 to his way of thinking, but also several lurkers who only joined the thread after FlatEarthTruther57 had conceded in order to post admiring comments about Mark's contribution to knowledge in the field. When he put down his computer and came to bed, I put my phone away, pretended I'd been reading, and tried to have sex with him. I put my hands inside his T-shirt and pressed myself against him and gently snuffled and bit the soft skin between his neck and shoulder. He wasn't able or interested and it was as if the man of enthusiasm and passion I had watched post on the forum had remained there in the ether, his lively double, while only the pale shade of that presence had made it back to our bed. Maybe I should have joined one of those forums myself.

Penelope1981: Who cares if Neil Armstrong is lying?
Penelope1981: Get a life.
Penelope1981: Your tea's ready.
Penelope1981: Come to bed.
Penelope1981: Where are you?
But I never did.

My point is, my excavation of my husband's online life had taught me only one thing: if Mark had ghosted me, as Eddie had suggested, then I wasn't dealing with the ghost of a man; a less substantial and out-of-time version of something and someone familiar. No, his was the ghost of an alien or an automaton. I had been living with someone strange and unknowable: a mere paranoid remnant of the man I had married.

I placed all the pieces of the broken laptop inside a plastic carrier bag and knotted the handles. It is harder to obliterate a laptop than you might think and I was panting slightly. I know now I should have burned the hard drive or soaked it in bleach. That forensic computer technicians can do quite a lot with the fragments of a shattered laptop computer. Nevertheless, I did my best with the knowledge I had available to me, and placed the knotted-up carrier bag inside a larger, tougher plastic bag. I didn't use the rubbish chute but carried the package with me to work and placed it in one of the industrial-sized refuse containers used by the student housing block. It was collected, along with the rest of the refuse, the next morning, and I have never heard a thing about it since.

There's one other piece of suspicious behaviour I would like to explain. What happened was this: Mark's mobile phone rang many times in that first five weeks, and I always answered it, letting his friends know he was in the shower, but would return the call soon.

'Soaping up *again*, Laurie?' one of them asked. 'You want to see what he's up to in there. He'll wear it away!' He laughed and

I laughed along with him, not minding – even relishing – the way the pair of us were conspiring to humiliate Mark. It really did feel like he might be wanking away in the bathroom, the shower running, while I chopped carrots in the kitchen with Bay FM playing softly in the background, his mobile phone tucked between my chin and shoulder. I played the good wife and took another message.

It went on. I asked the woman who rang from the library to renew his books, and promised he would be in to pay his fines when he'd recovered from his flu. Mavis, who called from her retirement apartment in the Algarve, was a little more difficult to put off, but in those early weeks she was satisfied with talking to me. We chatted about my work. She asked about the so-called summer in the north-west of England and gleefully listened as I told her how disgustingly wet it was. She asked, as she always did, when Mark and I would come out and stay with her for some proper sunshine. I played along and pretended to write down the lists of things she wanted me to buy and bring with me when we came. She seemed satisfied with the story – the lie, I suppose, if I speak plainly about it – that Mark had decided to take on lots of extra shifts at the power station, because we were struggling – as we usually were – for money.

I can see why, when the police started to speak to Mark's colleagues and my behaviour came to light, these phone calls and the way I chose to handle them could have appeared suspicious. I can see why Mavis was upset with me when she eventually found out that I'd delayed drawing attention to Mark's disappearance at a time when he could very badly have needed help. I can also see that my motivation – to both seek sympathy and disguise or at least not emphasise any difficulties Mark and I might have been having in our marriage – was just the expression of a more general sense of anxiety and guilt I was feeling at that time.

I can only say that in those early weeks, despite what I pretended – that all was well – I was almost always searching for him out of the corner of my eye, in crowd scenes on the television, as I waited in the morning for the first bus – even in the bed at night, when I tossed and turned in my sleep, searching for the warm heavy mountain of him under the duvet. I could not bear to do otherwise. My refusal to really acknowledge the gravity of what was happening – telling myself instead that he was playing a trick on me, and I needed to set the police on his trail without actually appearing to be that concerned about him – was actually a kind of hope. I realise that now. I was still engaging in minor acts of marital sadism, which relied on me being able to assume that he was still out there somewhere, on the receiving end of my manipulations. I tried to win at the game he was playing so he would be playing it with me, instead of being gone.

After the police telephoned me and I hastily got rid of his computer, something broke in me. I spent most of the time I wasn't at work sitting out on the balcony smoking rollies and watching the evening traffic cross the bridge over the river. I tore at my fingernails with my teeth. I sat with his mobile phone in one hand and mine in the other, calling him repeatedly. Over three days I called him over four hundred times, sick and mad with craving, feeling the sheer want of him in my throat and tongue and teeth. I cried a lot. I deleted my missed calls from his telephone so that when he came back he would never know how much I had wanted him, and I watched the sun go down and willed one of the cars that passed on the main road to indicate and turn onto our street.

Some nights, one of those shimmering, flickering selves inside me made strange bargains with the universe.

If I can hold my breath until this taxi crosses the bridge, he'll be inside it.

I'd make my vow, then fill my lungs full of smoke and refuse to exhale until my eyes were streaming and blood was buzzing in my ears and at my throat.

Come back.

Come home. Come home.

These thoughts had no real shape, no grammar – they were urges, not sentences. The cars never stopped.

Things were getting out of hand. I never missed work, but the flat was an utter tip. A disgrace. I did not call Sharon but I did find out, with the help of Google, that there were three mediums called Joyce working in Lancashire. I could have clicked through to their websites and read them carefully. I could have cross-referenced on Facebook the website Joyces against local Joyces with an interest in clairvoyance, mediumship and the paranormal. It was not beyond my ability to do that. But I resisted, knowing that as long as I didn't continue my search, I was still in the realms of sanity and acting like a reasonable person.

3

I had always been convinced that Olena, given enough time and opportunity, would end up being one of the seventeen murderers the statistics promised I would come across in my lifetime. Because of this, sometimes I went into my father's house really quietly, hoping to catch her in some act of cruelty or neglect. Occasionally I'd creep up the stairs in my stockinged feet, certain that I was going to find her in his bedroom, leering over his sleeping form, brandishing a feather pillow with pound signs in her eyes.

The seventh week of Mark's absence – forty-eight days since I'd last seen him to be precise – found me tiptoeing across the unhoovered upstairs landing in my father's house, listening to the sound of the water running in the bathroom.

'She's twelve years old this month, Mr Spencer. My mother says she's taller than I was at that age. Can you believe it? I feel old.'

Olena was speaking about her daughter, who lived back in Dnipro with Olena's mother. I frowned, wondering then as I had done many times previously, what kind of mother lives a thousand miles away from her only daughter.

'Does she take after her father?' my father said. 'Laurie's always been more like me than her mother. It works out like that sometimes.'

'She's nothing like him,' Olena said quickly. 'She's like me. My mother has a photograph . . .'

'Water's a bit hot, Olena my love. Could you . . .'

I heard splashing. Olena swore lavishly. I opened the bathroom door.

'Laurie! I wondered when you were going to come in. Did you think you were going to catch your father and me making love in the bathtub?' she said. She was wearing a disposable plastic apron and latex gloves. My father was sitting on one of the kitchen chairs, his head tipped backwards over the bathroom sink. She was washing his hair with the shower attachment. He leaned over, wrapping his head in a towel turban, and laughed.

'She's got you there, Laurie. Bang to rights!' he wheezed.

Sometimes I wonder why it took so long for Olena and me to hit it off.

'Not a social call,' I said. 'I have some important news.'

I'd like to say that I'd made the visit to my father specifically to tell them what was happening with Mark, or the lack of him. I'd like you to imagine me surfacing from the shocked silence of my denial, finally ready to avail myself of the care, compassion and help of my loved ones. I will be honest here though: telling them about Mark was the only thing I could think of that would distract Olena and my father from laughing at my sneaking around on the landing. They'd have gone on about it all day otherwise.

'News?' Olena's face softened and she smiled. Reached out and took my hand. I remember the feel of her hand in mine: the soapsuds and the latex, all her gold rings digging into me through her glove. 'Is it, Laurie? A baby? Oh . . .'

She was as bad as my father. Neither of them happy until I was fertilised. I turned away and slid my hand out of hers. 'Meet me downstairs. Dad, you as well.'

I didn't have a name for the aspect of my father that didn't feel like an aspect, but just his usual self. I could have called it Normal Father – though his lucidity was a fragile state he only lapsed into rarely. He was Normal Father that afternoon though, or at least he was to begin with.

'What's the matter, love? Has something happened?'

44

'I'll just come out with it,' I said, in a hurry. I'd committed now and if I tried to change the subject they would assume I really was pregnant and being coy about it. The prospect of that was unbearable.

'I've had the police round. It's Mark. He's gone missing.'

'Laurie!' Olena said. We were sitting in the living room, me and my dad on the settee and Olena on the matching armchair.

'Has he left you? What have you done?' said Unfounded Accusations Father. I ignored him.

'I don't know where he is. The police are looking for him. He's not used the joint account or his savings account since he left, which obviously looks bad, but they're not ruling anything out.'

I liked that. 'Not ruling anything out.' Neither of the officers had used the phrase with me, but it felt like the kind of phrase they would use, if I tried one of my crazier theories on them.

What if he's met a woman on an internet forum and run away with her?

'We're not ruling anything out, Mrs Wright.'

He could be gay. It might be a man. He could have left me for a man.

'Not ruling anything out.'

Anything was possible. That was the problem. I think I was a bit deranged and didn't know it.

'Are you all right? Do you need money?' my father said.

'You give Olena all your money,' I snapped back, 'and she spends it on Silk Cut and second-hand gold jewellery.' It was true. She had one of those clown pendants. They're really not cheap.

'There's no need for that,' Olena said. She stood up from the armchair. 'I'm going to make us some tea. Have you eaten? Could you manage anything?'

I did feel a little ashamed then.

'I'm all right. Thank you. Sorry.'

'I just don't understand it,' my father said.

I was about to explain – to tell him about the police and the bath panel and Eddie's theory about ghosting and immature personalities – but he went on.

'It came as such a shock. Your mother never seemed like that sort of woman.'

'Don't start this now, Mr Spencer,' Olena put her head through the kitchen hatch, uncharacteristically impatient. 'It is not the time.'

'She sat me down two days ago – right in that chair there,' he ploughed on, pointing to the seat that Olena had recently vacated. 'And she told me that I wasn't your natural father, my love.'

'I see,' I said wearily.

'Ignore him, Laurie,' Olena called. 'I'm switching him to decaf. I read an article that said it might help.'

'It won't make a difference where the will's concerned,' he added hastily, 'none of that will change. But I thought you'd want to know.'

'Mr Spencer! Will you have a Tunnock's Teacake?' Olena shouted. Of course she wouldn't want him to linger too long on the subject of his will – not if she'd managed to convince him to leave the lot to her already. My father, ricocheting wildly between his Pervert and his Unfounded Accusations Aspects, ignored her and carried on talking to me, his pace quickening, his face growing redder.

'The thing we've got to narrow down, my love, my little one, my little best thing – you are, you always are – you always will be – is which one of the bastards she was fucking is the one who knocked her up. We need to make a list. I write the names down, but there are so many of them, and it was such a long time ago, and then Olena here tidies the list away, and we have to start from scratch. But let's do it now, darling. How old are you now, my sweetheart? My best one? Exactly. It's important.'

'Dad,' I began, as gently as I was able to. He reached for his notebook, lying on the coffee table. 'Dad? I wanted to tell you something. About Mark. Will you listen to me?'

'Have you spoken to Mavis?' Olena asked, appearing in the doorway with a saucer of chocolate biscuits. 'How is she? Poor Mark. Poor Mavis. She must be going totally crazy.'

I wanted to put my hands over my eyes or crawl under the settee. This had been a terrible idea. Poor Mark? Poor Mavis? What about me?

'I have the names here,' he said, running his fingers over the notebook. He opened it and showed it to me. Inside, a mess of scribble that only occasionally resolved itself into language. I flicked through the book. He'd spent hours on this.

'You've got to stop this.'

'How old are you? Quickly now.'

'I'm thirty-six, Dad. You know that.'

He laughed.

'No spring chicken. And not a mother yet. When your mother was your age she was . . .' he paused. Looked at me, stricken. As if he'd heard a clock chime loudly in the next room and the noise had brought him back to himself.

I should have been more sympathetic: it must have been like coming out of a drunken blackout, and I know what that is like. But the way we indisputably glimpsed each other clearly in the brief silencing of the roar of his delusions (the look on his face was recognition – as if he'd heard his name in a lull in conversation at a raucous party) was more of a factor in my anger than what came next.

'There were so many of them,' he said, limply. His enthusiasm for the tale was gone. Instead, this was like a speech he'd been forced to rehearse, but had long ago lost interest in. 'She was at it all hours. One night I couldn't sleep. We were on holiday, I think. I came downstairs and she was at it in the kitchenette. Standing up against the fridge-freezer . . .'

'Shut up,' I said, and stood up. He flinched. I remember that. I threw the notebook at him. It bounced off his chest and slid to the floor. He immediately leaned over to retrieve it, his hands shaking. 'Leave it alone!' I shouted, or something to that effect. Olena came in to find me standing above him, raining down blows on his head and shoulders, on his skinny speckled forearms, which he had raised to protect himself from me.

'Laurie! Calm yourself!'

I didn't stop. Olena is, as I have already said, a large woman. And I am not. I was doing no real harm to my father, who, firmly in his Mournful Aspect, had started a keening wail that would have roused a corpse. I carried on swiping at him, he continued to cower and dodge me, his arms now tucked around his head. Olena wrapped her own arms around me from behind, lifted me off my feet, and deposited me on the other side of the room. I am making the incident sound, I think, more dramatic than it actually was.

'Get off,' I said quietly. I was out of breath. 'I'm sorry. I'm calm now. I'm calm.'

'Go into the dining room,' she said. She sounded furious and I wondered if she would report me to the police or to social services for elder abuse. Age Concern had a helpline: I knew they did, because I'd looked it up when I first became concerned about Olena's relationship to my father's savings account. I caught my breath and nodded but my father was still wailing.

'Go on. I will settle your father and then I will bring your tea.'

In my mother's time, the dining room had been used regularly. The mahogany table, chairs and sideboard set were her pride and joy, unveiled only for polishing, then smothered in floral oilcloths and placemats. Now the room was unloved and the table covered in shoeboxes. I sat and waited.

'Here,' Olena brought in a tray. 'Mr Spencer is watching television. He'll sleep soon.'

'I'm sorry about that,' I said. 'It's a very hard time right now.'

Olena poured the tea. She'd used a teapot, instead of just putting the bags in the mug, which was her way of saying, *I am taking this conversation seriously,* or even, *I expect better from you, young lady.*

'He won't remember,' Olena said. 'Or he will, but he'll think I did it. Or your mother.'

'That's no excuse,' I said.

She shrugged. 'You didn't hurt him. Tomorrow he'll tell me about it, but tell me he saw it on television. It isn't the same for him as it is for other people.'

'If that was true it would be fine to smother babies, or beat them up, or throw them out of windows,' I said. 'After all, they won't remember it.'

She shook her head. 'Will you drink your tea?' she said.

She fished around in the front pocket of her tabard and brought out a packet of cigarettes and the long clicky lighter thing that we used to light the gas on the cooker. This was just not fair. My father did not like me smoking, did not like smoking at all, and banned it in the house. Except when it came to Olena. She was even allowed to use a saucer as an ashtray. She leaned forward and, craning her neck a little awkwardly because of the length of the barrel of the lighter thing, lit her cigarette and inhaled deeply.

Watching her stoop over the flame to light her cigarette put me in mind of a documentary I saw once, about a doctor discovering that a gunshot suicide was, in fact, a murder. When people shoot themselves in the mouth they tend to shoot upwards, right into their brains. Easiest to do with a little handgun. If you use a shotgun you end up leaning forward, and jutting your chin out a bit, and it means the bullet goes in at an entirely different angle because of the length of the barrel, and how difficult that makes it to keep everything lined up straight and still reach the trigger. Nobody shoots straight up into their brains with a shotgun, and this particular man had done, which was eventually how the doctor could tell that his wife had actually got him drunk then leaned him, half conscious, against the pillows in their marital bed and done it herself.

I wiped my eyes.

'I can't believe he said I'm not his daughter,' I said.

Olena let the silence hang for a while then stood and started sliding the shoeboxes around on the table, the cigarette drooping from her bottom lip. They were all labelled, and when she found the one she wanted she took off the lid and pushed it towards me.

'Did you know about this?' she said. 'Mark's project? The work he was doing with your father?'

There were photographs inside the shoebox. Hundreds of them carefully stacked on their edges. Old family photographs from holidays and days out that had been developed in chemists that didn't exist any more. Me, starting as an ordinary enough looking baby (they all look like slightly deflated potatoes, don't they?) and then getting skinnier and taller, plainer and more frizzy-haired as the years went by. There I was on my mother's knee on the promenade at Morecambe. There I was again, standing in front of the lion enclosure at Blackpool Zoo. Me once more – holding my father's hand and looking stiff and awkward on a bowling green at Lytham St Annes.

'There are older ones in the box over there,' she said, 'before you were born. Your father, he was a good-looking man.'

'He always liked to say so,' I said, which was spiteful of me, because he was, and my mother was good-looking too – in a stiff, slightly harried way – which I've never been. I could say that I am not photogenic, but the fact is I am just one of those unpretty women and the camera makes an accurate record of it. Mark had taken the photographs out of their packets and tidied them and placed them, as far as I could tell, into chronological order. They stopped rather abruptly when I was about seventeen – the year my father got a digital camera.

'He was doing all this?'

'Yes. He turned up when his job ended. He came nearly every day for a fortnight. Sat with your father right here and put the photographs in order. He bought that,' she pointed to a scanner sitting on the floor under the windowsill, 'and the two of them spent hours digitising them all. Sorting out the file names. There's a memory stick. Do you want it?'

I shook my head. 'He never told me.'

The thought of him sitting here patiently with my father all those mornings was as strange and unmooring as the thought of him throwing a punch at work or sneaking about with Katrina upstairs or developing a liaison with a woman from one of the conspiracy theory websites. I have heard people say that in a long marriage, there is always a point when you turn around and wonder who this stranger – this terrorist – is who you've allowed into your life and your bed – but in all the years that Mark and I had been together I had never felt like that. And suddenly I did.

Olena laughed softly. 'Maybe he wanted it to be a surprise for you. I asked him once why he wanted to spend all this time listening to the muddled and made-up memories of a difficult man who wasn't even a blood relative. Do you know what he told me?'

I couldn't look at her.

'He said he thought you were worried about your dad forgetting who you were. That every time you put your key in the door you wondered if today was the day that he'd forget your name or mistake you for your mother and make a pass at you. Or worse, imagine that you were from the council and throw you out of the house.'

'I never told Mark that.'

That's what I said to Olena. I do not think I was lying. But I was not accounting for the many evenings in the early part of the year when, before he headed out for his late shift at the power station, Mark listened to me wail and rave while I was already two or three bottles of wine into a drinking session. It is very possible I shared something along those lines with him then. I don't have a memory of saying those words, but it does sound like the type of thing that I might say in those sorts of circumstances.

I know the thought had troubled me privately. That is the best I can do in terms of being truthful about this matter.

'Was he right?'

'My father and I weren't close,' I said, 'even before he got ill.' It wasn't much of an answer.

'You didn't see him for a long while, yes? Mr Spencer told me this. That you vanished from his life. That he wondered if it was drink, or drugs. That you had a number of missing years that were of great concern to him. And then your mother died and you came back to him.'

I laughed politely. 'That's not quite how it was.'

Olena put the lid back on the box of photographs. 'Do you want to take these with you? Or shall I leave them here, as they were? I was wondering where Mark had gone.'

She waited, smiling sympathetically at me as if to give me the chance to say more. This was a technique she had probably read about on the internet when researching methods of how to handle my father. I said nothing.

'Do you need anything? Any help? Are you going to let anyone help you?'

'I can clean my own flat, Olena,' I said coldly. She sighed and put her hand on the box of photographs.

'Perhaps we can save them for when Mark comes back.'

I thought she couldn't believe that any harm could have come to Mark because after seeing my outburst with my father, it had become very obvious to her that I was exactly the type of wife a man would want to leave.

I shook my head. 'I don't think so,' I said. 'It's been weeks now. And his job didn't "end". He walked out before they could sack him.'

Olena raised her eyebrows.

'For fighting,' I said grimly. 'He punched someone.'

There. Now she wasn't going to think of me as this unhinged crazy hysteric and Mark as the long-suffering saint off finding himself somewhere. Now she knew exactly how it was. That's what I thought. But Olena only nodded.

'Ah. It happens,' Olena said. 'Men working together all day every day. Tensions develop,' she threw her hands in the air in that European way she liked to cultivate for my father's enjoyment, 'there are worse things.'

'He didn't tell me about it. I never even guessed. What else don't I know?'

'There were problems in your marriage? Has he another woman?'

She leaned back in her chair and sipped her tea. The idea of another woman seemed ordinary to her – an inconvenience that wives all over the world, herself included, had borne with mild irritation. I thought again of all the times Mark – claiming we needed milk, or a newspaper, or a top-up on the meter – had escaped out of the flat when I needed him, and where he might have gone in those hours. He can't have been here sorting photographs the whole time. It had felt, sometimes, like living with a ghost – there, and not there – a ghost you couldn't catch hold of, or an empty door that would not open no matter how hard you banged your fists against it.

'I'd be the last to know about that, wouldn't I? The police had to tell me about this fight at work. He never said a thing. They're talking to people he knew. God knows what else I'll find out. They'll want to come here, I bet.'

Olena sat forward in her chair.

'Why would they want to come here? Your father has his good days, but he's not a reliable man. Not a good witness to anything.'

I shrugged, irritated. 'I don't know, Olena. I don't know anything. Maybe they'll want to talk to *you*. Sounds like you saw him more than I did. Cosy mornings over the photograph album talking about me. Was it like that?'

'I don't talk to the police. I have nothing to do with the police,' Olena said, as if it was an aspect of a deeply held religious practice – beyond compromise or explanation. It is not a pleasant thing to admit, but I assumed she had a concern about her student visa – she was a part-time MA student doing a project about alcoholism among middle-class, stay-at-home wives – and whether her working for my father was entirely legal.

'I doubt it will come to that,' I said.

'I have nothing to tell them,' she insisted. 'He'll come back. They always do. Look at your father. His heart was always for your mother, wasn't it?'

I could have argued with her at that point, but I was overcome by weariness and a wish to be alone on my balcony.

'Thanks for the tea.' I stood up. 'If you leave out your timesheet I'll put some cash in an envelope for you tomorrow. Just let me know the hours.'

She remained in her chair.

'Are you looking after yourself Laurie? I don't want to pry into your business, but answer that for me, will you? For your father's sake?'

I could have confided in Olena. She had more than once told me she was always available to me as a friend. But the expression on her face made me want to tell her she was my father's cleaner-cum-housekeeper and nothing more. That in his confusion he might have made her into a borderline member of the family and by extension something equivalent to an aunt or a godmother to me, but I did not intend to go along with that delusion. And because I wanted to say that, and it would have been cruel, I left abruptly, without saying goodbye to my father. He was still watching television, the tears wet on his cheeks, though he had already forgotten why he was weeping.

4

The night Eddie and I had planned to go out drinking arrived, coinciding neatly with the end of our work cleaning up after the summer graduation ceremonies and garden parties. Mark had been gone nearly two months, the police clearly thought I was some kind of maniac and since I'd humiliated myself in front of Olena, so did she. I was still dodging calls from Mavis and, to top it all, running out of money. I thought I deserved some distraction, even if only for one night. One night when I did not sit on the balcony, watching the traffic and waiting for my husband to come home. Would I regret it if it turned out something terrible had happened to Mark and, on the night they'd pulled him out of the river, I'd been out on the lash with a friend? I shrugged the thought away and put on some lipstick and my going-out earrings. I was owed a treat.

'Someone put lipstick on a pig,' Eddie called out as I arrived. He was sitting at the bar in his work clothes, two pints in front of him. I wobbled over in my high heels, realising I had gone overboard and was perhaps indicating to him that I considered this to be a date.

'And someone needs to make friends with Mr Soap and Mrs Flannel,' I snapped back. I lifted the glass and drank deeply.

'Cheers,' he said, 'and here's to seeing the Wankers off for another year,' which was our traditional summer toast.

The coming months of July and August were a special period of peace and routine for us. We cleared out the student rooms and sorted and disposed of all the interesting things they left behind. We got the satisfaction of doing the restoration and deep cleans after larger works of reconstruction and maintenance that were saved for the long vacation. We got to pretend we were chambermaids, and do room service for conference guests, noting how similar the intimate habits of academics were to the students they taught.

'Another year,' I said.

'It's strange, isn't it? We see them off, take a breath, and another load come in. I think the lot that started the same year I did have probably bought houses and got kids by now.'

'I wouldn't bank on it,' I said.

We talked about our work for a while – not the tasks themselves, but about the people we worked with, the gossip around who was sleeping with who from the various departments – the minutiae that campus novels of a certain type are made of.

'It'll be nice to have a bit of peace,' Eddie said.

People think that cleaning is monotonous, but really, it isn't at all. We become more or less invisible to the Wankers who shoal around us in the quads and corridors, and them to us. It is as if the university (which is more of an idea than a location or set of buildings in the first place) splits into two locations, one slightly superimposed on top of the other. In the summer the whole campus feels as if it is both holding its breath waiting for the return of the people it has been made for, and at the same time as if it is sighing in relief now that the interruption of term time is over and normal service – the sleepy ghost town of the long vacation – can resume.

'Have you seen the new rotas?'

I shook my head. 'Have you got them with you? I'll give you the headlines.'

'No need. Celia was round last night. She gave me the gist.'

This was something – him asking Celia to read for him – but I didn't press the point.

'And?'

'Split shifts. Once the Wankers come back. That's what she's planning.'

'For fuck's sake.'

'Yes. I spent the entire afternoon swabbing out toilets and composing my resignation speech.'

'Again?'

Eddie had been with domestic facilities since he was seventeen and knew the university more intimately than any of us. He'd been planning his resignation speech all the time I'd known him and, each year, as Shaw's antics with the rota became more draconian – a document designed more to torture the staff than to ensure the cleanliness and good working order of the buildings we were hired to tend – the more lavish his speech became.

'If I see her tomorrow morning, I'm going to tell her. She can shove her split shifts. Her rota. Her compulsory working at heights courses before we're allowed to change a light bulb. Her "lunchtime enrichment sessions".' He picked up his pint, drained it, then gestured at the empty glass. 'This is what I have in mind. Ale. And plenty of it.'

'She doesn't invent all that stuff herself, you know.'

'I don't care,' Eddie said. 'Don't try to talk me out of it. If I see her strutting about with her stupid fucking key-rings jingling out of her pocket . . .'

We laughed, but we knew – both of us – that Eddie would never make his speech and that – to mangle a quotation from somewhere else – he'd probably retire at seventy with the song still in him. It was another piece of knowledge that lay between us, sticking us together without us ever having to talk about it: all institutions get you in the end, and Eddie had been got.

'And how is Celia?'

Eddie grinned. 'Lively, my friend. *Lively.*'

Celia lived in Manchester and was a freelance medical journalist, writing articles about new drugs for science magazines. She also wrote a column about conjoined twins and men who survived being shot in the face with nail guns and women who could remember every single word ever said to them – Marvellous and Miraculous, it was called, and she used a pen name because she was embarrassed about it. She'd picked Eddie up on Tinder and he hadn't ghosted her yet.

'She says she'll let me piss on her,' Eddie said.

'That's very decent of her.'

'In the shower. With the water running. But you can't have everything.'

'Sounds serious.'

I was only being half sarcastic. Eddie didn't meet many women whose appetites matched his.

'I like to keep the relationship status marked as "complicated",' he said – his familiar lecture. 'No need to lock it down. It is what it is. It's what she wants too.'

'A match made in heaven,' I said, and toasted him. 'I wish you both very many long and happy years together.'

Eddie coughed, quite artificially. I knew what was coming.

'I suppose you'd have said by now if you'd heard anything,' he said, 'but without wanting to shit all over the night, I do feel it's only polite to enquire as to the current whereabouts of Mr Wright.'

'Nothing. No news. I emailed them a picture of him.'

'What for?'

'I don't know. Posters. To show at the morgue.'

Eddie winced, which was why I'd said it.

'You'd have known if it was something like that. You'd have been able to sense it.'

'Women's intuition?'

'You knew him, that's all I'm saying.'

'I didn't know he was going to fuck off, did I?'

Eddie sighed. He was doing his best, and I was not playing along.

'The police asked me if this was out of character. They asked it three or four different ways. Was he the sort of man who did this type of thing?'

'Is there a sort of man who does this sort of thing?'

I thought about my father, who would express irritation with my mother by remarking that whatever she'd done to annoy him – forgetting to buy milk, or getting the car insurance renewal confused, or even just failing to read his mind and have a particular jacket dry-cleaned and ready for him when he wanted it – was 'absolutely typical' of her. Katrina had done a similar thing: Mark and I met her and Tim in the communal lobby once, her struggling with a few shopping bags, Tim trying to hold the doors open for her by ramming them with the front of the pram.

'That's Tim all over,' she'd said to me, 'never uses his brains when brute force will do!' She rolled her eyes in a conspiratorial fashion, as if I might have a story to share about Mark's unwise and inappropriate use of prams too.

They were brandishing this flawless knowledge of each other as a way of broadcasting their happiness. Later Mark and I decided, perhaps only out of jealousy, that they were actually very miserable, skint, hated each other and hadn't had sex in months, and only felt the need to parade the comfortable intimacy of their knowing – *what is he like!?* – in order to reassure themselves that the living hell their lives had now become with the arrival of their baby was amusing and normal and temporary instead of an irrevocable and self-inflicted disaster. But maybe they really were just happy.

Had Mark been unhappy? Had he realised – the knowledge slowly unfolding layer by layer as the months and years we spent together passed – that he was living with someone entirely unbearable? Was it that the more he got to know me, the less he had been able to love me? I imagined him getting out of the shower that last morning, after I'd already set off for work. Looking at the curtain and wondering if he should fix it. Standing there with the towel around his waist, the water dripping from his hair. He might have looked at that curtain for a long time, and seen his life stretch before him like a punishment.

And then he had dressed and left. Just like that. Was that what had happened?

'If he'd just dumped me two months ago I'd be over it by now. Back in the saddle,' I said, while tracing the blue-black outline of the tattoo ink on Eddie's arm, the swirls of scales and clocks and compasses and shipwrecked galleons and Medusa heads that covered his skin from the back of his hand right around his wrist and up the inside of his arm up to his elbow. He watched my hand, the bitten-down fingernails and the cracked skin on the back of my knuckles. I do not have pretty hands. My skin is not soft.

'Where do you think he is?' he said.

'Another woman,' I said. 'One of the administrators at the power station. Someone from HR?'

Eddie shuddered. He considered infidelity to be only a venial sin; sex was a healthy, vigorous activity, best enjoyed regularly – rather like PE. But fucking someone from HR? Unacceptable.

'I try to picture it. I think about them in bed, or holding hands, or even just sitting watching the telly, but I can't. My mind goes blank. I've only ever seen him do those things with me.'

'You'd know if it was someone else,' Eddie said. 'You'd have smelt it on him.'

I thought of Katrina again. In her silky slutty nightie, her hair piled on top of her head. Earrings still in, no matter how impractical it was: just like the women in porn films. I shrugged, which made me topple on my stool. Eddie put a hand on my back to steady me, then pointed towards the pint glass that had appeared in front of me, as if by magic. 'Drink,' he said. 'Don't get morbid.'

'The police seem to be taking it a bit more seriously. There's the canal. Morecambe Bay.'

'He'd have been found, surely?'

'Maybe. Maybe not. You know there are about six hundred unidentified bodies in morgues up and down the country right

60

now? In cold storage. There's a website where you can look them up by height and download pictures of their tattoos and wristwatches.'

'Please tell me you are not spending your nights on the internet,' Eddie said.

I shook my head but he was right, I had been spending my nights on the internet, my denial slowly wearing away and with that gone, the frenzied research into possibility beginning. There are so many ways for a person to come to harm and so much damage that can be done to a body. I spent drunken hours rooting them out, looking for pictures that might help me write one sort of ending to Mark's story. There were infinite options. The fallings, the jumpings, the overdoses, the electrocutions, the falling asleep and dying of cold, the being hit on the head in a remote place, the hit-and-runs, the gassings, the waking up in hospital with no words, no memory, no identification.

I often thought about Connie Fallon's mother and the press conferences she did in the weeks before her daughter's body was found. She never spoke at them, she left that to her husband, but she would sit, white and remote in the great unknown of her daughter's absence, like a piece of marble lit up by the press photographers' flashbulbs, and while she wasn't exactly the victim (this was before we all knew what she'd done), she was dignified by the gift of pity that the entire country bestowed on her, and she looked stiff and pale and beautiful, the vastness of her motherly love transformed into a sinkhole of silent and private longing overnight. *How horrible*, we all thought, *must it have been not to know*. Except she did know.

'I don't know what I think,' I said. I did my impression of the woman officer – her posh voice and the strange language she used. 'What we find in these cases,' she'd said, 'is that it's very unusual for an ordinary man in the midst of a life that is going well to absent himself on an impulse. There's usually some planning involved that leaves a trace we can use to find him. For your average person, this type of impulsive decision – never mind carrying it through for longer than a couple of days – is nearly unheard of.'

'And yet that's what he's done,' Eddie said.

'A strange way to make a bid for uniqueness,' I said.

Eddie laughed. 'Sorry,' he said, and laughed again. 'And here am I supposed to be getting you leathered and taking your mind off it.'

He went away and brought back some more drinks: pints and chasers. I tried to brighten up and change the subject, but I couldn't.

'I just want it to be over,' I said, not knowing what I meant, but stroking his arm – stroking and stroking it with the edge of my fingernail. 'He could have said if he wanted a divorce. But if there's no sign of him we still have to stay married. It's five years. Seven. Something like that.'

'It's early days to be thinking about that, isn't it?' Eddie said. I could see he was a little horrified at the state I'd got myself in – those drinks had slipped down quickly – and also at the prospect we'd be remembering this conversation in a couple of weeks' time when the police had pulled the innocent body of my faithful and still loving husband out of Morecambe Bay. *It's all right*, I wanted to say, *we'll forget all about it*.

'Schrödinger's wife. That's me.' I made a mess of 'Schrödinger', and my stuttering and slurring made him laugh. And I was still running my fingers up and down the designs on his arm.

I won't pretend I didn't know what I was doing. When the pub closed and we each had several more drinks inside us, it was not such a big thing to invite him back to the flat. We walked through the wet streets of the city smoking, me on the rollies, him on his stupid vape, and we went up in the lift together, me leaning heavily on him, his hand first around my shoulders, then my waist, then in the back of my hair. I wanted to be touched – I was drunk and lonely and pissed off and all of these things should be very understandable to everybody. But I also wanted to be single: not a wife apart from her husband, or a wife waiting for her husband. If I couldn't be a divorcee for another half-decade, then I could at least be an adulteress: that would be some kind of solid ground to start again from, wouldn't it?

'The keyhole seems to have moved,' I said, on the third attempt to get into the flat.

'How appallingly inconsiderate of it,' Eddie said, in his Staff Wanker voice, and took the keys out of my hand to open the door himself. We tumbled, laughing, into the living room, which I – showing some premeditation I could not blame on the drink – had tidied that afternoon, clearing away the wine bottles and takeaway cartons and overflowing ashtrays. Immediately, the sound of a baby wailing throbbed through the ceiling and down to us.

'It's Tim and Katrina's,' I said. 'It's driving me mad.'

We stood there and the wail – siren-like, it was – continued. I put my hands over my ears. 'I hate it!' I shouted.

Eddie gestured towards the kitchen.

'You've had a bit much,' he said, 'shall I make us a cup of tea?'

'Put some music on or something,' I said. 'I'll get us something to drink.'

'It's fine. It's fine,' Eddie said.

'It's the noise,' I put my hands in my hair and made fists. 'I can't bear it. Can we go back to yours?'

Eddie laughed. Mark used to pretend he couldn't hear it too. We argued about it, sometimes.

'Tea. Cup of tea for you. Then a pint of water and two paracetamol. I'm tucking you in.'

I leaned over and grabbed him by the shoulders. I tried to kiss him.

'Laurie. Laurie. There's no need for that. Shall we get out on your balcony and have some fresh air?'

I followed him out. It was cold but it had stopped raining and I was glad to be away from the noise, the noise that Eddie was pretending – out of a misguided sense of politeness about the terrible place that I lived in, the way that some people pretend not to notice a fart, or a stack of laundry left undone in a house they are visiting – not to be able to hear.

On the balcony I sat on my little kitchen chair, the stinking jam jar full of fag ends between my feet, as usual. I made us both a rollie. He leaned over the rail, looking at the view.

'Bloody hell,' he said.

'I know. I wish it was light so you could see the sea. If the weather's good you can see the whole bay. The power station. The port.' I was proud of it, despite the traffic noise and the graffiti in the stairwell and the strange smells on the landing. The sky wasn't clear enough to see the stars, but I looked out at them anyway, thinking of the incomprehensible space between them and the probes and satellites zooming about, taking measurements and sending messages about the weather conditions between themselves and back to earth. It was a comforting thought and now the wail of the baby had gone, I could think a little more clearly and felt steadier.

'It's so high,' he said. 'I never knew you were this high up.' He leaned over and lifted one foot, pretending to overbalance, his hands in the air. 'You'd catch me if I fell, wouldn't you?'

'I'd try,' I said, 'I don't plan on clearing the whole of Derwent Block out on my own on Monday.'

I handed him his rollie. He leaned against the railing, his back to the view, observing me while he smoked. Outside on the grass and paving slabs below, a man let his dog off the lead. It started running backwards and forward across the grass, yapping.

'We're not allowed pets, not really,' I said, trying to fill the silence. 'But people have them. Birds. Hamsters. That sort of thing. There's a man on the fourth floor who has a snake: I met him in the lift with it round his neck once. Upstairs – two above Katrina – right at the top, they had a cat. An inside cat, she said it was. She covered the gaps between the railings on her balcony with netting and let it sit out there watching the birds. And one day I was coming back from work and walking across the way from the bus stop, I saw what I thought was one of those fluffy Russian hats lying on the pavement.'

'Shut up,' Eddie said, thrilled. 'You did not.'

'Its guts looked like little brown and purple sausages,' I said. 'I made Mark go up and tell her. She came back down with a carrier bag and a shovel. We watched her from the balcony. It took her ages.'

Eddie shook his head admiringly. I exaggerated the story a little bit to make him laugh: I had asked Mark to go up and talk to her, but he had refused and we'd argued about it. I'd called him unfeeling and insensitive, and he'd said he wasn't about to poke himself into the midst of some stranger's emotions, and she could find out herself. We had watched her though, scraping up the remains of her cat into a Bargain Booze carrier bag and dropping it into one of the big Biffas. I liked my version of Mark better: the one who had gone up and broken the news and helped her find the bag. The one who had held her hand as she'd cried and told her what to do to sort out the problem. That was the Mark I wanted to talk about. The one I wanted to present to Eddie.

Eddie had only met Mark a couple of times. That moment on my balcony, looking out and thinking about spacecraft and dead cats, was neither the time nor the place, but I was gripped with the urge to tell him more about Mark. I had been thinking a lot of the formative incidents in Mark's childhood that he had told me about, searching through them and trying to understand if there was, as Eddie had suggested, something broken or badly formed in his personality that would explain his vanishing the way he had. Whatever Mark had done would either be my fault, or his, and I was so determined that it could not be my fault because I couldn't bear anything more on my conscience.

Mark had not known his biological father – the phrase he used about his mother was that she was 'friendly, and poor at record-keeping', and there had been a stepfather or three over the years, none of them mean, none of them abusive, and none of them very good at keeping in touch once their short-lived relationships with his mother had come to a natural end. This had not been traumatising for him, Mark had insisted. The men had treated him well – often as a way of getting into his mother's good books, Mark realised, but even as a boy he had known the wisdom of not looking a gift horse in the mouth.

One of the men, Mark told me, had invited Mark and Mavis to spend New Year's Eve with his family. Even at a young age – he was about ten years old – Mark had understood this to be a watershed moment in the evolution of his mother's and Jimmy's relationship. The New Year's Eve celebration was a traditional family get-together at Jimmy's brother's house, involving Jimmy's parents and sister-in-law and his brother's children, and the fact that Mavis had been invited to it, Mark understood, constituted both something of a token of the seriousness with which he was taking their fledgling relationship and an audition of some kind: if Jimmy's brother and mother liked Mavis – and by implication, Mark himself – then the relationship would continue.

I pressed Mark on how Mavis had communicated these things to him. She was not an insensitive woman – had never seemed to me to be the type of person who would put undue pressure of this kind on a child. Mark struggled to explain to me exactly how he had got this impression – it was something to do with the way she had prepared for the party, making a tray of sausage rolls to take with her for the buffet table, taking a bottle of vodka that she had been given for Christmas by a colleague to share with the others and the care and time she had taken over choosing and ironing both her own outfit and Mark's.

There are two other things to know before the conclusion of this story. Things Mark only reluctantly explained to me and which, even if I had tried, I would have found impossible to convey to Eddie with a sense of the gravity of their details. The first is that the best-liked boy in Mark's school had made popular a peculiar impersonation. Nobody could quite place how it had started, but as the weeks of the autumn term had elapsed and the Christmas holidays had approached, all this boy needed to do to bring the entire playground to a fever pitch of excitement was to lie on the floor, flat on his back, make a sizzling noise between his teeth and gradually, with a little to-ing and fro-ing, curl himself into an s-shape and lie on his side.

'Bacon,' someone would shout, and another friend would take up the cry.

'Bacon! Bacon! Sizzling in the pan!'

And on it would go like that, until half the school was gathered around the boy in question chanting and screaming encouragement while the boy lay on the floor, sizzling and frying, and the impression was complete. When the boy finally judged the chanting and praise to be sufficient, he would hop to his feet, dust off his trousers and take a small, mock-modest bow. The entire school – or so it seemed to Mark at that time – would burst into wild and delighted applause.

The second thing to know is that since Mavis and Jimmy had been seeing each other more regularly – since the summer holidays or thereabouts – Mark had struck up what felt like the seeds of a genuine friendship with the man. He played the guitar and would often show up at the house with the instrument, which, now and again, he would allow Mark to remove from its case. There was the promise, at some point in the future, if he behaved himself, that Jimmy would teach Mark how to play a few songs.

'Anything you like, pal,' he'd offered. 'Three chords and a bit of swing covers everything worth playing.'

From this – and I never quite understood Mark's leap of thought here – Mark had concocted an entire fantasy around Jimmy. Jimmy, Mark imagined, was actually his natural father, returned from whatever army mission or secret M15 posting had taken him away from his family all these years. All Mark needed to do was prove himself a good and loyal son to this man, and Jimmy would both return to the family home full time and reveal his true identity.

'We looked a bit alike,' Mark had told me. We were on a train heading up to Carlisle for a day out and some Christmas shopping. This would have been two or three years into our relationship and, I think, the first Christmas after we started to live together properly.

'He had dark hair, a bit curly – like mine. We got mistaken once. Some bloke in the park kicked the ball back and said, "He's the spit of you, he is," and Jimmy didn't correct him. He was just trying to be polite or save my feelings, but at that age you work things up in your mind, don't you?'

I couldn't honestly say I'd had a similar experience, but I thought I understood a little of what he meant, so I nodded and let him continue.

'I mean, if he'd been embarrassed by me, he'd have put the bloke straight, wouldn't he? Said I was his girlfriend's boy, or just shaken his head or something. But he didn't.'

That slight resemblance, noted by a stranger, as well as the promise of guitar lessons had combined in Mark's mind, and with each passing day the fantasy grew stronger and more real to him. As the weeks passed and Christmas approached, Mark began to feel more and more certain that Jimmy was just searching for the right time to unveil his true identity. And Mark, not wanting to rush the process for fear of spoiling it, gave no sign at all that he had guessed the truth, and instead worked to treat

Jimmy with a polite but cool indifference: a demonstration that he was not easily provoked to emotional outbursts, and that he could be trusted with whatever secrets or revelations Jimmy saw fit to unveil. The phrase he used to me was 'biding my time'.

For the first couple of hours of the New Year's Eve party, all went well. Mavis had been welcomed into the kitchen by the women of the family, and when Mark had gone in there to pour himself more Coke from the makeshift bar of bottles and cans laid out on the ironing board set up for that purpose, he'd smelled the happy smell of perfume and cigarette smoke and heard them talking and laughing together and felt reassured. Mavis looked relaxed: her going-out top had been admired, her figure complimented, and the sausage rolls she had brought laid out on their foil tray on the breakfast bar. Mark wouldn't have used the word at the time, but the impression he got was that his mother had been accepted.

In the living room, the men had taken over the three-piece suite and the television played Jools Holland's *Hootenanny*, though nobody paid attention to it. A card game had been started and abandoned, and Jimmy's two nieces, a few years younger than Mark, had fallen asleep on the carpet and had been covered with a quilt brought down from the bedroom. Mark was content to sit and listen to the men's conversation, and while not included in it, felt that even by being awake and in the front room, he had made his allegiance with the men and their card games, not the women in the kitchen and not the children sleeping sticky-mouthed over their emptied Christmas selection boxes under the coffee table. Like Mavis, he relaxed and started to enjoy the night.

At a seemingly prearranged time in the evening, the television was turned off, the girls woken up – they cried a little, but were soon soothed – and the women, soft-eyed and smudgy and smelling of vodka and Appletiser – were called back into the living room.

'It's time for your turn,' Jimmy's brother said, nodding towards Jimmy.

'Me first? Didn't I go first last year?'

'Age before beauty, Jimmy,' his sister-in-law called. Jimmy laughed and, evidently delighted by the attention, went out into the hallway for his guitar case.

Mark looked at his mother, unsure of what was happening, but she smiled at him encouragingly, and thus reassured, he settled to watch Jimmy remove his guitar from its case, perch on the arm of the floral settee, and play 'Crocodile Shoes' to the small gathering. He was met with raucous applause and cheering, quite out of proportion to the extent of his achievement. Next, one of the two girls was encouraged to stand and recite a poem she had evidently learned off by heart for the occasion. Next – and here is where Mark started getting nervous and looking around again for his mother, who was leaning in the kitchen doorway and clapping along – Jimmy's sister-in-law stood and sang, in a wavering and not altogether tuneful singing voice, 'Close to You' by the Carpenters.

It became increasingly clear to Mark that this was some kind of family tradition, and in the hour before the clock struck midnight, each member of the family was supposed to 'do a turn' and provide a small performance or entertainment for the benefit of every other member of the family. Jimmy's brother stood on a kitchen chair brought in for the purpose and told a lengthy and not entirely coherent joke about three men, a pub and a barmaid with a peculiar talent for making gin bottles disappear. The joke was met with shaking heads, groaning, and – again – wild and rapturous applause. Mark glanced at his mother, trying to catch her eye, but she was edging back into the kitchen in the hope of missing her turn, or maybe only wanting to top up her glass or empty an ashtray.

'Mavis? Mavis, come up here sweetheart and show them your pretty face. Will you do "Mistletoe and Wine" for us?'

Jimmy looked for her, and when he couldn't find her, settled on Mark.

'She's come over all shy. Never mind. Come on son, up you get,' he said.

It was the word 'son' that emboldened him to do it. Mark never said so, that's my own slant on the story – and one that I never put to him at the time on that train journey to Carlisle (it might have been the cold wet weather, the early dark and the Christmas lights in the train station that had brought the story to mind for him that day). Mark, his stomach sloshing with Coke and sweating inside his good shirt and best jumper, lay down on the carpet and, without much preamble or deliberation, did his bacon impersonation. Or rather, he did the bacon impersonation the boy at school had used so successfully to win such admiration and popularity.

It is not hard to imagine how strange this might have appeared to the others. And how Mark, so keen for approval, would have been alert to any subtle sign of disappointment. Were the adults really so puzzled? Did they really applaud with slightly less enthusiasm than they did for the other turns, exchanging glances? Ten-year-old Mark thought that they did. The evening had descended a little after that, with Jimmy finding Mavis vomiting in the kitchen sink ('She was probably nervous,' Mark had said, always forgiving of his mother's poor judgement) and the way the next morning, back at their own house, Mark had awoken – still in his party clothes – to hear Mavis and Jimmy having a spectacular argument in the kitchen downstairs.

'They won't have been arguing about you,' I said.

'Jimmy was pissed off that my mother had been sick and needed taking home. He'd had to leave the party early to see us into the taxi and back to our house, and he was furious about it.'

'I suppose that's understandable,' I said.

'But I thought they'd been arguing about me,' he said quietly.

'You daft sod,' I said. I laughed. And now I realise that wasn't entirely what Mark had been looking for. He was never one to confide thoughts or feelings or memories to me – this was a rare occasion, which is why I remember it so well – and my misstep closed a door that had only just been left ajar between us. This was the first in a long line of tiny mistakes like that – little incidences where I had wounded him or let him down, almost without knowing it. Had they added up?

'Water under the bridge now,' he'd said briskly.

Mark had seen Jimmy again – his and Mavis's romance had limped on until February, when he had, like the other stepfathers, melted away from their lives, never to be seen or have his name mentioned again. 'He went before Valentine's Day,' Mark had said, and made a joke that I'd laughed at and he hadn't, 'probably to save on the card.'

The incident of the bacon impersonation would be one of the stories I would probably try to tell at a wake, if there was one. It would illustrate something essential about Mark and his character and perhaps how he came to be the man he was in later life, although exactly what that was, I couldn't say. It was a ghoulish thought and Eddie must have picked up on the quality of my silence because he jumped up and sat on the edge of the balcony, his back to the open space and the drop, and grinned at me.

'Do you ever get dizzy standing up here? Ever wonder what it would be like just to climb up and lean over and . . .' he whistled. 'You know.'

'Yes,' I said. 'I think about it all the time.'

'Come on,' he said, 'it's getting cold. Let's go in. Let me get you your water.'

In the living room, I tried to kiss him again, and for a few seconds – no more than that, he let me. I heard the noise of my lips working against his: a gentle, irregular slopping. I thought about how they must edit it out of romantic scenes in films, because it was such a strange sound – like water rocking backwards and forwards in a plastic cup. Not nice. Eddie is not a bad-looking man but the mechanics of it were all wrong. It was not a mouth I was used to. He moved his head and turned the kiss into a hug.

'Is it Celia? Is that the problem?'

'Come on Laurie. You're drunk. You're going to feel like balls in the morning.'

'Don't you always say these things are recreational? Nothing but good clean fun? Is there something wrong with me?'

I lurched towards him again.

'A goodnight kiss between friends,' Eddie said, pecked my cheek and stepped away from me. 'And that's your lot.'

'You could stay over,' I said. 'I won't tell anyone.'

Katrina's baby started crying again. I flinched.

'I think they torture that baby,' I said. 'It's not normal – the amount it cries.'

'You're in a bad way,' Eddie said.

'It's not me,' I said. 'I'm fine. But I think there's something wrong with it. Reflux. Colic. They walk him up and down. Or put him in his pram and wheel him backwards and forwards. Hours at a time. It sounds like they're playing with bowling balls up there some nights.'

We were still standing in the middle of the front room.

'It'll be quieter in my bedroom,' I said, trying to put the inflection of a question into the statement, without diminishing the air of confidence I was trying to exude. Men like confidence. I knew Eddie enjoyed it when a woman said what she wanted and took charge of things a bit. I was out of practice at seducing and being seduced. 'Take me to bed.' It sounded all right in my head.

'Let's get you tucked in,' he said cheerfully. He held my hand and pulled me out of the living room and along the hallway.

The hallway was dark and there was a crack of light around the badly fitting door. I was sure the light had been off in there when I'd left.

'Not that one,' I said, more harshly than I'd intended. My irritation drew his attention. Eddie had his hand on the small room's door handle.

'This one?' he was teasing now. Rattling the handle.

I batted his arm away.

'Eddie. No. Not in there. Bedroom. This way.'

He grinned, having caught the scent of something intriguing.

'What's in there? Your S-and-M dungeon?' he whistled, as if he was a ten-year-old boy and I was his best friend, or, at most, the girl whose ponytail he was pulling that day.

'Just leave it,' I said, getting between him and the door. 'Don't touch it. Eddie. Get the fuck out of my house.' I put my hands on his shoulders and tried to push him, but he stood firm and I only succeeded in toppling myself over. I fell backwards, against the door which, because it was ajar, didn't support my weight. I landed on my backside, which might have hurt, except I was so drunk my entire body was numb.

'Whoopsy daisy,' Eddie said, and reached out a hand.

'No,' I said, from the floor. I reached behind me to close the door. 'Just go away. Just get out and leave me alone. This is my house and my room and you've no right to . . .'

He shook his head and backed away.

'Drink some water, Laurie,' he said, the amusement in his voice gone. 'Get some sleep.'

'Send my love to Celia,' I said, still sprawled on the floor as he closed the door to the flat behind him.

I got up. Upstairs, Tim and Katrina had started to argue. I only heard the odd word here and there, her high-pitched shriek rising above the lower rumble of Tim trying to tell her something. Despite the unwanted intimacy with the ups and downs of Tim and Katrina's marriage and the difficulty they had in getting their baby to sleep through the night, it was impossible to tell who was the aggressor and who was attempting to make the peace. I didn't think having a baby had been very good for their relationship. I closed the door of the small room tightly, checked the mechanism on the handle had clicked through properly, checked again, and shakily went into my own bedroom and got into bed. The baby carried on crying.

Late last year, I had lain in this bed with Mark, listening to the racket of a different disagreement echo down towards us. Katrina was crying, I think, as well as the baby, and although we'd already settled in for the night, I sat up and turned on the bedside lamp and asked him if he thought I should get dressed and go upstairs and see if she was all right. She was my friend. Did I say that? We were friends, Katrina and me. Really good friends to each other.

'They're fine. It's just a row,' he said, pulling me back towards him.

'It sounds like he's really shouting at her.'

'Everyone has rows. He's not a wife-beater.'

He was tucked in behind me, as was usual for us, and I felt the stubble on his chin rub against my shoulder as he spoke.

'We don't have rows,' I said. He scoffed lightly. But our bad time still lay ahead of us and most of our rows were bickering sessions about whose fault it was that the bathroom was so disgusting, or whose turn it was to go to the shop. We almost enjoyed them.

'They're knackered, that's all. That baby won't sleep. Their nerves are shredded,' Mark said.

'It'll be a lot to get used to,' I said, and made some comment about the way they used to spend their evenings binge-watching Netflix series, and about how we always knew when they were settling in to *Making a Murderer* because the ominous creak of the country fiddles in the theme tune of the opening credits seemed to find a special way into our flat through the pipes and airspaces in the walls, and in the end we grew to quite like it and watched the series ourselves.

'They won't have any time for that now,' he agreed. 'No shagging, either.'

We used to have a joke about their sex life. I can't remember exactly how it started or what the punch line was, but it was something to do with the predictable regularity of their Thursday night sessions, and how it always seemed to involve banging wardrobe doors and books falling from the bedside tables either side of their bed, and about how we, who were far from unadventurous ourselves, just saw no need for a noise like that on a week night. The joke was our imagining that they weren't having sex at all, but just jumping up and down on their bed fully clothed, and throwing things at the floor, just to give the flat below – which was Mark and me – an impression of their marriage that would leave us feeling both envious and inadequate.

'No time for anything like this,' Mark said, and grabbed my hips and turned me towards him. He kissed me.

'It'd be a shame if we never had the time to do this sort of thing,' I said, and reached inside his pyjama bottoms for his cock, which wasn't quite big yet, but was getting there.

The argument flared above our heads: Katrina was angry about her lack of sleep, and at the way Tim thought he was allowed to sleep every night when Katrina tended to the baby just because he was at work and she was at home, because being at home was work too. That's what the arguments were usually about.

'We won't get like that,' Mark said, and kissed my neck. 'You don't have to worry.'

He reached for the hem of the T-shirt I slept in and lifted it over my head. I wanted us to have our unremarkable and ordinary time together between the sheets of our second-hand divan bed in our tiny flat in the slightly down-at-heel area of a perfectly nice little city near the north-west coast of England. It wasn't too much to ask for.

I wondered if Eddie was going to text me to check if I was okay. I lay there a while, playing with my phone. He didn't get in touch and the baby carried on crying. Constant. It has been crying, more or less, since last November. You expect some leaking of noise in flats but this was intolerable. They should have the noise of a baby's crying noted down as a method of torture. After a while – and it was a long while, and I had been drinking – I lost my temper, got up, went into the kitchen and picked up the broom.

I'm turning into one of those people, I thought, and *the baby won't shut up just because I'm banging,* but that didn't stop me lifting the broom above my head and using it to bang on the ceiling.

'Shut up! Shut that baby up! Stop that fucking noise!'

The bristles softened the impact, I think. The sound was hollow and disappointing. So I turned the broom around, held it by the wider end and used the handle to beat at the ceiling. Three times, then a pause, then again, but harder. It's the Morse code distress signal. *Mayday! Mayday! Help me! Help me!* I made marks on the polystyrene ceiling tiles: they're probably still there.

Afterwards, I ran the water in the kitchen sink, cooled my wrists and filled my cupped hands to splash my face. There's no window in the kitchen so I didn't need to look at my reflection. I didn't want to see what I had come to. I found a half-bottle of wine I'd forgotten about – I was often mislaying things – and settled on the settee with it. I turned on the television. There was a film on about a woman who was stalking her ex-husband, his new wife and their baby. She was planning to take the baby – though whether she wanted to look after it or do it harm was unclear, and formed much of the suspense of the piece. I turned up the volume because it drowned out the crying. I tried to comfort myself. I gave myself a talking-to.

I decided it was probably better that Eddie and I had not taken our relationship to the next level that evening. I wasn't prepared. No condoms in the house and I'd taken the last contraceptive pill in my packet a few days before. I'd start bleeding again soon, and if I wanted a repeat prescription, I would have to go to the doctor's and get a weigh and measure and a blood pressure reading taken.

'How are you bearing up, Mrs Wright?' she'd ask, and I would cry, or not cry, and the whole thing would be a bother.

But if I was going to be single, and back in the saddle? It was going to be a matter to address. A part of moving forward and taking care of myself. Details like this would be important.

I wondered if I was ever going to sleep with anyone else again. People grow and change in relationships. For example, I had come to share some of Mark's interests in strange science fiction and his theories about the bleak impossibility of travel beyond our solar system. I learned to understand the sadness and the optimism of his world view: there were almost certainly other beings like us and other civilisations like ours, only better, elsewhere in the universe. In the great scheme of things, they were probably in touching distance, and they could save us from ourselves. But with both our technology and the laws of physics against us, and with us concentrating our efforts on the printing press, petrol, Instagram and cures for malaria rather than the colonisation of Mars, the chances of us making contact before our species made itself extinct were slim to none.

It was hard, anyway, to get into bed with someone. There was no shame in being out of practice, or finding conducting the transaction with a new partner a little awkward. Mark and I had always been easy in bed together.

'Do you want to have sex?' I said. We'd got out of the taxi after Sharon's wedding in town, because we wanted to buy some chips. Now we were walking back to his house and I wanted to be clear. To get things straight. I don't like not to know what is going to happen.

'Sure,' he'd said, smirking. He threw a hot chip into his mouth and chewed thoughtfully. 'Who with?'

That had made me laugh. It had made me notice how weird and silly I was being, and I saw that he knew I was being weird and silly too but didn't mind it. Might even have – I'd hoped – found it endearing. We ate the chips and went back to his and went to bed.

Afterwards he told me about his interstellar travel theory. He was very concerned about climate change – he'd talk to me about it a lot in those early days, and for a while was very assiduous about the recycling and not buying plastic bottles of milk, but glass ones, and so on. Then he'd read a leaked report from some organisation formed by the top scientists of all the different countries around the world that said that it was too late, that a natural human genocide was on the way, perhaps even in our lifetime or the lifetime of the next generation. The rich people would probably be all right: would be able to afford to flood-proof their houses or move to the rapidly diminishing lands that would still hold them. But for the rest of us . . .

That's when he started to get into the idea of space travel, he said. The most imaginative scientists had seen this coming, he told me, and had been calling for more funding to be put into researching interstellar space travel since the early 1970s. The moon wouldn't be far enough away but we could strike out into the dark and colonise Mars, using it as a kind of service station or hitching post in order to take off further and further into the great beyond, eventually, he'd hoped, finding another, kinder and gentler sort of civilisation that would save us.

'I felt better after I thought of that,' he'd said. 'It's not like it would be me going off in the spaceship. I know that. But that we'd carry on somehow. That there was a chance for the species.'

'But now you don't?'

He shook his head. 'Our technology isn't good enough yet. And there's a kind of logical problem. Say we did manage to send off a brilliantly energy-efficient and powerful craft today. Off it would go. It might take light years to reach anything worth stopping for,' he walked his fingers across my stomach, tracing a little path between my pubic bone and my sternum. It tickled, but I didn't mind. 'That's fine. Assume we can keep ourselves alive and sane and entertained on the ship for as long as it takes.'

'Okay.'

He smelled like vinegar and hot fat and I wanted to lick his fingers and bite the soft skin on the side of his neck. I tried to look as though I was paying attention.

'Well, back on Earth, the years pass. The water gets higher. Antibiotics stop working. A super-cancer emerges. A super-malaria. There are a few mishaps at nuclear power stations. That sort of thing. Europe uninhabitable – just toxic frozen water now. The remaining landmasses overcrowded. Now the average Westerner is more likely to die of dysentery or starvation than cancer or a stroke. And still, we keep pouring our money into interstellar travel. We build an even better, faster, safer craft. And we fire that one off into the dark too.'

'To catch up with the other one?'

'To *overtake* the other one,' Mark said. 'You can't imagine the distances we're talking about. We'd need to take breeding pairs on these crafts – like Noah's arks, they'd be – because it might take generations and generations of travel in order to get anywhere at all.'

'I don't understand what the problem is.'

Mark was still stroking my skin and I was waiting for his hand to get to my face so I could put his fingers in my mouth and pull him back on top of me.

'Well, because we've worked out that any craft we build today will be made useless by the crafts that we're likely to build tomorrow, we wait. We don't do anything. We wait for the obsolescence problem to resolve itself, and instead the only thing going obsolete is us.'

He suddenly looked very depressed and I wanted to cheer him up.

'All of this assumes that there are other, better civilisations out there. Spacemen with libraries and socialised healthcare and free housing for all. If they exist, and if statistically they *must* exist, well, why don't they come to us?'

Mark shook his head. I carried on.

'They're kind, right? They're nice? All the problems we have, they've found a way to figure them out. And if they're so good – so morally advanced, well, they're definitely going to want to come on a rescue mission. They'd worry about us. They'd want to help sort out climate change and Twitter and cancer and the economic crisis?'

'Look around,' he said, in a way that did not make me feel stupid but let into a secret. 'Look at us. We'd probably seem like a weird, out-of-control parasite. Why would they bother? What have we got to offer them? Best thing is for the whole lot of us to stop breeding and die out naturally. Little fuss as possible.'

It was a strange conversation to have on a first date. At the time I wondered if this was Mark's way of saying, early on, he definitely, certainly, absolutely did not want to have children. I could have reassured him on this point – I didn't either – but it would have felt presumptuous given that we hardly knew each other. Thinking about it after Eddie had gone, I could not remember how the conversation ended and I still can't. I think we might have just fallen asleep, confident that we would resume it, or not, in some other time and place. There was a safety there: in feeling we could always pick up a conversation some other time. And we had ended up bending each other's bodies and personalities into a shape that would fit nobody else's. The slow and uncomprehending recklessness of it astounds me now.

After I put the broom back in the cupboard and tried to settle myself to sleep, I heard the door to the small room click and creak and drift open. It does that a lot. I got out of bed to deal with it.

We never called it the spare room: it was too little for a guest, and though we considered making it into a home office or den for a while, the plans never got put into action. Perhaps the sixteenth floor is not level, or some seasonal shift in humidity or temperature changes the way the edges of the walls and floors line up with each other so that now and again it tilts. It is discomfiting to remember that buildings are not as solid as they seem – as we, especially those of us who dwell on the upper floors, living our whole lives in the air, far above the streets below, need to imagine they are. They breathe and they move.

I unsteadily pulled the door closed and rattled the handle to check the latch had caught. It must not have clicked true earlier on, and that is something else I had asked Mark to look at, and which he never did. It frustrated me at the time, but I can understand it. I wanted to make this place our home, but he was never invested in it in the same kind of way and the flat itself seemed to fight against our efforts.

When we moved in we discovered that the previous tenants had put a child in the small room, and this child had ripped the wallpaper on the wall by its bed and drawn in felt-tipped pen on the plaster. The drawing was troubling; a high-rise flat, very like the one we lived in. Because of the way they were drawn they could just have been guardian angels flying around the flat, protecting the people who lived within it, or doomed and desperate occupants in their nightgowns, adults and children together, throwing themselves from the windows and balconies towards the tarmac below.

I always said they were angels, and Mark was convinced they were suicides. We understood it was a matter of interpretation and we'd have to agree to disagree, and for several years we did just that, living our lives with the strange figures in the background of a room we rarely used and, when we did mention them, using the drawing as a kind of shorthand for the way we differed in how we saw the world – my mindless optimism, his persistent and wilful misery.

'It's just like that drawing,' I'd say sometimes, 'you're just *trying* to put the worst slant possible on things. Like your spacemen. They might like us. They might want to help us.'

'And you're kidding yourself,' Mark would say affectionately.

The time came when we needed to decorate the small room.

'There's no point doing up this shit-tip,' Mark said, 'we'll have to get somewhere bigger soon enough,' but he indulged my whim to freshen up the walls and carried the paint tins up the stairs for me anyway. But when we did come to paint that wall – whatever colour we tried and however many coats we applied – it was only a matter of days before the ink seeped through the paint and left the ghostly impression of the angels/suicides floating on the freshly painted surface. It was as if the flat didn't want us to make our plans for the future.

I shook the handle again to make sure the door was closed properly. You've got to push upwards sometimes – to lift the entire door slightly on its hinges to get it to click in. No doubt it will come open again. We rent this flat, but the landlord does not concern himself with urgent maintenance, never mind trifling matters like doors that swing open in the night and bang against the walls, frightening the life out of a person and destroying sleep entirely.

5

I went into work that Monday dreading seeing Eddie. I spent the bus ride there wondering if it would be better to apologise, perhaps with tears, and blame the stress of my situation for my behaviour, or if I should brazen it out. I could even pretend that I remembered nothing and if he raised the matter, accuse him of making up a story to embarrass me. As the bus turned onto campus, I grew more anxious and wondered if the best thing to do would be to get in there first and pretend that I was very offended and felt that he had taken advantage of *me*. Maybe I should have avoided the problem entirely by taking a day off work, though there was a conference on and Eddie and I were supposed to be attending to the guests. There was nothing to be gained by delaying the inevitable, I decided.

Usually at conference time Eddie and I pair up and do the rooms together, him lifting the mattresses so I can get a nice sharp envelope corner on the sheet, and me swiping the mirrors while he does the bins. Thirty seconds on a room – that was our record – though it turned out the bed had hardly been slept in and the bathroom was unused because the early career researcher on coastal erosion had actually spent the night in the single bed next door, belonging to the Emeritus Professor of Renewable Energy Innovation from a university I won't name, but which you will have heard of.

It doesn't matter now. My point is that Eddie and I were supposed to be working together that morning, but rather than do the rooms together and attempt to beat our record, he told me, without meeting my eye, to go along the corridor and do the beds on my own.

'Get a head start on it,' he said. He was going to finish vaping, then he'd come behind me, swishing the bathrooms and collecting the bin liners as we went along. It wouldn't have made much difference to our time, but it was clear in a way that was both awkward and hurtful that he was avoiding being alone with me.

I did as he'd asked, opening the doors with my master keys, making the beds, collecting the old towels into my trolley and replacing them with clean ones, and leaving the door ajar behind me so Eddie could go in after me, finish off and lock up. We worked like that, me hearing the doors banging and the plastic bin liners disappearing into his trolley, but us not exchanging a word.

After a while I started to feel strange. The odd feeling I'd been having of being watched, especially when I was at home, and of things being altered behind my back or out of the corner of my eye began to gather around me. The light in the room flickered as I was doing the bed, and in the moment of darkness – the sheet I was straightening flying out from my hands like a pan of spilled milk – a trace of something formed. I don't know what it was. A not-quite shape: an outline without an edge. I jumped.

It wasn't the trace or the flicker that had startled me as such. I'd been getting them at home too. Small movements – like the impression on the retina that is left behind when you stare at a bright light, then away. It wasn't the cold feeling – the prickle at the spine and wrists, the sensation that I was being both observed and disapproved of. But it was the fact that these – what shall I call them? Phenomena? – had travelled with me to work. I didn't realise I'd been thinking of my work as a sanctuary until it ceased to be one.

I have done some internet research on this. The way presences – memories of energy, the more scientific-type websites call them – can adhere to a time or a place or a room. That a space or a building can carry an ordinary relic of past experience (you know the word I am attempting not to bring into play here: I would like to be taken seriously) and, in certain circumstances, that relic can replay itself. There's no intelligence there, it's just a lightshow. But that morning in the bedroom, as I let the sheet fall from my hands and caught sight of myself in the mirror, I realised that the *effects* I had been experiencing did not cluster around the block I lived in, nor flat number 16, nor the smallest room inside that flat, as I had thought. Because here I was at work, on an ordinary morning, doing an ordinary thing, with Eddie next door humming and banging the empty bin on the side of his trolley to loosen the old teabag stuck to the bottom of it (I didn't need to see him to know what he was doing and why he was doing it. I've been working here since I was twenty-two years old and yet there it was, and it wasn't a ghost, it was me.

The thought made me very tired. I went over to the bed and lay down. I don't know how long I lay like that, watching the plain white institutional shade around the light bulb and seeing that there was no flicker, no light or disturbance other than the one I carried about inside me, which leaked into the people and places I came into contact with. Eddie came in and found me like that, lying on the bed with the duvet pulled up over my head. It smelled like a man's bed: not dirty, exactly, but close and heavy. I still had my trainers on and the bottom sheet would need changing because of it.

'What are you doing?'

'I'm tired,' I said. I poked my head out. He was standing in the doorway, a knotted-up bin liner swinging from his fist.

'We've eight to go. Come on. Shaw is on the rampage today.'

I pulled the cover over my face.

'I can't,' I said.

I looked teenaged and dramatic to him, I suppose, but I meant it. I was unable to move. I just wanted to lie there. Let the man whose room it was come back and sit at his desk and write his important thoughts down in his complimentary conference notepad. Let him shower in the en suite and make himself a little cup of tea with the tiny hostess kettle. Let him sleep all night, unaware of me until it is time for him to get up in the morning and give his paper and take his questions and accept, without modesty, his applause. Let him go on to more keynote addresses in Europe and America, and let him enjoy his glittering career and the distinguished visiting professorship posts that will come as the years roll on. Let him do all that and let me lie there, still, still and silent in this bed, the bed he had once lain in for a chilly, sleepless night and went on to quickly forget. The bed will not exist in his history, but I will lie here forever, keeping the presence of him close, the dust settling on me, and I will not sleep or dream or think or wait. I will just lie here. That's what I thought.

It was impossible to explain this to Eddie.

'Are you ill?' he said, clearly irritated. 'Are you hung-over?'

'No,' I said, though even the effort to say that single word felt like a great concession he should have been grateful for. Instead, he came into the room fully; the door banged closed behind him and he pulled at the edge of the duvet.

'You're not leaving me to do all this on my own,' he said.

I grabbed at the duvet, wrapped myself up in it and rolled away from him, towards the wall. I had some idea, I think, that if I just lay down there with my eyes closed the entire world would carry on around me without me needing to do or say anything or make any decisions. That all the important things would be taken care of by someone else – by the Olenas of the world – and I could just let the detail of my life drift away.

'Leave me,' I said.

'For fuck's sake, Laurie,' he said, letting go of the end of the duvet. 'You want Shaw to call you in again? You want to explain to her why we're behind? Again? You can lie there looking at the ceiling all you like, but some of us need our jobs.'

I kept my eyes closed and the duvet over my face. The air inside there was getting warm and damp: I could smell my own coffee and roll-ups and toothpaste and smoke. It was comforting.

'I'm going,' he said. And he did.

The bed was nice. It was narrow and firm, and if I moved around I could hear the plastic cover on the mattress crackle and squeak. It reminded me a little of a hospital bed, but being in hospital, among all that bleach and white and someone else's routine, would be no bad thing. I think I slept for an hour or two, then I got up, smoothed the duvet so it was neat and tidy and left.

It was Bartleby, I was thinking of. I couldn't place the name of the story until just now. A man at work, like me, who just lies down and refuses to go home because he doesn't feel like it. No particular reason.

After that, I did decide to take some time off work. I booked a fortnight and Shaw let me have it at short notice, probably because Eddie had told her I was cracking up. I had annual leave owing but no trip abroad to look forward to and, I reasoned, I was as entitled as anyone to a period of rest. I spent a lot of time in the flat, reprising the dark days at the beginning of the year, when sometimes I couldn't persuade myself to open the door and go down the stairs for days and days at a time. Now and again I searched, as I had done before, for Joyce + medium + Lancashire on Google. The same three results showed up, but I still did not click through to the websites to find out if one of the Joyces was the woman Mark and I had met at Sharon's wedding. I wanted to, only I refused to give in to myself. Things were not quite that bad, I told myself. Not yet.

When I needed the fresh air, I walked over the bridge and through the narrow streets and cobbled roads of the little city towards the train station. It felt like a good place to sit and drink coffee and watch the world go by – though I was no trainspotter and was only looking for my husband. I have read since that widows, in their grief, sometimes hallucinate sightings of the man they have lost. That they see a glimpse of a man wearing a familiar green jacket, stooping to retrieve a packet of crisps from a vending machine. They spot, from the corner of their eye, a sloped shoulder or a lolloping gait or even the cuff of a beloved blue cardigan, and apparently these half-sightings are a kind of comfort because in the seconds before the mirage dissolves and they realise they were mistaken, these widows have become wives again.

I sipped expensive coffee in the café on the platform and watched the churn of commuters and day-trippers but I didn't see Mark. I watched and waited and when I could wait no more, I visited my father.

One Saturday evening, when I let myself in he was in the kitchen with Olena, who was cooking. She was talking to him – or herself, really – about her family in Dnipro. He was hovering behind her, wanting to see what was in the pans. This toddlerish behaviour of his made my heart hurt and got on my nerves at the same time.

'She'll be starting senior school soon enough,' Olena was saying, 'so there will be the cost for the uniforms, books, music lessons too probably. How we will afford it, I don't know.'

'You said there was money from her father?'

Olena nodded. 'A little bit, yes. But it's all gone now. It didn't last long,' she sighed. 'I wish you could see her, Mr Spencer. Hair like an angel, and needing brushing ten, twenty times a day. I tell my mother – have it cut! Cut it off! – but she won't. And I'm glad really. Remind me later and I will show you a photograph. She emailed me some new ones yesterday. You won't believe the change in her.'

They hadn't noticed me. I felt superfluous somehow, or as if I wasn't hesitating in the kitchen doorway of my childhood home at all but watching a particular kind of theatre – art of the kitchen sink and the everyday, the kind where nothing really happens and you're just supposed to be interested in the relationship between the characters rather than wanting to know what happens next.

'You must go and visit her,' my father said. 'You can't spend your best years mopping my kitchen floor. I'll ask Laurie to stay with me for a while.'

Olena laughed quietly at this – whether at the idea of her taking time off, or of me staying and looking after my father, I could not tell.

'If wishes were pound coins, Mr Spencer, I'd be there already. There already!'

I coughed. It wasn't a passive-aggressive way of drawing attention to myself – though it might have sounded like it. I had been smoking hundreds and hundreds of little hand-rolled cigarettes and, since Mark had gone, had even started smoking in bed. There was a faint dry rattling in my chest – there all the time but much worse at night and first thing in the morning. They turned to me.

'Good afternoon?' my father said. He looked tired. His voice had the lilt of enquiry. He used to play this game with me when I was younger.

'Who's this little girl?' he'd say, if he happened to be in the house when I came home from school. 'Who's blown in from the street this afternoon?'

'It's me, Dad,' I'd say.

'Me? Me? I'm not sure I know anyone by that name. Let me think. Do I know anyone by the name of Me?' He would tap his chin, or turn out his pockets, as if looking for an address book. 'Can't say it's ringing a bell, Me.'

He would egg on my mother, who seemed to like the game a little bit less (she saw it, I think, as an interruption to her afternoon routine) to join in.

'Do you know her, Janet? Are you familiar with this young specimen here?'

'Can't say I am,' she'd say, wearily, turning pages in a magazine or chopping vegetables or spraying Mr Sheen on the sideboard, not looking up.

'I wonder who she is then. I wonder just who's been rude

enough to traipse right in and invite herself for tea. What an imposition! Heh heh heh.'

I never really understood what my father expected of me in those moments. He would get annoyed if I ignored him and took myself away to my bedroom under the pretence of doing homework. If I laughed, or otherwise indicated that I appreciated the joke, he would redouble his efforts – sometimes keeping it up for an hour or more. He once, I remember, lifted the telephone in the hallway and pretended to make a phone call to the police, complaining that a mucky little girl had turned up in his kitchen and was refusing to go back to her parents.

He would stop when I got upset or angry.

'For goodness' sake, Gerald,' my mother would say, and he would hold up both of his hands, palm outwards, and plead the innocent.

'Just a game, Janet. Nothing but a harmless little game.'

He would be smiling, but it would stop. I used to think it was because he realised he'd taken his joke too far but, as I think about it now, I wonder if my distress was the reaction he wanted. My tears of rage and fear satisfied his playful or sadistic urge in some way. It didn't happen often – he was mainly at work – but I remember these occasions as another of the annoying, taking-up-too-much-room sort of things my father did when he was bored, in the house in the afternoons, and not fitting into the usual schedule.

'It's me,' I said. 'I've come to see you.'

'Well, that's lovely,' he said, uncertainly. 'You must join us for dinner.'

'I wasn't going to,' I said, refusing to play along. 'Just a flying visit.'

'But Olena here will be offended if you don't try her stew,' he replied, keeping up his veneer of puzzled politeness. 'And you've come all this way.'

I realised then that he wasn't playing with me. He wasn't

telling me he didn't know me – he was trying to hide the fact that he *didn't* know me and doing pretty poorly at it.

'Is it cold outside? Would you like a hot drink?'

'It's July,' I said. 'Not cold.'

His gaze searched my face. He knew that he knew me from somewhere, but couldn't quite place me. Olena was on hand, if not to soothe the awkwardness, then at least to acknowledge it.

'It's Laurie, Mr Spencer,' she said loudly, as if he was also deaf. 'Laurie has come to see you. Your daughter.'

He laughed politely and shook his head.

'Oh, this isn't Laurie,' he said, in exactly the same tone of voice he used to use when he was playing the game with me. 'It's someone who looks like Laurie, I'll give her that. Has her hair. Her eyes. Those are her trainers and that's her jacket. Whoever this person is has paid attention to the details. Credit where cred-it's due,' he glared at me then – malicious or desperate, I'm not sure which – 'but she isn't my daughter.'

'Dad . . .' I'm not sure what I was going to say next. This was the first time it had happened. I had worried about it, but worried uselessly, without making any preparation as to how I would respond to the inevitable. Olena, who was more used to all of this than I was, broke in briskly.

'Mr Spencer. Are you going to get the butter dish down for me and put it on the table? We do want to eat sometime before the Second Coming, don't we?'

'I won't be spoken to in that way by an employee,' my father said, delighted, and went to the back of the kitchen to fetch the butter dish.

'Don't mind him,' Olena said, her voice lowered. 'Half of it is him just trying to irritate you. You know that.'

'It doesn't matter.'

She stirred vigorously, as if she wanted to disagree with me but was restraining herself from doing so.

'Is there any news?'

I shook my head and she turned back to her pans.

'I see. Well, let's have no excuses this time. You can eat with us. I'll set a place.'

'Yes, all right,' I said. 'I'm just going to the bathroom.'

A strange idea had come over me. The beginnings of a plan. I climbed the stairs and, from the landing, diverted into my father's room. It used to be my mother's room too; her perfume bottles were still laid out in a brightly coloured phalanx on top of the tallboy. Olena told me he sometimes sprayed a handkerchief with the dregs of her addled Shalimar and tucked it inside his pillowcase.

There was a wedding photograph in a silver frame on his bedside table and I sat on the edge of the bed and looked at it. My father's comments about the matter of my paternity had been playing on my mind, and that's what I was looking for, something of my own face in the young man that my father had been: trainee accountant in a big Manchester firm, the world about to be his oyster, and a woman in open-toed white high-heeled shoes on his arm, her hair piled high. Their faces were tiny and sun bleached. His eyes were green and mine are blue-grey. He had dark hair when he was in his prime – a whole heap of it – and my hair is an ashy, dirty, dishwater blonde. I don't take after my mother either: she was slight, strawberry blonde, and delicately pretty. I squinted at the photograph, seeing the detail of the confetti on the pavement around their shoes, the rainwater pooling on the steps of the registry office, the tiny posy of yellow roses my mother held in front of her abdomen, where I, apparently, was dug in firm like a tick and rapidly growing – the Unexpected Guest.

'Are you coming? Your father is about to starve to death!' Olena bellowed up the stairs.

I put the picture back and went over to the tallboy. I opened the top drawer. Socks. Boxer shorts rolled into little bundles and stacked on their sides (Olena, as part of her continuing professional development, had been reading *The Life Changing Magic of Tidying Up*). His hairbrush. There were several white hairs clinging to it, and I took the brush and stuffed it into the front pocket of my hoodie. My intention was to retrieve his hair from the brush and put it in an envelope and send it away to one of those online DNA-testing companies. My father was no longer a reliable witness but the structure of our DNA would be. I needed to know for sure. It was a spontaneous plan, half formed on my way up the stairs to the bathroom – but while I had the drawer open, I noticed that my father's money tin was open and all of his cash was gone.

It is a stereotype that older people start to mistrust banks and withdraw their pension and savings to have in cash, stuffed under the mattress or between the pages of old *Reader's Digest*s or tucked inside the toes of their party shoes, long unworn. My father wasn't even that old, not really – still strong and vigorous, capable of spending an afternoon digging in the garden, but not of remembering what seeds should be planted where, and how they should be looked after. But even though he was an ex-accountant and trusted his bank, he still kept alarming amounts of cash in the house and always had done. I think it was a habit from the times he'd pay in cash for his clandestine dinners and the orders from florists that were not for my mother, so as not to leave a trace of his antics. As his illness had taken hold, so had his paranoia and his wish to fly under the radar of the government. Olena and I had managed to convince him to stash the notes in his top drawer, and now and again I 'withdrew' money from it to pay her. I had always dealt honestly and fairly with my father's money and I was as confident as I could be that it was not me who had taken it or lost count. But all the same, it was gone – nearly four thousand pounds of it.

'Your father informs me you were brought up much better than this!' she called. 'Your tea is on the table!'

I closed the tin, arranged the socks around it, and went downstairs. My father was tucking in to his meal. Olena gestured for me to sit down. She'd had her hair done: usually it looked like the foamy top of an ice-cream float but that evening it was slick and smooth and glossy.

We ate.

'This is lovely stew, Olena,' I said, watching her carefully.

'I have a secret ingredient,' she said. She'd parked herself at the head of the table, my father and I either side of her, like children.

'Oh yes?'

'She spits in it,' my father said. Olena and I glanced at him. She swore in Ukrainian, then burst into laughter.

'Mr Spencer, you are a disgusting man,' she said. He nodded his head in a mock bow, then turned to me.

'I'm sorry about before,' he said. 'I'd had a sleep this afternoon. Just woken up when you got here actually. I think I was still dreaming.'

'It's all right,' I said. 'It doesn't matter.'

'You just look a bit different sometimes.'

'I'm not in my work uniform. That's what it is. I've taken some time off.'

'No. It's something else. I can't place it.'

'I haven't been to the hairdresser. Not like Olena here,' I said spitefully. Nobody seemed to notice.

'It isn't your hair love. It's you. You were fat, weren't you?'

Olena sucked in air through her pursed lips, shook her head and said nothing. I couldn't tell if this was Pervert Father or Angry Father. It could have been Normal Father being mean, I suppose.

'I've lost a bit of weight,' I said. 'It's been a hard time.'

'You were *much* fatter.'

He stared frankly at my body in a way that made me want to grab the edges of my coat and pull it closed over my breasts. His doctor had warned me about this – or rather, she had given me a leaflet that warned me about decreased inhibition, and sexually inappropriate language and behaviour.

'Dad.'

'No,' he insisted, 'you were,' – he sketched a shape in the air – 'you were a right fatty, weren't you?'

'That's not nice,' I said, in my baby voice, which sometimes drew out Doting Dad.

'Well, you're different. You are. I don't know what it is,' my father said sulkily.

I heaped up my fork with mashed potatoes, meat and peas. I didn't want it to be good, but it was. I have never been much of a cook, and it felt ridiculous to prepare proper food when it was just me in the flat to eat it. Olena looked on approvingly.

Olena had a theory about my father. She believed that he lied – confabulated, is the word – because there was so much about his previous life as a husband, father, mediocre accountant and persistent philanderer that he could no longer remember. His vascular dementia meant that in the distant and the recent past the blood vessels in his brain had both constricted and broken, and the tiny bleeds and suffocations this had caused had wiped out little chunks of his brain tissue. To know that he did not remember, that his years had dissolved and blown away and the best part of his life was already gone, his blood-soaked brain no longer able to retain it, would have been too much for him. It would have distressed him beyond measure, and so his confabulations had a protective function: they were lies, yes, but entirely innocent ones, in that even he did not know he was lying. His mind swooped into these potholes in time quickly, so quickly he did not catch it in the act, and coloured them in with nonsense.

This lying, Olena told me, fresh from her internet research (I worried constantly she would become unsatisfied with the hourly rate of a mere cleaner) was part of the pathology of vascular dementia, but it was also only an exaggeration of the way everybody's minds dealt with the fragmented, shifting and entirely unreliable nature of our memories. We fill in the gaps all the time. If we knew

– she told me – if we ever really knew how little relation our scant memories bore to the abundant facts of our existence, we'd all go insane with grief at the incomprehensible scale of our loss. There was so much we didn't want to know and we were all dead before we died because most of our memories were fiction. A little lie now and again kept us from madness and that was all there was to it.

After we had finished the washing-up, my father went into the dining room to look through his photographs and Olena and I sat in the conservatory, which in the years after my mother had the under-stairs cupboard turned into a toilet (she called it the 'water closet' and I do still believe it was the single thing in her life she took real and uncomplicated pleasure from) had been used to store all the usual under-stairs things – the coats and boots, the mop bucket and vacuum cleaner, the plastic fold-up table and chairs for the garden, and several boxes of tattered Christmas decorations. We sat at a wicker table among all this junk, like guests at a jumble sale.

'I think he's getting worse,' I said. She was smoking again, blowing her smoke at the moss-and-algae-spotted glass of the conservatory roof. I eyed her packet of cigarettes enviously and didn't take one. 'Do you think so?'

Olena shrugged. 'He's up and down. Some days good, some days bad. I don't see a pattern. Do you want me to make a doctor's appointment for him?'

'He won't go,' I said. 'You know what he's like.'

'It's been going on a long time, this, hasn't it?'

I heard my father in the dining room then, shifting the boxes about, and imagined him looking mystified at the faded faces on the old family photographs, sliding them around on the table as if they were tarot cards.

'I wasn't here for most of it,' I said. 'It was at Mum's funeral that I really noticed. Perhaps it had been a bit gradual – creeping up on him, but because I'd had that gap it struck me a bit more.'

'I never knew your mother,' Olena said. 'I feel like I do though. Your father talks about her a lot.'

'Yes, I bet he does,' I said, and she laughed.

'She was a patient woman, I gather,' she said delicately.

'She handled him,' I said. 'He was always a bit . . . like he is. Hard to know where the illness starts and his personality begins. But at her funeral . . .'

'Was he very bad?'

'It was all right at the service. He was all right. Stood at the front and talked about how much she'd helped him when he first set up the business. About how nice she made the house. Told a funny story about the time she forgot about the pressure cooker and the lid came off and blew a hole in the kitchen ceiling. All that kind of thing. He did well. But afterwards we all went to a pub. He'd put some money behind the bar so everyone could have a drink or two, but there'd been more people there than he'd expected, so there was a bit of a bill to pay at the end.'

'Your father is a generous man. It can be a fault sometimes,' Olena said.

She stubbed her cigarette out in the saucer and immediately reached for another. I thought about the missing money and watched her carefully. Was she going to confess now – to claim that he'd been up there and gathered up his notes and presented them to her, as a payment for the overtime she undoubtedly did, the extra hours she stayed, the laundry she took home with her? Was that why she didn't want to have anything to do with the police? She could have worked on a story by then. Something plausible, like saying he wanted to reward her. That she didn't want him to feel indebted to her, so she'd accepted the cash and agreed to keep it quiet in fear that I would be unreasonable about it. But she lit her second cigarette and said nothing.

'It wasn't a big crowd. Some friends from the office. A couple of nurses from the hospice. The neighbours and a couple of cousins. She wasn't old, but she had a small life and he was the main part of it. None of them big drinkers. So it won't have been a massive tab. But he got really upset about the bill.'

I remember him blustering, waving the printed-out receipt in the face of the bar manager and saying the till must have been on the blink. Then he took the receipt to a little table in the corner and spent an hour with a pencil trying to do the sums on the edge of an old newspaper. People kept coming up to him to see if it was all right. He got a sweat on. It was embarrassing.

'What happened?' Olena asked.

'Mark wanted us to pay it, without him knowing – just so we could get out of there. But we didn't have any money spare.'

'An accountant no longer able to do his sums,' Olena said. 'He must have been terrified.'

'No, it wasn't like that,' I said. 'If he had been scared, it would have been easier to get him to the doctor – to get the memory tests and the scans done a bit quicker. But he was just pissed off. Convinced the pub was trying to cheat him out of his money. Mr Haworth paid it in the end – his partner at the firm.'

'I know who he is. His wife – she visits sometimes.'

Mrs Haworth. I hadn't thought about her in years. I laughed, and it was a mean laugh.

'Does she?' I said.

Olena put out her cigarette in the saucer.

'I know that type of woman,' she said, and winked at me. 'I don't cook for her.'

We sniggered. Olena pushed her cigarette packet towards me and I shook my head.

'We never did pay Mr Haworth back. Poor bastard. It was excruciating. People said it was just grief. That it makes everyone act strangely. But I knew there was more to it than that.'

'So you decided to see him again. To come back into his life?'

'I thought,' it was hard to say this and I took my time over it. 'I thought something must be wrong. He was so horrible – so bloody nasty about it. Causing such a scene when it was supposed to be about my mother. I could see he wasn't right. And it made me wonder if he hadn't been right for years. If a lot of things I remember from my teenage years – he was very difficult and we didn't get on – were actually him being sick, rather than him being . . . I don't know. A bastard. Unforgivable.'

'Maybe you're right,' Olena said. I thought she was about to say more, but my father appeared then, a photograph of me in his hand, and I was glad I'd not taken one of Olena's cigarettes. He waved it at me triumphantly.

'See!' he said, dropping it onto the table. 'I told you you used to be fat. Look at this one!'

I went for Olena's cigarettes then, not caring what my father had to say about it, and Olena picked up the photograph before I could see it and tidied it away.

Olena's theory about my father's lying was a good one. And, as I say, she'd done the research. She was probably right about a lot of things. But, like the matter of his bad personality, I don't think it was as cut and dried as all that. My father could have chosen any number of fabrications to explain my mother's absence to himself. Subtracting the fact of her death from his emotional ledger meant he had to find new ways to account for his feelings of abandonment or neglect. But that helpful mind of his could have told him that she was on holiday, or visiting relatives, or even that she was with me. Instead, he concocted a vivid extramarital sex life for her, when the fact was that if there were illegitimate children lying around, then they were more likely to be the seed of his loins than of whoever was fictionally fucking my mother. Mr and Mrs Haworth had three kids – all around my age – and I never dared look at any of them too closely. It was guilt. Projection. Classic.

And yet. I doubted. Of course I doubted. I heard Olena with my father in the dining room, putting the photographs away and trying to distract him by telling a long story about her dog, which the day before had escaped from the house and come back with half a chicken in his mouth, probably swiped from a neighbour's kitchen. I felt the outline of the hairbrush in the pocket of my hoodie and tried to make my own ledger balance. In so many ways other than my looks, I was unlike my parents. It lay, I think, underneath my sense that I did not really know them, and that they in their turn did not know me.

I will also tell you why I didn't confront Olena about the money there and then. I don't come out of this very well, so because of that you can be sure that I am telling the truth.

Olena is a proud woman – proud of her work, proud of her ethics, proud of the way that the people she cleans for come to rely on her. She likes to be useful. She likes, I think, to feel essential. And she was essential to me as well as my father, because if I had accused her of being a thief, I was almost certain she would have packed up her things and left, and the job of caring for my father, seeing to his washing and meals and generally checking in to make sure he'd not signed up to have his drive re-tarmacked or solar panels put on his roof or invested in some dubious overseas business opportunity and, most of all, listening to these endless stories he told about my mother, would have fallen entirely and solely to me. I was, I will admit, a contrary and undutiful daughter, and if the cost of deputising some of that filial work to Olena was a missing wad of cash, well, I was willing to pay it.

Olena kissed me on both cheeks and left and I finished cleaning up in the kitchen and helped my father to bed myself. He was not so incapable that he couldn't be left overnight, and though I considered staying and searching the house for the missing money – there was always the chance he'd taken it out of the tin and placed it elsewhere himself – the gentle ticking of the carriage clock on the mantelpiece and the click and puff of the boiler started to drive me mad and I grabbed my coat and wandered off into town.

6

Truth be told, I did not want to go home. I often had to steel myself to climb the sixteen flights up to the dark flat. The empty rooms felt haunted: as if my loneliness itself was a hostile presence. In the daytime it was easy to dismiss odd sensations, flickering lights and missing items as symptoms of my mentally unsettled state. At night, with the persistent coldness – a coldness that gathered in the corners no matter how warm the day had been and how high I turned up the heating – it was too difficult to stop my ideas running away with me. Easier, then, just to stay away from the place all together.

After wandering through the town centre, in and out of pubs, my hair getting wet and drying again, I washed up outside a nightclub. There are two in our little city. One for the students, owned by the union – and which I dared not enter. Life was difficult enough without being recognised by a Wanker out on the razzle. The other, talked about scornfully by the Wankers and Staff Wankers alike, catered more to local sixth-formers and depressed forty-year-olds. I'd never been in before, but the cigarette-burned red carpet laid out on the pavement outside to indicate the extent of an optimistically roped-off queuing area made it easy to find. There was no queue, and, somewhat bedraggled and lacking in funds, I drifted through its neon-lit doors.

I was not experienced in these things. Mark and I tended to do our drinking at home, in front of the television. In fact, our early courtship was conducted on my settee against the background of the Connie Fallon case and lubricated by the cheap wine he'd bring with him to the flat. In the aftermath of our – what should I call it? Fucking? Lovemaking? It wasn't quite either of those things – we'd turn on the television and watch the late-night news and get up to speed on the investigation. At that time the police were trying to piece together a timeline of her last movements by gathering accounts from neighbours who had seen or heard her playing in the garden. They were also testing various pieces of unspecified forensic evidence they had found on and near her body. Mark was always more interested in the progress of the case than I was, in a way I found both sinister and endearing, and in fact one of our earliest private jokes was my pretending to be convinced that he himself was the murderer the police were looking for.

'You can tell me,' I'd say. 'I won't tell anyone.'

'Would you wait for me if I went down for some serious time?' he said. 'Come and see me all dolled up while I did my bird? Send me your dirty knickers in the prison post to keep me going?'

It was a tasteless kind of joking – I do realise that – but I've come to believe that most special bonds between people are made of the things they say to each other that they could not possibly say to anyone else. For some people, those things are comprised of sad, intimate facts about their childhoods. For others, they might be privately held ambitions or dreams for the future, almost too ludicrous to be spoken aloud. It just so happened that, in our case, it was a horrible joke about a dead little girl. I guess, looking at the way our lives have turned out, the joke was on us and we have both been repaid in full for our cruelty.

'I'd write to you. Send you parcels. A file in a cake, then you can break out and come and see me,' I said. 'You'd come and find me, wouldn't you?'

'I'd take you away,' Mark said, unbuttoning my jeans and pulling me towards him by the waistband. 'We could go on the lam together.'

It wasn't just a joke to Mark, though. On our second night together he brought an envelope out of his pocket, wrote something on a scrap of paper and sealed it inside. He got me to write my signature across the seal, as if he was a stage magician, and tucked it between the pages of the book I was reading – it was *Double Jeopardy* (I remember it clearly).

'You leave it there,' he said. 'Don't open it. Don't fiddle with it.'

I cajoled and pestered him to tell me what was inside, but he would not be moved. When he left, I brought it out of the book and held it up to the bedroom light bulb. I was hoping for a romantic gesture of some kind but he'd folded the paper in two and, although I could see there was writing on it, I couldn't read it. The weeks passed and eventually I forgot all about the envelope, until the night came when he turned up at the flat with his carrier bag of lager and crisps and asked me to go and find it.

'Go on. No crisps until you do.' He held the bag up high and I pretended to reach for it, which made him laugh.

I retrieved it. He turned the television on and pushed me into a chair. The news was on, reporting, again, on the Connie Fallon case. There had been the inevitable sighting of a white van, the arrest and elimination of the school caretaker, and the DNA swabbing of her male neighbours and relatives. Mark nudged me.

'Look. They've got them.'

The footage playing was of her father being led away from the family home in handcuffs, an ignominious pink and brown floral bath towel draped over his head and shoulders to hide his face. As he was helped into the waiting police car, her mother also emerged, her face uncovered, wearing her own pair of handcuffs and flanked on both sides by a second pair of police officers. I will remember the expression on that woman's face forever. She looked as if she'd just woken up from a long sleep to news of her own wrongdoing. She was befuddled with shock, the way I imagine I look to the judge and juries that I so often dreamed about. I wonder why she didn't cover her face?

'Go on,' Mark urged. 'Open the envelope.'

The slip of paper inside had been torn from a notebook and had a ragged edge. I had come to know Mark's handwriting by then – its regular, looping, almost feminine style.

I am not a psychic, he had written. *Connie Fallon has been murdered by her mother. Her father is in on it.* He'd carefully signed and dated the slip of paper. I looked up – he was giddy and smug and I was, I expect, somewhat crestfallen.

'Shall we give Joyce a ring? Tell her she's out of a job? I should change my career, I reckon. Get a cape and a funny hat and start charging people, like she does.'

'She doesn't charge,' I said, holding the piece of paper carefully. The television played on – a statement from the police about some forensic evidence found in the upstairs bedroom of the little house where the family lived – and a shot of the house itself, the bunches of flowers and teddy bears covering the tiny front lawn being carefully removed by a sombre officer. 'How did you know?'

'It's always the dad,' Mark said. 'But it couldn't have been the dad, because he was away with work.' He counted off suspects on his fingers, like a shopping list. 'If it's not the dad, it's an uncle or a stepdad. But there wasn't a stepdad, and nobody ever mentioned an uncle. If the police thought it was an uncle, they'd have put him on the telly and made him do a public appeal, like they did with her parents. So I reckoned it had to have been the mum. She was there. In the house. Nobody saw anyone else.'

'I see,' I said, and folded the paper in two. The detective in charge of the case was making a statement, talking about forensics and the Crown Prosecution Service and thanking the public for their support. 'Well, then it looks like you were right.'

'Mystic Meg eat your heart out,' he said, and grinned.

It wasn't as if we went on to have an argument that night, and if Mark noticed my disappointment, he did not mention it. We ate a bag of crisps and finished the lager and he stayed over. We watched a film, I think, and I may even have fallen asleep with my head on his arm, as had become common for us. When we went to bed we had sex in the usual way, and the excitement of strangeness was still there, but giving way – with a feeling that was both delicious and terrifying – to a familiarity and a knowing of each other's ways. If I put my hand on his balls like *this*, or he bit the skin between my thumb and first finger like *this*, we could be confident of getting started. But, from my end of things anyway, the atmosphere had soured between us a little. He was so keen to prove Joyce wrong about her first prediction that I felt sure the implication was he couldn't bear her being right about her second, concerning the nature of the connection between us. I never mentioned this theory of mine to him.

But I digress. The nightclub I ended up in that night was, I imagine, as all nightclubs of that type are. Girls in short dresses and complicated shoes, boys in band T-shirts and trainers. I was low on cash, but there was some kind of deal on with the drinks so I was able to spend an hour or so in a corner maintaining the state of drunkenness I'd achieved thus far and marvelling at how young and energetic most of the clientele were. I suppose I stood out in many ways, but I leaned my head back on the faux-leather banquette, let the music throb through my sternum and decided not to mind.

A man joined me. I may have had my eyes closed as I listened to the music because he appeared from nowhere, holding two plastic cups in one hand.

'Drink?' he bellowed, tipping an imaginary glass to his mouth with his free hand.

I bet the younger women there would have steered clear of a man like him – too old to be in there, like me – a possible letch on the prowl, a sad-case, a walking midlife crisis, a loser. He may have been all of those things. He was wearing an orange short-sleeved shirt with jeans that were a little too big for him and he'd been dancing – the sweat stains under his arms the shape of the continent of Africa.

'Why not?' I said, knowing that as I had been appraising him, he'd already looked me over and decided that I would do. Sometimes, boys did make passes at girls who wore glasses. He deposited the cups on the table and sat down next to me.

'Are you having a nice time?'

I smiled weakly and he nodded, and then looked away. He was, I could tell, searching his mind for something else to say. It made me like him a bit. We were, after all, in exactly the same boat.

'Not my usual sort of place,' I screamed over the music.

'I've not seen you here before,' he shouted. He pointed at the dance floor. A song I didn't recognise but which was obviously a firm favourite – a solid crowd-pleaser – had begun to play. Bodies jumped and bumped together, arms flung in the air. 'Dance?'

I shook my head.

'What do you do?' he carried on shouting, and flecks of spit from his mouth hit the side of my face. I'd finished my drink in three greedy gulps and was hoping that he would offer me another one.

'I work at the university,' I said, in my normal voice because anything else was too tiring. 'I teach English. But I'm writing a novel.'

He nodded blankly. He hadn't heard a word I'd said, though I was laughing drunkenly at my own joke.

'I've not been there long. I'm a late starter. My dad always wanted me to go to university, which is why I refused to.'

'They're all from the university,' he yelled, waving his arm vaguely. 'Don't know they're born.'

He was wrong about that, in actual fact. Most of the students were back at their own homes with their mothers and their fathers for the summer, or off volunteering in hot countries. But I didn't correct him.

'Turns out though, that my dad isn't really my dad. I'm probably the illegitimate daughter of our local MP.'

He frowned slightly, lifted his cup, drained it, then squeezed it in his fist until it cracked along its side.

'Your dad won't mind. I get on well with people's dads.'

'Anyway. I ended up in prison and did my degree there. Started at the uni shortly after I got out.'

He nodded at me eagerly. I laughed again. This was a cruel kind of fun, I suppose, but it had been a while since I'd had any fun at all and as he couldn't hear a word I was saying and was only, in any case, pretending to be interested, there was no harm in my entertaining myself.

'Have you ever been in prison? Have you ever killed someone?'

'I come here most weeks,' he said eagerly. 'It's not bad when you get used to it.'

I lifted my glass and made a meal out of noticing it was empty. He stood up and made a little mock bow.

'Same again?'

When he got back – carrying four plastic cups this time, two in each hand – I knew I would have to invite him back to the flat.

'Thanks,' I said, exaggerating the shape of the word on my mouth and pointing at the cup. 'It's very generous of you.'

'Do you like it at the university?' he asked desperately.

'It's hard work. But there are worse things I could be doing. And between classes I go to the library and work on my novel. It's about a woman who murders her husband and buries him in the garden.'

'I'm divorced myself,' he said.

'It would have been easier,' I agreed.

'And are you with anyone?' He'd been working up to this and now he'd finally arrived at it. Awkwardly, and with a sense of inevitability that crushed us both, I imagined, I only sighed and shook my head.

'I'm with myself,' I said. 'All the time.'

He nodded and smiled, as if I had told him that I was in a figure-skating team and we were training for the next Olympic Games. It was exhausting to carry on a conversation like this and I was getting tired of my own nonsense. The strange, medicinal-flavoured drinks had clearly had an effect on me and I felt my eyelids drooping.

You'll do, I thought. *Enough of this.*

I stood up.

'Do you want to come back with me?' I shouted, pointing towards myself with my thumb. 'Me? My house?'

The man's face opened then – like a flower. I was no catch – I do realise that – but something was better than nothing and I expect, not being much of a catch himself, he most often went home from those night-time fishing excursions empty-handed.

'We can if you like,' he said hopefully. He smiled – a real smile – and patted at my knee. My jeans were a bit damp because I'd spilled one of the drinks on its route to my mouth. 'That would be nice.'

'All right then.'

I wobbled slightly as I got up and headed towards the door, but when I paused to weave my way through a group of people – kids they were, really – I felt his hand resting on my back. It wasn't unpleasant to feel the gentleness of his hand resting there – the warmth. Perhaps, I remember thinking, this wouldn't be so bad.

Outside, rain was hammering down. The red carpet had been packed away and the streets looked as though they were made of wet tar. A police van parked at one end of the street and a group of volunteers on the church steps at the other were handing out lollipops to keep everyone quiet. My ears were ringing after the noise of the club.

'Are you far? Shall I get us a taxi?'

I nodded. 'I've just got to make a phone call first. Is that all right?'

'Check your mum and dad have gone to bed?' he said, and winked. I know he was trying to compliment me a little by pretending he believed I was a youngster still living with her parents and, indirectly, please himself with the idea that he was still able to attract a girl in her twenties. And while I was not repelled, I was not quite comforted either. I felt pity I suppose. For him, in his naked and vulnerable eagerness, and for myself too, in mine. Self-pity is never a pleasant emotion, and as soon as it bloomed, the anger followed.

'I'll just be two ticks,' I said. It was a phrase I never used but I was trying to sound perky. I thought about telling Mark about it when I got home. 'I said *two ticks* – can you believe it?' and enjoying him laughing at me. The thought made me angrier and I ducked into a shop doorway and left the man in the street waving frantically at all the black cabs that sailed past.

I dialled Olena's number. I knew she'd be asleep and in my cowardice I was relieved when her voicemail message asked me to leave my name and number.

'I know what you're up to,' I began. 'I know about the missing money . . .'

It went on from there. We all knew, I remember opining, about the way Harold Shipman had insinuated himself into the lives and the last will and testaments of the elderly and vulnerable people in his care. About how that had turned out. I will admit: I was not coherent and I was not kind. I had recently watched a late-night documentary called *Carers Who Kill*, and my subconscious had clearly filed away much of the detail. My only defence is that at the time I was under a considerable amount of stress and I believed my suspicions to be sound.

The man I was with – his name, if he ever gave it, escapes me entirely now – put his arm around my shoulders and turned me from the doorway back out into the street. I ended the call and pasted on a smile, my lips sticking to my teeth.

'Your chariot awaits,' he'd said, or words to that effect, motioning to the black cab he'd managed to hail. Young people in groups and pairs were milling around, ignoring the rain and leaning against walls, crying and kissing and shouting into mobile phones. We ducked between them and got into the cab. As it drove bumpily through the streets of the little city, I concocted a nasty little fantasy.

Mark would have returned, and he'd be asleep in our bed when I brought my new man-friend back to our flat. Somehow, as we fumbled and kissed in the bedroom doorway in the half-light from the bulb in the hall, we would fail to notice him lying there. And some noise I would make – perhaps a yelp of pleasure or a deep-throated giggle – would wake him, and he would sit bolt upright, like a vampire disturbed in his coffin, and see the lot. That night I learned there is only a tissue-paper-thin gap, physiologically speaking, between anger and sexual arousal.

I'll elide the next few hours. Allow me my dignity. Sometime the next morning I awoke, thankfully alone and un-murdered, in my own bed. It smelled horrible: the unfamiliar smell of someone else's sweat and aftershave, and the sickeningly familiar stink of sex which is the same no matter who you do it with.

I'll change the sheets, I thought, attempting to stave off despair, but when I turned over in bed my body felt as though it had been pumped half full with slime and seawater. My mouth filled with saliva. My foot touched something cold and rubbery – a forgotten hot-water bottle from days before – and I reached down for it, unscrewed the top and tried a few tentative sips of water. I had to spit them out onto the wood laminate by the side of the bed and spent the next few moments with my head dangling over the edge gazing dumbly at the frothy and slowly spreading puddle of fluid on the dusty floor.

At various points in my life I have tried very hard to get black-out drunk. There's a knack to it, and it's not really to do with how much you drink, though that's part of it, but more to do with how quickly you get it down you. I suppose Eddie's science-journalist girlfriend Celia could do a feature on me for her 'Marvellous and Miraculous' column. I might put myself forward as some medical marvel because no matter how much I drink, nor how quickly, I am never able to kill time, and I always remember the things I do not want to remember. That morning, it wasn't only the man who had been in my bed the night before, but – more urgently – it was the message to Olena.

I lay back on the pillow and groaned. The day's tasks, I imagined, would involve not only getting myself upright, washed and fed – which could take most of the morning, judging by the way I felt – but also locating and employing a new carer for my difficult father.

I was still lying there, marinating in my filth and self-inflicted misery, trying to distract myself from the task of deciding what to do about Olena by recalling all the times she had irritated me in some way, when the buzzer sounded. It sounds like angry wasps trapped inside a plastic box, and even at the best of times the noise it makes is startlingly unpleasant. I put my head under the duvet and waited for whoever had pressed the buzzer for my flat in error to realise their mistake. But the buzzer sounded again – long and loud. I hauled myself out of bed and pressed the intercom button.

'Hello?'

'Mrs Wright. Can we come up?'

The policewoman. They have him. They have Mark. With them? No. He'd have spoken himself if he was there – no need for an escort from the law; he'd committed no crime. Not that. I looked at myself: not as hung-over as I was going to be, because I was still partly drunk. She'd already taken against me and I was on the brink of making things worse for myself: if I feared they already held me in low esteem, how would it be for me if they saw me like this? I leaned against the door frame, panting and sweating, my mouth filling again with that bitter, pre-vomit taste.

'Mrs Wright? Can you hear me?'

'I'm not very well,' I said.

'It's important. We have news for you. Can we come up?'

'Bad news?'

'Will you let us up?' She wasn't having any of it. I pushed the buzzer.

The lift in our block works about 50 per cent of the time. If the lift was working, the pair would be with me (I looked around desperately, at the discarded clothing that marked a trail from the front door to the bed, at the old pizza boxes and wine bottles, the saucers filled with fag ends and ash, the mugs with congealed matter lying in the bottom of them) within five minutes. If the lift wasn't working, then I could give them a little longer. Sixteen flights. Police officers though – not carrying anything particularly heavy or awkward, and presumably having passed some sort of fitness test to equip them for the chasing of burglars and drug dealers. Twenty minutes? Fifteen? I calculated desperately while stumbling into the bathroom.

The sight in the mirror was unpleasant. The usual – greasy hair, black smudges around my eyes, bruises or love bites (the mirror was too dirty – speckled with soap scum and toothpaste – to get a clear view) already starting to bloom on my neck and my upper arms. I scrubbed at my face with cold water and put on a dressing gown. Squirted toothpaste from the tube into my mouth and swilled it around in there while removing most of the debris from the coffee table. I spat the lumpy foam into the kitchen sink and dumped the dirty mugs in the cupboard underneath it. I was running the tap when they knocked on the door. Evidently, the lift was working.

'Mrs Wright,' the man took the lead this time. 'There's a video we'd like you to take a look at. A bit of CCTV from the train station. Can we come in?'

It had been bothering me, who these two reminded me of. I let them in and gestured towards the settee. I took Mark's armchair and sitting there, swaying and sweating and worrying that I was about to vomit on their feet (the floor was laminate, at least, and could stand most things spilled on it), I distracted myself by trying to remember who it was they put me in mind of.

'Do you still need the photograph?' I asked. I had missed something. Missed quite a lot. It was Sapphire and Steel I was thinking of – space detectives fixing history wherever it had gone wrong. Sapphire was still talking and I laughed. Yes. That's who those two reminded me of. She was blonde, he was in need of a haircut – so there was that. But it was more to do with how they acted than what they looked like. It was as if they were constantly talking about me between themselves without moving their lips, the way the two characters in the TV programme could get into each other's minds and communicate facts and instructions to each other without speaking. I looked around desperately at the cluttered surfaces.

'. . . so the next steps would be to contact the agencies around there. Homeless shelters, soup kitchens, Salvation Army and so on. You could start to do that yourself. Or there are agencies that will help you. Of course, if he doesn't want to be found, or doesn't want to come home, there's nothing we can do.'

'I did look one out. I put it somewhere. I can't think . . .'

The woman leaned forward and patted my hand. 'This is good news, Mrs Wright. Very good news. The chances are he's going to get whatever it is in his head out of his system and come back of his own accord. You must tell us if he contacts you, whatever form that contact takes – all right?'

'He's going to phone me? I've been keeping my phone on charge. Both of them. His phone too. I don't suppose he'd ring his own phone, but, well, there's a chance, isn't there?'

They looked at each other.

'There's a support organisation we can put you in touch with. To help with the . . .' she paused, and pointedly did not look around at the state of the flat. I clutched the collar of my dressing gown more tightly around my neck, '. . . emotional strain. What we can do is . . .'

I looked at the tablet in her hand. The screen was dark and showed up the smudges of her fingerprints.

'This must be a shock,' Steel said. The video. They'd been trying to show me some CCTV.

'Can I see it again?'

Sapphire frowned. 'Yes, all right then.'

She tilted the tablet so I could see it but she would not let me hold it, as if I was a child who could not be trusted with the expensive equipment. There he was: his grey North Face jacket, slightly torn at one of the cuffs. That particular way he had of walking, as if he knew his height and size made other people uncomfortable, so he attempted to scrunch himself up slightly so as not to invade their space or draw attention to himself.

He'd have hated knowing he was being filmed. Hated the sensation – or the idea of the sensation – that in the future he'd appear on this little screen, in the front room he had vacated, under the watchful eyes of the wife he had abandoned. Because it was clear now, as if it had ever really been in doubt, that my husband had chosen to leave of his own free will. The camera caught him in profile as he bought his ticket: unshaven and furtive, but no more so than usual. He bent his knees slightly as he pushed the paper money into the tray underneath the plastic sheet that separated him from the person behind the counter. He always feels his height at counters: paying for things, washing up, signing things at the bank. I wanted to touch him, of course I did. He bent again to collect his tickets, and walked away towards the platforms, tucking them into the back pocket of his jeans as he went. My guts clenched. The hangover, perhaps, making its presence felt in my bowels. Or love. It might have been love.

'He's not ...' I said and swallowed a mouthful of spit. I retched slightly, though they may have mistaken it for a sob. 'He's not dead.'

'This was him two and a half months ago,' Steel said. 'Obviously where he is now or what he's doing, we couldn't say ...'

'This was in May,' Sapphire added, helpfully. She gestured towards the timestamp on the screen. 'This was the day he left, wasn't it?'

'Yes,' I said. I knew the number. I knew it exactly. I always did: the days beat along in my heart like the slowest, saddest of metronomes.

'Seventy-two days today,' I said. They glanced at each other. I didn't care if it sounded weird, even suspicious. You'd have thought she'd have looked sheepish or apologetic about how long it had taken them to find the footage. But she didn't, and I didn't dare mention it: I hardly had a leg to stand on where quick action was concerned, did I? Presumably they were only taking their cue from me.

'That's all there is,' the woman said, and turned it off. 'But now you've positively identified him – and you are one hundred per cent sure?' I nodded wordlessly, '– we can check the train CCTV and the station at the other end.'

She stood. I followed the progression of the tablet from one hand to the other, then to a pocket or compartment inside the yellow jacket she was wearing. It vanished, tucked away forever. I should have asked her for a copy of it: that's what I thought. I should have asked her to email it to me so I could watch it as often as I wanted, because with that glimpse of him, pushing notes across the train-station ticket counter and picking up his tickets – I had become a wife again.

7

I spent the rest of that day in my horrible smelly bed. Since Mark disappeared, it had become my habit to sleep with both my mobile phone and his charged and beside my pillow, and I would wake – sometimes as many as four or five times in the night – to check I had not missed a call or a message from him. I reached under my pillow for my phone and did then what I had taken to doing every morning and used my mobile to ring my husband's. It was somewhere in the bed, and I felt the vibration of its ringing down near my leg. Twenty rings: that's how long it took to get the answer-machine message. I waited, counting, the nausea subsiding as I lay very still in the bed.

'Hi, this is Mark. I'm afraid I'm not here, and this isn't really me, but a recording of my voice I like to call No-Mark (chuckles). When you hear the beep, leave No-Mark a message, safe in the knowledge that he never bothers listening to them. Ta.'

There was no room to record another message. I had filled up the voicemail inbox within the first few days of Mark vanishing in case he had set up remote access. I'd imagined him dialling into his account from a payphone and listening to me wail and shriek and beg, and sometimes I pictured him laughing at me and hanging up the phone. In those fantasies he emerged from the phone box into the embrace of a woman who was always taller and more beautiful and fragrant than I knew myself to be. In other fantasies, he would lay a hand against his chest – the cheap objective correlative to the piercing sorrow and longing he felt when hearing the depth of my need for him – then let the receiver drop from his hand while he dashed away from the phone box to hail a taxi and come home. I had it all planned out: the abandoned telephone receiver swinging in the empty phone box, the cut to a shot of him hailing a taxi, him telling the driver, 'Fast as you can, Chief.'

He wasn't checking the messages though: the voicemail inbox was always full. The automated message telling me as much played again. *No more messages can be recorded at this time. Please call back and try again later.*

At least, thanks to the little business of the keylogger, I could go into his email account and delete the messages that I still sometimes sent him when morose and drunk – the ones appealing to our shared history, the ones that outlined some of the special moments of our relationship and attempted to use them as a bargaining tool to extract him from whatever life he was busily building without me and return him to our shared one, the ones where I promised him and myself he would slot in safely and easily as if he had never been away.

We'll never mention it again, I'd type. *I don't need to know what happened.* Even now I am not sure how the logic of that worked in my mind: we had happy times together, and that means you are now responsible for me forever, and therefore must come back safely to me. There's no formula or physics that makes sense of the human heart when it longs for something, I have learned.

That morning I hung up at the sound of the automated message and phoned back so I could hear his voice again. I listened to Mark – the smugness of his silly little joke, the way he was already (I could tell by the tone of his voice) anticipating how amused some of his friends from the power station would be by it. Perhaps he was even trying to get himself a nickname. He was never popular enough to have been awarded one, but maybe his message was an attempt to get No-Mark coined and in circulation. There were sounds behind the words that I listened to as well; the rushing perhaps of static or interference on the line, the impressions of the background radiation, relics from the big bang, a white noise to find a voice in, as the EVP maniacs do. I tried to piece together the fragments and whispers of sound that lay between his words, thinking that perhaps, underneath it all, it would give me a clue as to where he was when he recorded that message.

And what I started doing then, which I'd never done before, was talking into the phone while the automated message telling me there was no room in his voicemail inbox played. Just talking, as if he were there somewhere and could hear me.

'Mark,' I said, my mouth dry and so foul I could smell my own boozy breath, 'I've had enough of this now. You've made your point.'

I paused. There was silence. A tiny echo on the line – perhaps only my own breath hitting the edge of the mobile phone and coming back to me. The line would cut off automatically soon. It wasn't a proper phone call. I was only connected to a recording and I wasn't leaving a message on the answer machine. It was a gap or an absence, something that I thought of as just 'black sound'. I would, from that day, call it often and talk to Mark.

'That man from last night wasn't anything important,' I said, brisk and businesslike. 'Didn't matter. Didn't count. I don't remember his name. I'm still . . .' how to put what I wanted to say? 'I'm still yours. Still here. So you can come back now. All right? I'll clean the flat. Make the bed nice. For us. We'll never talk about it.'

It felt the way praying can feel – or the way praying did feel, the single time in my life I had tried it previously. And that hadn't worked either. The phone made a beeping noise and the call cut out.

'I'm still waiting, Mark,' I said, experimentally.

I don't know how many times I called my black sound but it was a lot. I can see I was not adjusting well. I turned over in bed to face the window – that irritating unhooked curtain still sagging, as it had been doing on that last morning when I had been so angry with him about it.

I was angry with him a lot. It's awful to remember the energy we used to put into our arguments. We were like most other married couples in that living in the same small space and making the texture of our two very different personalities mesh together to form one shared life was a nearly impossible task. Instead of accepting the outcome of our efforts as an imperfect, good-enough sort of job for the time being, we blamed each other viciously for any unknitting of our unity. Or at least, that's the way I think about it now.

Let's take the matter of the colander. We had two colanders, a plastic one with a long handle, like a saucepan, and a metal one with two small looped handles on either edge. I didn't like using the metal one for actually draining things because the handles were so close to the bowl of the colander itself I worried about burning my fingers when I was pouring a pan full of boiling water and pasta into it. Instead, I used it to steam vegetables (we didn't have a proper steamer) by putting it on top of a pan of boiling water, then using a pan lid to cover the vegetables inside it. It worked very well. And because of this, I kept it in the drawer where we kept the rest of the metal pans.

Mark, who had hands made of asbestos and didn't mind the boiling water splashing at him when he was draining things, found it totally incomprehensible that we'd have two colanders in our tiny kitchen. My position was that he didn't need to comprehend it, he just needed to accept I saw things differently, I was allowed a say in what objects we had in the kitchen and he wouldn't always get his own way.

In our good times, the long entrenched disagreement just expressed itself through his insisting on putting the metal colander with the plastic one in the high-up cupboard, so when I looked for it in the pan drawer I was not able to find it. But as we moved into our bad time, when he spent his evenings in front of his laptop and I spent mine in the room next door watching his internet activity appear on the screen of my mobile phone and pretending to read *Rebecca*, this little colander-shaped flaw in the weave of our shared life started to unravel.

'Can't you just put it in the top cupboard? It doesn't fit in the drawer.' His face appeared in the doorway of the darkened bedroom where I lay. I made the screen of my mobile phone go blank so he wouldn't know I had been observing him.

'It fits fine in the drawer. It's a pain to get it out of the top cupboard.'

'It's only a pain because we've got too much stuff. We need to have a sort-out.'

'You say that like it's a fact. Your opinion is that we have too much stuff. My opinion is that we don't. Why should yours count for more than mine?'

'For God's sake, Laurie. Look at the cupboards.'

'I use them for different things,' I said. 'I can't believe we keep having to have this conversation.' Our voices were raised now. Mine first – I will admit that.

'They're the same! They're exactly the same thing! Is this just about you having to get your own way?'

'Do you want me to burn my hands when I drain the pasta? Is that it? Is there some sick bit of you that wants to punish me?'

I was out of the bed now, standing there with my hands on my hips. It is hard to argue with dignity when you are undressed and so I turned my back to him, retrieved my dressing gown from the dirty-clothes chair and put it on.

'You're being ridiculous.'

'That's always how it is, isn't it? I want something, it's stupid. I feel something, it's ridiculous.'

'Laurie . . .'

'I'm serious. Look at yourself. For the sake of a bit of cupboard space, you want me to burn my hand every time I cook for you.

Is that what this is really about? I think it is. You just won't admit it to yourself. You really can't stand me, can you?'

'Can we just stick to the facts here? The actual facts of the real world, instead of your hysteria and paranoia?'

'Funny, isn't it? How the facts always seem to line up exactly with your preferences and opinions. Ever noticed that? Ever noticed that whenever you bump into any bit of discomfort, it's the whole world that needs to adjust itself to you, rather than you just give a bit?'

'This is me adjusting, isn't it?' Mark said quietly, gesturing not towards the kitchen or the colander that he still held in his other hand, but towards me. 'I'm adjusting.'

'Oh yes. Of course you are. You're adapting just fine. It's like nothing's happened in your world, isn't it Mark?'

His name felt strange in my mouth. I never used his name, not unless I was talking about him to someone else. Only if I was angry, or he was leaving the room and I wanted him to come back.

'Can you hear yourself?' he said, venomously.

'I can hear you. Calling me hysterical.' I lowered my voice then. If I shouted at him too much he would just leave – take his coat and leave the flat and not come back for hours. Or he would go back to the living room and put his headphones on and sit in front of his computer pretending I wasn't there until I fell asleep or one of us had to go to work. He could keep up the silent treatment for days, saying that he wasn't going to talk to me until I stopped behaving like a child, and him doing that made me feel so much like a child that I wanted to bang my head against the wall and tear myself to pieces. He had trained me not to shout. So I lowered my voice.

'For centuries, when a woman has disagreed with a man, that man has called her hysterical. Can't you see it? Look at yourself instead of pointing the finger at me.'

'You pulled this last time, this exact same thing. With the bedside cabinet. That wasn't my fault.'

'Who said it was your fault? Who was blaming you?'

'It's the same thing . . .'

'No. What it is, is you being pulled up for being a control freak about the kitchen, and ignoring what I need, and pretending there's some logical reason for it all, but actually it's just that you fucking hate me and won't admit it. Won't leave, like a decent man would, but just stay here, sitting on that settee like a lump, refusing to talk or move or say what's wrong, and then wanting to talk to me about the fucking colander. And when that doesn't get you anywhere, you bring up the bedside cabinet. Can't you see what you're doing?'

My voice had grown high-pitched. It's a disadvantage, that. When I'm angry – even justly – I cry, and he couldn't stand it, and because he couldn't stand it he made fun of me and that made me cry more.

'Oh, what is it now? You're losing your temper? What's wrong with you? Run out of wine?' His tone was nasty, cruel, mocking. 'Your little bottle empty? So you need to pick an argument with me to keep yourself entertained?'

I took a breath. Harder to master myself than him – but it always had been.

'I was perfectly fine in here reading my book until you came in. Why don't you just get back to your . . .' I stopped myself then. I had been about to describe what he'd been doing on his computer – more investigation into conspiracy theories around the moon landings – but bringing that into the conversation would have revealed the way I had been observing him and diverted the discussion entirely. So I threw myself down on the bed and told him to leave me alone. I heard him go back into the kitchen and make a point of clattering pans and bowls about in the cupboards, having his sort-out, and putting things into proper order, which meant taking his own way, no matter what I wanted. I wanted to get up and see if he was putting my plastic colander down the rubbish chute, but I refused to give him the satisfaction and instead pretended to be asleep.

After half an hour or so, he put his coat on and came into the bedroom.

'We're out of milk. I need some fags. Do you want anything?'

I used my baby voice.

'Will you get me some more wine?'

He didn't answer, only turned and left the flat, but half an hour later he brought it in to me, already open, with a big water glass because he knew that I found our little wine glasses too small and having to top up the glass every five minutes or so was annoying.

I used to think that people didn't do things unless they got something out of them. My mother, for example, must have got some sense of gratification out of successfully casting herself as my father's long-suffering victim. Her gratified relief at her diagnosis of cancer seemed to come from a sense that the bad news had proved what she thought about herself and the world – *it's not my fault* – scientifically and indisputably true once and for all. I thought that our circling in endless loops of destructive or just plain incomprehensible behaviour always made sense: that we were like pleasure-seeking machines, and if we took some kind of perverse pleasure in causing mayhem in our own lives then the logic underneath it could be uncovered by looking for the payoff. And understanding the payoff might not end the madness, but would make it easier to bear.

I have changed my mind about that because even though I knew it would not do me any good, I rang the black sound and pretended Mark was just sleeping behind me. I dozed and fooled myself into thinking that if I leaned backwards I would be able to feel the warmth of him, and if I held my own breath for long enough I would be able to hear the faint repetitions of his coming and going. I did all that for hours and it didn't make me feel one bit better: in fact, it did the opposite, as I'd known it would.

In the evening, I made it into the kitchen to eat toast and then into the living room. I opened up my laptop with the intention of checking Netflix and, almost as soon as it sparked into life, it started ringing with an incoming Skype call. Mavis. I knew if I hit the red button and declined the call she'd only try Mark's mobile, then my mobile, and I'd been making excuses for weeks, so I answered.

'Hello love, it's me. Can you see me?'

'You've to choose the button that's got a picture of a video camera on it, Mavis.'

I kept my smile warm and fixed but inside, I was seething. Every time. Every single time. 'Have you got it?'

'I'm pressing it now, love!'

She appeared, sitting at a table at some kind of outdoor café, and her face looked suntanned and shiny. She'd propped up her mobile phone against the cruet set, presumably, and was sitting alone with her *café duplo*, screaming at it, and confirming whatever assumptions the locals had about British tourists and expats in spades.

'Oh love. Are you having a bad day?' She put her head on one side and crossed her arms over her chest, hugging herself. 'I could just squeeze you.'

'What?' I'd forgotten about the dressing gown. My unwashed and unbrushed hair. 'Oh, no. I'm just not feeling very well.'

'You can't let it get on top of you like this,' she shouted. 'You've got to plough through it. Be strong, for Mark's sake if not your own.'

'Yes,' I said, 'I'm trying. Ploughing on.'

'How's the weather there?' It was her favourite topic.

'Windy,' I said. 'A bit damp.' This pleased her.

'In July too! Well, that's your chance of summer over, isn't it?'

She laughed. 'It was thirty-four degrees here yesterday. The Siberian Plume, they're calling it. A sort of travelling heatwave.'

'Iberian, Mavis.'

'What's that love?' She cupped her ear but carried on talking. 'The locals stay in at dinnertime. They have their sleep. But I get out on my balcony and get my legs out. You've got to pick up a bit of a tan when you can, haven't you love?'

'You do, Mavis,' I said. She was the same shade as He-Man – the colour of strong tea.

'You're not right, are you?' She pursed her lips sympathetically. 'I wish you'd come out here. You and Mark. The flights aren't bad, and you can stay with me. Food covered. Won't you think about it? Nothing that a bit of sunshine won't cure. There's a bar around the corner,' she picked up the phone and moved it – a wide sweep of sky and white-fronted buildings, a flash of a cobbled street swept across the screen and vanished again as she brought the phone close to her face. 'Look at this place. Think about it. Will you?'

'It's just work, Mavis, that's all.'

'Where's that boy of mine anyway?' she asked. Perhaps she was thinking he'd be easier to persuade than me. 'You're not going to tell me he's at work again, are you? I ring at night; you tell me he's working late shifts. I ring in the morning; you tell me he's sleeping after working nights. I ring in the afternoon . . .' She shook her head and pointed her finger at the screen. 'I know you've been ignoring the phone.'

'I'm not always up to talking, Mavis.'

'Where is he?' she demanded, ignoring my bid for sympathy.

'He hasn't been in touch with you?' I said. I knew he hadn't – she'd have mentioned it otherwise – but there was one small part of me, a nasty member of my team of shimmering selves who fought and swirled around inside, that wanted to hear her say it. I could be comforted by the knowledge that if he'd seen fit to send no word to me, at least he wasn't singling me out.

'You know full well he hasn't,' she said.

I know now the reason I was so reluctant to tell her that Mark had left me was because I feared she would blame me for driving her adored son away. Whatever mad idea was currently gripping him and sending him across the country, it would be me that had planted it in his mind. My responsibility, at least, to pluck it out before it could take root. My task, as his lover and wife, to make home a sanctuary and a paradise that he could not bear to leave. If he'd found another woman – someone better groomed, more sympathetic, more likely to store colanders in the correct cupboard – well, he couldn't be blamed for that. And underneath all that, the fear: once Mavis had decided this was all my fault, she would leave me too.

There would be no more annoying phone calls or Algarve-themed gifts through the post, no more late-night Skypes to show us what the moon looked like from her apartment window. No more guilt-tripping over Christmas, or mentioning, or Not Mentioning, grandchildren. No more inspirational memes, or texts with links to diets that would improve your skin tone, help you deal with brain fog, and meet the world with a more positive mental attitude. No more tight-lipped enquires after my father, who had made a pass at her at our wedding reception, and who she hated. No more boxes of Milk Tray from pound shops at Christmas, and cast-off half-bottles of perfume for my birthday, and stuffed animals through the post with not enough postage on that needed to be collected from the local sorting office, which was really not that local at all and only open during the exact hours I worked over on the other side on the city. None of that ever again. I would – I feared – be dead to her. And if she did pass me in the street, she would walk by me without any sign of affection or even recognition and I would become even more dead to myself than I already was.

'What is it love? Please tell me. You're worrying me now. He's not ill, is he?'

She leaned into the phone and stage-whispered. 'It's not cancer, is it? Tell me it isn't cancer.'

'He's not here. He's gone.'

'Gone? What do you mean, gone?'

'He jacked in his job and I didn't know. He told me he'd been made redundant. He left me. I reported it to the police and they found some CCTV of him buying a train ticket, so he's alive and probably all right, but he left his phone and I think we're not together any more,' I said.

'Laurie! Laurie!' she batted her hands at the air between us. 'Laurie. Sweetheart.'

'I know. I'm sorry.'

'I can't take it in. He can't leave you. Not after what happened . . .' She paused, stricken.

'Well, he's not here, is he?' I said, unkindly.

'How long has this been going on for? What have the police said?'

I tried to outline what Sapphire and Steel had told me: the lacklustre nature of their investigation, their advice to contact the homeless shelters in Brighton.

'May? He went in May?'

The image on the screen froze and unstuck, the audio lagging behind the video. She was, I could tell, furious.

'Why didn't you say anything?'

'I . . .' I wiped the sweat out of my hairline, felt the tears smear what remained of last night's mascara further over my face. There wasn't anything I could say.

'I have tried to be patient with you Laurie, I really have. God knows you deserve it, but this . . .'

'All right, Mavis. All right!' I shouted.

I'd been struggling with the starter all afternoon, but now the main course of the most terrible hangover I have ever had caught up with me and the sweats started – I felt it forming in my hair and getting all cold and sticky on the back of my neck and between my breasts. I needed to drink water and have a shower and get something to eat, but all I could do was lean back against the settee cushions and cry. Mavis relented immediately. I knew she would – it was part of the reason I gave in to it.

'I'll come. I'll get a flight. I'll talk to him,' she said, flustered. 'You hang on in there, my darling.'

My darling? Oh, it was so lovely to be called that by her. I wiped my face. 'You can't talk to him. He's not here, Mavis. He's not anywhere. I don't know what I'm supposed to be doing,' I said. 'The police came this morning. They brought a video of him buying a train ticket. To Brighton, they said. I've to ring some places there. Shelters and soup kitchens. But I didn't write it down and I don't know . . .'

'We'll sort that out when I come,' she said decisively. She'd picked up her phone and was walking somewhere, talking into it. The perspective jumped and wobbled between the sky and the shopfronts and her orange-painted toenails in her rose-gold sandals and this did not help the nausea that had me in its clutches. 'I'm on the move. I'm going to look on the internet and get a flight. Hold on tight.'

'You don't have to come,' I said, crying freely again. But I wanted her to, and she could tell that I did.

8

Mavis texted the next day and told me to expect her late the following week, not being able to afford the cost of a flight at short notice. I carried on. What other choice did I have? As I was at the end of my leave, I rang Shaw's office at a time I knew she would not be in and left a message on her answering machine, pretending I had a stomach bug and needed another few days off work. I'd never have got away with it in normal circumstances, not on top of the fortnight I'd just had off, but Eddie must have told her that Mark had disappeared and she only texted me hoping that I'd feel better soon.

I spent my time getting drunk and investigating the cold spots in the house. I tried to clean the flat in preparation for Mavis's arrival, and each morning awoke to more mess than there had been the night before. In desperation and wanting, I think, to make the flat into a place that would feel welcoming to Mavis, I started googling psychics again.

I clicked through to the websites this time. Things had become that bad. I found out that the three Joyces who worked in Lancashire claimed to have skills in tarot, past-life regression and clairvoyance. There was a difference between a medium and a clairvoyant, apparently, though I didn't know what it was. I loaded the websites one by one and scoured them for clues, slightly shamefaced even though I was alone. One of them had a photograph of herself sitting in a leather armchair with a cat on her knee. She was grey-haired and slim, wearing a heap of silver bangles on her wrists, and she was definitely not the Joyce I met at Sharon's wedding. The second had a website full of soft-focus headshots that made her look more like a catalogue model than a serious professional, and she was too young, and too short, and too blonde. The third didn't have any pictures of herself on her site at all, so I gathered my courage, got through the first bottle of wine I'd been able to stomach since the previous day, and telephoned her.

'Is this Joyce?' I asked tentatively.

Sharon's Joyce? Wedding Joyce? Mark and Laurie's Joyce? Would I recognise Joyce's voice from a brief conversation at a wedding nearly sixteen years ago? I did not trust myself to be sure.

'It is I,' she said.

'I was wondering if . . .'

'You have a question,' she said. She'd answered the phone in a slightly distracted, everyday voice, and once she heard my faltering beginning she switched to her at-work voice – a quieter, more portentous tone.

'Obviously,' I said, snippily, then regretted it.

'Have you had a look at my website. Services and prices?'

Prices? I thought Joyce did the work as a kind of public service. A contribution to the common good. Perhaps she had fallen on hard times. Perhaps I'd got the wrong Joyce.

'Would you like to book an appointment?'

'I work during the day.'

'I can do you over Skype love, that's not a problem. The cyber realms are very hospitable to non-material beings, you know.'

If I ever, ever told Eddie about this, he would never let me hear the end of it, I thought.

'I think I need my house clearing. Cleansing. Sorting out,' my cheeks burned. 'I think it has a . . .'

'A presence?'

I nodded. Coughed. 'Yes. It's cold. All the time. The doors open and close. Stuff goes missing. That might be me, mislaying things. I don't know,' my voice cracked. 'Everything's gone wrong for me,' I said, pathetically.

'A presence malign in intent?'

'I don't know.'

I imagined her nodding and making notes in a leather-bound volume, the phone tucked between her shoulder and her ear.

'Hard passing?'

'What?'

'The passing over. Sudden? Painful? Sometimes they don't know they're in the wrong place, lovely. I can see you're a beginner at this.'

'I don't know. I don't have that information.'

It was, now I come to think about it, like that time I rang the Housing Association to ask them to send someone out to look at the electric heaters. Not having the vocabulary to describe what was wrong, or know what to ask for, I struggled and lost my temper.

'It's just not right. In my house. In my life. The flat. Everything. It's all . . . getting away from me.'

I sounded like a nutter. I knew I did. But then again, I wasn't the person charging money to talk to people's house spirits, so this Joyce, if she was going to judge me, didn't have a leg to stand on. The thought galvanised me.

'I'm not sure what . . . services you offer? To clean a place up?'

I looked around me. My efforts at sorting out the flat had been half-hearted and minimal. I needed Kim and Aggie more than I needed a psychic.

'All right love. Sometimes it's a matter unresolved. Words left unsaid. Leaves a ripple in the veil between our place and theirs. Does that fit?'

I didn't want to tell her about Mark. About what had happened to us. I didn't want to tell her anything. I'd read about it, you see – the art of the cold reading. You shouldn't give them anything to go on. I decided to take control and ask the questions myself.

'Do they hang about? If they feel like wrong was done to them?'

I looked around the living room. The way the light from my open laptop cast shadows into the corners, and a strange bluish light over everything else.

'They're not so different to the way they were in life. Can I take your name? I can't really do a phone consultation without taking a few details. Your card number?'

'Did you work on the Connie Fallon case?' I asked.

'You're not a journalist, are you? Press requests need to come through the website. In writing. There's a contact form.'

'I'm not a journalist,' I said. 'I'm just interested.'

'Are you asking for references? Have you seen the testimonials page on my website?' she asked irritably.

'It's not that,' I said weakly. 'I just want to ask. Blake Barrett?' I said. 'You might remember Blake Barrett. York. A suicide. You helped find him. The police.'

'Who is it you're wanting to make contact with?' she asked briskly. 'I'm not mucking about with time-wasters.'

'I'm looking for you, I think,' I said, incoherently. 'I'm sorry. I don't know your second name. I don't think you ever gave it. Have you a friend called Sharon? Sharon Booth? She got married. Sixteen years ago it would have been, near enough. I met you at the wedding, with a man called Mark. Do you remember him? Do you remember us?'

That was a happy day, I wanted to say. *Did you think we were going to be happy together?*

Her voice changed again – not mysterious and portentous, not patient and friendly. It grew cold and suspicious.

'If this is a joke of some kind, I'm afraid I don't get it. You rang me. Nobody asks you to believe. There's plenty of room in the world for sceptics without you—'

'I'm not sceptical,' I said.

'Yes. Right,' she said briskly. 'Well, as it happens, I do have someone here with me. A presence. Nothing clearer than that. It might be for you. No promises. Now if you'd like to take my payment information, we can get the ball rolling on sorting out your house.'

I picked up my wine glass from the coffee table and emptied the dregs into my mouth. 'Tell me again what you said about them being afterwards the way they were when they were alive.'

'They're just people,' Joyce said patiently. 'Same foibles. Same quirks. Same likes and dislikes. It's all a lot less mysterious than it sounds, you know.' She paused, and the kindness returned to her voice. 'Sometimes talking about the one you've lost can help you know, sweetheart.'

'I don't know what she was like when she was alive,' I said. 'She didn't get the chance to be like anything.'

I was crying.

'All right love,' she said. 'All right. How about PayPal, if that makes things easier? Then we can keep talking.'

'It doesn't matter,' I said. I hung up. I don't half talk nonsense when I'm drunk.

The presence, if there was one, became more vindictive: I'd wake on the settee to find the books and clothes I'd carefully put away strewn around the flat, broken glasses in the kitchen sink, my toothbrush down the toilet. I found my father's hairbrush in the cutlery drawer, of all places. I picked it up and examined it carefully. The tidying stopped as I opened my laptop and started my research.

It's more expensive to do a test using hair rather than a cheek swab. More likely to receive an inconclusive result too. But an inconclusive result would leave me no worse off than I was to begin with. Where was I going to find the money? I hardly had any spare at all, and things were already more difficult than they usually were. My father himself would have given me money if I'd asked for it – but there was hardly any cash left now Olena had got her sticky fingers into his drawer. Olena. I thought of the message I'd left on her machine and opened up a new tab on my browser. Mail-order paternity testing. *All Your Questions Answered!*

I wrote a cheque on one of Mark's old chequebooks, forging his signature, which was easy enough to do. I printed and filled out the form. I put the hairbrush inside a clean sandwich bag and put the lot inside a Jiffy bag from the recycling box. I even – as if I knew I would change my mind or deliberately forget about it if I delayed – went into town and got the thing posted off before I could start wondering if stealing someone's hair and forging the signature of a missing man constituted a crime. Only when the envelope disappeared over the post office counter did I stop to wonder what the police, who might still have been keeping an eye on Mark's accounts, would make of him writing a cheque to a mail-order paternity-testing company. Ah well. I would, I decided, deal with that when I needed to.

One of the other things I did – unnecessary and perhaps over-kill, but it felt good to do it – was to take everything out of the kitchen cupboards and wipe them out, then replace everything inside, but in different places. I didn't need Joyce to help me cleanse my flat, I thought to myself, as if sorting out my own mess was getting some kind of revenge on her. Or if not her, then Mark. I felt that Mark's presence, in some scientific way I was ill-equipped to understand, still clung to our possessions. The last particles of whatever trace he might have left on my skin and in my body had been, I imagined, completely neutralised by my antics with the man I had picked up from the club. But the flat was still choked tight with the sense of his absence, the fact of that, and I wanted it gone.

I took the colander out of the upstairs cupboard where it was difficult for me to reach and placed it triumphantly in the pan drawer, where any sane person would have stored it. Then I sat on the kitchen floor and cried.

*   *   *

At the start of this year, when Mark and I were entering our hard time, I often had these sort of weekend episodes. It was almost always the same thing that had upset me. The noise, from upstairs. Tim and Katrina's baby would start crying, and I would turn the television up and put my head under the pillow, and Mark would put his headphones on, and I would tell him he needed to go upstairs and do something about it, and he would refuse, and say it wasn't that bad. Some nights he would say it was all in my head and he couldn't hear anything at all. The arguments would spiral from there, on to all manner of other things. I pulled his headphones off his head and broke them once, so insistent I was that he pay attention and listen to the noise that was driving me insane. Afterwards he would sulk and I would drink and, eventually, we'd sleep.

'I'm never going to drink again,' I'd say in the morning, 'and I'm going to start jogging. A bit of fresh air before work every morning. And,' I waved my finger in the air, oblivious to Mark's amusement (it started as amusement – though if I am being honest, after the first few performances, his response to these declarations was often more muted and indifferent than that), 'I think I'm going to go to a smoking cessation clinic again. Get the nurse to put me back on the patches.'

On those days, we would come to some kind of a peace, tucked up together in our box in the sky, the outside world only a story that when we bothered to consider it we doubted was true. On afternoons like that, we'd curl up in front of the television and he'd stroke my head while I had a bit of a cry as the tail end of the hangover left me.

We watched a film during one of those times about a married couple who killed themselves in a car accident and didn't immediately realise they were dead, and their afterlife involved living for a hundred years in the house that they'd cared for and had cared for them while they were alive. The challenge for them was to learn to share the house with the couple who had moved into it after they'd died, and who had very different ideas on the matter of interior design and the treatment of guests at dinner parties, and so on.

'You never get ghosts from the 1990s, do you?' I murmured sleepily. Mark, his hand in my hair, had probably dozed off.

'What?'

'They're always in historical fancy dress. Headless horsemen or ladies in white dresses or children with balls and tops and little sailor outfits. Civil war soldiers or poets from the trenches. They're always old-fashioned.'

Mark laughed at this. It pleased me, that even though things were so bad between us, I could still make him laugh.

'You never get them in high-rises either,' he said. He didn't move his hand away from my head the entire time we were talking to each other. I remember that. I can still feel it there now – the weight and the heat of it and the comfort of his forgetfulness – touching me was only as remarkable as touching himself, or some other object that belonged to him, and for which no permission needed to be sought.

'Maybe you do. Maybe the place is full of ghosts and we can't tell because they don't look any different to us.'

'I saw someone who looked like me today,' Mark said lightly. A change of subject like this always meant that he had something important to say and I was supposed to pay no particular attention to it, in case it scared him off. He was easily startled by my interest, so I only turned around so I was facing him, my head still on his knee, and said nothing.

'In the canteen at work. Like me, but older.'

'Your doppelgänger. It means you're going to die,' I said, and put on my spooky story voice. 'Maybe not today. Maybe not tomorrow. But sometime soon.'

He ignored me and went on. 'I thought – I was stood there with my tray waiting to pay and I saw the back of him going out – I think he's one of the new electrical engineers they took on last month – I thought it might be Him.'

'Your dad?'

Mark looked away. The trick is, with him, not to ask questions. Not to look at him. It's like trying to get a cat to come and sit with you. You've got to act as if you're not bothered.

'I wouldn't know him if I passed him in the street. He could be dead, for all I know. I wouldn't know. He could be that guy I played darts with last week. He had hair like mine.'

'You could ask Mavis,' I said.

'No point digging it all up,' he said. 'It makes no difference anyway.'

'You should have done your bacon impression for him,' I said. 'That'd have brought him running.'

He flinched, though I was only trying to make a joke. I carried on. Digging and poking at that crack that had appeared between us.

'Maybe he's haunting you. This time it's the canteen. Next time it will be down the garage when you're getting the electricity card topped up. Out of the corner of your eye. A chilly presence. One of these days you'll get up in the night and there he'll be at the foot of the bed. *I am your father's spirit, Hamlet. Doomed for a certain term . . .*'

He did laugh then, though it was a fake one. I smiled along with him and pretended that I believed he really was amused. The little thing I had done wrong fell out of view and for a while I forgot about it. I don't think Mark did.

'I don't believe in ghosts,' he said. 'Why would they bother? If you woke up dead why on earth would you carry on doing what you've always done? Up and down in the lift with your snake? Hanging about on the bridge where you topped yourself? What would be the point in that?'

'When I die, I'll haunt you,' I said. I know many couples have bargains like this. Couples who loved and knew each other more than Mark and I ever did. I wanted Mark to say that he'd haunt me too, and for us to devise some kind of sign or code or system of knocks and bangings that each of us would use to let the one left behind know that the other was still there. But he only sighed and said, 'I bet you will,' then got up and went into the kitchen.

I wish, now I am thinking about it, that I had handled that conversation differently.

At the end of the week, I went back to work. Arriving on campus felt like alighting on another planet. It's always been a strange world all of its own. The campus is as big as a small town; a little concrete planet south of the city and connected to it only as the Moon is connected to the Earth. I stepped down from the bus and headed towards the staffroom to collect my keys, radio and trolley. I told myself I was needed and Eddie would be pleased I was back. But I knew that none of us was indispensable – Shaw didn't tell us that in so many words, but always made it known there were plenty of applications for vacancies in our team and lots of people ready to leap into our shoes.

But Mark had been missing for seventy-six days and the longer I spent alone the less I felt I mattered – almost as if I was disappearing myself. I was searching for an excuse to busy myself: first Joyce, then cleaning the flat, then my work – rather than doing as Sapphire and Steel had suggested and contacting people and organisations in Brighton who Mark might have asked for help. I did not know how I would explain this neglect to Mavis when she arrived. I did not know how to explain it to myself. Now I see that I was afraid – very afraid – of what I would find if I started to dig.

I was a little late, and Eddie had already got started by the time I got my trolley out of the lift and joined him in one of the vacated rooms in Derwent Tower. There were stories about that place. They closed the top two floors after a student threatened to jump from their bedroom window a few years before. There was just a steel gate over the stairs and a contraption on the lift that stopped it reaching the higher floors. Eddie said they forgot to shut one of the windows and the whole place had been taken over by pigeons, that the floors and walls were caked with shit, but I liked to imagine the empty space above me, the dust slowly gathering in the empty rooms.

I found him on the seventh floor. It was the first time we'd been together since I flaked out on him and fell asleep in one of the beds we were supposed to be making.

'Sorry to be late,' I said. He was flipping a mattress. I unrolled a bin bag and went in to attack the en suite. The bathroom was in the usual state: the shower tray yellow and grey with soap scum, the bin overflowing onto the floor. I filled the bag.

'Anything interesting?' I called, as a way of breaking the ice.

At that time of year the students left all kinds of things behind. Sometimes the students had been nicely kitted out in their rooms by their parents – little bedside lamps and microwaves and other home comforts – and when they abandoned their stuff it was as if the tower was giving us presents.

'Nothing much,' Eddie said. 'There's some nice shampoo in this cupboard here. I've left it out for you.'

I came out with the bag. Something about his tone – a certain studied lack of interest, unsettled me. Would it be better to clean the slate and address this directly?

'I went out and got laid last weekend,' I said. I wanted to shock him. Or show him that I was bouncing back, and wouldn't be a self-pitying nuisance any more. He made a noise in his throat but carried on wiping at the waterproof cover on the mattress.

'Didn't you hear me? I went out last weekend and—'

'I heard you,' he said. He wouldn't look at me.

'He was really sweaty. It was all right until—'

'Do you mind if we don't?' Eddie said.

'What?'

'Tall tales. Mucky stories. I'm not in the mood for it.'

'Hark at you!' I said, annoyed. It was a phrase my mother liked to use whenever I complained about anything, and I didn't know it was lodged in my memory until I heard it come out of my mouth. The double standards of the man, after all the detail about his weekend exploits I'd had to sit and listen to over the years. He didn't respond but turned on the Hoover and I busied myself inspecting the bottles of shampoo. Nothing fancier than I had at home, so I dropped them into the bin bag and knotted it closed.

'There was a sighting.'

I liked that. *Sighting.*

'They found him on CCTV. Booking a train ticket to Brighton. Mavis is going to come and help me look.'

'They know where he is?' he said. 'That's good then, isn't it?'

'They know where he was going, back in May,' I said. 'Not where he is now. But Mavis is going to help me ring up soup kitchens and stuff like that.'

'Good,' he said, and flipped the mattress back onto the bed base. 'I'm surprised she wasn't here earlier. She must be worried sick.'

I paused. There were some dark stains on the carpet under the window – old blood or coffee. We were going to have to haul the wet cleaner up in the lift and do the carpets properly.

'I didn't tell her. She knows now. I told her last Sunday. But I didn't tell her before.'

He only frowned, and still would not look at me.

'You've only just told her?'

'I would have said something sooner, only . . .'

'I don't know what's fucking wrong with you sometimes, Laurie,' he said.

It hurt. I expected some awkwardness but this – and after all I had suffered?

'There's nothing wrong with me,' I said. I was gearing up for an argument. We had disagreements all the time. Heated debates over which of the *Rocky* films was the best, or whether immigration or austerity was the reason it took so bloody long to get a doctor's appointment these days. We enjoyed our disagreements. If we could just have an argument now, I thought, well then it would clear the air, and we could move on.

'Fine. Nothing wrong with you,' he glanced at the stains by my feet. 'You're practically perfect in every way and you always will be. There. I'll get the wet cleaner then, shall I?'

Out of stubbornness and a sense of my own injury, I let him do it, and only carried on picking up rubbish – some broken hangers, a weird stash of carrier bags in a drawer folded into little triangle packages, a few odd socks and a forgotten T-shirt left in one of the built-in cupboards.

'How's Celia?' I said. It was my intention to change the subject and to show an interest in his life, but I will admit that it is possible he read my tone as sarcastic. 'When will I meet her?'

Eddie looked at me strangely and I wanted to grab him by the shoulders and shake him. If I could have spoken frankly to him I would have said something like, *It's all right, I'm not going to try to have sex with you again. I did it with someone else and it was horrible*, but now I've come to understand the sad truth that people hardly ever speak frankly to each other. The closer they are to each other, the less frankly they speak, in fact, and the more pretence and evasion there is. And Eddie and I were, or at least had been, close friends, knitted together by mutually convenient denials and untruths.

'I don't mean anything funny by it, Eddie. I'm just . . .'

We were interrupted by my phone buzzing away in the front pocket of my tabard. I nearly didn't answer it. I still made those little bargains with myself – if I could completely forget about Mark, make my life full and happy and meaningful without him, and that included stopping guarding my phone as if it was a newborn baby and even ignoring the siren of its call sometimes – then he would come back. The phone buzzed away.

'Answer it,' Eddie said.

I fished it out of the pocket. It was Olena, who of course I had been avoiding. Speaking to her was top of the list of the very many things I did not want to do.

'It's nothing,' I said. I was trying to stare him out, the phone still rattling in my hand.

'Answer it, Laurie.'

He turned his back on me and started to pour detergent into the wet cleaner. I took the call.

'Laurie. It's Olena here. Your father's *cleaner*.'

'Look. I know I—'

'Are you at work? Can you call a taxi?'

Her voice was clipped and curt. Annoyed with me, yes. Fucking furious, no doubt. But she was scared too. I could hear it.

'What's happened?'

'I've had to call an ambulance for your father. We're on our way to the hospital now. Will you meet us there? You should be there. As next of kin.'

Eddie had straightened up and was staring at me, the opened bottle of detergent in his hand.

'What is it?' he mouthed. I waved him away.

'What's happened, Olena? Did he fall?'

I couldn't hear a siren. If they were in an ambulance but the ambulance wasn't using its siren, then it couldn't be that bad, could it?

'I think he's had another stroke. I came at three in the afternoon to start preparing the evening meal. He doesn't answer the door, and I find him sitting in his chair, his face all crook-sided.'

I'd rarely heard Olena's English lapse like that: she's been speaking it since she was seven years old and knows more about grammar than I do. She was rattled.

'Lop-sided. It's a stroke. How long had he been there for?'

'Last night, I think. He'd not touched the soup I left out for him.'

'Has he said anything? Was he cold?'

'He's not talking, Laurie. You must come though.'

Eddie, on hearing the word 'stroke', was packing up my trolley and retrieving my fleece. He handed it to me and I shrugged my way into it, moving the phone from one hand to the other as I put my arms into the sleeves.

'Yes. I'm leaving now.'

'Fine.'

I was going to ask her to wait there for me. To wait with my father, not to leave him alone. Asking her that probably would have insulted her, and it wasn't that I thought he needed or deserved a companion, but only that, cravenly, I didn't want to have to see the state of him, or speak to the doctors, on my own. But before I could form the wish into a request, she had hung up on me. I looked at Eddie.

'It's my dad. He's . . .'

He didn't wait for me to finish my sentence.

'Go. Off you go,' Eddie said.

No offer to come with me. To take me in his car. I hoped for that, in spite of everything. The company. The lift. And now I was going to have to call a taxi and face whatever there was to be faced – Olena's anger included – without assistance. I handed him my radio and master keys.

'I'll sort it with Shaw,' he said, which was kind, but it wasn't the same as having someone with me, watching over me.

9

He was in an assessment unit, waiting for a place on the ward. The nurse drew the curtain back, where my father, who had become a crumpled little man I didn't know, wearing a hospital gown that didn't fit him properly, cowered in the bed and Olena, her back ramrod straight and her coat bundled up on her lap and crumpled between her fists, sat waiting.

'We'll have to wait for the scan results,' the nurse was saying. 'He's already been for his CT so the doctor will come and talk to you soon.'

'Is he . . .?'

'You can talk to him,' she said brightly. 'He knows you're here.'

The curtain fell behind her and she swished away.

'Olena,' I began. She stood up and gestured towards the chair.

'You sit. I will leave now. You want to check my handbag for missing items?'

'Please . . .'

I don't know what I was asking for. My father was – as she had put it – crook-sided. I can't think of a better way of putting it. His clothes were in a carrier bag at the end of the bed. I glanced at him. His eyes were open but he seemed more interested in the pattern on the curtains – rows of repeating, falling leaves – than he was in me or his own condition.

'You all right, Dad?' I said. 'I've come from work.'

I sounded like an idiot, I know. Olena wasn't helping. Standing there, grasping the handles of her handbag as if it was a weapon.

'He made himself wet,' she whispered. 'I'll take his clothes away with me. Get them washed.'

'You don't need to do that,' I said.

'So I'll stay? You want me to stay?'

She was wearing her work clothes, and no makeup. Her eyelashes were wet and were standing in little triangle points around her lids.

'I had a bit of a scare,' she said. 'I thought he was . . .'

'I'm glad you were there,' I said. 'Did they tell you how long the doctor is going to be?'

She shook her head. 'Hours. Days. I don't know. What passes for a health service in this country defies my understanding, I'll tell you that.'

I didn't sit, and neither did she. We stood there for a while, at my father's bedside. As he exhaled, he softly groaned, but I don't think he was in any pain.

'Well . . .?' she zipped up her handbag.

'Yes. Will you stay?'

She had practically forced me to ask her. If that was the extent of her revenge, I thought, well, I could take it.

'You can bring in another chair,' she replied. 'There's a row of them over there,' she motioned beyond the curtain. 'We'll wait for the doctor. Make sure he's not of the Harold Shipman type. I gather that is of the utmost importance to you.'

While the doctor was examining my father, Olena and I left the assessment unit and went to find coffee. It was when we were counting our money and feeding coins into a vending machine that she – in a rare lapse of judgement about her timing – brought up the matter of my estrangement from him.

'I should have known he was taking a turn for the worse. He was very agitated last night.'

'In pain?'

'No no, nothing like that. His emotions. He tells me sometimes, about the years when you refused to see him. About the times he did not know if you were alive or dead, what you were doing, where you were living, or anything. He was worrying about this last night. As bad as I'd ever seen him.'

I lifted the cup of coffee from the dispenser, spilled some of it over my fingers, and swore.

'I'm here now,' I said.

'You visit, yes,' Olena said, 'but he still does not know you.'

'I can't help it if he doesn't remember a thing I tell him,' I said petulantly. Why did she want to have this conversation then? Guilt, I suppose, about him sitting cold in his chair all night with the latest infarct spraying blood into his brain wiping out history, emotion, desire. The guilty always want to reach out and blame someone else for their own acts of omission and neglect. Still, at least she hadn't brought up the phone call and the things I had accused her of.

'He worries. He says all kinds of things about what you were up to. He thinks,' Olena picked up her own coffee and whispered, in the fluorescent-lit and empty corridor, 'that there was prostitution involved.'

'Yes,' I said. 'He likes his little stories, doesn't he?'

'If you have something, something heavy on you, wouldn't it help to talk about it?'

I must have glared at her. *Something heavy? On me? Hark at you!* But she did not flinch, only took a step closer and put a hand on my shoulder.

'I don't mean talk to me, Laurie. I'm not trying to get into your business. We all have secrets. But to your father. To talk to your father, is what I am suggesting.'

'I talk to my father all the time. Three times a week I come to the house and I have a meal with him and I talk to him. If there's anyone around here with secrets, it's . . .'

Olena shook her head and would not lift her hand from my shoulder.

'We will speak about the matter of your father's money and your despicable accusations another day,' she said. 'For the sake of his comfort and your own, I am willing to put that to one side. For now. Because I am not sure you are accepting the seriousness of the situation here,' she said sternly. It was her tough-love voice – full of *I know best* and *I only want what's right for you*. It made my skin crawl. 'I am telling you that if there are things you want to say to your father that would give him peace, and if giving him peace would give you peace – would ease a little of what's on your mind, well, I think now is the time to think about doing that. Don't you?'

'Let's go back to the ward,' I said, walking slowly away from her, the coffee in my cup sloshing against its rim and dripping onto my already scalded fingers. I wanted to know how things were with my father but I also knew it was impossible to tell Olena the truth about the break with him and what he described as my 'missing years'.

The truth was, and I hardly understood it myself, I hadn't been missing at all, but only living with Mark in our little flat, working at the university, and living my days within arm's reach of him. The break, when it had happened thirteen or fourteen years previously, had had much more to do with Mark than my father.

We had been together a year, and my father had planned a dinner at the house with Mr Haworth, his partner at the accountancy firm they had set up together. My mother was cooking, I was invited, or required to put on a dress and come, and as Mrs Haworth was going to be there it was suggested that I might as well bring the man I had been seeing all this time because they hadn't met him yet, and the table would look a lot nicer with even numbers.

'Am I supposed to wear a suit?' Mark had asked, stricken, when I had broken the news to him. 'I don't have a suit.'

'Wear your job interview shirt,' I said, brushing my hair in the bathroom mirror. 'It doesn't matter.'

He came up behind me and grabbed me around the waist. 'He's not going to take me into the back room and show me his gun collection and ask me what my intentions are?' he asked.

'My dad doesn't own any guns,' I said, shrugging him away. I was nervous too, and toying with the idea of getting a migraine that would release us from the commitment. Still, I would have liked to know myself what Mark's intentions were. We hadn't – outside the imagined future of him being in prison for the murder of Connie Fallon and me dressing up as a prison guard and sneaking into his cell at night for an unofficial conjugal visit – discussed the matter of our relationship or where it was heading. Perhaps the dinner would be the place I would find that out.

'It'll be fine,' I said, knowing that it wouldn't be.

We were late, which was my fault, and my mother, frantic and wispy in one of her formal dresses and apron, took our coats at the door and ushered us into the dining room.

'He's been waiting for you,' she whispered. The house smelled of garlic and scented candles. I reached for Mark's hand – wanting to reassure myself as much as him, I admit – but he'd gone in ahead of me.

'So I said, if he wanted to avoid his tax responsibilities, we'd help him, but evasion was an entirely different matter, though by the looks of his books he was handling that admirably himself!' my father was saying, and the Haworths laughed politely.

'Ah, the wanderer returns!' he exclaimed, as we took our seats. 'And here's her young man.' There was an awkward handshake over the table.

I'd hoped my father would wait for the main course before starting his antics, but he launched into grilling Mark about his work – he'd just started at the power station and the job was still new to him – and the prospects for advancement and promotion, while my mother was still sliding our melon and Parma ham starters onto the table.

'And there's a director of security, I suppose. Someone who orders operations and makes the contingency plans, is there?'

Mark nodded. 'I never see him, though apparently he's all right.'

'He's the person who designs the machine and makes sure all the parts are working in harmony,' my father said, 'and you're more of a cog, is that right?'

'Yes,' Mark said. I could see he knew that he was not being complimented, but had decided, for my sake, not to mind. It made me feel tender and guilty and furious, one after the other, then all mixed in together, and part of me blamed Mark for the guilt and the fury, even though he wasn't the one who had provoked them, and another part of me was proud of him, for taking it and not caring in a way that I'd never been able to – and all those parts jostled up against each other.

'You aiming to get that job yourself, Mark? Is that the plan? A year on the shop floor, then a quick upwards move to middle management and beyond?'

'I suppose they'd want graduates for that,' Mark said uneasily. 'I haven't really looked into it.'

At the word 'graduate', I cringed, and tried to meet my mother's eyes across the table. There was a complicated flower arrangement in the way, which she'd opted to cower behind, but even if she had been able to understand my silent cries for help, she was only rarely able to redirect my father once he got onto the subject of university education. She was probably, I thought uncharitably (but, I maintain, accurately) happy enough to let Mark or me stand in the cross hairs if it gave her a break for an evening. I should have overturned my wine glass or faked a gall bladder attack or fainted or set fire to my napkin. Any of those would have done.

'Our Laurie was all set for university,' my father opined, leaning back in his dining chair so the front legs lifted from the carpet. 'Her teachers told us she should be thinking about

Oxbridge. Or at least Russell Group. She's never had a head for maths but there are plenty of doors opened by a good humanities degree. She tell you that, son?'

'She never did,' Mark said slowly. 'But I'm not surprised. Always got her nose in a book.' I suppose he meant it to sound affectionate. Perhaps even he had a sense of pride about me and my brain, though if he did he'd never mentioned it before. And why should he have? People don't get praised for having dishwater-blonde hair or grey eyes. Random genetics, that's all it is.

'Books. Novels. Poems. All of that. Her teachers said she could have gone very far on it. That's what they said. History. Philosophy. Politics, perhaps. Cambridge. Or Trinity, if she'd wanted to spread her wings a bit. We could have funded it. Any of those on your CV and the doors of the world just swing open, don't they?' He waved his hand dismissively. 'It wasn't to be and I suppose she's too old now.'

'Really,' Mark said politely. I was twenty-two at the time.

'Now the only doors she opens are bathroom ones, and she's got a bloody mop in her hand!' my father said. He chortled.

The Haworths witnessed this entire performance, sitting there either side of my father like ornamental lions flanking a fancy vestibule. Jim sat to my father's left and contented himself with cutting up his melon wedge starter, then his chicken breast main, into tiny uniform pieces, arranging them in rows, then ferrying each one to his mouth on the back of his fork in a complicated manoeuvre that seemed to absorb him entirely.

Which was just as well, because as my father moved through the wine and onto the brandy, abandoning his triangle of cheesecake in favour of the liquid swishing about in the bottom of his enormous glass, he began to pay more and more attention to Mrs Haworth, to his right. He clearly had his hand on her knee under the table. My mother was clattering the cheesecake plates into the dishwasher in the kitchen. Mark rose from his seat at the sound of her crying out as a dropped plate smashed, and my father made a gesture with his outstretched hand like he was commanding a dog to lie down.

'Stay where you are. She knows where the dustpan and brush is and she's got to learn!'

Mark remained standing and our eyes locked.

'Natural consequences, son,' my father guffawed, 'butter fingers will take better care next time.'

I looked away from Mark and towards my plate, resembling (I knew it even at the time) nobody so much as my mother. He took his place.

'There you are,' my father said.

To put the cocked hat on it, Mrs Haworth shook a cigarette out of a packet and, even though he hated smoking and would never usually allow it in the house, my father insisted on lighting it for her himself, singeing the front of his oiled turf of hair on one of the candles, and placing it gently between her lips.

'Laurie really likes her job, Gerald,' my mother said weakly as she reappeared from the kitchen behind a loaded tray of coffee. 'Not everyone in the family needs to be a high-flyer like you, my dear.'

She needn't have said anything. The conversation was on the brink of moving on to new topics. But she'd either been mulling over a retort in the kitchen and didn't want to waste it, or this was her way of making sure the attention stayed on my cleaning job and not her clumsiness with the dinner plates.

'There's high-flying, there's low-flying, and there's crawling,' my father said. 'You don't get a nice place like this,' he gestured around him at the overcrowded dining room, his hand alighting on Mrs Haworth's shoulder, patting it proprietorially, then moving on in its trajectory towards the glass-fronted cabinet they kept the Christmas plates and cricket almanacs in, as if he was Adam showing a guest around Eden, 'by emptying bins and wiping someone else's piss off the toilet seat. Now do you?'

'Gerald!' It should have been my mother protesting, but it was only Mrs Haworth who dared, and perhaps only she, enjoying the special privileges of my father's sexual attentions, who would have got away with it. Mr Haworth, who wasn't even the junior partner in the firm, looked up from his cup and saucer, where he'd been scrying his future in the foam on his coffee, and interrupted.

'I'm sure Gerald only means—' he began, but his wife ploughed on over him.

'Laurie will find her own path in life. Make her own opportunities. It's different for a woman. We don't have to be so career minded, do we Janet? Sometimes home and family are enough. Sometimes motherhood itself,' she looked at me meaningfully, 'is a woman's highest calling. Don't you agree, Janet?'

My mother, stricken and divided, was an expert in keeping the peace. I watched her now with a sense of sick anticipation, wondering if she'd choose to side with my father, or his mistress. I could not have told you then, or indeed now, what her opinions were on the matter of women working, the single European market, the theological problem of suffering, whether or not she believed in life after death or even which of the perfumes my father liked to buy was her favourite, and which she secretly hated and only wore to please him.

'Well,' she began carefully, 'it's very important to be happy, isn't it? Maybe Laurie and Mark will get married and have a baby soon.'

It was her pathetic attempt to keep the conversation light and friendly at all costs that infuriated me more than anything. I pushed my cheesecake away and cleared my throat.

'I'm never having a baby. *Never*,' I said to her. The words in my mouth felt as glorious as throwing a brick through a stained-glass window.

My mother didn't exactly gasp, but she filled the silence that followed with the weight of her indrawn breath. I didn't dare look at Mark. I turned to my father. He was the person I was really angry at, and it was his reaction I wanted to see more than anyone else's.

My father roared with laughter.

'This is what I'm talking about, Mark,' he said, delighted. 'This is exactly what I am talking about. Failed every single one of those A levels – lowest mark that it's possible to get, apparently. And you're not telling me that she didn't do it on purpose! Her teachers were mystified. They told me that even if she'd answered the questions at random, statistically she'd have got more right than she ended up with. What do you think she was up to? Eh?'

Mark seemed to be looking towards Mr Haworth for help, whose brief moment of rebellion had drained away, leaving him limply hunching over his saucer, attentively stirring another spoonful of sugar into the last two inches of his coffee. I wasn't curious enough to wonder why he was so feeble – why he was so subservient to my father. They worked together but they were partners – my father couldn't have sacked him. They had known each other for years: there were photographs of the three of them together – my father, my mother and Mr Haworth – on a Spanish holiday the year before my parents had been married. My father didn't have friends, but Mr Haworth was the nearest thing.

If I'd given it some thought, I might have decided that my father had caught Mr Haworth out in some professional indecency – a minor case of embezzlement from a client's accounts, perhaps. He'd have enjoyed holding that over him and using his knowledge to ensure compliance. But I didn't give it much thought – my father getting away with whatever he wanted was just the way things were and the way they had always been. Mark and I left shortly after that, with my mother wringing her hands at the door and trying to tempt us back with a description of the three different kinds of local cheese she'd procured for the final course.

*   *   *

At the bus stop we waited in silence for several minutes before speaking.

'I'm sorry it was so awful,' I said stiffly. 'He's just like that. I tried to warn you.'

Mark raised his eyebrows.

'He's been fucking Mrs Haworth for years. Her among others. It's just the way it is. I should have mentioned it.'

Mark continued to say nothing. It was early autumn, and already quite cool. I could tell he was angry – his breath came fast and made clouds of vapour in the air.

'Mark. Come on. It was horrible but it's over now. They've met you now, so we don't have to do it again.'

He didn't reply.

'Mark? You can't blame me for what he's like.'

He shook his head.

'Is it what I said about a baby?' I said tentatively.

Mark pretended I hadn't spoken.

'Your poor mother.'

'She signs up for it. She doesn't have to stay,' I said, annoyed.

'You could have stuck up for her. Someone needed to. She's your mother.'

He was – I realised at the time and I remember it afresh now – not just angry. He was absolutely furious. And not at my father, but at me.

'She was crying in the kitchen you know, didn't you hear?'

'She's always crying.'

'I'm not surprised.'

'What did you expect me to do?'

'Haven't you ever said anything to him about the way he treats her? Ever?'

He didn't shout. He very rarely shouted. But he made his hands into fists and put them into the pockets of his good coat and moved towards the other end of the bus stop, as if he just couldn't bear to stand any closer to me than that.

'I'd have thought you'd have been more concerned about the way he treated me,' I said petulantly.

'Come off it. You were enjoying yourself. You're not stuck there with him. You get to go home at the end of the night,' Mark said.

'Yeah, to my shitty flat and my shitty cleaning job,' I muttered, self-pityingly.

'To the shitty job you chose. Just to piss him off, clearly, by the sounds of it. It's fucking weird, Laurie.'

'You have a problem with my job?' I said. I'd only recently made the change from Dorry's and, while a cleaning job wasn't exactly a step up from being a checkout girl at a garden centre, it wasn't exactly a step down either. Not much of one.

'Don't pull that card on me,' Mark said. 'I don't have any problem with your job. My mother cleans. Who cares what you do for a living?'

'You brought it up,' I said. I'd expected to leave my father's house to a gale of sympathy from Mark. This – his anger, and his persistence with it – was a nasty surprise.

'Let me be clear,' he said slowly. 'I don't give a fuck what you do for a living. I do care if you're in some extended Oedipal battle with your father. Did you really fail all your exams on purpose?'

I had, you know. And for precisely the reason Mark had guessed: solely to piss my father off, or impress him – one or the other.

'You don't want to listen to half the things my father says. It's just the way he is.'

'I'm more bothered about the way you are,' Mark said.

'Look, the bus is here. Shall we get off early and go to Bargain Booze?'

Mark didn't answer, but got on before me and, although he paid for both our tickets, he sat on the outside edge of the seat so I could not sit next to him, and had to sit behind, watching the back of his head and the hunch of his shoulders. I'd never really had a proper boyfriend before. Perhaps letting him have the last word would be the quickest way to resolve this, I thought. I was still convinced that none of it had been my fault – that it hadn't been me making everyone else uncomfortable. By the time we'd got home, the moment for repair had passed. I couldn't ever feel compassion for my mother, but the fact that Mark could – and so easily – made me love him more. I hid that fact.

After the disastrous dinner, it became too difficult to even imagine how I would have a life with both Mark and my father in it. How would I accommodate these two worlds and allow them to overlap? The Laurie that I needed to be around my father was a particular type of person. Not the sort I'd actually get on with if I met her at work or socially. I could try her on now and again to keep the peace, the way I was willing to wear formal and uncomfortable clothes at weddings and funerals, but wearing the Good Laurie Aspect was work, a horrible work, and I always feared I would end up possessed by that craven, smiling being. Even while I was wearing her I had to spend all my time resisting her and sometimes the resistance broke, and out came Arsey Laurie, and I didn't much like being her either.

So I simply stopped seeing my father. There was no great confrontation, no vow made, no drawing of a line in the sand. Instead, because it pleased Mark, I met with my mother once a month for coffee and scones in the café of a garden centre slightly outside of the city, as if we were having an affair and needed to go somewhere nobody would know us. We talked about our immediate surroundings: the weather, mainly, and the price of vanilla slices. Sometimes an interesting plant she was planning to buy, or a new scarf that she happened to be wearing that day. Mark approved of this, and sometimes came with us, so I kept it up. And because my mother had been well trained by my father to accept the most insultingly transparent of excuses – I've come to believe she preferred to live her life like that, always at arm's length from the truth – we never had to discuss my father or why I was refusing to come to the house.

As time went on and my mother grew sick, and then it became clear – without her ever telling me – that she was dying, I visited her at the hospice and we had our coffee and scones in the little flower garden there. Mark wheeled her in circles around the garden in her chair on sunny days, and she was thrilled by his chivalry. My father must have visited – I assume he did, in the time left between his trysts with Mrs Haworth. She would have welcomed him. Accepted his flowers and bottles of perfume and tall tales with gratitude.

When she died Mark bought me presents and made me take time off work and I had to pretend to feel more upset than I did so he wouldn't be horrified by me. Mr Haworth telephoned me, late at night, cried a little and offered to buy me a car. I presumed he was drunk, pretended not to understand what he was saying and did not answer the phone to him again. Mark asked me if I had visited my father to discuss the funeral arrangements and I said I had. Once you love someone, you have to start lying to them like that. But here's the truth: I didn't miss her. Her wish to appease my father had resulted in any individual personhood with which she might have started life wearing away through a slow process of marital attrition that had begun before I was born. I didn't know her at all, which is why, I think, I could not bring myself to grieve her much: her presence in my own life had only ever been spectral, manifest in the domestic tasks she performed for me – the washing of school uniforms and the filling of packed lunches and so on, and the need for these services had faded considerably as the years had passed into my adulthood.

Now I come to think about that dinner party, and Mark's reaction afterwards, I start to wonder if the seeds of Mark's decision to leave me were planted as early as that night. I thought the theme of all our arguments – which when you boiled them down to their essentials were always about who was facing up to reality, and who was avoiding it, who was playing the victim and who was soldiering on and deserved a bit more praise for doing so – was set almost as soon as we started to get serious about each other. But perhaps I was wrong about that. Perhaps he'd just imagined I was a much nicer person than I actually was, and that was the first time one of my less pleasant aspects had made an appearance, and it had disappointed him.

The doctor couldn't tell us much. My father was comfortable. They would admit him. Time would tell.

'Expect another increase in his symptoms,' he'd said. 'The cognitive and behavioural issues you've been dealing with. The stroke nurse and the occupational therapist will come and see him. You know the drill.'

I did know the drill. We both did.

'I will drive you back to the flat,' Olena said as we trudged exhaustedly away from the medical assessment bay. 'It's late.'

I tried to make conversation with her in the car on the way home. I asked her about her dog, who she sometimes brought with her when she came to work at my father's. It's called Holly or Nobby or something like that. I asked her about how her research project, which involved doing interviews with drunk middle-aged women in their homes in the afternoons before their children returned home from school, was coming along. I asked her about her stew and who had taught her to cook so well. I admit I was babbling, and the more I attempted to fill the silence, the more taciturn she became. She would not be drawn, and violently ground the gears every time she changed them, her gold rings glittering in the sickly green light from the dashboard display.

'I'm going to give up smoking,' she said abruptly. 'Right now. I will never lift one of those filthy things to my lips again.'

'What?'

She shook her head. 'I do not want to end my days in a hospital bed sucking on a tube for air with no family around me,' she said spitefully.

'My father's not having strokes because of smoking,' I said. 'He's never smoked.'

'That is not my point,' she said darkly. As if it should have been very clear to any normal person what her point actually was. I wanted to ask her if I could have her cigarettes if she wasn't going to smoke them herself, but thought better of it.

'Look,' I said, deciding at last to address the matter of the phone call. 'I wasn't at my best the other night.' She indicated, braked and parked at the kerb outside my block without answering.

The tower loomed above us, most of the windows lit. It wasn't so late. When people live up high, they aren't so wary of their privacy, and tend to leave the curtains open in the evenings. The guy on the fourth floor – who sometimes rode the lift with his snake around his neck – was standing, shirtless, at his ironing board. Above him, an old lady was out on her balcony, slowly – as if her joints hurt – retrieving her clothes from an airer. We were parked too close to see the upper floors and my own flat, whose windows would be dark and unlit, but I craned my neck to look anyway. I was hoping for the light to be on. If it was, it would only be that I'd forgotten to turn it off when I left for work that morning, but maybe not. Maybe I could make the slow climb up the stairs in the daft hope of Mark's return.

'Not your best,' she scoffed. 'Steaming drunk, more like. I could hear that,' she said. 'Where were you?'

'A nightclub.'

It would have been easier if she'd laughed, or rolled her eyes, or even told me off in that motherly way she had about her sometimes. But she did none of those things. I'd had so many conversations with her over the months she had worked for my father that the sound and tone of her voice had become another one of those little selves inside me, and I heard it talking anyway, saying what I wanted or needed it to say.

A bit long in the tooth to be out gallivanting, Laurie?

And Mark? What would he say? I could come up with nothing.

My flat was dark. Mark was not at home up there and he was not at home in me, either, because I could not imagine what he would say to me.

'Things got on top of me. I don't usually—'

'The things you said to me were very wicked,' she interrupted. 'You pour that stuff down your neck and a devil comes out. Your father will need some clean pyjamas. Toothbrush, things like that. He'll probably want the photo of him and your mother from his bedside table. There's a bottle of the lemon cordial he likes in the kitchen cupboard.'

I sat in silence, my hand resting on the door handle.

'I still have a key. Shall I collect those things and take them up tomorrow morning? Do I have your permission to do that?'

I looked more closely at her. It was later than I thought: the streetlights were beginning to warm up. The sky was already turning a smudged blue colour, and the low light brought out the shadows under her eyes and the lines under her mouth. Her eyes were full of tears.

'Are you crying again?'

She caught the surprise in my voice and was outraged by it.

'Your father is a difficult man. He was also sitting there alone all night and through the day, alone, unable to call for help.' She rubbed her fringe out of her eyes. 'It's a terrible thing to think about.'

'I was thinking about it too, you know.'

She turned her key in the ignition and the car sputtered into life.

'I'll gather the things and take them tomorrow. I can leave them with the nurses. They'll see that he gets them.'

'It's all right,' I said. 'You can go and visit him if you want to.'
She didn't answer.

'You can count it as your usual hours if that's what you're hinting at. I'll pay you, as usual.'

I knew she wasn't hinting at that. I did. And it was a horrible thing to say. I think I wanted her to be angry at me. You must understand I felt guilty all the time then. I deserved, according to my own estimation, all the care and coddling and pity there was in the world. But there was never enough available. People being angry at me was the second-best thing and provided a relief of its own: proof that I really was as terrible as I felt. But Olena was either exhausted or she knew me better than I knew myself. She put the car in gear and revved the engine.

'Out of my car now Laurie,' she said quickly, 'before I say something I will regret. Go on. Out now.'

She drove away while I was still standing on the pavement.

10

Mavis texted every day. She had been unable to get a flight as early as she wanted and had resorted to visiting the airport daily hoping to pick up a cheap standby ticket. She was passing her time at the airport on her phone, tapping out messages to anyone and everyone she could think of. Every pub and café in Brighton – she claimed – would be receiving a picture of her son with the instructions to print it out and put it in the window. Her messages to me grew increasingly desperate and accusatory: *Why wasn't I helping? Why was I leaving all this to her? Why hadn't I already started on this?*

I held her at bay by telling her about my father, about how he was suffering, and about how much stress I was under in looking after him. It was a convenient truth: the days passed in a blur of work, avoiding Eddie and visiting the hospital. The doctor said my father was stable but unlikely to improve, and the nurses would only say he'd either been 'comfortable', which I took to mean asleep, or 'restless' – which I dreaded meant he'd been lecherous, racist or foul-mouthed.

There was no more news about Mark. I imagined him wandering down the seafront and seeing a poster with his own face on it stuck up in a pub window. Mavis had used a photograph I'd sent her of him taken last summer. He was standing on the jetty at Morecambe with a cone of chips in his hand. Would he catch sight of himself and turn in the other direction? Would he go into the pub and peel the poster off the window and take it back to wherever he was living, folding it carefully inside an envelope? Would he stick it on the fridge, so he and his new woman could laugh at it, imagining my desperation?

Mavis badgered me into phoning the police every couple of days for news, but they would only say they were doing everything they could, would be in touch with any developments and took care to remind me that my husband was well within his legal rights to leave me. They urged me again to ring a telephone helpline for the relatives of missing people. I didn't. They just wanted to get me off their backs: I imagined the helpline would be full of soft-hearted do-gooders, wanting to know how I felt about things.

Olena made an uneasy peace with me during our frequently overlapping visits to my father's bedside. Whatever it was she wanted to say to me, or felt needed to be said, she had obviously opted to hold her tongue until the Sunday that she insisted we go out on a walk together. She'd been sly about it: given the state of the Sunday bus service, Olena had offered me a lift in her car back to the flat from the hospital. We were about to cross the bridge when, without warning, she turned the wheel and diverted us out towards the coast – accepting none of my excuses, because in her opinion I needed some daylight and fresh air.

We parked in the cheap public car park outside Heysham village. There's a big children's playground and a couple of cafés and a shut-up ice cream shop, and the little main street slopes upwards towards an old church and winds past a couple of pubs. I hesitated as we passed one of the pubs, smelling the comforting beery fug from its open door, but Olena hooked her arm through mine and tugged me forwards.

'We're walking. Sea air. You can lock yourself inside and smoke and drink yourself to death some other time. Come on.'

We walked. The road splits into two – one leading to a sharply inclined path up towards the old church, the graveyard, and the high headland that looks out over the port and power station. The other led downwards, towards the mud-sticky and pebbly beach of Half Moon Bay. Olena took a left, up towards the church, and I followed her, feeling my chest rattle and my armpits grow damp as we climbed.

'Your father seemed more relaxed today, didn't he?' Olena said.

'He was all right,' I said. He'd slept through most of my visit, snoring peacefully, a little bubble in the corner of his mouth coming and going and making it easy to count his slow and shallow breaths.

'Did they tell you when he could go home?'

I shook my head. 'They're going to do another scan on Monday, I think. We'll know more then.'

Olena made a clicking noise in her throat and shook her head. Hers was a practical, 'what can you do?' sort of sympathy. I had a vision of my life then – an unappealing and exhausting routine of bus journeys between hospital and work, my life lived in other people's corridors and anonymous, institutional rooms.

'Let's not dwell on it. And Mark? No word from Mark?'

The churchyard backs onto a wide sloping graveyard – full to new residents now, but busy with the live visitors, who do not come to lay flowers but to traipse the new desire paths between the stones and lean over the dry-stone wall that divides the edge of the churchyard from the drop of the cliff. There's a big shiny granite memorial to some gas workers from the rig out in the bay who died in a helicopter accident a few years ago – victims of the sudden bad weather that can relied upon in this place. We stood and read the names for a little while and I thought of the dark water, the sucking shallows and unexpected depths.

'No,' I said eventually. 'Nothing. Mavis is on her way. She's waiting for a standby flight.'

'Well, that will be good, won't it? Maybe she can look after you a bit.'

'She'll want to know chapter and verse.'

'So you tell her. Tell her everything that has happened. She's your mother too.'

'She's Mark's mother,' I said obstinately.

Olena tutted. We walked around the church and emerged onto the headland. It was not a particularly sunny day and the sludge-scented wind whipped through the grass and blew our hair around.

'You don't have to hold her at arm's length. She's your family. How long have you been married to her son? She can be a mother to you.'

'You don't understand,' I said. 'You're not married. It's . . . it's hard to explain. You're a different person in a marriage. You turn into a different person.'

Olena pointed at a path snaking between ragged patches of bald gorse and bedraggled heather. To our left, Heysham One and Two, the port behind, and a single turning wind turbine.

'You're still yourself,' Olena said. 'You're just not very well, that's all. And that's why you need looking after.'

'I don't feel like myself. I don't feel like anything.' We walked side by side along the path, and I fell silent as a couple with a dog approached us coming from the other direction, all wind-whipped and rosy-cheeked, smiling a delighted greeting at us as if they'd just discovered a new tribe in the rainforest. Olena smiled back and waited for me to carry on.

'When the person who you're married to isn't there any more, the only person you know how to be is the one that relationship turned you into, only there's no use for that sort of person any more. You won't get it.'

'I was married,' Olena said. She frowned. 'Don't you ever get tired of assuming you know everything there is to know about me?'

'I didn't know.'

I should have done. She had a daughter, so there must have been a man somewhere, at some point. I'd made her angry at me again, and I hadn't even meant to.

'No. You didn't know. I was married for twenty years.'

'Your little girl's dad.' I'd forgotten her name, shamefully, and didn't want to advertise the fact. Olena let it slide.

'My mother and my sister take care of her while I am here getting my degree. And my husband is gone. I live here and I am a student and a cleaner and a companion to your father and a single woman. But soon I will go back to Dnipro and be a social worker and a mother again. And, for your information, I do know how it is to be . . . *made* by someone. Formed.'

I wiped my hands across my face. It was despair, mainly. I really didn't want her to dislike me and yet whenever I opened my mouth I ended up offending her. When I put my hands down I dared a look at her and she was standing there, the giant sea and sky behind her, and she was laughing at me.

'Come on. Sit down here with me.'

We sat on the grass.

'Here. Feel this,' she said, took my hand and guided it along her jaw. 'There's a pin in here. A little plate.'

I said nothing but felt her warm and powdered skin under my fingertips, and beneath the skin, something foreign and hard and strange.

'I had to have an operation for that. He hit me in the face with a spanner because I didn't want to have sex with him. I'd just had the baby. Alina, her name is. Try to remember. I have told you before.'

I nodded.

'She hardly slept so when she did, I went to bed too and I tried to snatch sleep every second I could. He took it as an invitation – his wife in bed during the day – and when I turned away he got up from the bed and went to the place he kept his boots and work bag. When he got back I was drifting away. Into dreamland. I didn't see it coming.'

'Didn't you call the police?'

'A *family matter*,' she said scornfully, 'that's how the police are. I hate the police. I told the doctor I'd fallen down the stairs.

I suppose they see it a lot. Maybe I should have just let him have his way. It would have been easier.'

'Are you all right?'

'It hurts in cold weather,' she said briskly. 'But that one was the worst. Here,' she rolled up her trouser leg and showed me the skin on her shin, mottled and shiny, like the pale top of an under-cooked rice pudding. 'He threw a pan of hot water at me. I don't remember what I'd done then. Not the sex – we were in the kitchen. It might have been something to do with the cooking. The baby cried a lot. His dinner was often late.'

It was the wrong thing to think at a moment so serious, but looking at her with her leg bent and her jeans rolled up below her knee exposing that terrible scar reminded me of nothing so much as the scene in *Jaws* when Quint and Hooper get drunk on the boat, show each other the marks on their bodies and remember their run-ins with sharks. Maybe she was thinking of this too, because she put her head on one side and looked at me.

'You have anything like this?'

'No,' I said. 'Nothing like that.'

'There are things that don't show, maybe.'

'Yes. But nothing like that.'

She waited for me to elaborate. There's a way of looking at films and books that counts how many times women talk to each other about something other than a man. Useful, no doubt, but it does not take into account the fact that the only time women can talk about the wounds and pains men have caused them is when the men are out of the room and they're alone together, on a headland, watching the colour of the sea and the clouds gather and blow inland.

'He left me,' I said. 'He went.'

'Sometimes that's a blessing. My husband is long gone too. Haven't seen him in two years.'

'That's why you came here?'

'Yes. Fresh start. Fresh country. Fresh job. I will not be the woman he made any longer. I will re-form myself. And when I go back, everything will be different.'

'Isn't that strange? Not knowing where he is?'

Olena looked as if she was considering this, looking inside and weighing up her internal weather so she could give me an accurate report. She narrowed her eyes and bit her bottom lip.

'I don't miss him. Not at all. And my daughter is safe with my mother. I'll finish my dissertation soon.'

'Don't you worry about him coming to find you?'

I am ashamed to say I thought of my father's missing money then. About how tempting such an amount might be to someone who needed it for something much more important than the rubbish my father and I spent it on. I imagined how many plane tickets to Dnipro or violin lessons or school uniforms four thousand pounds would cover.

'He won't come and find me,' she said. She laughed. 'That bastard won't be coming to get *me*.'

'I'm glad,' I said, feeling ashamed of my grief and breaking apart when Olena could have suffered through so much and, from the outside at least, look like she was okay and was managing things. I wanted to ask her secret, but I wasn't sure I really wanted to know, so I changed the subject.

'Mark told me there was a foot washed up here once,' I said. 'A whole foot, inside a shoe, washed up on the beach down there.'

'Just a foot? Where was the rest of it?' she asked, only mildly interested.

'Nobody knows. There was another foot though. Turned up at Middleton, near the old Butlins.' I gestured vaguely in its general direction. 'Couple of weeks later. Same sock, same shoe. You wouldn't actually believe how many feet are lying about in mortuary freezers just waiting to be claimed. If the DNA isn't on the national system – and why would it be? Most of us aren't criminals – then there's no way of telling who they belong to.'

'Maybe there's a serial killer out there,' Olena said, laughing throatily. 'Maybe he goes up and down your seaside finding people, chopping off their feet and throwing them into the sea. Maybe he's got a whole cellar of footless corpses. He collects them, like some little girls collect Barbie dolls.'

'You'd think so, wouldn't you?' I said. 'Mark had a theory about this though. Did a bit of internet digging about it. We were in our kitchen cooking together. We liked doing that. Him stirring the pans, me chopping things up for him and putting them in little bowls, like we were telly chefs.'

Olena nodded. It was good to talk about Mark. It was good that she let me.

'We were making our tea and he told me that if these were murder victims, if they'd been dismembered in some way, then the forensic people would be able to tell. They'd see marks of the saw on the bones.'

She shuddered.

'But there weren't any marks. The feet had just come off – naturally. Process of decomposition, apparently. His theory was a whole body that had gone into the water, probably intact, and the feet were just the bits lucky enough to wash up and be found.'

'But why feet? Why not hands, or arms, or heads?'

'Well, I'm glad you asked,' I said, in my pretend-teacher voice. She laughed. 'The only thing that makes a foot different from a hand or a head is the fact you wear a shoe on it. A shoe that has probably got a shoelace or a buckle or a bit of Velcro, which means, in at least some instances, it's not going to wash off if you've got a body bobbing about in the sea somewhere. We fasten our shoes on tight.'

'Yes . . .?'

'And, especially these days, that shoe is more than likely going to have some plastic or foam in it, isn't it? And what does plastic and foam do?'

She was playing along with me, but getting sick of it, I could tell. I have never been able to entertain people through my conversation, to hold their attention for long. I gather facts like this, and rarely find a use for them.

'It floats. So, to put it together, if you wanted to kill yourself there's all kinds of things you might want to do, but at least one of them would be to go to a bridge or a pier or hire a boat or find some other means of chucking yourself into the sea, or a big river on its way to the sea. And if you succeeded, your body would be floating about, gradually falling apart, your feet coming away from the bottoms of your legs, the rest of you sinking beneath the waves, getting eaten up by the fishes, but your feet, transported by those floating, tied-on-tight trainers you got in fifteen instalments from the catalogue last year, eventually get washed up to shore.'

Olena was looking at me, the smile on her face gone.

'Is this what you've been thinking about, sweetheart? Is this what's on your mind, while you've been sitting here?'

'It solves the problem of why it's always men's feet – because men tend to commit suicide more often by jumping and hanging. Women stay at home and they cut or use pills. The oven. Men go away and do it somewhere away from their houses. And why it's always trainers they find these random washed-up feet in. Hardly ever business shoes or work boots. Because trainers are full of plastic and foam, and they're light, and they float.'

'Are you all right, Laurie?'

'So there you go. It's a gruesome story, isn't it? Mark told me all about it. He was really pleased with himself for solving the mystery. I said he should email someone and tell them what he'd worked out, but he never did.'

'You miss him, don't you?'

I'd been speaking very quickly, sometimes ploughing right over her interruptions and questions, but at that point I ran out of breath and steam and felt limp and without any interest in continuing that line of conversation further. I couldn't have told you why I had even started or persisted with it.

'You've had a lot to deal with this past year, haven't you?' Olena said. 'If you won't talk to me and you won't talk to Mavis, do you have someone else who you can talk to?'

She sounded like my GP. It pissed me off.

'I'm used to it,' I said. 'Sitting in front of the telly on your own at night isn't really that different to sitting in front of the telly with someone else.'

She raised her eyebrows slightly.

'I've been that busy with Dad – the way things have been – that there's really not been time to worry about it. Relationships end all the time. You've just got to get on, haven't you? Like you have. After your husband. You've just got to get on with things.'

'My husband was a very different man to Mark, Laurie,' she said.

'Maybe your husband is out in the sea somewhere, getting all eaten up by the fishes.'

'We can only hope,' she said, and put her arm around my shoulders.

I will interrupt myself to correct something here. A minor thing, but perhaps it will turn out to be important. I had not been entirely truthful in the way that I had told Olena about Mark's discovery about the phenomenon of the washed-up feet. It was true that this was something he was interested in, and something that he'd spent a lot of time researching. It's also true that he'd developed a kind of theory that made sense, and had used this theory to dispel a lot of rumours circulating on his favourite online discussion forum about a coastal serial killer, or even a team of killers – a hidden underground network of them, as the phenomenon was so widespread and, it seemed, increasingly common as to require more than one active murderer.

His post on the forum – a forum dedicated to the discussion of unsolved mysteries and the conspiracy theories that flourish around them like weeds on the site of an old bonfire – had garnered a fair bit of attention, with some members trying to pick holes in his logic, and others expressing admiration and grudging respect for both his research and the way in which he had elucidated it. Eventually, the doubters and critics had been silenced, the balance had tipped in favour of his supporters and the long thread had moved on from a discussion of the phenomenon itself to a litany of praise for NightGuard1980's deductive thinking and detailed research. His posts in response to this adulation had been modest yet, reading between the lines of his familiar, understated prose, proud. The whole incident had been a source of great pleasure and satisfaction to him. All that is true.

What is a lie is the scenario that I had sketched for Olena – that we had discussed this over preparing food together in our little kitchen. It was a very little lie, but I had, without really planning to, conjured up an image of marital closeness and harmony that was little more than a fantasy. Evidence, if any were needed, of my wishful thinking. In actual fact, Mark had never shared any of this with me. Not his careful research nor his triumph on the internet forum, nor the way that from then onwards his posts were treated with a special respect verging on deference and his opinions always considered carefully and taken seriously. None of that he divulged to me. NightGuard1980 was busy during that period, but it was not with me.

As I sat there on the headland with Olena, thinking about Mark's secret research into this phenomenon and the fact that he had never told me about it, I began to realise what it might mean. It had been eighty-six days since he had bought his train tickets at the railway station. And the ticket he bought had been to Brighton. I hadn't considered it until then, but Mark had been heading to the seaside himself.

I thought of his feet, which for such a large man were only a size ten. I had held those feet in my hands, massaging them as we lay at opposite ends of our settee watching one of our Netflix dramas late at night during better, closer times. I pictured that CCTV footage again: the sight of him shuffling away to the platform, tucking his tickets into his back pocket. He'd been wearing his own trainers then. Why wouldn't he? And had been heading to the bottom edge of the country – far away from me and towards (the knowledge of this fact crept across my skin, as if I was slowly submerging myself in a cold bath) the water.

The thought affected me deeply and, although I didn't see fit to share with Olena the conclusions I was coming to, she must have been able to tell that I was upset. She passed me a packet of tissues she produced from the inside pocket of her cagoule. I took one, and handed the packet back to her.

'Are you worried about your father?' she asked. 'He's not in any pain. And in safe hands. The best possible place. You can go and see him again tonight if you want to.'

'He's different, isn't he?'

'He's scared.'

'I'm so used to being angry with him, I don't know how I'm supposed to act when he's being all . . . helpless, like that.'

'Ah,' Olena said. She shuffled up close to me and I felt her shoulder against mine. The strong bulk of her – not quite exuding heat, but certainly the idea of it – was comforting. 'I understand. You have some compassion for him. You're not used to it.'

'Sometimes I feel sorry for him. Then he says my mum was shagging around and he's not my real dad and it goes away again.'

'He can be both, can't he? Vulnerable and sick man, scared and grieving your mother. And a man who did not cherish you properly. Did not act decently in his marriage. He could be both of those things. Same as you. Same as me, though you'll only see big strong Olena who can unplug the toilet with one hand and

174

cook beef stew with the other and steal his life savings with the third.'

'I've said I'm sorry about the message,' I said stiffly. 'No need to keep bringing it up.'

'You still think I did it though, don't you?' Olena looked at me. Up there on the headland, the wind blowing my hair back from my face and the light in my eyes, there was nowhere else to look and no point in lying. No point in saying anything. She laughed. Reached over and, very gently, took my face in her hands.

'You silly girl. You silly, silly girl. Lovesick. That's what you are. So sick with it you can't see what's in front of your face. You know who took your father's money. You know it as well as I do.'

I shook my head and shrugged myself away from her hands. 'I don't. If you're hinting that I took it, then I suggest we call the police and get them involved. Get them to take some fingerprints. You've probably cleaned up though, haven't you?'

I expected, even wanted, an argument, a fluttering of frantic excuses or an explanation, but she only exhaled slowly and smiled at me.

'Come on, my darling. What do you think Mark's been living on all this time? Thin air and good wishes?'

'Your hair . . .'

'You think I spent four thousand pounds on this?' She gestured towards herself. 'I can't even be flattered by that, it's so stupid. My dog groomer does this for me when I take the dog to be clipped. She used to be a hairdresser. You won't believe how little she charges. Let me tell you what I told the police when they came to speak to me.'

'I thought you said you weren't having anything to do with the police, Olena?' I said. I heard the tone of my own voice and hated it: smug, wheedling – as if I'd caught her out.

'I don't want to talk to them. Don't want to be informally or formally interviewed by them. Don't want to be in the same room as them, if I can help it. But if they knock at the door and your father lets them in and tells me to make them tea, who am I – Olena, helper to your father and no authority whatsoever over what the man does in his own house – to say no?'

'When did they come?'

'The day before your father was taken ill,' she said. She could have made a comment about the stress or anxiety this had caused him and hinted that perhaps this – as well as many other things – was all my fault. But she didn't.

'What did you tell them?'

And why, I thought, hadn't the police told me they'd visited my father and Olena? I was Mark's *wife*!

'They were asking about Mark. His health, his mood. His *state of mind*. I don't know anything about that, I said. The daughter and son-in-law visit, I make them meals, help your father make them welcome. I stay out of the way and iron his clothes. Mark comes to visit on his own now and again because he is a nice man. They're a normal family. Everything just normal.'

'What else?'

She was enjoying this.

'They wanted to know about the visits Mark made to the house on his own – while you were at work. Wanted to *build a picture*, they said, of how he was spending his time and his general mood after he left the power station. It can be bad for a man's mental health and well-being, that's what they told me. It can make a man, especially a man, very depressed. And a woman, when she's depressed, might lie around the house crying, or eating cream cakes, or internet shopping, or drinking wine during the day . . .'

'I get the gist.'

'Yes, you know how that is. For a woman. For you. But a man, when he is depressed, is not likely to talk to anyone. He will keep it to himself entirely.' She pulled an imaginary zip over her closed lips. 'A woman goes upstairs to her neighbour and talks it through. A woman occupies herself. She gets kindness and sympathy and Get Well Soon cards and presents. She goes to the doctor and gets her happy tablets prescribed.'

She made it sound like I'd enjoyed an extended holiday. I wanted to put her straight, but she was in full flow now, and I didn't dare interrupt.

'A man, he retreats. He goes into his own mind. He pretends all is well, and to the outside world, everything is well, but inside, bad things are happening to that man and nobody knows. Not even his wife.'

Olena, as infuriatingly old-fashioned about the nature of the sexes as she was, was right about some of this. There had been a period when cards and flower deliveries had appeared at the flat on a more or less daily basis. Even Shaw had arranged a collection at work, and a bouquet of roses had arrived. I had left them in the kitchen sink to rot. I had gone to my doctor fairly regularly, my last visit being back in February when I was about to return to work.

'And how are you holding up emotionally?' the GP had asked. She was typing notes into her computer and I admired her ability to do that: to speak and think and write at the same time.

'I'm doing fine,' I said. I had my eye on the clock: you get ten minutes for an appointment, the waiting room was full of coughing infants and limping adults and I felt them out there, looking at their watches and grinding their teeth at me.

'At home? You're well supported? Your husband is . . .'

'My husband is very supportive,' I said stiffly. 'He brings me tea in bed every morning. He's had to go back to work now – he only got two weeks – but I'll go back soon myself so there's no problem there.'

'He brings you tea in bed,' she said. She paused in her typing, then continued. I wondered if she was writing that on my notes,

Her husband brings her cups of tea in bed, and if she had, why she'd done it and what it might signify. It might have been better if I'd said, *My husband brings me cups of tea in the living room* – so she didn't have a mental image of me lying in bed in the dark all morning, though that phrasing would have sounded weird. I knew her repeating my statement back to me like that was a basic counselling technique she'd probably been taught in some medical practice enrichment session. Testing out her professional development, whole person well-being nonsense on me, and I was enraged.

'Yes. Every day. Milk and no sugar. Quite strong. Just how I like it.'

She smiled and pushed her wheelie chair back from her desk to turn to me fully.

'And are you talking about what's happened? Between yourselves? You've got to talk about it.'

I glanced at the clock again and she caught me doing it.

'Don't worry. They can wait.'

I was trapped.

'Yes, we talk.' I said. I might have told her about the kind of talking we were doing. The incident regarding the colander, for example, or the incessant racket from upstairs, but I didn't. I wanted to get out of there so I gave her what I thought she wanted. 'I get upset and he brings me a cup of tea and asks me what I am upset about and then I tell him and I feel better.'

She smiled again, nodded, and made another note on her computer.

'He's the rock you rage around, is that it?' she said knowingly. She let out a little laugh. 'It's often like that. My husband's the same.'

A rock. I suppose he was like that to me. A rock that would never buckle or shatter, no matter what geological pressure was placed upon it. Not like the big chunks of limestone up on the fells, riven by snowfall and rainwater, or the slowly dissolving

178

churchyard walls at Heysham, but something else. I drifted for a while, trying to remember my GCSE chemistry lessons, that scale we were to learn off by heart about the hardness of rocks. It was something to do with glaciers. I had been good at chemistry but it was all gone now. I bet the doctor would know though. You don't get to be a doctor, even just a doctor in a crummy surgery like this one, unless you're good at remembering that sort of thing. My husband was a rock, and I was his bad weather, his acid rain, his slow-moving glacier.

'Yes. He's a diamond,' I said. And I forced myself to smile.

'Good,' she said. She clicked her mouse a few times and her little printer spat out a green slip: my prescription.

'Come back in three weeks,' she said. 'Book a double appointment if you like, then we're not rushed.'

I was thinking about rocks again – sitting up there with Olena looking at the way the water had scooped bites out of the coast along the high path that ran along the coast from the church and the village towards the port and the power station. Every now and again the sea had made little beaches – coves, I suppose we'd have called them, if we'd been kids with a wooden boat in an Enid Blyton novel. These beaches were made of soft drifts of pale sand turning colloid and grey as it met the water. Walkers had worn paths down the shallow cliff sides towards them, and black plastic bags of dog-shit adorned the ragged gorse and brambles along their edges. The hardness of rocks was something to do with the way they were formed, wasn't it? The underground pressure and heat they had been subjected to? I thought about that and tested the word in my mouth – *igneous* – without saying it aloud. Something to do with volcanoes?

It felt impossible that the information I had spent a whole spring cramming into my head as a fifteen-year-old could just have evaporated like that. I'd done well in that exam. More likely the facts were still in there, resting in some little-used compartment of my brain. I just wasn't able to find a way to it. And Mark wasn't a diamond, as it turned out. He was a volcano, rumbling away secretly underground then exploding one day while I wasn't looking. Some types of rocks float on water and some are made of the bones of dead things but rocks don't break and they don't disappear, except when they do. I should have got my doctor to put that on my notes: *igneous.*

'Do you think that's what was happening?' I asked Olena. 'Do you think that's why he went?'

'He was sad, Laurie. Didn't you know?'

I didn't reply.

'I didn't tell the policeman anything like this. My opinions about things. I would never tell him what I guess or feel or imagine. I keep all that sort of stuff to myself. Instead, I tell them what I see. Only what I see and hear with my own ears and eyes. I saw Mark come to the house to visit his father-in-law alone. He's a good man. They seem to get on well, which is new. It's nice for me, because I get to take some time to myself. Get the bed changed. Have a break from your father's yak-yak-yakking about your mother's sex life. And because I wasn't hovering over them listening to every single word, I don't hear much about what they say. What I do hear is that Mark is going to buy a scanner. He's going to go through the old photographs. A project, to keep his ailing father-in-law occupied.'

'There's nothing wrong with that,' I said, leaping to his defence, though I had wondered what he was up to as well. I got out my smoking things and made a rollie. Lit up. The wind blew the smoke into our faces and Olena coughed ostentatiously.

'I wish you wouldn't smoke those things. You stink. It makes your skin look grey. How long have you had that cough?'

'My chest is fine,' I said, sulkily. Having only just given up smoking herself, Olena had become anti-nicotine with the fervour of a death-row convert to evangelical Christianity.

'You gave them up before. It wasn't so hard for you.'

180

'That was last year.' We were on dangerous ground now. I almost felt it, and she did too. But she persisted. I wanted to cough, as it happened, in that moment, but clenched my jaw tightly.

'You quit them once, you can quit them again. You want to end up in hospital like your father? And your drinking . . .'

'It was different last year. There was a point to it. There isn't now.'

'Oh Laurie. You're the point. Can't you see?'

'Don't change the subject. What was Mark looking for? In those photograph boxes?'

I didn't buy what she'd said to me the first time we'd spoken about this: that he was trying to do a kind thing for my father and me, and make sure he would always be able to remember who I was when I came to the house. The best theory I had been able to come up with on my own was that Mark – in a fit of para-noia and conspiracy thinking, and perhaps influenced by the flavour of my father's particular delusion about my mother – suspected that I had been having an affair. That there had been someone else, perhaps in my life for a long time, or an old flame from my teenage years, and he had been searching through images of times past in order to identify that person. It's possible to put a photograph into a Google Image search and have the engine turn up matches for you. He might have been planning to do that – to identify my imaginary lover through his Facebook page. It sounded outlandish, but it was the best I could do.

'You stupid, stupid girl. He wanted to hear your father talk about you.'

'My father doesn't know anything about me,' I said. 'He lets his imagination run away with him.'

'Well, imagination's all the man has. If you want people to know more about you, you have to tell them. I heard Mark telling your father once that he felt like you'd disappeared on him.'

I was outraged. 'I didn't go anywhere. I was there. At work. At home in the flat. Nowhere else. If he'd wanted me he could have got up off the settee and come into the bedroom and talked to me.'

I had said more than I meant to, and painted Olena a more accurate picture of my marriage than I would have preferred to, if I had been in complete control of myself. I glanced at her, but she was looking calmly out at the horizon and seemed to show no surprise.

'There are other ways of leaving a man,' she finally said.

I sat still and smoked for a long time. Olena likes to talk and if I waited long enough, she would tell me what I wanted to know.

'I told the police about his visits. About the way he would sometimes go upstairs to use the toilet, or to bring down a photo album, or to take up a laundry basket for me if I looked busy. Once I used my key to come into the house and your father was in the dining room looking at the photographs and your husband was up the stairs in your father's room. The look on his face. I think he was getting the money then. I told the police that. That there was a sum of money gone missing, not insignificant, and that it was my belief that your husband had taken it. They asked me the date, and I looked at my timesheets and they tell me that his *suspicious behaviour* – that's what they called it – took place the very day before he left.'

'Why didn't you tell me this earlier? Why didn't you tell me it when I messaged you and . . .'

I put my head down, feeling sick. The police knew this – had known this for a while now – and hadn't told me. Why had they left me wondering?

'I think you're sad too, aren't you Laurie? So sad it makes you crazy? So sad it makes you into a monster? I can understand that. And if you'd rather be angry with me than crying at home into your teacup, well, that is okay with me. You'd rather decide Olena – Olena who has never stolen a thing in her entire life and never will do! – has taken your father's cash and spent it on her dog groomer's beauty services, well, I'll let you think this. When you're ready to see the facts, you'll see them.'

I sat very still and watched the squat narrow shape of a ferry leave the port. It moved slowly, sounding its horn, and moved in a wide curve, avoiding the water outflow of the power station, which is exposed as a stone channel at low tide and totally hidden in high tide, then moved away to the west, out towards the Isle of Man, invisible in the cloud and haze, somewhere beyond where the sea turns milky and melts into the sky. I thought about Mark's trainers and his little feet. I knew, for the first time, the way all my sadnesses had found themselves in anger and curdled into self-pity. I felt Olena watching me but I said nothing, and eventually she stood up, brushed off the back of her trousers and said that her ticket would run out soon and we should get back to the car because she wasn't in the mood to pay a parking fine.

The fresh air and the long walk must have exhausted me, because when I got back to the flat I didn't turn the television on or boil the kettle or run a bath or open a bottle of wine or do any of the things I usually did in the evenings. I didn't check my phone or call my black sound or have a rollie out on the balcony. I didn't call the hospital and ask the nurses how my father was getting on. Instead, I took my coat off and dropped it on my bedroom floor and lay on my bed, fully clothed. I went to sleep immediately, without tossing and turning or searching for my earphones and finding my place in my audiobook or without any other preamble. I just passed out because every single one of the little selves inside me was utterly worn out.

And I had one of my dreams. One of my guilty courtroom ones. There were lots of people around me, every single one of them asking *just how could a mother have done such a thing?* I was like Connie Fallon's mother: all pale and shocked and uncomprehending. I couldn't even remember what it was I was supposed to have done. In the dream I had the idea that if I couldn't tell them why I did what I don't remember doing, then I would show them, and there was something – perhaps in a pocket in my shirt or in the front of the hoody I was wearing – something I had about my person that would be able to demonstrate what I was unable to say. I patted at my body, looking for it, but it was gone. When I woke up I was groping through the bed sheets for it, feeling the cold and the absence against my belly and breasts, a kind of longing or a hunger. I lay in the dark, tangled in the duvet, sweating and over-heated, and had to run to the bathroom to vomit.

There's a strange thing that happens in our bathroom some-times. The water in the toilet bowl – or our bath itself, if it is filled during bad weather – moves and ripples a little. The first time I noticed was last year, during a different spell of nausea which I spent on my hands and knees in the bathroom, feeling my guts churn and wishing – willing myself, in fact – to vomit because I thought it would make me feel better.

'Mark. Come in here and look at this,' I called weakly. He was waiting for me outside, and came in with a glass of water, a look of concern on his face.

'What is it? Shall I call the doctor?'

'It's the toilet. Look.'

I pointed. He leaned over. The water in the bowl was moving – forming a shallow, barely perceptible whirlpool. It juddered from side to side, as if someone had hold of the toilet bowl and was gently rocking it.

'Am I seeing things?' I said. 'What is that?'

Was that the first time the idea of a presence in the flat had occurred to me? I do remember wondering if the plumbing was possessed.

'It's the wind,' he said, 'moving the building. Maybe you're a bit seasick.'

We laughed about that. Mark, who had noticed the rippling before and had looked it up, told me that tall buildings like the ones we lived in were designed to sway a little in the wind, that if you looked at the really mega-tall high-rises in America you could actually see them moving, and it's fine, it's nothing to worry about, and I should just enjoy it.

'Enjoy it?' I said, incredulously, and leaned over the bowl again to vomit up the cup of tea and gingernut biscuit he had just brought me in bed. The biscuit was supposed to help with the sickness, and it never did, but we didn't mind. When I looked up, he was holding out a wet flannel.

'I'm sorry it's so grim for you,' he said.

'It is your fault,' I said, pretending to be angry.

'It is. And I will buy you presents every day for the rest of your life to make up for the imposition,' he vowed theatrically.

'Shut up.'

I flushed the toilet and we waited for the cistern to refill and the water in the bowl to settle while I brushed my teeth so we could see the whirlpool effect again, and the whole time we were smiling – giddy as children – because I was pregnant and hanging my head over the toilet all the time with my morning sickness was a sign, so the book said, that the hormone levels in my body were rising steadily and the pregnancy was progressing well and the baby forming inside me was safe and strong.

11

A day later I was in the flat, emptying a carrier bag of my father's pyjamas into the washing machine, when the buzzer sounded. Now – I thought, as I leapt towards the intercom – *now* would be a brilliant time for Mark to come back, and to see that I was really getting on just fine without him. He could explain himself regarding the matter of my father's cash, too. But as soon as I'd had that thought, I realised I'd jinxed the whole thing just by hoping for it and so of course it wouldn't be him.

'It's me,' Mavis's voice crackled through the intercom. 'Are you going to let me in?'

I buzzed her up.

She was dressed as if for a holiday, in lemon-coloured Capri pants and metallic sandals, with each toenail a different colour. She had a wheelie suitcase and, in each hand, a bulging carrier bag from Iceland.

'I came with supplies,' she said. 'Wouldn't turn up empty-handed. Are you eating? Look at you,' she raked her eyes across me, up and down, 'yes, you're eating. At least there's that.'

'You could have rung and . . .'

She bustled in.

'You knew I was going to turn up. I had to raise merry hell to get a flight sorted. Funds. Last-minute cancellations. But I'm here.' She threw herself on the settee. 'Have you heard anything? Tell me everything. How are you?'

'Is this all stuff for the freezer?' I said, eyeing the bags spilling their contents onto the unswept wood laminate. Oven chips and ready meals and ice cream. Lasagne and garlic bread. 'You didn't have to bring food.'

The flat, mercifully, was not as bad as it had been – though the sheets on the double bed weren't as fresh as I'd have liked, and there's no way I'd get them washed and dried in time for her to use them that night. But it could have been much, much worse.

'It'll keep us going,' she said, nodding towards the bags. 'I won't put you to any trouble at a time like this. All easy solid food. Just bung it in the oven and Bob's your uncle.'

'I don't think I'm going to have room for all this,' I said.

'Will you come and sit here and talk to me?' she patted the cushion next to her.

'Yes,' I said. I sat down, then stood up again.

'Do you want coffee?'

'Laurie!'

She was, I saw then, under the bustle and bluster, the tan and the bronzing powder, worried and pale.

'Let me just pack this stuff away,' I said, and bent to retrieve the bags. 'It'll go to waste if I don't get it in the freezer before we settle in. I want to give you my undivided attention, Mavis.'

This was disingenuous on both counts. We only had a little freezer compartment in the top of the under-counter fridge, and mainly used it for making ice cubes and chilling bottles of beer. I messed around in the kitchen for a while, unpacking the things onto the counter.

'It's all going to defrost, Mavis,' I said.

She frowned.

'I'll take it up to your neighbour,' she said. 'You tell me. Who do you know? I'll knock and ask for a favour.'

Mavis's enduring faith in other people's kindness was something that both infuriated me and endeared her to me. Most people would have made negative assumptions about what sort of people rented the flats in this block. Not Mavis. I enjoyed picturing her chapping on the door of the weed-smoking couple who lived on the ninth floor, or getting right to the top and enduring the cantankerous and vicious depression of the woman who had let her cat go over the edge. Perhaps, I thought, I could even let her go and call on Kevin. I bet she'd scream the place down if she saw a snake.

'You could try upstairs,' I said. She was already putting the things back into the carrier bags, and tutting at the array of wine bottles on the kitchen counter, lined up ready for the recycling.

'And don't think you'll be sitting there pissed every night while I'm here,' she said. 'We've got too much to do for you to be hung-over the whole time.'

'You could try Tim and Katrina. Seventeen. They'll be in,' I said, mainly out of desperation.

'I'll leave these ready meals out for us for now,' she said brightly, 'and I'll be two shakes of a lamb's tail. Then,' she put her head on one side, as if I was a naughty child, 'then we'll talk this through properly.'

I waited with a rising sense of anxiety burning away behind my sternum and wondered what I would say to her when she returned. Katrina would want to invite Mavis in for a cup of tea and show her the nursery and brag about her baby, and Mavis would want to hold him while Katrina packed the shopping away and sooner or later (probably sooner) the subject of Mark and his disappearance would come up. Katrina would probably hug my mother-in-law, and Mavis . . . Mavis liked that type of attention and she would let her. Katrina would tell Mavis that no, of course she didn't know, she had no idea: she'd only imagined Mark was working nights and that's why she and Tim hadn't crossed paths with him for a while.

Mavis returned twenty minutes later and triumphantly showed me her empty hands, as if she'd just done a magic trick.

'She couldn't do enough to help us,' Mavis said. '*You've only got to ask*, she said. They're standing by, both of them, dying to help you. We can go up and get the stuff whenever we want. We've to think of it as our freezer too, she said. Lovely woman. I didn't know the two of you were such good friends.'

'I don't see her so much any more,' I said.

'Bound to be difficult,' Mavis said briskly. 'But she asked after you. She let me hold her baby.'

'Don't, Mavis.'

'You can't blame her,' Mavis said. 'I bet it's difficult for her too. She won't know what to say.'

'Mavis. Please.'

Mavis came into the kitchen and squeezed my shoulder as she edged past me, chattering as she turned on the oven for the ready meals and pulled trays out of cupboards and rooted through the dirty water in the sink for plates and cutlery to wash.

'She doesn't look after him very well, I don't think. He cries all the time,' I said sourly.

'He was happy as anything just now,' Mavis said, running the tap.

'Wait until it gets dark,' I said. 'Just you wait until you're drifting off to sleep. He keeps the whole block awake. I'm surprised they've not been evicted.'

'Laurie,' Mavis said. I waited. She touched my shoulder again and went to sit on the settee in the living room.

'We can talk about her, you know. You're allowed to say her name in front of me,' she said. 'Don't you get tired of living like this?'

She gestured towards the seat next to her but I moved across the room and opened the door to the balcony.

'Let's not,' I said.

My father's forgetfulness had been so convenient to me. Most people I knew were too stricken or embarrassed to ask me about my own baby. Olena knew better than to press me on it, but my father – who might have been the one person you could rely on to zero in on a painful spot and blunder all over it, had let the baby Mark and I were going to have evaporate into the status of an almost-forgotten pipe dream. I used to be fatter, and now I wasn't. That's all that remained.

Even Mark and I did not dare to approach the subject directly. Or rather, he did not dare. When some practical matter forced him to draw that time to my attention, he would talk about it in euphemisms.

'When you were off work,' he'd say, trying to remind me of some promise I had made to clear out some books from our bedroom and make more room for his things. 'When you were *off work* you said you'd have a bit of a sort-out – you said you wanted a project to keep you occupied.'

Eddie was the same. He'd often remark on some new policy or procedure that Shaw had instituted, and if I didn't seem familiar with what he was telling me, rather than argue the point or tease me for my forgetfulness, he'd say, *Oh, it must have happened while you were in hospital* or *during your sick leave* and we would skate past the gap as if it was a hole in a lid of a frozen lake, giving the entire thing the widest berth we could.

Those were the types of people I chose to have around me. People who would give me my space. Katrina was not one of those people. She was too scared or awkward to come and see me face to face, but she'd managed to post a little card through the door – some generic thing with lilies on the front of it, and a note inside, full of phrases like *anything I can do* and *can't imagine how you feel* and *let me know when you're ready*. Mark had intercepted the card and hidden it in the drawer of his bedside table. I'd found it – it must have been several weeks later – and the fact of him opening it and keeping it and hiding it from me had triggered a fury so ungovernable that I'd not only ripped the card into shreds, but also smashed up the bedside table.

'She should have come to see me,' I said. 'She's supposed to be my best friend.'

'You don't want to see anyone,' Mark said, 'she's trying to respect that.'

'It was a stupid card,' I mimicked her voice, '*nothing will take the pain away but eventually time will heal*. Katrina doesn't talk like that. Nobody talks like that!'

'Nobody knows what they're supposed to say to you, Laurie,' he said. 'I don't know what I'm supposed to say to you and I'm married to you.'

He stood in front of the door, which is why I went for the table. It was only a cheap flat-pack thing from Argos. It came apart easily. And – I do want to note this here – I put it back together afterwards and, apart from a scratch on the side against the wall, which you can't see anyway, and a slight wobbliness to the drawer-opening mechanism, which could just as well be to do with the cheapness of the materials as anything else, it's as good as new. I did make my amends.

Mark keeping that secret from me felt like a kind of infidelity: that there was something between him and Katrina, a little dirty secret – the hidden letter – that should not have existed. It felt like that. A betrayal. That the two of them would have some reason to communicate with tilted heads and meaningful looks in a way that excluded me, but which was about me. That together my husband and my best friend were united in not knowing what to say to me – Mark with his silence, her with her second-hand platitudes. It is hard, even now, to understand how much of that was paranoia and how much of it might have been true.

Did he tell her, for example, that he'd hidden the card? I suppose he'd have had to, or he would have been worried she'd come down and ask me about it, or wonder why I hadn't texted her my thanks. How would he have phrased that? Would he have said something about how nice it was – *what a kind thought*

– but he didn't think I was quite ready yet, so he was going to keep it safe until I was better? Would it have been like that? My mind had raced along, wondering how it had gone, and before I had made a decision to do it, the bedside table was in pieces, the drawer in my hands, the contents – receipts, paperwork, tissues and handkerchiefs, the usual type of junk – flying through the air between Mark and me like a cloud of moths.

I was not prepared to admit it to myself at the time but it was not only an intimacy between Mark and Katrina that I wanted to destroy, but the friendship itself. My friend and I were on the same path, and living the same story, though hers had a happy ending and mine had not. I did not want to know that then. I avoided people who might have known it on my behalf.

Mavis, however, was not my father. She didn't have his problem with time, or remembering, or the fear that lay behind other people's willingness to skate right around that hole in the ice. She wasn't *my* anything, which matters too, I think. She was Mark's mother, not mine. She was brash and tactless and she was going to force me to know again all the things I had spent most of the year obliterating with wine and rage.

'You must tell me what's happened, Laurie,' she said. 'I'm his mother.'

I came back in from the balcony, and while she boiled the kettle and made us tea to drink while our teas cooked, I told her what I'd told the police.

'I was a bit angry with him on that last morning,' I said. 'He'd said he was going to fix a curtain, and he hadn't, and I reminded him about it. It might have got on his nerves.'

'Yes yes, but what about his job?' she asked, as if the matter of curtains and poles and hooks was entirely beneath her notice.

'They said he was fighting,' I said vaguely.

'Fighting? Mark doesn't fight. He'd never lift a hand to anyone.'

I thought of Olena's jaw. Remembered all the times Mark had clenched his fists then turned his back on me and walked out of the flat. She was right. Mark would never hit a woman. I wondered if he'd thrown a punch at a colleague – a man, who it was almost all right to hit – imagining it was me.

'You'd have to ask him about it,' I said. 'I can't tell you what was in his head.'

'I want to ask him,' she said. 'I want to, but I can't.' She handed me a mug of tea and we sat down. I could see that she was on the brink of tears. 'What do you think's happened to him? You know him best. Where is he?'

I was sitting close to her. It would have been a small matter to put my tea down on the floor and shuffle closer to her. I could have put a hand on her shoulder or touched her knee in a consoling way. I could have told her not to imagine him down and out and living in a shop doorway as he'd helped himself to several thousand pounds of my father's cash. I don't know why I didn't do that. Why instead of touching her I stared at the rim of my mug and only said, 'Well, you're his mother, Mavis. You tell me.'

12

Mavis made herself at home. She started cooking my tea so it was ready for me when I got back from work or the hospital. All those microwave dinners and freezer cheesecakes were comforting, even though she insisted on having the television on all the time and provided a constant commentary on the soaps she liked to watch while we ate, leaving me chewing in silence and wondering if I was supposed to nod, rapt, or venture an opinion of my own about the on-screen antics of fictional strangers.

Mavis also insisted on making an appointment with Sapphire and Steel to meet them at the police station, and, in her words, 'get a full and in-person update on the investigation'. I tried to tell her there was no investigation to speak of – that apart from the CCTV footage, Mark had left no sign, no note, no forwarding address. But she put on a pair of good shoes and some pearly brown lipstick and went anyway. I watched her from the balcony, looking small and determined and afraid as she crossed the road towards the bus stop.

When she came back, she was furious.

'They're not doing *anything*,' she said. She must have been imagining an incident room. A dedicated phone line. Teams of uniformed policemen combing the backstreets of Brighton and a harried detective with an estranged wife and an alcohol problem overseeing the entire complex operation.

'He's allowed to leave,' I said weakly. I should have sympathised with her: I'd had weeks to surrender to the enforced helplessness that she was only then beginning to encounter.

'Not if he's not in his right mind, he's not,' she said.

Mavis had an enormous phone – more of a tablet, really – and she took it out of its iridescent case and started swiping at it.

'There's a lot we can do for ourselves, Laurie. There's an organisation that will put posters up in train stations. I've been getting his picture out there, but this company – it's a charity – they can coordinate it all. Make sure that we don't get hoaxers calling us up. Have you been on to them?'

I shook my head. 'I didn't feel up to it,' I said simply, which was sort of true. 'If he wants to go into his shell and—'

Mavis looked up from her phone.

'Shell? Shell?' she said incredulously. 'That man doesn't have a shell. That's the problem. Anything that happens in the world, he feels it. Anything that happens to someone he cares about, he feels it. He's like a . . .' she wiped her eyes, 'a little snail ripped out of its shell and put in the sunshine. That's what life's like for him. We can't just leave him to his own devices.'

Her perception of Mark was very different to mine – I'd have described him as a man who was all shell – a shell ten inches thick, like the concrete ring around the reactor rods at the power station. But instead of glowing, unstable energy inside, there was nothing. I wanted to tell her that. That before he left, being married to Mark had felt like nothing so much as banging on the locked door of an empty room and waiting in vain for someone to open it.

'I told you all this already. They rang around his friends. They talked to my father. They came here. They looked at his things.'

I was about to tell her about the business with the bath panel, but decided against it.

'I rang his work from Portugal,' Mavis said decisively. 'International rates but I just rang anyway. I *demanded* they put his manager on the phone. They wouldn't tell me anything so I turned up. Today. After the police station.'

'Did you?' I said. This was impressive.

'I turned up at reception and they pretended not to know what I was talking about. I said *fine, I'll sit here until you work it out then*. And I did. Only took them twenty minutes to send the manager down. He was very nice, actually.'

'What did they say?' I asked.

'I wanted to find out what that fight was about. Who hit him. Who upset him. It's not like Mark to get into a scuffle. Somebody must have done something.'

'Nobody hit him, Mavis,' I said. 'He was the one throwing punches.'

'His boss. He hit his boss.'

I had not bothered to find this out, so it was news to me, and the shock of it made me want to giggle. I pressed my hand against my mouth and turned away from Mavis. She probably thought I was overcome with a different type of emotion.

'You didn't know that?'

I shook my head.

'Well, he did. Not a serious punch. But it was gross misconduct anyway. And they could have sacked him on the spot – they can't have someone unstable in a working environment like that. It'd be too dangerous. But in the light of the circumstances, they just decided to accept his resignation. Said they were trying to make it easier for him to find another job.'

'I see.' I tried – as I had before – to imagine Mark hitting someone. And I couldn't. It was me – me who threw things and slammed doors and insisted on carrying on the argument when he only wanted to go to sleep. I was the volatile one. 'What started it?' I asked.

'He'd not been turning up for shifts at work. Late sometimes. Other times just wandering off. Going down to the beach or onto the Barrows for a walk. They said it had to stop. Said there was a woman he could see to talk it all through.'

'A woman?'

'A counsellor. They have someone there. For workplace stress.'

'He wasn't stressed. He loved that job.' I thought of him in his uniform then. How proud he was of it. My Night Guard.

'He was stressed about things at home,' Mavis said darkly. 'Obviously.'

'That's what he said?'

'That's what they asked him. His boss. Was everything all right at home? Would he like to go and talk to their on-site coun- sellor? He didn't say as much, but they probably made it a condi- tion of him keeping the job. And he lashed out.'

She wiped her eyes again. She was angry with me. I could tell.

'Well, I'm sorry, but I didn't know any of that, Mavis. He didn't tell me a thing. I'm not sure what I'm supposed to do if he didn't.'

'You could use your imagination,' Mavis said, then stood up. 'I've run out of fags. Do me one of your little rollie ones, will you? I'm going to make these phone calls. I'm going to check the police know about this – about how much he was struggling.'

August dragged onwards, and that sense of being watched as I went about my business faded, or rather attached itself to the solid and explicable presence of Mavis herself, who did watch me, sometimes with care and sometimes with suspicion, as I ironed my work tunics and emptied the kitchen bin and poured bleach down the toilet and generally tried to re-establish the ordinary routine maintenance of home and self that I had neglected so utterly in the period of time before her arrival. I could say a lot of things about my mother-in-law, but there was nothing spectral about Mavis.

She didn't get anywhere with her phone calls to Brighton to follow up on the posters she had emailed. Nobody she talked to had heard of or seen Mark. She tried to get shopkeepers and pub landlords and taxi drivers to promise to put the posters some- where prominent – to print as many of them out as they could – and even threatened to come and pay a visit. But I could tell she was getting nowhere. She would tap away on the keyboard of her giant phone and pace, and mutter under her breath, and cry. She made contact with some support group, and they coached her through the steps of setting up a social media campaign. Overnight, my inbox filled with messages.

We didn't know! Are you all right?

Anything we can do.

Just call on us, any time.

You're in our prayers.

I deactivated my Facebook page and deleted my email account and at night I lay on the uncomfortable settee trying to sleep while she snored loudly in the next room. Sometimes I heard her talking on her mobile phone to someone back in Portugal and other nights I heard her crying. At those times I would keep very still, not moving or turning over or rustling my blanket so she wouldn't know I was awake.

I did look for him, I wanted to tell her. It would have been a bad idea to get up and go into my bedroom and turn on the lamp and confront her. I imagined her, leaning on one elbow and weeping blue mascara stains into my pillows. She'd meant what she'd said about my drinking when she first arrived so I was almost always sober in the evenings now – and I was that night too. I could have tried to say something. But what good would it have done her for me to intrude on her grief?

In the time before I had told anyone that my husband had vanished, I used to walk through the city at night when I couldn't sleep. As I wandered, peering into the dark corners of my little city in search of his hunched figure in a doorway, or disappearing around a corner, I often thought about the Connie Fallon case. After her parents had been arrested there was a long period of speculation and argument on the television and in the newspapers that coincided with Mark and I becoming more serious about each other. He'd moved a few things into the flat that I was living in at the time, and we had begun to make noises about finding somewhere we could share on a more permanent basis.

The two things were always connected in my mind: me slowly realising that Mark and I were going to be a proper couple, and the entire country wondering what had happened to the little girl whose body had been found up on Caton wind farm.

It was a school photograph that all the newspapers used: I didn't need to have it in front of me (though it was easy enough to find online) to see her little pale face, her blonde hair and her red school pullover. It was as clear in my memory as my husband's face was, the sound of his voice, the particular detail of his hands, his feet, the way his limbs and torso were slotted together in a way that was unique to him. It was no explanation to say that someone is beloved because they are unlike anyone else, as everyone is unlike anyone else. But that's the way it is.

Some of the news articles wondered if Connie would have been searched for so carefully and her disappearance and murder publicised with such vigour if her parents had lived on a council estate and had ordinary jobs, rather than him being an academic and her a GP. Other articles focused on the act of murder itself – the sheer unnaturalness of a mother killing her own child. Mrs Fallon was not speaking, not even to her own solicitor, so rumours ran riot. *How could a mother do such a thing?* Nobody could understand it. Nobody *should* understand it.

One of the nights I was out walking, I had found myself in the all-night garage where we bought our tobacco and milk and topped up our cards for the electric meter. It was around four in the morning and getting light. The woman who worked there was using her Stanley knife to cut the plastic ties holding the bundles of newspapers together and I waited for her to serve me, reading the headlines of the newspapers as she worked.

I was looking for Connie Fallon, I realised with a start. Somehow – because I had always associated the case with Mark, and I had been looking for him – history and time had gone wrong and I had forgotten that the case was fifteen years old now, and all but forgotten. There had been other interesting murders and sensational crimes since then. Other babies and children whose parents had murdered them, or who had gone missing, only to be found naked and battered in fields, in woodland, beside out-of-town railway lines.

I bought what I needed, left the yellow artificial light of the garage and emerged into the chilly gloom of the early morning, clutching my little packet of tobacco, my fingers hooked through the handle of a pint of milk. It wasn't time that was going wrong, it was me.

As I lay on my sofa that night, listening to Mavis crying, I realised that if she had lived, that little girl would be in her early twenties now. Her hair might have stayed blonde, or it might have darkened as she aged, or she might have dyed it red or black or purple or cut it off or had it put into dreadlocks. She might be fat or thin, she might wear glasses. She could be a university student, or a mother, or a cleaner like me, or a nurse, or in prison, or off travelling, or any one of an infinite number of things.

The possibilities of her life – even a fairly ordinary life with only an ordinarily lucky set of comforts and privileges – seemed dizzying and impossible. The vastness of what had been lost made me feel sick and strange and sad, all of which was peculiar, and nothing I would be able to tell anyone except for Mark, because it wasn't as if Connie Fallon was my daughter, and the witnessing of all those possibilities was mine to lose and mourn and keen over.

I never did go in to see if Mavis was all right. I felt her crying as an accusation – almost an attack. I never told her that I had looked for Mark and I didn't try to persuade her that none of this was my fault. Maybe if I had been kinder and more ready to admit to her that yes, there were things I should have done for Mark that I had not been able to do, we'd have been able to talk to each other more easily. In my defence, no matter how long she cried for at night, she was always bright and breezy over breakfast, full of plans for how she was going to spend her day managing Mark's social media campaigns: it never seemed the right time to bring up her nocturnal grieving.

One morning towards the end of the month, she decided she was going to come with me to visit my father in the hospital. This was a shock: she disliked my father intensely.

'Infirmity comes to us all in the end,' she said ominously. 'And anyway, it's good for you to look on the misfortunes of others when you're suffering yourself. Puts things into perspective.'

I think she probably meant that she was feeling sad and was going to force herself to do something nice for somebody else because being generous and kind was a sure-fire way of restoring your spirits. She isn't an awful person, even though it sounded as if she wanted to go and have a stare at my father, still confined and confused in his hospital bed, in order to really feel her own strength and health. I was quiet as I gathered the nightclothes of his I had hung over the airer to dry overnight.

'Do you ever wonder what would happen if he came back, while you were out?' she said, as we stood in the lift together.

'No,' I said. I made my voice cold and hard. I wanted to be tough. 'He's still got his key, I presume.'

Mavis pursed her lips and sighed out of her nostrils.

At the hospital, I could not find my father in the ward, and for a moment I thought he had died and nobody had bothered to tell me. One of the nurses saw Mavis and me loitering at the front of the bay and took us to one side.

'We've put him in a side room,' she said, in a serious voice. 'Let me show you. We thought he'd be more comfortable there.'

We trotted along after her, the carrier with the clean pyjamas in banging against my leg.

'Has he been swearing again?'

'He's very quiet,' she said carefully. 'Doctor thinks there might have been another CVA in the night. He's not in pain.' She opened one side of the double door leading into his room and stood back. 'I'll tell Doctor you're here and he can come and talk to you.'

My father was asleep. He didn't look unsettled or in pain or mad or dead or any of the things I always feared and dreaded as I made my way through the hospital towards his bedside during that time. He seemed to be asleep, his twisted left arm hidden under the sheet and the left side of his face against the pillow. If I didn't look too hard, he could have just been having a nap after an ordinary Sunday lunch.

'What's a CVA?' Mavis asked in a stage whisper.

'Cerebrovascular accident,' I said, in my normal voice. 'A stroke.'

'Isn't the point of him being in hospital to stop him having accidents?' Mavis asked, as outraged as if my father's ill health had been directly caused by the negligence of the nurses and doctors who were treating him. I ignored her and sat by his bed.

'Dad. It's me. Are you all right? Did you have a bad night?'

My father woke up slowly and looked at me. One of his eyes was working properly, in that it swivelled around and found my face, then stayed there. The other one had a harder time in doing what he wanted it to, and his lid drooped.

'Where's the baby?' he asked.

Mavis gasped.

'Gerald, it's me, Mavis,' she shouted. 'We've come to see you!'

I saw him flinch and reached for his hand. It felt cool and dry. He had never been frail before but he was now.

'Are they feeding you properly?' Mavis asked, her voice still raised, as if she was talking to him down an unreliable telephone line. 'Is the food all right?'

'He can't eat much, Mavis,' I said quietly. She drew back.

'Where's . . .?'

She was terrified, I think, of what he was going to say, and came too close, plucking at his sheets and pulling them up close under his chin as if he was a child refusing to lie still in bed and go to sleep. He was only a couple of years older than her, and I wonder if it was frightening for her to see him like that. If it made her wonder who would be at *her* bedside, when her time eventually came.

'He likes sweets,' I said quickly. 'Wine gums. Sherbet lemons. Stuff like that. He gets a dry mouth. I meant to get some in the shop but I forgot. Would you?'

'I will,' she shouted, clutching her tasselled handbag to her side. 'I'll pop down right now and get them, Gerald. All right? Anything else?'

Neither my father nor I answered her and she tap-tapped away, stopping to make conversation with the nurses out on the main ward. I am not sure how aware my father was, or how capable he was of sighing with relief, but his shoulders dropped a little and I took it to mean that he was glad I'd got rid of her.

'You remember Mark's mother don't you, Dad? That's Mavis. She's come to stay with me for a bit.'

'I forgot about your baby,' he persisted. 'Where's your baby?'

It sounded as if he was drunk. I pulled my chair up to the edge of his bed and sat beside him. I had the urge to stroke his head. His hair was flattened at the back and sides where he had been lying on it and sticking up in tufts on the top. Olena would have sorted that out.

'The baby died, Dad,' I said quietly.

'Oh. It died,' he replied.

He sometimes did that, in conversations where he was losing the thread. Repeated the last words you'd said back to you with a particular inflection – one of attention and interest. Apparently even when vocabulary and understanding goes, as happens when the bleeds cause parts of the brain matter to die, the social reflexes to do with how we conduct ourselves in conversation and, incredibly, how we cover up what we do not understand or are embarrassed by, remain. It was impossible to know how much actually went in, and I found the thought of that both horrifying and absurdly comforting. It was only like talking to my black sound, this was.

'I never know what to say, when people ask me if I have kids,' I said. 'I could say yes, but then they'd ask me about her, and it would make things awkward and horrible. Sometimes I want to make them awkward and horrible. Or I could say no, and it would be a lie. It would be like rubbing her out. Pretending she had never existed. I don't know if I'm a mother or not. Can you be *sort of* a mother? Or is it like being a virgin? You either are or you aren't?'

'Your mother . . .' my black sound began. I shouldn't have mentioned virginity. I regretted it immediately.

'Don't, Dad.' I patted at his hand. 'Mavis is coming back in a minute. She's going to bring some sweets for you.'

I had a leaflet that said redirection could sometimes help in cases like this. They way, apparently, you should handle toddlers who are about to have a tantrum. It sounded disrespectful, infantilising and patronising when I first read it, but that was before he'd started getting obsessed with my mother's sex life.

'No no, your *mother*.'

'What about my mother?' I spoke sharply to him. I should have been more gentle. But I was not.

'Your mother,' he struggled. I took the corner of the sheet and wiped the side of his mouth with it.

'My mother?'

'Your mother liked holding you when you were a baby,' he said.

Was this Doting Dad?

'Did she?'

'All the time. She never wanted anyone else to have a go. She was really pleased with you.'

I think that's what he said. The paternity testing company said it would take eight to twelve weeks for the results to arrive in the post. There was a free telephone number you could ring to talk about your feelings with a trained listener if the results were unexpected. It was strange to think that the conclusive proof as to whether I was this man's daughter or not was probably being developed in a lab somewhere as we sat there together.

'You don't really think you're not my real dad, do you?' I asked. I sensed that time was short, without letting myself know that I knew it. It felt urgent then, to get the truth out of him. His bad eye closed completely. There was a bruise on the back of his hand – a cannula that they'd tried to fit, and which, apparently, he'd repeatedly pulled out, not understanding what it was for. He didn't answer. I grew impatient and stood up.

'Where's Mavis? I'm going to go and find her.'

'Don't leave me like this,' he said. Very clearly.

His eye fixed on me, and I couldn't stand it, so I went to his bedside locker. In the move from the main ward to this side ward, his possessions had been jiggled about, and I busied myself ordering them and arranging them nicely. His boxer shorts and socks, his nice watch, his glasses and their little blue leather case, which always also contained a blue, red and black biro pen, just in case there were any crosswords or sums that needed doing. His toothbrush and special pink toothpaste.

'Don't leave me,' he said again. It sounded like a little moan.

'Me? Who's me? I'm not sure I know any gentleman by that name?' I said. I tried to make myself sound bright and cheery, as he always did when he played The Game with me.

'I'm not . . .' He glanced around the room, as if looking for someone to help him.

'I'm sure I met a Me once. A long time ago. You're much too young to be him though. Surely?'

'It is me,' he insisted weakly. I moved away from the locker and stood close by the bed. He nodded and I patted his hand, the feathery skin grey and loose against his knuckles.

'Well, I'm sorry, Mr Me,' it became harder and harder to talk. 'I just don't have any idea who you are.'

He looked around the room, as if there were more people in there than just us. I sat down. He scrabbled for me and I let him hang on to my wrist.

'It's your dad, Laurie,' he said, and I do think he was smiling, though perhaps it was only the effect of the drugs he was on (I am sure they were giving him something to keep him calm and sweet) or the bits of his brain that weren't really online any more, but just firing electric shocks along very old pathways, the pathways that knew a smile was required when talking to a daughter, even a disappointing and contrary daughter like me.

'Sure?'

He nodded again.

'Fine. Good. At least we have that cleared up,' I said, wiping my face on the sleeve of my coat and trying to sound brisk and practical as Olena always did, because he liked people being that way with him. He always got on very well with her, anyway, and if anyone had asked me, I'd have said that, actually, she was the more contrary and argumentative one out of the two of us.

He went to sleep after that, and I leaned back in the chair beside his bed and looked out of the window. There was nothing much to see – only the main road, and the bus stop, and the bays where the ambulances that weren't in use got parked. I watched two paramedics wash out the back of one of the ambulances with a red plastic mop bucket full of soapy water. When Mavis came back, bursting through the door brandishing a bag of sherbet lemons in one hand and liquorice blackcurrants in the other, he was dead.

13

I did an awful, terrible thing. An unforgivable thing.

Mavis stayed with me in the hospital for the rest of the day and she was loud and annoying but she helped. I got her to tell me what to do with all the arrangements – the certificates, and the bank stuff, and the funeral directors and such – and in the chaos of those first two days I forgot to tell Olena.

For a long time I had thought Olena was the forgetful one. I thought she forgot that she wasn't my aunt or my godmother, but was only my father's cleaner, acting up in her duties until we could extract something more solid from social services. But it was me. Even after our talk at Heysham, when she had been so kind to me, I forgot that she had become a member of the extended family and that it wasn't my job to include her, but to accept that she had been included.

She went to visit him in the hospital with a packet of wine gums and a new tube of Euthymol toothpaste in her purse, and a nurse had to break the news to her as if – this is what she said later – *as if I was just a tourist in your family! A scrap of nothing blown in from the street!* I regret that. And I regret – when she appeared at my father's house on the morning of the funeral with a tray full of triangle-cut egg-and-cress sandwiches to be eaten at the wake afterwards – pretending to be more dazed and distraught than I really was so that she couldn't be angry with me.

We over-catered at the wake. Eddie had turned up to the funeral but, other than giving me an awkward hug, did not say a great deal to me and scarpered soon afterwards. In the end it was only the vicar, Mavis, Olena, Mrs and Mr Haworth and a few ancient suited men who commented on how much I had grown and lied about how much I looked like my beautiful mother. I did not remember them and they made so little impression on me that after they had left I could not have picked them out of a line-up if my life had depended on it. Mr Haworth – I was supposed to call him Jim, but didn't – wrote me a cheque with an amount that made me gasp and insisted I take it, as if I was twelve and he'd been unpleasantly surprised by me and caught gift-less at a Christmas party. Mrs Haworth had dyed her hair black – it was the dull scuffed colour of a well-used wheelie bin – and sat on the settee crying ostentatiously into Olena's magnificent cleavage (she looked like the mermaid on the prow of a boat that day: her formidable black dress and Elnett-ed hair had commanded more attention than the coffin).

'You should go and talk to her,' Mavis whispered. I was hiding in the kitchen inspecting the cheque. What was Mr Haworth thinking? Compensation for something? Commiseration? We were both, I suppose, willing victims of my father's manipulations, one way or another. And – the thought made me snigger, and look at my mother in an entirely new light – Mr Haworth and I did share the same unremarkable looks and forgettable grey eyes, and he had known my mother a very, very long time. If five grand made him feel better, well, I'd go along with it.

'Put that away and go in to her,' she said. 'She's really upset.'

Mrs Haworth had stopped bothering with my father around the time he started confusing her with my mother. I didn't know if she took the comparison as an insult, or if being compared to a dead woman made her feel more guilty than deceiving a live one.

'She's a dirty bitch,' I said brightly. 'She has the morals of an alley cat.'

'Laurie! She'll hear you!'

'She's a . . .'

Olena had many talents, and one of them was to be instantly aware, at any given moment, of the social temperature not only of the room she was occupying but of the adjoining rooms too. I knew when she did get back to Dnipro and became a social worker, she was going to get loaded with all the difficult cases; she had never met a person that she could not handle into polite submission. Before I could continue sharing my thoughts about Mrs Haworth, her voice floated through from the living room.

'Mrs Wright?'

'She means you, Mavis,' I said gleefully. I could only describe myself as an honorary Mrs Wright these days.

'What it is, Helena?'

'Olena. It's Olena!'

Mavis waved me away.

'You couldn't call a taxi, could you? Mrs Haworth here is quite overcome.'

Did I wish Mark had been there at my side at my father's funeral and wake? I did. I have told you about the difficult parts of our marriage, the time after our daughter's death, when everything went so badly wrong. The times even earlier than that, when I first started letting him down. But that was not all there was between us. And one of the reasons I was so furious with him for being unable to find the right thing to say was that I had enjoyed many years with him when he – unlike everyone else I had ever met in my life, including myself – always said exactly the right thing.

Often, in better times, we'd lie in bed and he'd tell me details of training exercises he'd taken part in at the power station. He was only a security guard, and his main job involved patrolling the perimeter of Heysham One and Two at night, searching the various vehicles that came in through the perimeter fence during the late evening, and inspecting post and parcels in the early hours of the morning before they were accepted by the internal mail. He didn't have a gun or powers of arrest, and he generally made a policy of taking his black jumper with the badge and his belt with space for keys and radio with him to work in a rucksack rather than wearing them in the vicinity of our block. He didn't want anyone in our flats to get the mistaken impression he was a member of the police force.

'The Civil Nuclear Constabulary get to do all the interesting stuff. Guns. Tasers,' he'd say, gently undressing me. 'But today we did a lockdown drill. In case of a terrorist attack.'

The plant accepted deliveries of treated uranium that arrived in big metal flasks on the back of trains. It also sent out the used-up uranium in the same flasks, and they went out on a different sort of train. The days of these comings and goings constituted what Mark had been taught to call a 'systemic vulnerability' in the security of the station. Weak points, in other words. All staff were to be on red alert.

'They'd never get at the reactor,' he said easily, leaning above me and, in a complicated and awkward manoeuvre, using one hand to pull down my knickers while resting his weight on the other, 'but they might get at the trains.'

'They?'

I knew the answer. This was like a bedtime story for us. He lay down on me and pressed his cock against me, not putting it inside, but just pressing it close, and making me wriggle about.

'Terrorists,' he said. 'Today we had a practice. The CNCs running around with the dogs and guns, and us security guys disabling the gates and setting off the alarm system.'

'Would it help?' I said. 'Would closing the gates and setting off the alarm stop them if they wanted to steal the . . .'

Mark never called it uranium. It was seen, in the culture of the station, as a slightly overdramatic term. He – in common with the others – called it 'stuff' or 'the load' or, when in a more formal briefing meeting, 'material'. I don't think, unless he was speaking to me, trying to coax me into a fear he could then comfort me out of by fucking me, he ever thought of the processes going on behind the seven-foot concrete ring surrounding the rods in the reactor hall.

'Nah,' he said. 'If they're near enough to breach the gates, intelligence has failed and we're all fucked. They'd as soon crash a plane into it as send a man with a pistol in through the perimeter. The jobsworths just like to keep us busy. Endless drills and practices for when the worst happens.'

I shivered and pushed myself against him. There's a practice siren that goes off every Tuesday and Thursday morning at Heysham, wailing through the little village and housing estate within range of the power station. Mark had told me the siren – like all sirens, from ambulances to police cars, from smoke alarms to car alarms and even the way a telephone rings – was designed after the cry of a baby; the one sound that human beings (unless they are psychopaths) are unable to tune out. That rise and fall, the undulation of distress and demand that we are constitutionally unable to ignore, calls out from Heysham twice weekly, even when all is well. Sometimes, when the weather is right, you can hear it from the flat.

'What do the people who live near the station have to do when they hear the siren for real?'

'They have to close the windows and bring their pets inside,' he said sleepily. I moved my leg between his and pushed myself against his chest.

'And then what? Wait?'

'Take a tablet,' he said. 'There's a leaflet. They take an iodine tablet and stay in.'

'Would that help?'

He was responding now, his cock getting hard and poking at me through the gap in the front of his boxer shorts. I pretended to be frightened of the thought of the siren going off.

'Shouldn't they run away?' I asked.

'Nah. If there was something properly wrong, you wouldn't want to survive it. You'd be better off at home going quickly.'

He lifted my T-shirt over my head and bent his head to my chest.

'Would you stay there?' I asked. 'While the sirens were going off? Just wait for it all to happen?'

'No,' he said, nuzzling at me. He hadn't shaved for a few days and the prickle on the side of his face was scraping at my nipple. It hurt a bit, but it sort of didn't hurt too, and I pressed myself against him.

'What would you do?' I asked. I giggled. This was a long time ago now. Before our bad time. Before our own blast.

He pulled at my clothes, and I lifted up my shoulders so he could get my T-shirt off, holding on to his shoulders to steady myself.

'I'd take my iodine tablet,' he said, moving my knees apart and sitting between them. 'And then I'd come home and do this.'

He went right inside. I was wet enough – I almost always was – and I liked it that way. The feeling that he was trying to put his whole self in there, and that no amount of close was close enough. I didn't shut my eyes but watched him moving – the way he still got a bit embarrassed sometimes and pulled up the edge of the sheet to cover my face if he thought I was staring at him.

'If it went up, it'd get the flat though, wouldn't it?'

My chin fitted against his neck. There was a certain way we liked to lie when we talked like this, him pushing softly against me, his face in the pillow, my mouth at his ear. We never really looked at each other while we did it, and it didn't seem odd at the time.

'It'd get the whole country. And most of Northern Europe,' he said excitedly. He put a hand on my hip and squeezed. 'Better to live near. Get it over with. If they get into the reactor, you don't want to be around for the aftermath.'

It was strange of us. Perhaps not. I don't really know how other people do it. How they manage to keep themselves interested in each other when the novelty has worn off. He did like to scare me, but I wanted both the scare and the comfort. It was a game and not quite a game, all at the same time. And the day of the funeral I wanted him to say the right thing to me, even though what was right for me and for us would have been strange to anyone else. I walked about with a teapot feeling wet and throbby between the legs and having to swallow the bubble of a giggle that kept threatening to emerge from the back of my throat. Every time I thought about the coffin disappearing behind the shabby red curtain at the crematorium I wanted to be in bed with my husband.

Mavis obeyed Olena and busied herself calling the taxi and bundling the Haworths into it. She came back to me while I was washing teacups in the kitchen, thinking about Mr Haworth's cheque and speculating about the types of dinner parties the four of them might have held back in the late seventies. My arrival might have been a nasty shock for all of them in more ways than one. I was, perhaps, a little hysterical – they say grief does funny things to you.

'You shouldn't be doing that, love, sit down.'

'It's fine. I don't mind.'

'Let me do it. You need to go and talk to – who is that woman? The foreign one? Helen? The cleaner?'

'Olena. Why? What's wrong with her?' I wiped my hands on the front of my good black cardigan, took the cheque out of my bra and unfolded it to inspect it again. Mavis was unimpressed.

'She's in your downstairs convenience,' she said, picking up the tea towel and using it to chase water and soapsuds off the draining board. She nodded at me meaningfully. 'I think she's being sick. Is there something wrong with her?'

'What? No.'

In the hallway, I knocked on the toilet door. Perhaps Olena had been hit harder by my father's death than I thought.

'Are you all right? It's me.'

Shouldn't it have been me with my head down the toilet bowl, mascara smeared over my face, and Olena and Mavis gently chapping at the door seeing if I needed some help?

'Just a minute.' Olena coughed and flushed the toilet. After a moment or two, she opened the door.

'What's wrong?'

'Under the weather. Just a little bit, that's all,' she said weakly, wiping her mouth. She was white, white pale – I've never seen a human being look so grey and not be lying naked on a slab in an episode of *Silent Witness*.

'What is it? Do you want a cup of tea?'

'No, no. It's all right.'

She wouldn't meet my eye, and was holding her mobile phone in both hands, as if it was a bomb.

'Is it your daughter? What's happened?'

Olena opened the door fully and motioned for me to come inside.

'Come in here.'

She shut the door, locked it, and sat on the closed lid of the toilet.

'I'm done for,' she said. She wrapped her arms around herself, visibly trembling.

'What have you done?'

It was a tiny room this, a little water closet (as my mother called it) shoved in under the stairs, with a half-sized corner sink. There was a small oval wicker basket filled with faded shredded paper and pastel-coloured soaps in the shape of seashells. We were never allowed to use those soaps – they were ornamental only, my mother had insisted, and now she had been dead for years and still they lay there. I picked one up and worked it out of the plastic film it was packaged in, scared of what Olena was about to tell me.

'I've had a message from my sister. The police. They have been in touch with her.'

At the mention of the police my first thought was about Sapphire and Steel. I wondered why – even taking into account the fact Mavis had been harassing them daily – the police would contact Olena's sister, an older sister who'd never left Dnipro and who, Olena told me, she didn't really get on with.

'What's happened?' I said.

'It's Maksym. They've found him,' she whispered. She put her hand over her face and leaned over so her forehead nearly touched her knees. I thought of patting her on the shoulder or rubbing her back, but I didn't.

'Who's Maksym?'

'Him. My husband.' She straightened up and uncovered her face. She was trembling. 'I think I'm going to be sick again.'

'He can't come and find you here,' I said. 'He won't come. It's all right.'

'No, no,' she said, almost wailing. 'His *body*. They found his body.'

'He's dead?' I whispered stupidly. Mavis had got the Hoover out and was running it up and down in the living room. The swish and zoom of it filtered through the thin wall.

'There's woods, outside the city. A couple of birdwatchers found him. Half buried.'

'He's been murdered?'

Olena nodded slowly, rubbing her hands over her eyes.

'My family. They will say I was at a wedding. My cousin's wedding. We were invited. I had a dress. And Maksym, he woke up with a terrible hangover and didn't want to go. So we argued. And then . . .' She made a fist and let it fall weakly onto her thigh. 'I have been so stupid. So stupid. They were always going to find him. Fucking birdwatchers.'

My smoking things were in my pocket. I leaned on the sink and rolled a fag. Olena did not complain – so much for her giving up. We shared it in silence, puffing smoke at the extractor fan.

'What am I going to do?' she said.

It was terrifying. Olena was the person who looked after me. And now this. She moved out of the way and I threw the fag end down the toilet and flushed it. It was my turn to be the one who had to – somehow – say the right thing.

'Don't say anything else, Olena. Wash your face at the sink. You look a state.' I handed her the novelty soap I had unwrapped. It was a pink cockleshell, not quite the size of an egg. She took it from me numbly and stared at it.

I knew it. I *knew* Olena would be one of my seventeen murderers.

'Mavis is right outside,' I said. 'So you're going to wash your face and I'm going to go out and make you a cup of tea. Two sugars. And you can have a couple of sandwiches and a bit of cake. You can pick a nice memory you have about my father and you can sit on the settee and tell Mavis about it. And then you can drive home.'

'Is that it? Nothing else?'

'Nothing else,' I said. I sounded more certain than I felt, but I was only letting the part of me that was really the part of her that I'd taken inside and made my own lead the way for both of us.

14

Mavis treated me, in the days after my father's funeral, as if I was a cloud about to dissolve or blow out of the window. I couldn't breathe heavily without her appearing at my elbow, offering mugs of tea or sausage rolls heated up in the microwave or bacon and brown sauce sandwiches. It wasn't, as she had correctly intimated on her first sight of me, as if I was wasting away. Eventually, even she grew bored and floated the idea of spending her Sunday morning in town, scouring the charity shops for a decent coat.

'Not something I have much need of back home,' she said, rubbing her arms dramatically. 'But I'm cold. Will you be all right?'

'I'll be fine,' I said.

'You sure?'

'*Mavis*,' I said. She hugged me, and in a gale of duty-free perfume and a jangling of charm bracelet, clattered away out of the flat.

I took the opportunity to have a bath in peace. And after that, I intended to telephone Olena. I was lying there, hearing the leaky tap drip into the water, thinking about Olena and half listening to a Radio Three adaptation of Coward's *Blithe Spirit*. I heard a strange scraping sound at the front door. I tried to ignore it. I remember ruminating, there in the water. Deciding that, in my view, *Blithe Spirit* wasn't a play suited to an audio-only production. It was hard to tell, you see – especially if your attention was drifting back and forth between the action and the problem of Olena, not to mention the sneaking suspicion I might, after all, have been the product of a wild night or two my mother had spent with the docile Mr Haworth – which were the ghosts and which were the real people. A key jiggled in the lock and I sat up, the water sloshing at the overflow hole.

'Mavis? Is that you?'

There was no answer. I'd left the bathroom door open – a rare luxury since Mavis had been cluttering up the place – so I got out of the water quickly and put my dressing gown on. Water streamed down my legs and onto the lino.

'Who is it? Who's there?'

I wasn't scared. I was irritated. Once, a man had let himself in to do some work on the heating system when Mark and I were sitting on the settee in our nightclothes eating cornflakes and watching the television. They're supposed to give you twenty-four hours' notice – it's in our contract – but he'd only let himself in as if he owned the place, traipsed through to the kitchen and started taking the control panel for the heating apart without so much as a 'good morning'. Mark had said it was deliberate: the Housing Association's way of reminding us we didn't own the space we lived in, that there would never really be any privacy, and we needed to know our place. He might have been right but, for my own peace of mind, I preferred to consider the intrusion the result of an unfortunate clerical error. I pulled the bathroom door closed.

'I'm in the bath,' I called. I wish I'd sounded happy and relaxed. I had been chuckling a little over the antics in the play, after all, but I was also thinking about Olena, trying to decide if her capacity for violence – I was not surprised by it, after all – would change things between us, and wondering how or if I would see her now that my father was gone. Selfishly, I was also wondering when the right time would be to tell her my theory about Mr Haworth and his five thousand pounds. I was looking forward to making her laugh. All of that, so I was pissed off that I couldn't have a half-hour in peace without someone disturbing me. The mirror above the sink was steamed up, and my reflection was just a dark clouded shape, hovering near the door. I heard the front door to the flat open, then close again. Someone laid something down in the hallway. Footsteps. I held my breath and watched the reflection in the mirror tremble and dither. I didn't recognise myself.

'Laurie. It's me.'

It was Mark.

Nearly nineteen weeks. One hundred and thirty-two days. My clock stopped.

I kicked the bathroom door closed and locked it.

On their second visit, the police had asked me about identifying marks. I hadn't immediately understood.

'Tattoos. Scars. Birthmarks. That sort of thing,' Steel had clarified.

'Nothing like that.'

'And his dentist? Can you let us know who his dentist is?'

I wanted to laugh. Neither of us had been able to get an appointment with an NHS dentist in years, so we just brushed them when we remembered and hoped for the best.

'He's just ordinary,' I'd said, unhelpfully.

They were, I realised after they had gone, trying to get information out of me that would assist them in identifying a decomposing body, should one appear.

I forgot about the scar on the side of his thumb where he slashed himself with a Stanley knife opening a box of flat-pack furniture in our living room. His blood will still be between the boards of the laminate, I bet.

I forgot about the way he has a tiny bald patch in the stubble on his chin from a chickenpox scar. It looks like a little white star and no hair will grow there.

I forgot about the way he always keeps his wallet in the right pocket of his jeans, so the denim there is more faded than it is on the left.

He's got four moles on the small of his back. Tiny ones. You could join them up with a biro and make a diamond.

His feet are small for a man his size.

'Laurie? Are you going to open the door?'

I couldn't.

'Is it you?' I asked. I had been shivering. My wet hair dripping down my back. I pulled the dressing gown around me more tightly. When he didn't answer right away, I thought I must have imagined it, so I unlocked the door and he was standing there. His hair was too long. He looked thin. He smelled – I could smell him right away – of sweat and dirt and the cold outside. He didn't smell like himself.

'It's me,' he said. He wouldn't meet my eye.

'I thought you were dead,' I said.

It was like standing too near to the platform as the train rushes past: the sense of being sucked into danger, the movement of the air rocking you off your feet.

'I'm not dead,' he said. 'Can I come in? Can I be here?'

He came in. I unzipped his coat and let my dressing gown fall open and lifted his jumper over his head. I was shaking. I felt sour pre-vomit saliva in my mouth. I unzipped his jeans.

'Is this what you want?' I said.

His eyes were strange. Cloudy. Far away.

'I want to sleep,' he said.

We went to bed. I had to go on top, and he was unwashed and he stank. He just lay there like a dead man.

'You're just tired,' I said, and lifted his hand from the bed and put it on the small of my back, which was still damp from the bath.

'I am tired,' he said.

I cried all the way through it, knowing that the money he had taken from my dad's tallboy had run out and it was getting cold and he was only here because he had no other choice. He'd come crawling back, as I'd hoped he would, but not to me. He hated himself. His cock went soft after a while and I made myself come by rubbing and pressing against his pubic bone, keeping going even after he'd slipped out.

'I don't know what to say to you,' I said afterwards, wiping my face on the sheet. I always hated it when I came and he didn't. It felt as if he was stealing something from me. He knew I didn't like it. That's why he did it. Before he left, I'd been through a phase of faking my orgasms. Not faking having them, but faking not having them. But it never worked. He could always feel it, he said, my muscles holding and squeezing his fingers or his cock. My body gave me away.

'I didn't expect that,' he said. He closed his eyes and went to sleep and I lay there wound in my sheet, staring at him.

After a while, we got up and Mark went for a shower. I followed him into the bathroom, trailing the sheet like I was a girl in a film, and watched the dirt run off him as the grey water circled the plughole and washed away. His toenails were black and there were bruises on his legs.

'Where have you been?' I asked.

He soaped his hair and looked through me. I plucked at my shroud.

'Let's not do this now,' he said.

I didn't dare ask him again.

'Your mother's here,' I said. 'She's gone out to get a coat. She could be back any minute.'

'She's here?'

'She came to look for you, Mark,' I said. There was a tone in my voice that he didn't like, I could tell. So I took a breath and got rid of it. I smiled. I did. I smiled.

'She'll just need a bit of warning, that's all. She's going to be so happy. But we don't want her to be so happy that she has a heart attack, do we?'

I hadn't told him about my dad. I hadn't told him about Olena or Eddie or anything else that had happened. It had only been a couple of hours.

Mark turned the shower off and I passed him a towel. He wrapped it around himself and I stayed where I was, sitting on the closed lid of the toilet and looking at him. He was thin. Had he been sleeping rough? Should I ask him if he needed a doctor?

'Laurie?'

'Yes?'

I would have given him anything that he asked for. I would have gone back to bed with him and never brought up the matter of his time away ever again if that was what he wanted. I would have cooked for him. I would have sent Mavis away or let her live with us. I would have held his tired feet in my hands and cut his nails and rubbed cream into the sore places.

'What is it Mark? What can I do for you?'

'A bit of privacy? While I get dressed? Are my clothes still here?'

Sometimes in a marriage it is important not to show that your feelings are hurt. My mother taught me that. They may be hurt, but you don't show it.

I smiled brightly. Brightly. My lips stuck to my teeth and my cheeks felt as if my mouth was crammed with pebbles.

'I folded them. I put them away. They're all really nice and tidy. Shall I bring them?'

He nodded.

When Mavis came back, she screamed at him for fifteen minutes. Called him a cunt and a bastard and a fucker and all sorts. I'd heard her swear before but this was something else. I was glad of it, really. Those were words that needed saying, and I couldn't afford to be the one who said them. Mark sat quietly through the swearing, his head bowed. He was waterproof: the torrent just rolled off him.

When she ran out of swearing, she held him and rubbed his head (she had to stand on tiptoes to do it) and force-fed him lasagne and cried, and demanded that he comfort her, then she swore again, and eventually she blew herself out and sat on the settee with him, red-eyed and limp and exhausted.

'Shall we sort out the sleeping arrangements?' she said. 'I can get a spare duvet from your upstairs neighbours. Shall I trot up there and do it now?'

She was like me, I think. Not wanting to let him away from her. She'd make up a spare bed for herself in the hallway, barricading the door with her body. I didn't say anything.

'We need some space, Mum,' Mark said eventually.

I hadn't showered. I was sticky between the legs and smelled, when I moved, that strange post-sex smell. A ripeness, no matter how clean you were to begin with. I sat there and smelled it and felt glad Mark was telling his mother to go. It meant – surely this is what it meant – that he wanted to be alone with me.

'Space! Space! You've had bloody months of space!'

I could see she wanted to hang on to him, in case he floated away. She hunched next to him and I hovered nearby, superfluous and anxious.

'Just for tonight. So we can all get a proper night's sleep,' Mark said. 'You'll have your own stuff to be getting on with, won't you?'

He did look tired. I wondered where he had been sleeping.

'I'm not getting on a plane until you tell me what's been going on,' Mavis said. She shook her head emphatically: her earrings jangled. 'I just won't do it. The police are still out looking for you!' It was as if the thought had only just occurred to her. 'We have to tell them you're back. Tell the doctor. Shall we phone the doctor, Laurie?' she appealed to me, her face pale. It had not taken so long for her to lose her tan, and without it she looked both greyer and older.

'Mum,' Mark said patiently. 'How about you stay at Laurie's dad's house? Just for a bit. Until we get sorted?'

This was a brilliant idea. I pushed aside a prickle of disquiet: I had not thought of this myself, and Mark had not discussed the plan with me prior to presenting it to his mother.

'I can come and see you. You can come and see us. We can have our tea together. But we . . .' he nodded his head towards me without moving his eyes, 'Laurie and I have things to sort out.'

She made a tiny harrumphing sound in her throat.

'I suppose you'll be wanting me to start packing right now,' she said. She had a fold of the jumper he was wearing clasped between her fingers and was tugging at it unconsciously. I tried to feel gently towards her: this was the boy she had walked with through the park every day on a pair of red leather reins until he went to school – in all weathers – just because he liked saying hello to people's dogs. She'd done that, and she hated walks, and bad weather, and being damp, and most of all, dogs. She'd done that. But inside I was saying, *yes, yes, start packing now.*

He slept that night. Thirteen hours. And I didn't. I watched him in the dark. Counted his breaths. Ran my hands over him as if he was a corpse I was trying to revive. He was thin and warm and home. I didn't dare close my eyes. When he woke up, he was rested and calm, though still quiet, and I was about as wrecked as I had been in the days after he'd first vanished.

Sapphire and Steel came round while we were still eating breakfast. I'd cooked sausages for him. Real coffee. They took their hats off at the door and Sapphire turned the volume down on her radio. Still, they would not take any tea or coffee. They'd probably had that covered in their training – they'll see all types, many of whom would have a grudge against the police and might spit in their mugs, or even worse. I was jangling that morning, scrubbing the front of the kitchen cupboards with a cloth and cleaning the fat spatter off the tiles behind the cooker while the kettle boiled. I flew around the house like a moth.

'You can just sit down, Mrs Wright,' Sapphire said, but her tone was neutral. No sense of relief or congratulations. No remorse for the way she had suspected me. Nothing.

See, I wanted to say. *See! I'm not a murderer!*

We sat down. Mark stared into his coffee mug. He was having it black now. He never used to have it black. I'd made him a milky one and he'd thrown it away and made himself another and I had to go into the bathroom and have my tearful overreaction to that in private and in as near to silence as I could muster.

'This is what we call a Safe and Well check,' Sapphire said, talking to Mark and ignoring me entirely. 'And on the completion of it, we close the case. Do you understand?'

Mark nodded humbly. Shame was coming off him in waves.

'I'm safe and well,' he said.

Steel nodded and cleared his throat.

I had been waiting for this. I knew Mavis would be on the phone as soon as she got to my dad's house. And the police – they would ask their hard questions and take no evasions. They'd have training, I decided – specialised training at winkling the truth out of reluctant suspects. There were things in his head that they would want and that I had a right to know, and if they were the ones who worked it out of him, who made him entirely transparent to us all, well, then he couldn't blame me for it and I would have my answers.

'We're not here to get into the whys and wherefores,' Steel said. 'We just need you to confirm your identity. Can you give us your date of birth, pal?'

Mark did, never lifting his eyes from the floor. He had his shoes on. Was he planning to go out?

'It doesn't matter about the money,' I said quickly. 'The money from my dad's. Nobody wants to press charges. Nobody wants to take it further.'

Mark lowered his head.

'That's between yourselves, given the circumstances,' Sapphire said. She meant seeing as my father – the owner of the money – was dead. Mavis had been thorough. But Mark didn't know that yet. I didn't want to put him under any more stress.

'Thank you,' Mark said, and that was it.

'Well, we'll leave it there for today.' They stood up. I saw them to the door and, once I had closed it, through the spyhole I watched them disappear along the hallway toward the lift. They were chatting to each other. Something to do with a programme they had both watched on the television the night before. I heard their voices and the crackle of the radios fade as they drifted away towards the lift. Sapphire laughed, and then they were gone.

I turned around and leaned against the door. My limbs shook and I heard the blood crashing and rushing in my ears, like the sound of the sea you can sometimes hear inside a big shell. I wanted to kill them. I wanted to open the door and run after them and tear them into pieces and throw them down the lift shaft and call the lift and have it slowly crush them into nothing. In the living room, Mark turned on the television. I took three deep breaths and rubbed my hands over my face and smiled before I went back in to him.

15

We had a lot of sex during that time, and it was very strange sex, even by our standards. We didn't talk about the power station, or nuclear disasters, or the certainty of worldwide population collapse. We didn't talk at all. He didn't ask me what I wanted, or if I was sure, or if I thought I'd had too much to drink, or if we should think about getting some rest so we could be fresh in the morning. He didn't ask me if I liked it and, if he came first, he didn't tie himself in knots trying to finish me off so I wouldn't sulk. He just did it, and so did I, and it was frequent and brutal and often horrible – lonely, I think; lonelier than I have ever been, anyway. Just two people rutting away on each other, in the same bed. He'd put a pillow over my face sometimes: just so I wouldn't be able to look at him. But we didn't stop.

It had been bad before he left too, of course. Sometimes it got so bad I would shout at him. In my special nightie, which I'd bought to try and help with the hardness problem.

'What is it? What is it about me that you don't want?'

He'd sigh elaborately.

'You said. You said we could have another baby. When I was ready.' I put my hand on my hip. 'Well, I'm ready now.'

'Laurie . . .'

I opened my eyes wide so that the tears that were forming didn't overspill and fall down my cheeks.

'You said, Mark. You said.'

He sat up in bed and reached for his jogging bottoms. Put them on awkwardly without looking at me.

'If we're going to be up all night having a row about this, can I just go and get a drink first?' he'd say, and disappear into the kitchen. Sometimes he'd put his shoes on in the living room and leave the flat entirely, claiming he'd just gone to the garage, or he'd forgotten he was on an early shift. He became evasive like that – sly – slipping through my fingers and denying he was doing it until I felt mad with rage.

But now he was back, and we were so often in bed, my hands and eyes and mouth full of him. I had imagined that body dead so many times and in so many ways. In the sea, on a beach, under a bridge, in a car parked in the woods, in an alley, on a mattress in some stinking squat somewhere, in pieces on a train line, gently rotting in a lift shaft, sunk forever in concrete on a building site – that every time I woke up I wanted to reach out and grab him and have his mouth on mine, his tongue on my skin, his sweat dripping into my eyes, his come inside me. Every time.

I think we went nocturnal, or, worse than that, turned ourselves into babies who would sleep a few hours, get up and eat and want some comfort, then go back to sleep again. I refused to go to work; refused to let him out of my sight. Mavis, who was desperate for a task, said she'd call Shaw and explain everything. I didn't care about anything else and it went on like that for a couple of weeks – the fucking and ordering in of pizza, the dozing and the waking up at three in the morning to fuck again and watch terrible films on Freeview channels we'd never needed to try before.

We made ourselves sick and sore and lethargic with it, and only showered and put clothes on when Mavis turned up to have her tea with us. When Mavis came round she brought us food, otherwise I think we would have starved. During those times, we ate like animals and talked about nothing. We chatted about the weather; Mavis as terrified to press Mark about where he had been as I was. She hinted that she had a man-friend in Portugal who was missing her, and that she might be going home soon, and while she lingered over her apple crumble and custard I would gaze at my husband, slack-eyed and wet with lust, counting the seconds until she got the fuck out of my house.

Some nights, no matter how well my husband fucked me, I couldn't sleep at all. I was afraid of my dreams. I was having bad ones about dropping something important over a cliff, or losing something under the wheels of a lorry, then being brought up in court to explain myself. Always, always, I woke at the same point – just as the conviction that I was innocent – that the entire business was an accident, just a terrible misunderstanding – gave way to the horror of my guilt. I used to wake Mark up when I had dreams like this, then I stopped falling asleep and just passed out drunk instead. After he came home, I thought I should do things differently, so instead of bothering him with my nonsense, I got up out of the bed and crept into the living room to surf the internet. I thought I'd managed to sneak away without waking him, but he came in.

'What are you doing?'

I closed the lid of the laptop. 'Nothing. I couldn't sleep.'

'It's late. Aren't you cold?'

I was, but I didn't move. Mark came over to me and gently eased the laptop out of my hands. Opened its lid and looked at the articles I had been reading.

'Connie Fallon again? You still doing that?' he said quietly, as if what I did or didn't do was no longer of direct concern to him. His interest, if I could put it that way, was mild and intermittent. Incidentally, *mild and intermittent* describes the ideal and precise conditions for addictions to form. That's why people whose first experiences of gambling involve winning just a few pounds on fruit machines are more likely to get hopelessly hooked than those who lose the lot or make it big-time on the first attempt.

'Her mother is still in prison,' I said. I remembered the time we'd gone out and got drunk together on our tenth wedding anniversary, and Mark – my defective fruit machine – had said 'you'd get less for murder' and we'd toasted it. 'She's appealed twice. She must have started talking to her solicitor.'

He made a noise in his throat. Not interest, precisely, just a grunt of acknowledgement, so I couldn't accuse him of ignoring me and get angry about it. I know his noises.

'Maybe there's new evidence,' I said. 'Maybe she didn't do it at all.'

'Why do you look that stuff up?' he said. 'Why's it so important to you?'

'I want to know how she was caught,' I said. 'Whether she confessed first or her husband changed his mind about protecting her and dropped her in it. Whether they had some CCTV footage or an anonymous tip-off. Whether they found some of her things,' I paused, and spoke carefully. 'Not at their home. But at his workplace. Her shoes and her school bag at his place of work.'

Mark looked at me as if he didn't understand what I was saying. I wanted to remind him about Joyce and her prediction for us and was using her words deliberately and very carefully, but he should have remembered that on his own. He should have cherished that strange misunderstanding that triggered our entire time together, as I had done, and me bringing it up now wasn't going to repair the fact that he had forgotten it entirely. He put his hand on my head and I looked up at him.

'Mum told me about your dad,' he said.

'Yes.'

'I'm sorry. I wasn't here for that. The funeral,' his hand was still on my head and he moved his fingers through my hair.

'Sorry?'

'I know. Not enough.'

'Well, try a bit harder then,' I said. 'You haven't asked me how I was when you were away. About what it was like for me. You haven't asked me anything at all.'

'I know. I'm sorry. How was he? What happened?' He was trying very hard. I could see that. I could see what an effort it was for him, to open the door to hearing about my feelings again. This was a man who had been up close to the worst of my feelings for a very long time.

'He was unwell,' I said. 'Another stroke.'

He nodded. Mavis had already told him all of this, of course. I watched him search for something else to say.

'And how's Olena?'

'She's in trouble,' I said, then I changed my mind. 'She's fine.'

'I'm sorry,' he said again. He didn't ask what kind of trouble Olena was in. I wanted him to, and he didn't. He didn't ask about me. About all those nights I sat up on the balcony waiting for him. About the nights I wandered through town, thinking I would die if he wasn't safe at home in our bed when I finally got back.

'It doesn't matter. It's fine.'

What else was I supposed to say? I wanted him to stay. He'd done something too big to get over. So I had to pretend it wasn't there, and he had to pretend he didn't know I was pretending, and those were our choices if we wanted to keep hold of each other.

'It matters,' he said. We stayed there like that for a moment, me just looking at him. He put his finger into the side of my mouth. I touched it with my tongue. He pulled, and I stood up, and I let him lead me back into our bedroom like that, his finger inside my cheek like a hook.

Another night, I woke to find him not in bed with me. I crashed out of our bedroom, my heart in my mouth. The flat was in darkness, except for a yellow light around the door of the smallest room.

'Are you in there?' I said.

'Yes. Go back to sleep.'

'I'm not tired.'

I didn't open the door. Didn't go inside. I stood still and held my breath to hear him in there, rustling and moving things.

'Don't mess about in there,' I said. 'I've got things how I want them.'

There was no answer. And because I could not go inside – not now, not sober and awake and in front of my husband – I went back to bed and stared at the sagging curtain until he came back.

One evening, very late, Olena called. I was asleep and the vibrating phone under my pillow woke me – Mark was out cold and I sneaked away out of the bedroom to talk to her. I had, I remembered, promised myself that I would ring her and make sure she was all right, and since Mark had arrived my entire messy and complicated world had shrunk down to the pinprick of his presence and approval. I do see that now.

'He's back,' I said. 'Mark's come home.'

I expected her to say something. To give me advice or comfort me. To offer congratulations. But she only sighed.

'That's good,' she said.

'It's very late, Olena.'

'I know. I can't sleep. I have been waiting up,' she said.

'What for?'

'The knock on the door. I hear it sometimes, when I am sleeping, and I wake up expecting them there, with a battering ram at the door, but nobody is there. So I get up and I drink coffee and I clean other people's houses and I work on my dissertation and at night I go to sleep and go back to waiting for them.'

'Have they been in touch with you?'

'Nothing.'

'And what's your sister said?'

'She doesn't know anything. Maksym, he had some unpleasant friends. The police are probably speaking to them. Searching for a man with a grudge. A man of his type – the police perhaps are not working too hard.'

'Well, there you go.'

I wanted to ask her how she'd done it. A saucepan to the head. Her hands around his throat. Perhaps she'd stabbed him or poisoned him or pushed him down the stairs. I wanted to ask her how she'd got his body into the woods, and if she'd put on her party dress and gone to the wedding reception afterwards. I wanted to know if her daughter had been in the house when it happened, or out playing with a skipping rope in the car park in front of the apartments. I could imagine these and many other scenarios, but perhaps it was better not to know.

'It might not be so bad to be in prison,' she said quietly. 'I could go and give myself up. The relief of it, after all this time. It would be like driving my car from a cliff. Better to do it quickly. Not think about it too much. Then it would be over. The fall would be bad, but it would be over quickly. A firm landing. At least I'd be on solid ground. No more of this wondering.'

'No more life,' I said.

I had moved from the bedroom into the living room as we spoke, and I was sitting there in the dark, whispering into the phone, when Mark came in. He was still fuzzy and ruffled from sleep.

'Who is it?' he mouthed. I waved my hand at him. 'Is it Mum?'

'I've got to go,' I said to her. 'I'll phone you in the morning.'

'Laurie, don't leave me like this . . .' she said, or something like it, but I was already ending the call.

Back in the bedroom, Mark got into bed. I followed him. He was sitting up, looking at me, and I let him watch as I, without explaining what I was going to do or why, pulled the wobbly bedside table out from the wall, put it against the window and stood on it while I fixed the fucking curtain.

'See. There it is. Didn't take half a minute,' I said, jumping down.

'Right,' he said. He had no idea. I know that at the time I was trying to prove a point to him: to demonstrate how easy it would have been for him to help me out with something that was bothering me – and how neglectful he'd been in refusing to do it. And now? Now all I see is how much of a fuss I'd made over something that I obviously could have done for myself all along.

'You don't have to be like that. I'm allowed to have friends. Allowed to talk on the phone to them.'

'I didn't say you weren't. It's good you're talking to people. How is Olena?'

'She's fine. Full of the joys of spring.'

It is a habit of mine, I see, to weaponise my hurt, then get furious when the shrapnel I throw out doesn't garner me any comfort. But I didn't know it then – I only knew that I felt hurt and abandoned and unhinged with fury, the way babies are when they are not fed as soon as they'd like.

'Are you upset about your dad?' Mark said. 'Do you want to talk about it?'

Things were going back to how they had been before he left. He'd had this way of speaking – almost robotic – that meant even when he was saying something, it felt like silence. I once told him that living with him was like living with a bag of cement, and it was. And he was doing it again.

'Why would you take even a minor interest in what things have been like for me these past few months? In all the shit you've left me to deal with on my own while you've been . . . whatever it is you've been doing. What have you been doing? Where have you been? Do *you* want to talk about it?'

If he'd sit there and take it from Mavis, he could take it from me. I was owed that. Entitled. It's a horrible word, but I did feel it to be true. He didn't reply.

'God knows what you've been up to. Were there others? Just tell me that, Mark. Were there others?'

'It's late, Laurie. Do we have to do this now?'

He sighed wearily, leaving the argument we were about to have to be my fault. He'd join in if I insisted on it, but only if I'd agree upfront that it was my idea. Evasive, that's what he was. But I was not drunk: that was different. I was stone-cold sober, as I had been for so many of the nights since Mavis had come to live with me. It made a difference.

'Were there? Just tell me that.'

He nodded. 'Yes. If that's what you want. Yes, there were others.'

It didn't hurt. I thought it would but it didn't. I was angry that it didn't hurt. *If that's what you want.* It was another way of saying something without saying anything. It could mean: *yes, I slept with other women.* It could just as equally mean: *I will tell you whatever you want to hear, regardless of whether it is true or not.* It meant: *you will never know.*

'How many? Lots?'

He shrugged.

I waited, lifting my chin, for him to ask me the same question. I would tell him, I thought, I'd tell him all about the man with the sweaty shirt who I picked up in the nightclub. *In this bed*, I'd say, and imagined myself pounding on the mattress with my fist like a judge with a gavel. I'd make him cry. Then he'd be sorry. Then I would comfort him, and things would be all right. *Right in this bed.*

I waited for him to ask but he only got out of bed and went into the kitchen to get himself a glass of water. I got under the covers, listening to the water run and the cupboard door open and close, biting back the words I wanted to say in case they made him go away again. When he came back I pretended to be asleep, and listened to him pretending to sleep. He always did fall asleep before me, and I could pinpoint when it happened – a sudden heaviness in the arm or leg that he'd draped across me, and a change in his breathing.

I must have drifted off at some point, unable to keep watching him in the dark, which was newly complete now I had fixed the curtain. I missed the moment when he drifted and had one of my dreams – a very bad one. When I opened my eyes it was morning and the bed was empty and I fell into a panic.

He was only sitting in the living room, drinking coffee and staring at the television. At that time the local news was full of reports about the anti-fracking protests and he seemed enthralled by the images on the screen.

'I didn't know where you were,' I said. My throat felt as though someone had their hands around it. He glanced at me.

I think it wasn't just the once that I woke up in a panic like that. There was a whole run of mornings where I slept late and woke in an empty bed, my head and heart pounding.

'I didn't want to wake you.'

'You can wake me. Wake me,' I said. I perched on the edge of the armchair, feeling the cold in my bare feet, the muscles in my abdomen, knotted up in panic, gradually unclench.

He leaned back.

'All right. Fine. I'll wake you.'

It was the sigh that did it. He was being tolerant – patient – and more than that, he wanted me to know it. He was making an accommodation. It wasn't that he wanted to wake me. But he'd do it because it was what I wanted, and it would keep me happy. How was it possible that an agreement to do what I wanted worked – as all of his moves did – to keep me at arm's length rather than to bring me close? A rage flared in me so quickly I had to hold my teeth together to stop myself from screaming.

'Aren't you supposed to be going back to work today?' he asked. He nodded towards the television. It was nearly eight. 'You're going to be late.'

Overhead, the baby started crying. Our eyes met. I didn't acknowledge it.

'I'll ring in sick. Take a day off.'

I wanted to suggest a day out. A pub lunch. Chips on Morecambe seafront. Fancy coffees that cost three pounds in the sort of Staff Wanker-ridden city centre café we'd never usually be seen dead in. But more than that, I wanted him to suggest these things. Any of these things. I had what he would say all planned out in my head before he had a chance to speak.

'We can't afford for you to get sacked. You've had a lot of time off,' he said.

I held myself very still. The hypocrisy of this was astonishing. But if I brought it up, we'd argue about that instead of his remoteness. Which is of course what he wanted – that distraction. So I did what he was so good at doing and made it clear by the look on my face that I had *plenty* to say, but was going to be very, very kind and let it pass. I was rising above it. And he had to be nice to me now because of that.

'It doesn't matter,' I said, but he was right. Shaw's patience would only stretch so far, no matter what Mavis had told her. 'We could go out?'

'If you want,' he said, and turned back to the television.

'You're not here,' I said.

He sighed.

'I'm here.' He gestured towards himself, sitting there in his jogging bottoms and stained T-shirt, the coffee mug resting on his lap, the remote in easy reach. 'I'm right here.'

'No, no you're not.' My voice was sliding upwards – I could hear it, whining and wheedling. I could see – of course I could – why spending the day with me would not have been an attractive prospect. 'You ran out of money. You didn't have anywhere else to go. All right sleeping rough when it's summer. Not so much fun in autumn, is it? That's why you came back.'

'You didn't want me to come back?'

'I *still* want you to come back. You're in the flat. You're on the settee, in my bed, but you're not *here*. You're like a fake using my husband's skin. You're doing an impression of him. But it isn't you.'

I sounded like my father. I know this. Knew it at the time: how crazy it sounded, insisting that he was some kind of impostor, an automaton manufactured in the shape of the man I had married, but not the real thing.

'I don't know what you want,' he said. 'Tell me what you want.'

'It's like living with a shop dummy,' I said. 'You ask me what I want but you don't want anything. What do you want? Tell me what you want. I know what you want. You want me to go to work and leave you alone, sitting here in peace. You want me to be quiet. You don't want . . .'

Katrina's baby carried on crying. He stood up and left the room, leaving me standing there in the kitchen doorway.

'Don't pretend to me that you can't hear that noise!' I shouted, then held my breath, waiting for the sound of the front door. No, it was all right, he didn't have his shoes. I spent most of my days in mad calculations like this, always knowing where in the flat his wallet and keys were, which pair of shoes he was wearing, where his coat was. The work of surveillance was constant and it exhausted me. But I could not stop doing it. I heard the swish of the shower curtain and the water being turned on. The baby's wailing grew louder. Maybe it's me, I thought. Maybe it's all the racket I made down here, upsetting it.

'You could have asked me,' I called through the closed bathroom door. 'You could have asked me if I wanted to have the day off work and do something with you. You could have woken me up. You could have asked me if I wanted to come in the shower with you. You used to ask me things like that.'

I waited. There was no answer and I banged on the door in frustration. He'd only claim he hadn't heard me over the sound of the shower running – that he wasn't ignoring me and couldn't be held responsible for me not speaking up and saying what it was I was after. I could imagine what he'd say – that it wasn't his job to do the wanting but my job to be worth wanting. And all this talk about who wanted what and whose job it was to do the work of wanting would send us round and round in circles until we sat in different rooms, me with my books, and him in front of the television, deliberately not asking me what had happened to his laptop.

'You could have asked me who I was talking to on the phone the other night!' I shouted.

'I did ask you. I asked you!'

'You didn't ask *enough*!'

I started to cry. I hated myself when I was like that. I needed him to sit me down and hold my hand and talk me back into myself. To take my clothes off and go inside me very hard, even if I was being reluctant and not entirely in the mood. He should have said: 'I need you now,' and told me all my worries were just my feelings, and that they would pass. I wanted him to say, 'Of course I'm here, Laurie. I'm home,' and he should have said it in such a way that it left no room for doubt.

'I'm having a shower, Laurie. Am I not allowed to have a shower?'

'Fine. Have your shower,' I said. I waited silently, counting in my head. I'll give him a minute, I thought. And in a minute he'll change his mind and act better. But he didn't.

I dressed in the bedroom, weeping and humiliated, and went to work without saying goodbye. Not because I wanted to, but because I hoped he would emerge from the bathroom and wonder where I had gone – to feel that stab of loss and fear and terror that I felt every time I opened my eyes in the morning and he was not there sleeping beside me. *Let him know what it feels like*, I thought, sitting on the bus with my phone in my hand, checking to see if he had tried to call me. But he had not called and he did not know what it felt like – to be so petty and helpless and child-ish, as I had become.

I'm all right, I said to myself, as the bus rounded the corner and came onto campus. The big sign advertising the university's achievements had been changed: they did it once a term or so. *Our scientists are working on a cure for Alzheimer's*, it used to say. *Our scientists are devising a method for the counting and measuring of black holes*, it said that morning.

And I had been all right when he was away. I had cooked and I had paid the rent and I had got to work and – apart from one or two incidents of regrettable behaviour, entirely understandable given the strain I was under – I had coped with everything that had happened to me admirably. Anyone watching me from the outside – seeing me doing ordinary things like wrapping my sandwiches in cling film and washing out plastic milk bottles and taking them down to the recycling bin, sitting on the bus and arriving at work only a little bit late – would have said the same thing. They would have been in awe of me. I comforted myself like this.

When I got back to the house that evening, Mark was packing.

'What is this?'

'I can't . . .' he said.

'You can't what?'

I tried to catch his eye but he wouldn't look at me. His holdall was on the bed and he was stuffing clothes into it – pulling his T-shirts and jeans from the dirty-washing chair and shoving them in without folding them.

'My mum's going back home. I'm going to go with her for a bit. Take some time out. She's booked me a flight.'

I dropped my work bag. Mavis. Of course she'd be on his side. He was her blood. She was only kind to me to get to him. I thought I saw it all very clearly and, breathless with pain, I positioned myself in the doorway between the bedroom and the hall. I would stop him.

'I'll come with you. Give me a minute. Let me phone work. A holiday is a brilliant idea.'

I made my face look happy and hopeful. The kind of face that he would not dare to disappoint – a naked vulnerability only a monster would be able to crush. That's what I did.

'Will it be sunny? What shall I pack?'

I had a vision then, of us sitting together on a beach somewhere. I'd never been to the Algarve but the postcards Mavis sent now and again gave a nice impression of what it was like. Just the place. Good weather and cheap drinks and fresh fish. In that part of Portugal, Mavis said, they don't have duvets on the beds, only sheets and blankets because even in winter you don't need to wrap up too warm. We'd be away from everything. Mavis would look after us and with our little city and sad flat thousands of miles behind us, and Mark under my eye always, I would be able to relax and things would get better.

'No, Laurie. Just me,' he said. I let myself crumple against the wall, acting as if he had punched me.

'You can't,' I said.

But all the things I usually did to show Mark that he needed to make me feel better did not work. I cried. I shouted. I ricocheted between trying to make him feel sorry for me in my grief and frightening him by threatening to divorce him and throw whatever stuff he left in the flat out of the window. I told him if he left I would never allow him back in, and never speak to him ever again.

He was immovable. A stone.

'I've got to,' he said. 'I can't go on like this any more. You can't say you're happy either, can you? This will be better for you too, even if it doesn't feel like it right now.'

'Is that it?' I said. 'Did you just come back to make a better job of leaving me?'

He shrugged. 'I don't know. I don't know what I'm meant to do here. Just let me . . .' He tailed off. What was he going to ask me for? All he wanted was not to be around me – and he didn't need to ask for that. All he needed to do was take his passport out of the kitchen drawer (I tried to snatch it from him and he held my wrist tightly until I was forced to let it go) and walk out of the flat with his holdall over his shoulder.

'How long have you been planning this?' I said. 'Do you hate me that much?'

'I didn't plan anything,' he said, pulling down his coat from the hook in the hallway.

'Just tell me where you were. Tell me what you were doing when you were away all that time. I know you took my dad's money.'

He zipped up his jacket.

'I did. I did take it. And I bought a train ticket. And I went to Brighton. As far away as I could . . .'

'From me?'

'From you. From here,' he waved his hand around, 'from that little room I'm not allowed to go into. From all of it. I just wanted some . . . space. Can't you understand that?'

'I could tell the police I've changed my mind and I do want to press charges. You stole my dad's money.'

He shrugged. 'You could. You should, if that's what you want to do.'

'They'll question you. They'll want to know everything.'

I thought of him with his little feet under the interview table, his chapped hands clasped on top of it. *No comment.*

'What were you up to? In all this space of yours? I have a right to know.'

'You don't, Laurie. You really don't. You don't have a right to open up my head and have a root about inside whenever you feel like it, you know.'

'I don't know who you are.'

'No,' he said. He'd picked up his keys and his mobile phone – that was something, at least – and tucked them into his pockets. He really was going. 'No, you don't.'

'Tell me what you did.'

I was past caring, I think. But if he was here, in front of me, talking to me, then he wasn't on his way to Portugal.

'I stayed in a B and B. I got some bar work. I drifted around. I slept rough sometimes.'

'Was there a woman?'

I'd asked him before, but this time I was determined to get a straight answer, and I think he knew that.

'There were women. Sometimes. At the beginning.' He stepped towards me and touched my hair. 'I thought it would help. It didn't.'

He was trying to be kind. I could see that.

'Was that what you were planning? To just fuck off and leave me to go on a seaside jaunt? Shag your way along the south coast? Was that it?

'I didn't plan. I just . . . drifted.'

'And what are you doing now? Drifting again? Are you going to come back? Is that us done?'

'Laurie. Would you just . . .?

He didn't finish the sentence, and because I was standing in the doorway of the flat and would not move, he edged past me, knocking me gently with his bag, and leaving the door open behind him.

I phoned him. I phoned hundreds of times. I phoned Mavis too. Nothing. I waited a day then started phoning again but they still would not answer and I couldn't speak to their black sounds. I didn't get drunk. He and Mavis would be expecting me to do that. Olena too, probably. All expecting me to do as I had done before, and spend all evening knocking back wine and pacing on my balcony. So I didn't get drunk. Not because I wanted to be better, to do better. But because I wanted to spite them – to prove to them that I was better than the way they imagined me. Instead, I phoned Joyce. I grabbed my laptop and mobile and just did it without thinking about it. It was late, but she picked up her phone after three rings. Like the sex lines and the suicide helplines, these sorts of telephone psychics must do most of their business in the night-time hours.

'It's me,' I said. 'I rang before.'

'Did you?' she said, warmly. Not recognising my voice, but not admitting to it either. 'What are you after, love?'

'A reading, please,' I said. No chitchat this time. No messing about. 'How much?'

I transferred the money with my PayPal and heard her clicking and tapping as she checked her account.

'Right love, that's gone through. Give me a minute to get myself tuned in.' I heard her breathing deeply.

'A loved one, is it?'

No shit.

'That's right. My husband. He's not here. He's gone. He's . . .' I felt the catch in my throat and swished it back with a swig of tea. 'I rang before. I wasn't very . . . nice. But you said that talking about a lost loved one might help. You said that. So I'm ringing again.'

'Recent, was it?' Joyce is all business.

I nodded, and gulped. 'Yes. He was . . . he . . .' I wasn't playing fair with her. I know that. But she was getting paid all the same.

'Right. You don't tell me anything, love. I tell you. That way you know it's coming from him.' She huffed and sighed again. I pictured her in the black and silver dress she wore at Sharon's wedding, her posh hairdo coming slightly undone. She might have been in her working clothes – I imagined a turban and a purple cape – or more likely, in some hippo pyjamas and fluffy slippers, sitting on her pleather settee with the telly on mute but still playing the film she'd been looking forward to. I rearranged my pillows and made myself comfortable.

'Have you tuned in? Is he with you?'

'I've something with me. A movement in the air. A heaviness behind my shoulder,' she said thoughtfully. 'It could be him.'

'I feel something, in the house sometimes. My flat. It gets cold. The doors open. I thought it was just me. Forgetting things. But . . .'

What did I want from her? Not this.

'They don't want to hurt you, love. It might seem like that, if they're getting frustrated at being ignored, but they never want to hurt the living. You can invite them in, or you can ask them nicely to go on to what's next for them.'

'What do they want?'

'This one, this one wants to tell you he loves you very much. That he was taken too soon, and he knows it's been very hard for you. But he's in a place of peace now. He wants to say that love never ends, and that you should, when you're ready, move on with your life with his blessing.'

I thought of Mark getting waited on hand and foot by Mavis the Betrayer. Sunning himself on the veranda of her apartment. Drinking cocktails in beachside bars every night. A place of peace indeed.

'I don't want to move on with my life,' I said.

She made an understanding noise in the back of her throat.

'He says he understands that, love. He knows how hard it is. He didn't want to leave you. Was it an unexpected passing?'

'Yes,' I said. But only because I wasn't paying attention.

'I'm getting the feeling of a very loving man. A protective man. Does that ring a bell for you?'

'That was his job. He was in security. A nuclear power station.'

'Ah,' she said. She sounded gratified. 'Well, there you go. A man more concerned with the safety of others than his own comfort. He's still watching over you.'

I'm not stupid. Please don't think that. But I cried anyway.

'Are you still there?'

I wiped my face with the sleeve of my dressing gown.

'I'm here. We've spoken before, you know. Years ago. You met him.' I laughed a little. 'You had a bit of an argument with him, actually. He didn't believe in all this kind of thing.'

'Not many do,' she said, amused. 'Scepticism is a good thing.'

'You said we were made for each other. A special connection.

Something like that. You thought we'd been together for years but we'd only met that night. It was a wedding.'

'Did I say all that?' She was polite, warm, uncomprehending. And underneath all that, suspicious. She would get a lot of piss-takers in her line of work. 'I've been to a lot of weddings in my time. And on a couple of drinks . . .'

'You were telling us about your work. You were . . .' I chose my words carefully, 'hearing from a little girl. Connie Fallon. She was in the news at the time.'

'I remember her,' Joyce said. She was noncommittal. 'A sad business. Very sad.'

'Did she know?'

'Did she know what, lovely?'

'When she spoke to you, did she tell you?' I was getting upset again. 'Did she know it was her mum that had done it to her?'

'What a thing to ask.'

'I was wondering. If she was sad about not being alive. If she was upset that her own mother hadn't wanted her. Can you pick up on that kind of thing?'

Joyce sighed deeply. I heard the rustle of a page being turned. She might have been making notes in a ledger where she kept records of all her dealings with clients, the better to serve me next time. She might have been opening a sudoku book. I'll never know.

'Let's leave Connie to rest, shall we? We're here to talk about you. Your husband.'

She let me cry for a while. I wiped my nose on the duvet cover.

'It's hard sometimes, isn't it? To hear from them. Do you want to leave it there?'

'Is there anything else? Does he say anything else?'

Joyce made a 'hmmm' noise, as if she was rooting through an untidy cutlery drawer looking for a corkscrew she was 98 per cent certain was in there somewhere.

'I can't say I'm getting anything. I can't. I could make it up for you, but I won't, because I don't work like that. It's a good sign. No unfinished business between the two of you. No words left unsaid. But . . .'

'What?'

'Well, I'm getting something else. Some other presence. A noisy one, this is. Young. Very young. Nothing to be scared of, but . . . wait a minute, love. I'm not getting words. Not words as such, but a . . .'

The bedside lamp flickered slightly. It does that sometimes. But it startled me, and in my fright, I hung up on Joyce. I put the phone down on the bedside table so I could see to the lamp, and the glass bulb shattered, the lamp went out, and I was left sitting in darkness.

16

I remember, after I'd tiptoed past the broken glass, looking out across the city, wondering about the broken light bulb. It meant nothing at all, and everything – both at the same time. I was too wound up and afraid to go back into the flat and I must have dozed a while on my chair on the balcony. While I was sleeping the night gave way to a cool wet morning, the lights in the houses went out and the traffic began to move. I opened my eyes to the usual noise from upstairs: the throb and wail of the baby's cry, the pram wheels being pushed backwards and forwards along the hall. Tim shouted something at Katrina then left the flat: the bang of their front door slamming closed rattled my windows.

I put a jumper on over my pyjamas and climbed the stairs. I hadn't climbed those stairs in months. The door to their flat was ajar. All the doors did that – if you banged them too hard they bounced back on their hinges and didn't close properly. The whole building had been cheaply fitted and badly designed.

'Katrina?' I called. I chapped at the door quietly a couple of times, and there was no answer. Still, the baby cried. I pushed the door fully open and took a step inside. Was it okay to go right in like that? We used to be friends. Used to be the type of friends who could turn up like this, unannounced, at odd hours. Were we still?

'Katrina?'

She was crying too – I could hear it then and I crept along the hallway and found her in the front room, pacing with the baby in her arms, his head over her shoulder. He was really screaming, kicking his legs about and thrashing his head from side to side. *How strange*, I thought, as if I was not there at all, but only watching the scene from very far away. How strange that she'd put the baby's head next to her own when he was making so much noise.

'Laurie. I'm sorry. It's his teeth. Tim's gone out for Calpol. I'm just . . .'

She dissolved into tears.

'He's just like this all the time. All the time.'

I waited in the doorway, no idea of what I was supposed to do.

'It was me banging that time,' I said.

She and Mavis must have had conversations about me during Mavis's freezer runs. Mavis would have, almost certainly, invited her down to the flat for coffee. *She'll be all right on her own turf* or, *she just needs to come face to face with the baby then things will be fine.* Something like that. But still, Katrina had stayed in her own flat and the only reason we hadn't passed each other on the stairs or in the lift more often than we had must have been because she was avoiding me too. I had made her scared of me. She was scared of saying the wrong thing and scared about what I'd do if she did. Imagining what it was like to be someone else – someone on the receiving end of me – was both difficult and painful.

'Sorry about that. About the banging.'

She didn't respond because she was still struggling with the baby. Teddy, his name was. Olena had a daughter called Alina and my friend Katrina had a son called Teddy.

'He's hot. I think he's ill but Tim says he just needs some Calpol. I don't know. What do you think? Will you feel his head?' she said. She didn't care about me banging, or not banging, or the state of me, or anything else. She cared about Teddy being ill, and shutting up, and getting to sleep, and there wasn't much room for anything else.

'I don't know what they're meant to feel like,' I said. But she was coming towards me and I stepped back because I could smell the baby: a strange hot smell of milk and powder and piss. Katrina looked like a wraith – dark-eyed and dishevelled and desperate in her dressing gown.

'I don't know. I don't know anything about . . .'

He paused in his screaming – noticing, perhaps, I was there. He turned his head and looked at me curiously, his face wet with tears and snot and saliva, his cheeks and ears red. I stared back at him. He was probably used to a warmer reception. Before I could prepare to say something, he took a deep breath and let rip.

'Here,' she said, and thrust him into my arms. He was heavier than he looked. He felt like a hot damp parcel of laundry. 'I just can't. I can't. Not for one more minute.'

She gave him to me, and I took him, and she rushed away.

I didn't really know what you were supposed do with babies. I knew you should keep their heads supported and make sure they aren't too hot or too cold, and it's better for them to have eye contact, and they like to be rocked, or talked to, or walked around a room and given interesting things to look at. I knew all these things in a second-hand sort of way because Mark and I had a book and looked various things up on websites and forums in order to get ourselves prepared. And I really wanted to put all these scraps of untried theory together and comfort Teddy, and hand him back to Katrina a few minutes later, him mollified and smiling, and me smug. But he wriggled and screamed in my arms as if I was hurting him, and I struggled to keep the blanket tucked around him and his head where it was supposed to be, and the noise – the noise up close – was really astonishing. No wonder the two of them were half barmy most of the time.

I took him over to the window and opened the curtains. The sky was almost completely light by then – it was possible to make out the dark shapes of the fells beyond the city and the distant murk of the sea in the bay to the north-west. It was the direction I always looked in myself when I was angry and sleepless

– towards the water, and the power station; to the thought, if not the sight, of Mark in his black trousers and jumper, walking slowly in the dark around the perimeter of the nuclear power station, a quarter-mile away from the centre of the reactor, pacing through the salty air, making sure all was well.

It was so strange to have a baby in my arms.

At that awful dinner with my parents and the Haworths that Mark and I had endured, I had told him and my mother I was never going to have a baby. I hadn't, in actual fact, given the matter much thought at all, but since I'd said it, and since Mark had heard me say it, we lived through an entire decade of marriage, each assuming the other was happy with the status quo.

And I think we *were* happy. I wasn't hankering. Wasn't the kind of woman who cooed over miniature clothes in shops and cried with envy at the sight of a pregnant woman in the supermarket. Nothing like that. Mark never mentioned anything, either. I imagined asking him, once or twice. But I didn't because I thought he'd talk to me about climate change, and overpopulation, and about how the human race was a vermin on the face of the earth, chewing through its resources and poisoning the air and the land and the water and the best thing we could do for the natural system we lived in and were about to capsize entirely was to stop treating diabetes and cancer and malaria, invoke a 'survival of the fittest' policy when it came to treating childhood ailments, let our population drop to sustainable levels and hope that we'd done it early enough to let the planet recover.

If he'd broached the subject with me, I might have said that we weren't the kind of people who had children. We liked our crisps and our wine and our horror films. We liked watching documentaries about interstellar travel and fucking whenever we felt like it. We weren't very clean – the bathroom was an utter disgrace – and we didn't always do the recycling, and sometimes we were a bit behind on the bills, and neither of us had what you'd call careers, and we were both terrible for saying we were going to give up smoking, then not doing it, and there were so many reasons not to bother until I was throwing up in the toilet one morning and we realised – all at once – that we were both very pleased about what had happened to us. An accident. Shock of my life. The main shock being that it turned out it was what we'd been waiting for all along.

Tim and Katrina joked that we'd got the idea from them, Teddy due in late October and our baby – we guessed, then had it confirmed that it would be a 'she' – due around Christmas. Mark made plenty of jokes about immaculate conceptions. Considered his own sperm to be equal only to God's himself. If I'd worried he might not know how to be a father, never having had an example for himself, I needn't have done. He'd planned an entire life for her. She – his daughter – was going to cure malaria. She was going to build a time machine. She was going to develop the world's first true lingua franca, which would be a language of symbols and digits, never spoken. She was going to be kind and clever and charismatic and she was going to astonish everyone in the world except for him, who knew she was going to be brilliant even before she had formed a brain stem. I thought of my father and his expectations and decided instead that I would want nothing at all for her.

Let her do nothing, I murmured to myself, like some kind of blessing. Let her do whatever she feels like. Let her life be little and of no consequence. Let her drift. Let her fester on her settee, like I do. Let her linger, anonymously, making little impact on the people she comes into contact with. Let her wait and watch and do nothing spectacular at all. Let her be forgotten by history. I wished for all those things because I knew that even if she did live her life as inadequately as that, it would be priceless to me. I wanted her to have that feeling of being loved without having to make any effort at all. *You're going to be amazing*, Mark would whisper to the bump. *You're going to be loved*, I'd say, when he wasn't around. I was so careful never to imagine her future and kept the path ahead entirely dark and blank. Was that wrong of me?

The labour hurt more than I'd imagined was possible. Everyone says that, and nobody believes it, and some things just defy description and that kind of pain is one of them. I said things. I said to Mark, between sucks on my Entonox pipe, that if there was a gun in the room I would happily shoot myself in the head with it, and he was sweating and smiling and patting my back and I wanted to murder him and the entire world and then myself with my teeth and hands, and I wanted a window to throw myself out of, a noose, a cyanide pill, then the pain came again and I wanted nothing because I was nothing – obliterated in the face of it.

The other thing that I said was that it was too much, and that her coming out was going to break me open, and I said I'd changed my mind, and I didn't want a baby any more, and I'd rather just forget about it and go home, and when I said that the midwives looked at each other and smiled – because that sort of nonsense is a sign that you're far on in your labour and that things are progressing well, and so she was going to come soon, but what they didn't know was that I meant it. I did mean it. I was there and I know.

I broke one of my nails holding on to the bar on the edge of the bed as I was pushing her out. You don't push, really – you think you do, but you don't – it's like vomiting in that your body just does it for you, no matter what you and your amazing book-worm brain feels like doing. So my body pushed and I broke my nail and my hand was bleeding. The blood was all over my fingers and the back of my hand and I looked at it, my vision flickering with pain, and I said again, *I don't want a baby any more*, and the midwife who had the Doppler on my stomach looked at me in alarm and told me to shut up and put my chin on my chest and push and I did, and I shat all over the bed sheets, and they say you won't care if that happens but I did care, and I swore I wasn't just babbling nonsense because of the gas, but I was fully in my right mind and I really and truly didn't want her. What kind of mother says that? I just wanted it all to stop and then in the next breath she was born and she didn't cry: where the terrible throb of the siren should have been there was nothing.

'Laurie? If you get him to sleep, you can put him down' Katrina said quietly. Teddy was calm. Not sleeping: I could feel his eyelashes against my neck as he blinked – but he was settled. There was a Moses basket on a stand in the corner of the living room. I stared at it.

'There was one of those in the hospital,' I said. 'When I had Sadie. But it had a metal box and a pipe underneath it – a cooling unit. It keeps the mattress really cold.'

Katrina edged towards me. She didn't touch me – and I was grateful for that – but she did put out her hand and rest it on her son's back. He turned to look at her, then buried his head back in against my neck. I felt him snuffling: the moisture from his nose and mouth making the side of my neck damp.

'I asked them about it. What it was for. I knew, but I made them tell me anyway. 'It stops Baby deteriorating,' the midwife said. I always think of that word now in a different way. *Deteriorating*. It's horrible, isn't it? My boss said it to me at work once and I had to go and throw up in the toilets and she thought it was because I was upset with her.'

Katrina put her head on one side. 'Your boss was asking you about . . . the cot?'

I shook my head gently, trying not to disturb Teddy, who was finally still, and growing heavier.

'No. My work. *The standard of your work is really deteriorating Laurie*, she said, and I just turned around and walked out of the room. I couldn't explain it. Not even to myself. Not really. That word.'

Katrina's eyes filled up but she blinked quickly and did not let them overflow. I caught myself at my old tricks again: trying to upset her. Did I really still want to hurt her – to put a bad thought in her head, in her cosy little flat with her noisy little baby and dependable little boyfriend? Did I want to throw some of the darkness in her direction? To get revenge, for that daft, awkward card she sent? I think there was still a little part of me that did.

'It's called a cold cot. They don't call it that in front of you. They just say "the cot". It's got a frill on the edge, like yours has, to hide the pipe. But I googled it when I came home. Cold cot.'

Katrina took a deep breath. It was more than a marriage could hold, this. I was too much bad weather for Mark. But for my friend? She squared herself up a bit, as if she'd been hit and was now regaining her balance. I wouldn't have cried if she'd shouted at me and told me I was sick and disgusting and should get the fuck out of her house. I would have been relieved to be treated that way because that was how I felt and how I had felt for a very long time.

'I didn't know what her name was. Your baby. Sadie. I didn't know how to ask you. It's a lovely name.'

'It's what's on the certificate. Sadie Mavis Wright.'

'Sadie Mavis Wright,' Katrina repeated quietly, as if trying to conjure up a presence.

'I have pictures of her. The midwife took pictures. I didn't want them to but she said we'd regret it if we didn't have any. I have them in an envelope in our small room. I never look at them though. Sometimes I go and hold the envelope. I can feel them inside. Otherwise I'd think I was imagining it all. That there never was a baby.'

'I'd like to see them,' Katrina said gently. 'I'd like to see what Sadie looked like.'

'She looked different. Her skin wasn't right . . . it happens, when it's like that.'

'I bet she was beautiful.'

'She had nice fingers,' I said eventually.

Teddy had gone to sleep. His head was limp and heavy but he was still snuffling and bubbling through his blocked nose. I rocked from foot to foot slightly, as people holding babies in adverts for nappies and formula milk do. I knew how to do that. Maybe that was something that had soaked in from one of the books and websites I pored over during my pregnancy. Maybe just basic nurturing instinct that I had in common with most other mammals. Even Connie Fallon's mother must have rocked her as a baby, and even Connie Fallon must have once fallen asleep in her mother's arms.

'What happened? Did they tell you?'

Nobody had ever asked me this before.

'It wasn't the cord. Wasn't a heart or a lung or a liver or a brain abnormality. They checked everything. All the chromosomes were normal. I gave up smoking as soon as I knew. I didn't drink or anything. Not even lager. Remember that leaflet we got in the class? About cheese and peanut butter and stuff? Pâté? I didn't have any of those things. I was really strict about it.'

'I didn't mean that,' Katrina said quickly. 'It wasn't your fault.'

'People did keep saying that,' I replied. 'But it must have been. Who else's job was it to look after her?'

'You didn't do anything,' she said.

'I wished for it. When I was having her. I said I didn't want to have a baby. That I'd changed my mind.'

Katrina patted at my arm. 'I said that too. I said all sorts.'

'Did you?' This surprised me.

Katrina was looking at Teddy, stroking his ear. He was properly asleep by then and she smiled and whispered: '*Everyone* says things like that. Half the women in our NCT group threatened to kill themselves, the midwives, their husbands. It makes you crazy.'

'People say you'll change your mind at the last minute,' I said, 'but they don't tell you that you'll actually mean it. I'd have felt better if the midwives had called the police, you know.'

'They never would have. Here, let me take him,' she said, and gently scooped Teddy out of my arms without waking him. The damp warmth he'd left on my neck and chest immediately grew cool. He was bigger than I had imagined. Less of a baby – nearly a toddler, in fact. The Moses basket was not what he slept in any more – I glanced at it again and saw that it was filled up with clean clothes. Perhaps Katrina was waiting for Tim to sell it on eBay or take it to a cousin or maybe she was saving it there for the next baby. The next baby! I thought of the cold cot again and turned away.

'Nobody mentioned what had happened when I got back to work. Eddie asked if I was sleeping all right. Shaw wanted to know if I was still fine to push the trolleys about or if I wanted light duties.'

'I never asked you either,' Katrina said.

'Nobody did. I thought after a bit I was going mad. That I'd just had a dream that I was pregnant. We had a funeral but it was only me and Mark and Mavis. We didn't know who else to invite.'

'I didn't know you could have funerals,' Katrina said. 'I should have asked. I didn't want to make things worse.'

'The vicar said we could stand up and say things about her if we wanted. But we didn't. We didn't say anything. She hadn't had a life.'

'She was here though.'

'I'm never sure if she was, not really.'

'What do you mean?'

'We didn't have anything to say about her. Nothing about her personality or the things she liked doing or the people she liked hanging out with. Nothing about her favourite food or favourite colour or anything like that.'

'I see what you mean,' Katrina said. 'I'm not sure I'd have known what to say either.'

I didn't reply, then Katrina came up with something.

'She was wanted. You could have said that. That you wanted her. You and Mark. Remember what he was like with the monitor? Stupid get. It was funny the first few times. Less so the fifty times after that.'

She was talking about the baby monitors we'd bought – both in the same week. Mark and Tim figured out that if they stood in the right place in the flat – in the living room it was, I think – they could use them as walkie-talkies. If Tim left theirs on and forgot about it, Mark enjoyed himself by making ghosty howling noises into the receiver and frightening them.

'I remember,' I said. I laughed, and then I started crying – a horrible noise – worse than Teddy. I put my hand over my mouth.

'It's all right. You have a cry if you want,' she said. She didn't seem frightened or upset by the noise I was making. But it occurred to me that Katrina would have a higher tolerance for crying noises than most people. If I'd told her that she'd have laughed, but I couldn't say anything at all.

'Cry as much as you want. You've earned it, Laurie.' She turned away from me and lay Teddy down on the settee.

I watched her tuck a blanket around him, my arms and legs trembling.

'You're all right,' Katrina said quietly.

'I'm not. I'm really not. I'll never be all right again. It isn't fair. That you've got all this,' I waved my hand, 'and I don't. It isn't fair.'

'No,' she said. 'That's true. And still, you're all right.'

It made no sense and yet it did, so I didn't argue with her and let her take me by my shoulders and sit me down next to her sleeping boy.

'I'm going to make you some tea,' she said. 'Keep your hand on Teddy. Don't let him roll off.'

I nodded and put my hand on his leg, through the blanket, and still, I carried on crying. She brought the tea through and I didn't drink it, and Katrina didn't say anything else, only sat on the living room floor at my feet with one of her hands on Teddy's back and the other on my knee, in case, perhaps, I started thrashing about or made a dash for the balcony. I cried for a long time.

I don't know how Katrina decided that either she or I had had enough, but eventually she got up again and came back with a toilet roll. She tore off a piece and handed it to me and I blew my nose as quietly as I could so as not to wake Teddy. She took a bit for herself.

'What time is it?' I asked.

'Breakfast time. I don't know where Tim's got to.'

'I'm sorry about all of this.'

She waved her hand, as if I was embarrassing her.

'Mark came over you know, before he went to Portugal.'

'He came up here?' I stiffened at the thought of them talking about me.

'He wanted to see Teddy. Borrow Tim's laptop. He couldn't find his and he said you'd put a password on yours. He was looking up flights.'

I was too tired to be angry with her any more. Anyway, none of this was her fault. It wasn't mine either, not all of it, but it was definitely not hers.

'He used to come up a lot, you know. Before he went. Did you know?'

I shook my head.

'We didn't talk about anything. You know what he's like. Tim would give him a bottle of beer and let him sit and watch the telly for a bit. I think . . .'

'What?'

'Don't take this the wrong way, Laurie. You know I love you, don't you?' I didn't say anything. 'I think he wanted a place where it was all right for him not to be all right. Do you know what I mean? We heard you arguing.'

I imagined myself in the flat below – mine and Mark's flat – throwing things about like a poltergeist, shrieking and drunk and crying. Why had I never considered that noise travels in both directions?

'He just came and sat up here?'

She nodded. 'He'd watch telly. Hold Teddy for a bit. He and Tim would sometimes play a bit of Xbox. That's it.'

I tried to imagine that. Mark up here while I was at work. Or in the evenings, on one of his two-hour trips to get milk and tobacco. Sitting just over my head, holding Teddy in his arms and watching the ten o'clock news, before work with someone else's family, a treasured guest in their lives.

'Listen. I think I've still got two mint choc Viennettas in my freezer from that time your mother-in-law came round and dumped a load of your stuff on me,' she said.

I stood up. 'I'll take them with me. Sorry. I should have thought. Mavis can be—'

'No. I mean, do you want one?'

'Oh. Isn't it a bit early for that sort of thing?'

'They've been talking to me all night. I'm having some even if you aren't. It won't help make things any less shit,' she laughed hollowly, 'but you can have a shit time without a slice of Viennetta, or a shit one with. And I want sugar.'

She disappeared behind the freezer door and I looked at Teddy, the way his eyelids weren't completely closed, so a tiny bit of the white of his eye showed between his eyelashes as he slept. Babies breathe faster than adults, even when they're sleeping. Did you know that? I didn't know that, and I watched his chest flutter up and down, like a butterfly beating its wings in order to dry them.

'Laurie? Do you want some?'

I nodded and tore my eyes away from the sleeping baby.

'Yes. All right then. Give me some.'

Once Tim returned from the garage with the bottle of Calpol, we drank more tea together and polished off the second block of Viennetta. They asked me to admire Teddy's bedroom and a photograph of him sitting up on his own in the bath, framed in the hallway, and I was hugged lots of times by Katrina, as if I had been away for a very long time and had only just come back. Even Tim tried to get in on it.

'What are you going to do about Mark?' he asked. 'Is he going to stay in Portugal with his mother?'

'I don't know. I think so,' I replied.

'Well, you don't have to be on your own all the time, you know. You can come over. Look at us. We don't keep regular hours. Everything goes to pot when one of these comes along,' he nodded towards Teddy, still sleeping on the settee under his blanket. 'You could come at five in the morning and we'd be up, and two in the afternoon and we'd be asleep. There's no logic to it.'

'All right, I will,' I said, almost meaning it.

I left them in their hallway, the yellow artificial light in the communal stairwell lighting their faces oddly, making them look sick and bedraggled and tired and happy, and I did not feel jealous of them.

17

When I got back home, my flat was different. I don't mean that someone had been in and stolen or rearranged things while I was out. It was more to do with the atmosphere of the place. I wouldn't say that handling Katrina's baby had taken something off my mind and left me, and my environment, feeling a little less haunted. It wasn't as if the place felt more like home again – more welcoming and safe. It just felt like . . . nothing.

My books were still on the shelves and scattered around the floor and piled up against the walls. My rubbish – the pizza boxes and Coke cans I used as ashtrays – was where I had left it on the coffee table. The wires from the television were still collecting a fur of dust and hairballs in the corner. Cobwebs had gathered along the top of the curtain rails, the glass from the bulb that exploded a few hours before was still scattered over my bedside table and floor, and the dirty-laundry chair was still filled with dirty laundry. The place looked occupied, but not loved. Not 'lived in'. It felt, for the first time in a long time, as if it would be very easy to leave.

I didn't pull the curtains and go to bed. I didn't take a shower and get ready to haul myself into work on no sleep at all. Instead, I made myself a cup of tea and went back out onto the balcony to smoke. It was properly light and cold – a real smell of autumn in the air now – and the school run and commuter traffic was starting to clot over the bridge, and now and again the sound of someone leaning on their horn floated up to me. I wondered if I was going to start crying again. The balcony was the place for it, after all.

I had done a lot of crying over those past few months but the conclusion I had come to was that there was a difference between self-pity and grief. Self-pity was much easier. There was a sticky pleasure in it that could be addictive. It was a tangled emotion, mixed in with anger and blame and resentment. Grief felt different: a much purer thing. There was no bargaining with it, no escaping or evading or manipulating or denying. If you were a stone in the way of your grief you only shattered, and in the shattering turned yourself into shrapnel that, hurled through the air by the force of the event, harmed every single fucker with the misfortune to be standing anywhere near you. That was what had happened to me and Mark. A blast big enough to wipe out a continent, and me, its resistant and malignant epicentre. For grief you have to be soft, and let it come towards you like a train, and when it hits you've got to let it knock you off your feet, and when you're down, you have to lie still, blinking, as it rumbles above your head – like the waves of a great storm at sea, or a tornado. Which after a time – a very long time – passes over.

I smoked one rollie, dropped the end in my nasty little jam jar, then made myself another. I wondered if I should give up the fags as well as the booze? I blew smoke into the cool morning air. Nah. One thing at a time.

There were two people I could call before eight in the morning and feel fairly sure they would reply. Despite everything. Despite – I'll say it – how I had been acting. Olena, and Eddie. My friends. I dialled Olena's number first.

'What is it Laurie?'

There was no urgency in her voice, only anxiety. I'd woken her up and she had reason to be afraid of early morning phone calls.

'I'm going to sell Dad's house.'

'Right.'

'We're going to split it. The money. I looked on Rightmove the other day and the one three houses down sold for two hundred and seventy grand last year.' I was talking quickly – too quickly for Olena to keep up with me. I ploughed on anyway. 'Dad's won't be worth that much. The conservatory's shot and the bathroom wants redoing. But not less than two hundred and fifty, I think.'

I earned sixteen thousand pounds a year. Olena would be on less than me, and more in need of it. I decided we could both easily change our lives with the money from my father's house. He'd be horrified not to have it in the family – his empire, his little piece of England. Maybe I'd sell it to a landlord who would fill it with international students. My father would turn in his grave. I grinned.

'Maybe more. It's got a big garden.'

'You can sell your father's house. You can do what you like with it. You don't need to tell me,' Olena said.

'Will you help me? I'll need someone to talk to the estate agents. Sort it out a bit. Take anything you want from the house. Keep the photographs for me. Other than that, just make it respectable. And we can split the money. You need it, right? For your mum. Your daughter. What's her name?'

'I've told you her name. I've told you her name hundreds of times, Laurie.'

'I know. I'm crap. I'm sorry. But will you do this for me? And let me do this for you?'

She sighed heavily. I was not sure what I'd expected. For her to shriek? Wouldn't it be like winning the lottery for her?

I was in the kitchen, the phone on speaker, kneeling on the cracked lino in front of the fridge and taking out my perishables and sorting them. I kept the items that could respectably be given to Tim and Katrina (unopened packets of cheese, a box of eggs, a brown paper bag of tomatoes) and tossed the rest (years' old jars of mustard, half a packet of butter, a bottle of brown sauce, a few Tupperware containers best left uninvestigated) directly into the pedal bin.

'You don't need to pay me to be your friend,' Olena said. 'You don't need to find some work for me to do so I can still be in your life. Is this what this is?'

'No. I don't mean it like that.'

How to explain? There was no word for the type of kin we were to each other, or how awful I was feeling for the ways — small and large — that I had hurt her, but my sense of urgency overwhelmed me and I found one.

'Sister. You're my sister from now on. I've decided. I want to share with you. Help you stay away from Dnipro, if that's what you need.'

'I can't get away from this. I'll never get away from it. The police will come, or they won't come. I'll be waiting for them for the rest of my life.'

'Your family are going to help you,' I said. 'And I'm going to help you too.'

'This isn't a film. What do you think I'm going to do? Buy a new passport and change myself into Jane Smith? Book a one-way ticket to a country with no extradition treaty?'

'Those sound like excellent ideas, Olena. But I was thinking more along the lines of a holiday. A nice rest. Finish your dissertation somewhere sunny. See how the land lies when you get back. We've all got to learn to live with a bit of uncertainty, haven't we?'

She sighed. Olena was, I had come to understand, the most unexcitable women I knew. She might as well have been English.

'Have you started drinking again, Laurie?'

I laughed, stood up and pulled the black bag out of the pedal bin. 'I am totally sober. Are you back on the fags?'

I'd heard her clicky lighter going, her puffing away while we spoke.

'That isn't the same thing,' she said.

'I've got to go. I'm going to post you the keys and some other stuff, all right?'

'Where are you going?'

'A change of air. A new chapter. Shake the dust from my feet.'

I knotted up the bag and left it in the doorway, ready to sling down the chute later. Olena's sense of propriety means she will only ever swear in Ukrainian, and she did so, wearily.

'Sisters confide in each other. They talk to each other about what's going on in their heads. If a woman has a mad plan, then she shares that plan with her sister so her sister can tell her she is a lunatic, and grieving, and needs to leave it many months before making any hasty decisions with life-changing consequences like—'

I interrupted her.

'Not that kind of sister,' I said. 'We'll work it out. I'm going away. I will phone you when I get there,' I said, truthfully. 'I'll ring you every day. I want to know you're all right. You and . . .'

'Her name is Alina. A-leen-ah. It's not difficult.'

'That's right. Alina. You and Alina can go somewhere else. In case you need to. Or take your mother away on holiday. Get a house or something. Whatever you want.'

'I am not thinking about the money right now, Laurie. We will talk about that some other day. I am thinking about you. I am wondering what this new madness of yours is. You sound happy. Are you happy? Are you deranged on drugs?'

'I'm all right. I promise.'

'You're not going to do anything stupid?'

She was fully awake now. I could see her in her dressing gown with her hair tied up on top of her head, wrestling with a coffee machine or pulling orange juice out of the fridge or bringing milk in from the doorstep. She would be frowning and suspicious, yes, but there was something else in her voice, something guarded, and almost like hope.

'Yes. Something really stupid,' I said. 'I'm going to give you half of my inheritance, whether you like it or not. I'll force it on you. I insist. I'll call the police and drop you in it if you don't take it.' I laughed. 'You don't have to worry about me. But I have to go. Will you help me with this?'

'I am agreeing to nothing. Nothing until I have seen you in person.'

'I'm going to drop a key off with you. I need you to do one other thing. My post. Will you—'

'Your father's *cleaner* and your personal assistant. Is that it?'

'Give it a rest. One letter. It's a DNA-testing company. I'm expecting it.'

'Mother of God, Laurie. What have you . . .?'

'It should be coming any day now. Just keep it for me, will you?'

'You want me to open it? Forward it on?'

'I don't know. I haven't decided. You'll hold it for me? Keep it safe until I know what I want to do, right?'

I liked the idea of that. Of the envelope arriving with her, and her holding it in her big hands, carefully tucking it into her tea towel drawer or putting it inside her desk or wrapping it in a scarf and putting it at the back of the wardrobe with her winter coat and spike-heeled boots. I liked the idea of it existing, and of her keeping it safe for me. For as long as I wanted. If Mr Haworth was curious too, and the presence of his money in my account suggested that he was – if only a little bit – then he could wait until I was ready. My mother, the darkest of horses. I laughed but Olena was still talking, protesting and asking questions when I ended the call. She would help me, though, once she'd had time to digest my idea and get used to it. I was sure of it.

I had one more phone call to make, but first I went out into the hallway and towards the small room. I liked to pretend I never went in there – that after Sadie died Mark and I closed the door on her nursery and, without discussing it, decided that it would be a little pocket of our tiny flat that we would no longer credit with existence. I put my hand on the doorknob. No-space. Un-space. Behind that door: deleted territory.

But that was not true. How many of the nights I could not sleep had I wandered in there, half drunk, half asleep, plunging myself into history gone wrong, futures deferred, and a room that wasn't haunted at all? I could never bring myself to call it *Sadie's room*, because Sadie had never been in it, and even though there was a certificate, Sadie herself had never really existed. She'd never breathed in the world and had been both a daughter and only the idea of a daughter, just as I was not a mother, and only held the idea of being one. I called this place the small room, and unless I was drunk and stumbling, kept the door closed.

I opened the door, took a breath and looked around. There were no surprises. It contained an unused cot filled with boxes of nappies and lots of little clothes, most of them still in their packets. The old drawings on the wall – the angels or suicides tumbling or flying around a block of flats that might have been ours, but might not have been – were still blooming through the paint like a cloudy shadow, and I considered all the nights I had sat on the floor of this room staring at them, trying to resolve their indeterminacy into the fact of a story – a story with an ending – while Mark browsed the internet in the living room, having given up on calling me back to him a long time before.

There was a little half-sized wardrobe in there: my father had given us some money for that, and the cot, and on top of the wardrobe was a small red suitcase with wheels. I had packed it when I was thirty-five weeks along and kept it near the front door of the flat, ready for when I went into labour and needed to take it into the hospital. I lifted the suitcase down and flicked open the lid and it was empty. It must have been Mark who'd unpacked the unused baby things and my bloodstained nightshirt, washed them and put them away, though I'd never seen him do it.

We had put up yellow curtains in there: expensive blackout curtains, because one of the books had said that if your baby was a bad sleeper, blackout curtains could help. Perhaps, I thought, I could ask Olena to take them down and offer them to Katrina sometime. Anything to get the little bugger to sleep. I went over to the small window and pulled them back. Dust flew. The nursery window has a different aspect to all the others in the flat, and I looked out of it, not towards the bay and the power station, but back in across the river and towards the east side of the city. In that direction the land slopes upwards towards the hill and the park, and all the little houses lie neatly in rows, stacked in tight either side of the river, as if they are waiting for something.

I had the feeling I should say something important. But to who? The empty cot? The suitcase or the unfamiliar view over the city? The room was empty – it always had been – and there was nothing to say and nobody to talk to, so I picked up the suitcase by its handle and wheeled it back into my bedroom, pulling my mobile phone out of my pocket and dialling Eddie's number as I went.

'What is it?' he demanded. Irritated with me, certainly – but worried too.

'Lovely to talk to you too, sunshine.'

'Are you all right? What's happening?' He seemed surprised by my good mood. I put him on speaker and left the phone on the bed while I moved around my bedroom, finding clothes and throwing them, half folded, into the case.

'I need a favour. A little one.'

'What sort of favour?'

There was a murmuring in the background – a female voice.

'Is that Celia I can hear?'

'Shut up.' He sounded shy – almost embarrassed.

'Hello Celia!' I called loudly. I imagined him holding the phone away from his ear and lowered my voice. 'You've let her stay over? You *never* let them stay over, Eddie.'

'Hello Laurie!' she called back. 'Lovely morning, isn't it?'

I could *hear* him blushing, and heard the smile in his voice as he protested.

'Please, please, *please* tell me what you want and then fuck off, will you?' he said. And yes, there was something I wanted, but this was too good – too perfect. I'd missed taking the piss out of him too much to let an opportunity for it pass me by.

'Well, well, well,' I said. 'It must be serious. Staying over. And it's been . . . what is it now?'

'Eleven months,' said Celia, and she sounded nice. 'And he's still not let me meet you, Laurie.'

'Eleven months,' I called, making sure she could hear me. 'And he's not invited you round to mine. We'll have to sort that out, Celia. It is almost as if he doesn't want me to tell you all his grubby secrets, isn't it?'

She laughed, maybe sitting up in his bed, the sheets tucked in all around her, leaning towards him so she could hear what I was saying, while he playfully pushed her away.

'Have you met his sister yet, Celia?'

'No! I haven't met *anyone*.'

'Amanda's lovely. Get her to show you the school photos. His Goth phase. Black marker and Tipp-Ex nail varnish. You need to be fully aware of the Goth phase before you go any further with him, don't you think?'

'Oh, definitely,' she said, her giggling smothered by the tussle, presumably as she tried to get nearer to the phone and Eddie swiped her away. It was funny. It made me happy, in a strange way that I didn't expect.

'Eddie,' I said quietly. 'Eleven months! I'll have to get myself a hat.'

Eddie sighed.

'The point, Laurie. My girlfriend, who is currently wearing nothing but last night's perfume, has just put her head under the duvet and she is, quite rightly, expecting my total and undivided attention. Accordingly, this finger of mine is hovering over the

270

little red telephone and unless you and the point make contact in the next two . . .'

Girlfriend. There'd be some fun with that – I didn't think Eddie had ever had a proper girlfriend before, or at least I'd never known him to use the word. But as much as it would have entertained me to tease him further, I had things to get on with. I dropped a pair of jeans and a handful of underwear into the case and picked up the phone from the pillow.

'Remember that time you said you'd love to tell Shaw where she could stick her job?' I said.

'God yes,' he said.

'Right. Good. I want you to tell her. Shaw. From me. I am no longer in need of my position. I resign. I'm out of there. That's the message. The style in which you deliver it, any additional ornamentation and elaboration, I will leave to your discretion. Tell her I'm wanted for murder.' I thought of Olena, at home, worrying about her conspicuous absence from her second cousin's wedding photographs. 'No, don't tell her that. Tell her I've joined the circus. Tell her, in Technicolor detail, just what you think of her Split Shift Rota and her weird new haircut and her daughter's cockapoo's Facebook page and those god-awful eyelashes on her car headlights and that fluffy bobble key-ring she's got. Let her know we all know about her and the Staff Wanker from Classics. Say I said it.'

'Really?'

I didn't think I had ever heard him short of something to say. Not ever.

'Really. She won't sack you for telling on me, will she? She'll probably promote you.'

'Laurie? Are you sure? What are you going to do?'

'Have fun, Eddie,' I said, and hung up.

Mr Haworth's cheque, which my grief had not prevented me from paying into my bank account the day after the wake, had cleared and the money had been sitting in my account ever since. When you are used to not having any money, it is hard to spend an unexpected five thousand pounds. It had made me feel safe, having it in there and knowing that nobody – not Mavis or Olena or Mark – knew it existed. I puzzled over it now and again – the amount of it, and what it might mean. But Olena often told me I overthought things, and for once in my life I decided to take her advice, stop looking my gift horse/father in the mouth, and spend the money. Once I finished packing my suitcase and taking the rubbish to the chute, I got on the internet and bought a train ticket.

18

I got on the train to London with no plan in mind other than to shrug away the sadness in the flat and stay moving until I had totally outrun it. I arrived in Paris, wandered anonymously for a few days, then moved on, eventually reaching Dijon. A day or two later I went on to Lyon, then to Montpellier. I travelled cheaply, broke my journey often in small places that nobody in their right minds would want to visit, and tried to make Mr Haworth's cheque last as long as I could.

This meant nights in cheap hotels, days spent wandering cities, loitering in cafés, lingering in libraries and bookshops, spending rainy afternoons at the cinema watching films I didn't understand and losing myself in swirls of tourists and travellers at train stations and coach hubs. I ate in all-night fast-food places, enjoying not being able to understand the headlines on the covers of the magazines and front pages of the newspapers left behind in waiting rooms, most of the chatter from fellow passengers unintelligible to me. I headed towards Barcelona, went on to Valencia – meandering slowly southwards along the coast, then north again, on a whim to Madrid. I took no photographs and sent no postcards.

This was my way of being alone without loneliness and it worked. Autumn grew cooler and turned, gradually, towards winter and the end of the year. I bought a rucksack from a second-hand shop in Lyon and abandoned my wheelie suitcase in a hostel there. In Barcelona my trainers fell apart and I bought boots. Sometimes there was some flirting in cafés or in sleeper-train buffet cars, but most of the time I minded my own business, finding no need to speak since pointing at fruit on market stalls and gesturing towards café menus to indicate what I wanted did the job. After a month, I almost forgot the sound of my own voice.

Olena texted sometimes wanting to know if I was alive, if I had started drinking again, if I had gone completely crazy.

I'm fine, I texted back, and sent her a picture of my new boots.

Where are you? she asked, and I didn't reply, knowing then how it might have been for Mark – the comfort and freedom in walking through a city, along a beach, looking through shop windows on a high street, with not one person around him giving a damn what he did and no one who did care about him having a clue where he was.

There was no other transformation: I didn't lose weight, get a tan, swap my glasses for contact lenses or grow out my fringe. I didn't give up smoking. But something else changed.

I began to sleep at night. Sleep properly – through the snoring and coughing and late-night conversations in hostel dormitories, through the multilingual travel announcements in stations and on trains and, using my new rucksack as a pillow, in airport departure lounges. I slept through anything and everything and did not dream of my guilt. When I woke up it was with a sense of curiosity, as if the decisions about where I might end up were not mine at all. Winter began, I bought a new coat, and wandered around the Christmas markets in Madrid, wondering about presents for Teddy and Alina.

If I did have a plan, it was only that when Christmas came, I would be somewhere else. That Teddy could have his birthday in October and Mark could have his in November but Sadie's – Sadie's December birthday – would be consigned to no-time, the temporal equivalent of my black sound. The way travellers lost hours as they circled the globe had always interested me. I once told Mark that if I planned to commit a crime, I'd work out some means of doing it on the night when the clocks went back so that the disappeared hour would contain my wrongdoing and form part of my alibi. It was what happened in *Murder on the Orient Express*, and the confusion with the clocks and the time differences involved as the train made its slow way across mainland Europe was one of the reasons why Poirot was so slow to see what most readers would have worked out from the opening. So on Sadie's birthday I planned to be between time zones, the anniversary swallowed up in the lost hours of a time difference that would erase it from my consciousness.

On Christmas Eve, I turned up at the Madrid Barajas airport and looked at the departure boards. I thought I might go home. I might stay in my father's house until it sold and decide what I wanted to do next once my half of the money was in my account. But the departure board had a flight leaving for Faro in six hours and, surrendering to the great magnetic pull of a curiosity I did not know I was still capable of feeling, I flipped a coin, ignored the result, and booked myself onto it.

The plane was half empty. For the first time, I couldn't sleep through the journey. The hour and minute of Sadie's birth passed and I spent the no-time staring out of the little lozenge-shaped window into the dark, the red lights on the wing blinking. The plane landed, and when I got off it I called Mavis the Betrayer's mobile from a public telephone in Faro Airport's baggage reclaim hall, keeping an eye on the carousel for my rucksack while I waited for her to answer. Because the phone number was local and she'd have no way of knowing it was me, I expected her to pick up, and she did.

'It's me, Mavis. Merry Christmas. Where's Mark?'

She took a moment or two before answering. I liked that, that I'd put her on the back foot.

'You've come over? On a plane?'

'I'm at the airport. Where is he, Mavis?'

My bag appeared. I watched it make its slow progress along the conveyor belt while she prepared her answer.

'You'd better come here. Get a taxi,' she said.

'Fine,' I replied.

Mavis' apartment was tiny – smaller, even, than the flat where Mark and I had spent most of our days together – but from the fringed wicker lampshades to the raffia tablemats to the blown-glass cats on the windowsill, every inch of it was perfectly her own, and I was glad for her.

Mark was not with her, and though I felt impatient to go out and find him, and almost as desperate for a shower and sleep (she had not invited me to stay – I noticed that), she took a long time to turn on her coffee machine and make us coffee, hunting around in her kitchenette for biscuits which I did not want and didn't eat. During the wait I started to get paranoid again. He was hiding somewhere – in a back bedroom or a cupboard, nearby, but just out of reach, and she was using the little matching coffee cups and saucer of biscuits to distract me while he slipped out of the apartment and disappeared. There was no small talk this time.

'You didn't even tell the police about Sadie. About the pressure he was under. They barely did anything. He was in a bad way, Laurie. Anything could have happened. Why didn't you tell them?'

This was something she could have asked me a long time ago. The fact that she hadn't and brought it up at that moment, right away, showed me more clearly than anything else that for Mavis the period of tiptoeing around me and treating me as if I was as fragile as tissue paper, as dangerous as a bomb, was well and truly over.

'I know. You're right. I should have done. I wasn't . . .' I had been going to say, 'I wasn't myself', but that wouldn't have been right, would it?

Mavis stared at me. 'You've got away with far too much for far too long,' she said. She was right. She was. She frowned, then softened and gathered me into her arms. I could smell her hair-spray and the perfume she liked to douse herself with.

'I worried about you. Him leaving you like that. Dealing with it all on your own. I wish he hadn't done it. I wish he hadn't needed to do it. I wish none of it had happened.'

'I wish I'd said something,' I said.

'You couldn't tell the police,' she said, 'strangers, who didn't know you. You couldn't even say her name, could you? You couldn't say anything.'

'No.' My face was pressed against her neck, my words muffled.

'But now you can. Now you can say what you need to say. Is that why you're here?'

She stood back and looked at me again.

'I don't know why I'm here, Mavis. I've got to be honest with you there. I don't know.'

Mavis walked away and pulled a little notebook with a leather cover and a tiny gold pen attached to it from a box near her telephone. All her things were like that: decorated and perfectly appointed and in their correct places. Why had we never come to stay before, when she had invited us? God knows where she'd have put us to sleep, but we'd have had a nice time. She'd have looked after us and made sure we got fresh air and natural light, as if we were plants, and that might have helped us a little bit. Why hadn't I agreed to come? She leaned over the breakfast bar, writing in the notebook.

'He's been going out every day. There's a row of bars and restaurants on this street here. I'll call you a taxi. I don't know what he does. He comes back for his tea some nights, and some nights he stays out.'

She tapped the notebook with her pen, tore off the sheet of paper, then gave it to me. 'You might find him round there.'

It was dusk, and the streets were almost empty. The locals would be in with their families, the tourists in the city, getting drunk and causing mayhem. It wasn't that cold, but the beach was deserted. The taxi dropped me off at the top of the street Mavis had suggested and I walked along it slowly. It was evidently an area for tourists but it was out of season, and most of the bars and souvenir places were quiet. But one of the bars had a chalk-board outside with writing in English, advertising itself as a safe place for wives to leave husbands while they shopped. As I passed it, I slowed down to look inside.

There he was: my stone, my Night Guard; sitting at a table in the window with his back to the door, a glass of lager and a woman who was not me in front of him. She was laughing at something he had just said. I scuttled inside and sat at the bar, perching on a stool. I asked for a bottle of water and watched him in the reflection of the mirror behind the optics. If he had looked anywhere but at the woman he was with, he'd probably have been able to see me.

It isn't often a wife gets to see her husband like this – in the wild and about to be picked up by another woman. She was talking loudly to him – at him, really – about her divorce. Insisting, through a frantic, stretched smile, how free and happy she felt – how she had hoped for a festive girls-only holi-day, just to let her hair down for a bit, but one by one the girl-friends she had invited had declined because of commitments to their work or children or partners and rather than stay at home feeling sorry for herself, she'd decided to come anyway, on her own.

'You've got to put yourself forward, haven't you?' she said, 'get out there and see what happens. I've earned this holiday. Decided I've got to put myself first for once.'

She had a southern accent – not London, but East Anglia – a little soft and countrified. And every few sentences she ducked her head towards her glass – a big pink and orange confection stuffed with ice and slices of fruit – and took a delicate sip through a straw, never taking her eyes off him.

'It's pretty amazing, you coming out here on your own at this time of year. Not many women would do that.'

She laughed. 'I know. I don't recognise myself. I don't know anyone here. No idea if the place would be deserted or not. But I'd booked the tickets, and I thought – well, I might as well just see. I was bricking it on the plane.'

'I bet you were.'

She sipped again and nodded at him.

'I'm glad I took the plunge, though. Leap and the net appears. My mum used to say that to me.'

Watching Mark at that moment felt just like the time I had studied him as he'd flirted with Joyce at the bar at Sharon's wedding. I'd thought they were a couple and had been a bit disappointed that this tall, strange woman with her stories of dead children and important work with the police had got in there before me. What had drawn me to him then? I didn't know him. He didn't know me. Had there been – as Joyce had said – some kind of connection? No, I don't think so. I had just been curious. I had wanted to hear him talk a bit more, and I'd wanted to see what was going to happen and how that strange argument he'd been having would end. That had been all, and while it hadn't been the only thing to have got us through the following fifteen years, it had been a big part of it.

That little scene I was spying on was a cliché, as all love stories and tragedies were. The relatively exotic location: the unexpected event all cued up and waiting to happen. The characters onstage were as we expect them to be too: the quietly depressed man, ruggedly sitting in the bar, taciturn while he nurses his wounds. The beautiful younger woman, vulnerable too, in her own way. If Mark was looking for someone to take care of, and someone who would be grateful for the taking care, then perhaps he had found her.

I could have left the bar and gone home right then, a single woman, and told myself a story about how our relationship had ended and after a while I would have believed it, and the simple certainty – *he left me for a younger woman he met in a bar in Portugal* – would have been one kind of comfort. Or I could have marched over there, surprised him, grabbed him by the scruff of his neck and hauled him out onto the street. A part of me wanted to do just that and to remind him of who he belonged to and what he had done. To tell him what he still owed me. My hands and arms were numb. The Mark I was watching was not the Mark who I had watched flirting with Joyce all those years ago, and this woman who watched – me – was not the twenty-one-year-old who had hovered in her mother's dress, feeling sulky and unwelcome and searching for a safe place to land and finding that place in the middle of an argument about Connie Fallon.

Had I stopped being curious?

'I've been swimming,' the woman said, stretching out an arm towards him. 'The water's pretty cold. But you come out feeling amazing. Alive. You should try it.'

Mark laughed. Was he going to try it? I had literally no idea.

'I'm not much of a swimmer,' he said. 'They'd have to send someone to fish me out.'

'You can hold my clothes while I go back in later then,' she said. 'Make sure nobody steals my shoes.'

Mark laughed again but he did not say he wouldn't.

The woman – and yes, she had so much of his attention that he *still* hadn't noticed me sitting there, all that honey-and-choco-late-coloured hair and golden, sand-dusted limbs (*of course* I was jealous) – leaned forward and pointed, with one finger, at his hand. She didn't just point, she tapped his finger. Flirting. Definitely. You don't touch people you don't know unless you are trying to scare them or get them sexually interested in you. I became freshly aware of myself – my jeans were the wrong fit and length and colour and my upper arms were flabby and white. I had, I noticed as I turned in my chair to get a better view of them, underapplied my deodorant that morning.

'What's that?' she said. She put her head on one side and smiled.

He lifted his hand and looked at his fingers.

'Ah. That,' he said.

'A wedding ring? What's the story there? You married?'

I waited.

He looked at his hand thoughtfully, as if it had been a very long time since he had considered it. As if this was a question that had only recently needed considering.

'Sort of.'

'Sounds interesting,' she said, and giggled. She was giving him an opportunity to say he was separated, or on the way to being divorced, or only staying because of the mortgage or the children or his wife's insanity, which tied him to her and meant she couldn't be left, apart from for occasional holidays like this, but what happened on holidays like this didn't count, would stay just between them, their little secret.

'What does *sort of married* mean?' she said and laughed again. He laughed too – a real laugh, as much at himself as at her. The game was on.

'It means I'd better buy you another drink,' Mark said. He was tired – I could hear it in his voice. And he pushed his chair back, stood, turned, and came to the bar, where – eventually – he noticed me waiting.

Shock did not quite cover it. He looked – sorry about this, but I can think of no other phrase – as if he'd seen a ghost, and the colour went right out of him. What was it he was feeling? Fear? Shame? Relief? Disappointment? Impossible to read, because his face just froze and all he was doing was staring at me. I would have giggled, in other circumstances.

'Laurie,' he said. It wasn't a question.

What did I look like to him? In my badly fitting jeans and new walking boots and a T-shirt that needed washing. I had tried a bit with my makeup, then felt stupid, so had washed it off in Mavis's bathroom. Did he still know me, or were we just two strangers staring at each other in an almost deserted bar, out of season in the Algarve, British tourists washed up in a place where they didn't know the language and didn't quite understand the money?

I don't know how long we waited there – it couldn't have been more than a few seconds, but the woman Mark had been chatting up had clocked what was happening, and left. I didn't see her face, only her shoulder as she swung her fringed leather handbag over her arm – with embarrassment or anger or disappointment or resignation or amusement, I didn't know. I bet I was looking smug. If I was, I wasn't trying to hide it.

'It's me,' I said stupidly.

'Yes, so it is.'

He raised his eyebrows. A curiosity of his own? I had surprised him. I had even, perhaps, intrigued him.

'Are you going to say something?' he said.

Was I?

I had not planned a speech. I have come to believe that life seems to turn out better if I do not pretend my own plans have anything to do with what is going to happen. So when I opened my mouth, I was as taken aback by what I said as he seemed to be.

'On my way here the plane had this map on the telly screen on the back of the seat in front. They weren't showing a film. Just a map of the world with a little dotted line heading towards a big red X. The dotted line was the plane, and the X was Faro. Was it like that on your flight?'

'I don't remember,' he said. He sat down next to me at the bar. He'd left his beer at the table in the window, and the barman gave him another. He'd become a regular here, by the looks of it.

'It just put the thought in my head. Those spaceships you were on about. The interstellar spacecraft.'

'You remember that?'

'Yes, I remember it. You told me that the scientists think there's no point setting one off because it might never get there, and maybe we'd be able to make a better one in the future, which would be able to go faster and overtake it anyway. So they might as well wait for that, and because of that, they'll wait forever. And I said, well, maybe the spacemen would just come to us and rescue us. And you said there probably would be superior beings out there who could help us, but then if they arrived here and looked at us and the way we live – really saw us – then they'd understand we were just a parasite on the earth and probably run the other way screaming.'

It was quite a speech.

'Yes,' Mark said. He lifted his glass and drank deeply, wiped his mouth and looked at me. I hadn't felt that closely examined for a long time.

'I think I've solved it. The problem.'

'You've solved the incessant obsolescence postulate?' he said, amused.

'I certainly have. My theory is this. We might as well set one off. Because what else are we doing that's worthwhile? Even if it never gets to where it's going. Even if where it's going doesn't exist. We might as well.'

'Is that it?'

I put my hand on his.

'And we might as well, while we're going in the right direction and hoping to land somewhere decent, hope that there's someone kind coming in from the other direction. These beings. They might not be superior. They might be just like us. They might be looking too. For us. They might be on their way already, taking off from their own place that's gone as wrong as ours.'

Mark carried on looking at me. He was processing this. He has a certain expression when he wants to laugh, but is holding it in. There's a dimple on his left cheek – one of his identifying marks – that you never see at any other time. I saw it then.

'Are you all right?' he asked. I watched him brace himself for the answer, preparing for more of my bad weather.

I smiled. '*Sort of*,' I said. 'I'm *sort of* all right, Mark.'

He got the joke, and laughed at it, looking sheepish.

'And you?' I asked. 'Are you all right?'

He looked around him at the empty bar, the black and white posters of English rock bands framed on the wall, the little karaoke stage with its lonely microphone stand. There was a big potted plant in the corner near us, its spiky leaves wrapped in red and silver tinsel. I followed his gaze, looking at all of it, and through the writing on the wide front windows, over the cobbled street and towards the sea, which was not our sea, but which crashed and foamed on the seaweed-covered rocks and sandy beach in much the same way – hopelessly and pointlessly and beautifully persistent – as it did at home.

'No,' he said, still smiling at me, at the bedraggled tinsel, at everything else. 'No, I'm not.'

I nodded. He came into view. Not a rock, but a person, like me, who had been irreparably riven by the unexpected blast and shattered again by the aftershocks.

'I can see that,' I said.

ACKNOWLEDGMENTS

The first draft of this book was written during #100daysofwriting 2018 and was nourished by the encouragement, camaraderie and unglamorous selfies of all the other writers turning up every single day alongside me. The short story about the woman who kills her husband with a leg of lamb referred to in the first chapter is Roald Dahl's 'Lamb to the Slaughter'. The gruesome facts about feet and shoes washing up on the British coastline first came to my attention through the podcast *They Walk Among Us* and the local instance of the phenomenon, where a foot was washed up in Middleton, Lancaster and its companion in Heysham, Lancashire, was reported in the *Lancashire Evening Post* in March 2015. The film that Laurie remembers watching with Mark in chapter 8 is Tim Burton's *Beetlejuice*. The writer Adam Farrer shared his experience of living in a high-rise flat with me and the details of whirlpools in toilet bowls and the untimely ending of cats are included with gratitude. Thanks are also due to Emma Jane Unsworth and Conor O'Callaghan who read and gave suggestions on early drafts. Imogen Tyler let me write sections of this novel in her living room while feeding me mince pies and pork scratchings: thank you. Thanks to Charlie Gere for conversations about ghosts conducted via online séances while I edited the final draft in lockdown. Thank you to my agent Anthony Goff at David Higham Associates, to my editor Carole Welch, to Irene Rolleston, Penny Isaac, Maria Garbutt-Lucero and all at Sceptre.

Ghosted is set in a little city near the north-west coast of England, but whatever resemblances the reader finds in this novel to universities and power stations that exist in real life are intended to be playful rather than faithful.